COELACANTH

—— A NOVEL ——

PHILIP ALLEN

ANNAPOLIS, MD

To Susan Who Encourages Me into Every Day

ACKNOWLEDGEMENTS: The Heritage of Andrianaivo Rajaona and of Zele Rasoanoro.

Suggestions from Catherine Allen, Keith Schlegel, and Ron Springwater.

And pertinently to my admirable editors in the Graham Publishing Group.

As his weekly act of grace, the art teacher released Friday afternoon's class early— except for her. This time he stopped Cynthia with a challenge: "Let me see that sketchbook of yours again. And while I'm at it, do tell me, like, why a teenage girl keeps filling her pages with . . . are they spider webs? This ain't no biology class, Cynthia; it's supposed to be an art studio."

"They're not just webs," she muttered after recovering the sketchbook and starting to pack up her pencils. "They hold millions of black spiders swarming all over the ocean."

"Maybe," he said. "Lots of bugs on the high seas. Lots of great paintings too, but you know, usually with boats on 'em, not insects. Which ocean is this by the way?"

Cynthia hesitated. "My old man says it's the Indian one. But he usually lies about such stuff."

"And what do us in the Lower Ninth Ward care about some Indian Ocean?"

"An ocean of Indians," Cynthia shrugged. "Like a hideaway for Choctaws?"

"Okay," the teacher conceded. So this Black girl imagined Native Americans as wiry fugitives scattered out of Louisiana by the government.

"I see you don't know. But you rendered those frizzy webs, got color into the lacing just with pencils. You sure can nail the dumbest project! Next week I'll show you how to render water for your Indians to swim in. But maybe first you should ask Mr. Van Zan, like, why he puts bugs in his daughter's bonnet."

While glad to hear professional praise, Cynthia Van Zan exited school that day contemptuous of both men's motives—her teacher's and her father's. She sensed that the teacher liked her looks more than her drawing; too bad for him. As for Eugène Van Zan, who persistently thrust French magazines on his daughter to prod her into his native language—(the one he spoke in Martinique), he's always trying to intimidate.

Now, it's some story in the latest issue that purports to explain the assassination of a young man in a far-off African island because the boy threatened to bring down an empire. Since it appeared in French, written by somebody named Sophie, Cynthia deemed the narrative opaque———except for the revolutionary martyr's nickname: *Spider*.

This name gave her the warrant she needed to disregard Eugène's warning; now she would get that tattoo on her shoulder: the eight-legged black widow floating over an oceanic web.

Otherwise, Sophie Somebody's report would have to wait for Cynthia Van Zan to weave herself into the sea fabrics of Africa. Even if that took twenty years.

It did. Then, she asked to see the "Spider" article again.

CHAPTER 1

ON BABEL HILL

Sophie Makoa, Indesville, 2016

Shuffling through pedestrian clutter, I yearn for some protest or demo to join, some repression to suffer—anything worthy of Vinaigrette's pen, just to prove I still function. No use scanning the overstressed streets or the flimsy walls of the town for material. Or these slanting red-tiled roofs, imported by European settlers to hang over pedestrian cloisters that remain noisy but drained of old narratives.

My readers require action, so I welcome that jangling phone, especially on cross-continental business. From her current refuge in West Africa, Cynthia Van Zan has called for help, showing how even Amazon artists must resharpen their edge. She needs me to authorize a translation of my 1996 "Spider" story into English. Cynthia wants to resurrect it for her new book on student rebellions. She will, of course, do the illustrations—her forte. To get the translation right, she wants me to commission her old workmate Denis Guyane; to be sure, he's the only one I'd trust around here with my style.

Frankly, I don't mind granting consent, first because our national tragedy deserves attention beyond this island—and from an emerging English readership that I may need. Also, because I believe in the context: a revolutionary mission of young people even when they fail as this one did. And finally, because Cynthia Van Zan remains my hope of an America-Africa future. Her publication of Vinaigrette's old fable of the martyred Spider should open a fresh avenue into that mission.

Leaving me to do the rest myself. And Denis Guyane's translation. Here goes.

❁ ❁ ❁

From Sophia Makoa, *Les Fables à la Vinaigrette*, 1996
Babel Mountain, Indesville, AuxIndes

The Conqueror of AuxIndes rides high on the island's summit, not in some ordinary downtown park. Decades ago, imperial imagination hoisted General Pierre Charpentier in bronze onto a formidable plateau of cobblestone and eucalyptus. There he presides on horseback in lofty triumph, while admirers of statuary climb from urban depths to reach his martial presence.

That hill also happens to bear AuxIndes University—one of Charpentier's "civilizing" creations as the colony's first Governor.

In command of the campus gate, the Conqueror and his noble steed *Neptune* oversee the edifices of academe. Below hoof level, several stone figures, human and bovine, pay homage to the impassive General; they do not presume to represent the student body.

Student patriots on late beery nights are heard to command Governor Charpentier to "descend and fight," albeit without his compliance. The monument remains intact. This mid-week morning in

1996, however, a century after his colonial conquest, their resuscitated movement insists that something collapse. Something must. They have already posted a gadfly of their own—Freddie Khoin, better known as *Spider*—onto Neptune's noble neck. Wiry Spider straddles his steed nervously in front of an unimpressed bronze Conqueror.

Today, a fresh constituency surrounds the monument. This is not just another student protest, even if that's all it appears to be. Devoid of ceremony or decorum, demonstrators dressed casually as for the mere streets gather below the haughty equestrian to cheer their arachnid hero. Over the past ten decades, while scholastic dignity slowly dissolved, students have learned to shed formality. These days require no caps and gowns; not even the pith and tans that clothed the original academic body (sons of European officials and settlers); now it's just uncoifed heads and denim.

True, Charpentier's hill claims its historic reputation. Once a citadel for barbaric conflict, its academic energy now specializes—apart from a few stray rebels—in supplying reliable manpower to the island and beyond. Post-secondary education has persistently transformed this humble way station on the sea route to Asia into the Republic of AuxIndes.

As time passed, Charpentier's university extended its services beyond the piths and tans to offer a repository for local boys of color, tutoring them in how to act colonial. By now, the republican spirit has even allowed Indigenous young women to simulate their masculine counterparts. They blend delicately into the student population and choose to wear the same denim.

As the twentieth century closes however, half-hearted decolonization no longer suits the young Republic. An informal watchword for today's student strike is *Get out of our way!* Articulated by its president, Anya Wazimbwe, Students United seeks authenticity for a new nation, mobilized across a broad spectrum of its youth.

The student manifestos of 1996 propose an institution dedicated to high-minded objectives: fruitful international exchange; expanded laboratory and information technology; improved housing with uninterrupted electric power and water supply; student rights to evaluate faculty; global recognition of the value of their degrees; and never forget, fatter stipends promptly disbursed.

In effect, the movement's factions concur on one long-term priority: a future when their generation will govern the Republic before they too become old. Although AuxIndes's ambitious youth can't admit it, their essential reward after graduation will emulate the cultural status offered their European and colonial predecessors. They may catch up, but not transcend.

Anya Wazimbwe has acknowledged that after years of study, today's patriots would not have it otherwise.

A century of functional continuity has provoked some wits to retitle the institution "Facsimile U." Indeed, the world boasts many institutions of the kind. Students United has even charged the nation itself with that post-modern stigma: "Facsimile Republic" has dwindled into a haven, they say, for simulated statesmen whose charades have provoked the current morass. Its young have vowed to abrogate stagnation throughout AuxIndes without specifying what is to emerge henceforth.

Now in its third day, their protest threatens even the conquering bronze General. Culminating in demolition of Charpentier's statue, this strike must transcend all preceding actions. It is to be climactic—at least in the imagination of its militants. So are all such rituals, say their elders, until they are exhausted, suppressed, and in time superseded.

Complying with democratic principle, Anya Wazimbwe has urged students to articulate their grievances through representative channels. Each college has proposed its agenda, selected its spokesperson, defined its place in the movement, each in its own language. The outcome resembles the dissonance that has drawn the stigma "Babel Hill" to this academic mountain top. Striving for coherence out of cacophony, Students United supplies a vision and a language for transformation, but with yet undetermined effect.

In the process, Anya Wazimbwe delegates physical operations to brawnier activists like the bearded Benjamin Bamiara and science maven Roger Masson. Under their supervision, food and water supplies are stored, manifestos distributed, medical services enlisted, tools assembled, and cobblestones pried off roadways to serve as missiles.

On this third day of the strike, classes remain suspended illegally but with faculty complicity. Plotted over weeks, student strategy has absorbed advice from sympathetic academics who welcome the concept of work-free days while prodding students to go on the attack. This pressure has already induced the University's rector to surrender his feeble authority to the national agencies equipped to cope with controversy.

After weeks of desultory demonstrations in the city below, Students United now invites authority to engage on this hilltop. For the moment, as they await confrontation, militants have padlocked the gates and posted sentries armed with paving stones on the parapets. There is no sign of police so early this morning, but emboldened students eagerly prepare for attack. Sentinels peer out to detect the riot control units who ritually broadcast threats before anybody arrives to start talking sense.

The academic terrain does seem defensible. Starting from town, Babel Hill's fortress of erudition can be assaulted only perpendicularly, over winding cascades of roadway. To reach the hilltop in academic season, bush taxis agonize upward in lowest gear while town buses grind laboriously in and out of speeds. On their way down, buses ply their clamorous brakes while the taxis dispense with engine power entirely; their drivers cure the slopes by careening in "neutral" from one curb to the other, claiming to save as much fuel going down as they had burnt on the way up. Professors curse the trajectory for its punishment on their Citroëns, while humble staff tend to walk or to mix with the student passengers. Hardly a simple route open to invasion.

Today, Students United has decreed that nobody is to enter or leave the campus for any pretext until the Government pays its respects—by climbing that mountain to seek a meeting with the movement. If chief of state Bienportant remains out of reach (polishing his patriarchal brass knuckles), then at least his minions are expected to negotiate. Otherwise, as the insurrectionists boast, their Conqueror's monument will collapse into shards, and youthful masses will vandalize the cowering city of Indesville.

By noon, when a police perimeter finally forms, no private vehicles arrive and few descend. Yet, somehow students have gathered in clusters, then in droves, trickling out of dormitories and seemingly from exclaves in the atmosphere. Armed mainly with posters and handmade banners, flanked by untidy armories of stones and bricks, Students United denies access to any uniformed intruders. The police, they insist, will need heavy armor to take this rugged redoubt.

Inside the fence, student attention focuses mainly on that notable symbol of oppression, the equestrian monument. Charpentier's presence remains disempowering; they do not need his permission to learn, or his horse to advance. Should the authorities ignore their claims, students have voted to remove the statue. Their delegate Freddie (The Spider) Khoin, has been boosted with his web of cables onto Neptune's neck; below him, a wrecker crew has positioned sledgehammers. The sun showers euphoria onto the scene. Dutiful wardens circulate to exhort the apathetic. Most spectators find shady places to squat near their battery radios. A few appear to be reading a book.

"Prepare, capricious mortals!" proclaims the Spider in portentous French. He is uneasily perched on high, his back to the Governor, legs clinging to Neptune's curved neck against an unpredictable wind. Wiry and somber as his nickname, Freddie Khoin holds a heavy cable end in one hand, a rigid tuft of horse's mane in the other. "Too bad these iron cows don't go anywhere," he shouts down. Then, switching to Creole as though to confuse the General, "Won't it even blow around a little in this wind?"

"No, Freddie," answers Masson twenty feet below. "Statues are anchored against the tempest."

"Can't buckle under me? Can't even retreat?" pursues Spider. "What did you say this donkey was made of, Roger?"

"Bronze," says Masson, "Tough copper alloy. No, this one can't retreat or attack; he can't even prance anymore."

"Good for him. Good for us, or me at least. But what about the cowboy behind me, under that helmet squashing his face? You mean he can't move either, right?"

"Yeah, Spider. He's dead." Masson deliberately indulges Freddie's proclivity to play comic-strip booby, the boy's hedge against elitism. "So your statue needs the bronze to keep him erect. But what *you're* there for, heroic Sir Khoin, is to *make* him move—downward, when we're ready."

"You mean when *I'm* ready," mutters the young rider. "Actually, it's beautiful up here, watching the climate come in, if that's what climates do. Thanks for saddling me on this thing, Roger, even if you only picked me because"—his voice rising—"because I'm skinny and . . ."

"And dumb!" adds Masson. He has been joined by Anya Wazimbwe who can imagine this humble country kid suddenly unseating General Charpentier and riding into the mountains on his usurped steed.

"Fact is, I am stupid and glad of it," answers the would-be horseman, mainly to himself and the insistent breeze. Freddie methodically shifts position to face the Governor and loop a cable around those martial shoulders. "Copper alloy, is he? I do get it: when the sun "alloys" European bodies they darken. Not like us, huh; we were *born* bronze. At least, I was. Too bad spiders don't have their own statues to alloy."

Freddie Khoin insists on his nickname, for "Spider" had emerged intact from his childhood addiction to American comic books. It's how he learned to read languages and to battle his way through school.

"Done now," he calls. "Let the lynch party begin!"

"Not until we get you off it," Anya Wazimbwe cautions as students crowd around. "We don't want you caught up there when the thing collapses."

"Right," cries Spider, flashing a contagious smile. "I knew you'd be thoughtful, Anya."

After knotting the cable, Spider slips delicately down Neptune's flanks, over its right foreleg onto a narrow ledge, then lands on a stone shepherdess adoring her liberator from below, and finally into Masson's benevolent grasp. Freddie holds tightly to his length of cable, flourishing it as a trophie for the downfall of empire.

Venturing a more sober thought, Spider adds, "We're actually lynching a guy, aren't we—this statue, I mean? Of course there's a distinction: we only lynch some bronze colonialist, and we do it in reverse. Here we tug him down while across the equator, Americans hang our bodies up."

This is not posed as a question.

After filming militants loudly cheering Freddie Khoin for the record, Anya persuades the lad to hand her his end of the cable.

The movement leaders had met Spider through a literature class where Masson was taking refuge from the rigors of his zoology regimen. Roger then introduced him to Bamiara, but more than anybody, male or female, Freddie Khoin swore undying devotion to Anya the exquisite Wazimbwe princess—and rebel-in-chief.

In due course, Spider told his comrades how he had been forced to switch "majors" when the government transferred some big contract from an American to a French company; perfection in French was to assure retention of his scholarship and subsequent employment with the contractor. "At first, I was taking German to keep that job," Freddie said. "They converted me to the English major when Mannesmann dumped the project on Ingersoll. Then the Marseillais took it over. So I'm a Francophone now, but I hear they're going to surrender it to some outfit called Montecatini, and we don't even teach Italian here. Maybe we should just wait for the inevitable Chinese.

"Soon, though," Freddie concluded, "I'll be able to ask where's the toilet in four languages, and that'll help a lot."

Plotting "direct action" to de-imperialize the University's hill, Anya Wazimbwe had insisted on Spider as the statue's executioner; she sensed how the movement could publicize participation by this descendant of a traditional slave caste. Although her own highborn kinsfolk brush it off, Anya saw Freddie's academic tanas exemplary of the doubly-plagued national predicament—short-term confusion of commitments, long-term disrespect for the human and natural environment. To her mind, by switching Spider from one language to another, this facsimile of a university, towering on its plateau, has justified its nickname—"Babel." She is ready to behead the mountain.

For his part, from an originally agrarian perspective, Roger Masson anticipates a less belligerent agenda for their encounter with the authorities. Without rejecting Wazimbwe's leadership, he's inclined to stress *modernization*, a patient debate over national priorities, a student voice in the forum of academic governance. For him, threatening the Governor's statue is a bargaining chip to use as a last resort.

The movement's third voice, Benjamin Bamiara quietly invokes a doctrine of moral efficacy. This son of pacifist teachers reads the future through faith in the "arc of history." Focusing on tactics rather than objectives, Benjamin urges quiescence, humility to attract allies even if one must endure retaliation from vindictive powers. Militants consider Bamiara too willing to yield crucial points, as Anya Wazimbwe appears overly categoric in asserting them.

Class entitlement favors the trio of student leaders as though a common enemy made their respective strategies essentially congruent. But it's Freddie Khoin who humbly bears the weight of oppression. While vowing fealty to Anya "as any good slave does," Spider claims to have joined the student movement only to agitate for crisper baguettes in the refectory.

To combat this strike, President Dominique Bienportant's government has already applied the customary instruments of suasion in due sequence: first mere silence and dismissive shrugs; these were followed by official disseminations of wounded pride; then by appeals to parental authority (which surely wouldn't work these sorry days); subsequently came broadcast warnings of retaliation against students and threats against faculty who presumed to interfere with institutions of state.

Finally, insurrection will be confronted by ultimatum and the dispatch of disciplinary brigades to penetrate the shuttered citadel. In no case would Bienportant risk his supreme dignity in confrontation with callow rabble under the shadow of the Conqueror's monument.

Thus far, conventional repression has failed to intimidate Students United. Without specific authorization, police observe rules barring infringement on academic immunities. Now, when any officer approaches a gate, sentries defend the terrain from behind barricades, threatening to lobby rocks and bottles in medieval rites of civil disobedience. Ultimately, during noonday heat, with dented vehicles and after ineffective warnings, the baffled siege cordon appeals to its suzerain, Antoine Karamau, to intervene.

Invariably dressed in black, a dark leonine mane bristling down to his massive shoulders, Interior Minister Karamau embodies the proverbial menace of a police potentate. As if to inoculate themselves against intimidation, students refer to him sarcastically as "Le Philosophe," although few would presume to address him directly that way. Anya Wazimbwe is especially troubled by the prospect of an encounter, for the minister flaunts a reputation for flagrant womanizing; he has remarked on her attractions more than once, and has taken to referring to her as "la Divine Wazimbwe," while Anya's more austere admirers merely call her "La Diva."

Refusing to tolerate intimidation, any outrage over official treatment of Spider has armed her for confrontation. She now stands ready at the campus entrance, brandishing her end of the lynch-ready cable.

To undertake the pacification of some unruly youths, however, Karamau knows better than to labor up the mountain and beg admittance from kids waving sticks around the gate. After reviewing his agents' notes on the personal backgrounds of some dozen student activists, he waits through lunch hour, then takes off from headquarters in the one helicopter at his disposal.

When they hear an engine throb overhead, strikers tilt back in surprise. They had expected Government to arrive by armored vehicle, but their outposts have reported no sign of a motorized convoy. An aircraft landing is precluded, for the University's capricious architect had not left hilltop space for a runway. Some attribute the noise to a drone, bearing nothing but ill will toward the bodies gathered on the plateau.

"Probably carrying explosives, so watch for falling objects," shouts one sentry. "Could even be poison gas," calls another, "better take cover and keep the windows tight!"

Anya Wazimbwe doesn't share these anxieties. The confrontation has not evolved to the point of lethal reprisal. No police firearms have materialized, and only a few agents have been targeted by projectiles. If a drone is on the way, it is probably intended for reconnaissance, to assess the size of their demonstration, the weapons or equipment stockpiled around operational buildings. If so, that would be an untypical sign of respect. The movement leaders prefer to welcome this air tour as recognition of their solidarity.

Soon they all absorb the helicopter's thudding sound. Hovering above them, Karamau's Alouette sends a shiver through the crowd like a sudden gust over a wheat field. Then it lands noisily in the quadrangle, close by the equestrian monument. Urging Bamiara,

Spider, and the other delegates to take cover, Anya Wazimbwe holds her end of the lynch cable and gestures to Masson to stay.

When the vehicle settles on its skis, they can identify the dark bulk in its bubble as the bear of a man whom students regard as "boss cop." (They save the scornful "Philosophe" to use with more irony.)

Along the parapets, sentinels have diverted their attention away from the roadway that authority had been expected to use in its assault. One by one, without anticipating an order, they muster rocks to threaten the Alouette. After stepping onto ground, Antoine Karamau commands his helicopter to take off promptly, for its own good. Then he turns his back to the wind and faces the crowd. He is indeed large, swathed like a black hole.

"Not very effective," the man called Philosophe shouts under an ascending roar as Masson and Wazimbwe approach him on the quad, "to toss stones at a gunship." He waves his arms in mockery. "Does this show a lack of discipline in your mob?"

"To the contrary," replies Masson, "for they did get rid of the chopper—your departure craft."

"Who said I needed to leave?" responds Karamau. He gestures broadly, as if to say I run this place and everybody in it, then holds out his hand almost as a welcome sign.

"Don't exaggerate," Masson counters, not taking the Minister's hand.

After letting drop the cable, Anya also waves him off. "You aren't even the nominal proprietor of this institution, that blowhard who claims to supervise Education," she says. "We know your colleagues to be cowards, and see that you are not. Congratulations and welcome.

For the moment, you are here in our custody, our gentle custody. But you will have to leave eventually, and you'll need our help."

"Help from whom? From you, my charmer? That I will gladly accept."

"No, from the student body guarding the gate. Look around you."

Philosophe gives a guttural laugh. He surveys the territory skeptically. "I don't see what you call *a body*. Bodies I do see," indicating a proliferation of protestors, "all sorts, unified only in defiance of the law. A real Babel, as you've called this place, needing restoration of proper order, which is my job."

"That job," says Anya, "requires violence, doesn't it?"

"Not inevitably. We only need to talk a bit, me and your . . . factions. We'll see what can be resolved amicably and what may be left, regrettably, for the security forces to clear up. The peacemakers among you will be glad to see me off."

"We admire your confidence, Minister," she replies, "and perhaps all will turn out as you predict. But let's get to our business. We invite you to join us for negotiations—nearby, in the conference room of our Hall of Philosophy."

"Ah, an inadvertent homage to my nickname?"

"No reference to you is intended," assures Wazimbwe, shivering for an instant. "We just don't have a more offensive structure, one that would suit your taste. Our delegates are in Philosophy, waiting to meet with you. Shall we go?" She and Masson have moved toward the hall, but are interrupted by Minister Karamau's voice.

"You know, I have never actually appreciated this campus. People from my . . . my village don't usually get to university. Nonetheless, we welcome our invitations, we the untutored. I'd like to look around for a moment before we talk."

Karamau turns gallantly to Anya Wazimbwe: "I understand that the architecture follows a particular pattern. Might I have the pleasure of your company for a brief stroll?"

To redirect the visitor's attention, Roger Masson steps forward peremptorily and offers to guide Philosophe on a rapid campus tour. The gesture allows Wazimbwe to move away. She takes the opportunity to warn Union delegates that the intruder was no doubt preparing to exploit any weaknesses among the tribes of Babel. She and Bamiara will prepare the scene and keep tempers warm while Masson hurries his guest through the premises.

The long-departed campus architect had indeed executed his concept elaborately. Distributed over the plateau, each academic building is shaped to exemplify its discipline. The College of Medicine dangles downhill like a stethoscope, Literature is an open book, Law a balance scale, Political Science a wind tunnel, the Business School a Euro sign (reconfigured belatedly from the dollar), Theology the inevitable cross. These symbols are reliably discernible only from the air, but their photographs serve public relations purposes.

It was in such contours that the current uprising had taken its own form—inchoate at first, but gradually coalescing into a movement of defiance. There is yet no structure to symbolize that discipline, so Philosophy Hall, shaped like a rudimentary Parthenon, will have to do.

As they circulate, the minister records a specific identity for each faculty—distinctions of style between sciences and arts, the proliferation of laboratories, computer banks, and studios—also in the posters and verbal formulas indicating respective departmental priorities. As he navigates each portal, Philosophe evinces familiarity with key personnel and their respective agendas. Noting departmental data, including names of delegates, Karamau hums a fragmentary tune while they stroll. When he stops to write he troubles the gravel with the toe of a broad but smart black shoe.

He pauses at Zoology to recall Roger Masson's own father and grandfather from having worked near their paddy fields years earlier. At first curious, Masson has grown uneasy. Karamau claims to be touring the campus for the first time, yet he can read these buildings as though they conveyed messages just for himself.

By the time they enter Philosophy Hall, Masson already fears fragmentation of their movement into a welter of interests under pressure from their adversary. Philosophe cordially shakes a dozen hands and wedges himself into a seat next to Anya Wazimbwe. She opens the session and then warily moves off.

Undeterred by the Diva's displacement, Karamau takes notes as the delegates itemize student grievances. After an hour, he closes his tablet and speaks. The Government is prepared to accommodate the institutional needs that brought him to the hill, he says. Nevertheless, he perceives confusion in an agenda that confronts one complaint against another, down the chain of what the students may have naively regarded as a coherent bill of grievance.

Masson wonders. Where had this stranger perceived the influence exerted by "radical" faculty while students were determined to act for themselves? How did he anticipate that one faction would claim budgetary priority for computer labs while its neighbor insisted on expansion of staff? That some would privilege electronic pedagogy against another's preference for lecture-hall facilities? Or for hiring qualified expatriate faculty as opposed to job-seeking nationals? Or private against communal lodgings? Or deliberate focus on professional orientation rather than liberal studies? Or recruitment of gifted students over "affirmative action" for less equipped school-leavers?

"What I see here," summarizes Philosophe to the tribes, "is a disaggregated resistance to cohesive governance. You all brought legitimate demands to me. At least your constituencies think you did. So we'll take each one seriously, including somebody's protest against using millet flour to bake your Frenchified bread."

Philosophe has come prepared to offer remedies for student academic aspirations, within political feasibility. He welcomes accommodation to modern technology and international liaison, energy upgrades in the dorms, student roles in curriculum and faculty governance.

Not every response is accommodating, yet all are fortified by Karamau's awareness of the source of complaint, the recent history of the discipline, even the family identity of the spokesperson. Invoking frescoes and sculpture from some of their clan tombs (how did he retain all that?), he shows sympathy for family struggles against poverty, or parental loss, or disease.

Masson perceives the Minister's strategy as a way of cheapening substance into mere personal interests, while Bamiara understands it as a masterful deconstruction of the Union that had insisted on a cluster of objectives, rather than on nonviolent process. For Anya Wazimbwe this scene on Babel has reenacted the multilingual confusion afflicting the nations of Genesis. It is a microcosm of the universe in environmental disaster, and Karamau is the peremptory agent of Jahweh.

Then comes a series of personal incentives for abandoning the strike. All twelve Student Union delegates receive tailored pledges of support for financial or other favors toward higher studies and post-graduate opportunities. Anya will have a planning role in a government agency; sensing that he's destined her for his own bailiwick she nods silently, eyes closed; her deputy, Benjamin, is guaranteed top place in the national list for a fellowship in France; Régine Tosaka, while taking minutes ("the woman's role, even in revolution," she says), is assured a scholarship to Indesville's graduate teaching college; theatrical Olivier Kolona an internship in film-making; Bernard Neiru introduction to a metropolitan medical school dean; Solange Sériel receives subsidized preparation for doctoral study in mathematics.

This display of grace is understood by all as bribery in a campaign of cooptation. Some reject the payoff, some temporize, but others accept. Even Roger Masson, while aware of Philosophe's purposes, proves unable to resist the temptation—a fellowship for advanced studies in fisheries and aquaculture in Quebec. He had, in fact, already applied to that very institution.

"I know you expected a Philistine ruffian," says Karamau as Masson escorts him out, while Anya Wazimbwe conducts the vote that will end the strike. "No doubt because I look like one. I'm sorry if I have disappointed you. Sometimes boorish politics requires subtle transformations."

When Roger congratulates him on his mastery of the dossiers Karamau waves his arms like a symphony conductor. "It's a sort of musical form, intertwining motifs in development, recapitulation of phrases, boisterous climax. Try it sometime when you are feeling your own ambition in the world. Come see me, and" as he shakes hands and turns into the pathway, "do leave the General's statue in peace. For all you know it might be a Rodin." This jest is Philosophe's first reference to the icon of national humiliation soaring above them on its pedestal.

After ordering the gate unlocked, Masson turns to glance up at the monument, then freezes in his tracks. He sees a familiar figure mounted on the bronze horse in front of the Governor, facing the gate where Karamau will leave the hill for a waiting squad car. Something else has changed up there. Is Freddie Khoin actually pointing a firearm?

Masson shouts to Spider to climb down, for the boy sits in plain sight of Karamau's police at the gate—but he calls in vain. After lobbing a stone to get the minister's attention, Freddie aims his pistol in the same direction without firing it; a cry bursts out of him—something like "Ishmael!"—in what Masson could hear as anguish. But anguish over what? Abortion of Spider's grand mission on that statue? dismissal of his campaign for better bread? or, more pertinently, a bullying authority that has handed the young man's scholarship arbitrarily around from one contractor to another?

"Stop, Spider!" shouts Masson as he starts to open the gate for Karamau. "Put that gun away, or you'll get hurt!"

It is too late, for the minister's bodyguards, clustered outside, have seen Spider's weapon. With one deafening salvo, they blow the boy off his perch, virtually into their chief's path. The pistol falls nearby, and Karamau collects it in a handkerchief. Rising to full height, almost towering over the gate, he commands his men to hold their fire and calls for the ambulance crew that accompanied his police brigade. He then joins Masson, both on their knees over the fallen equestrian. Philosophe speaks softly, reassuringly, in Creole until attendants arrive and bear Spider off on a stretcher. Rising unsteadily, Masson controls his shudders to begin an apology for what appears to be a foiled assassination, but he can't get it out.

He asks only, "Who is Ishmael?"

Karamau shakes his head. "I know what has been bothering that youth you call Spider, and I regret neglecting his needs in my replies to your protests. His was—is indeed—the most poignant of them all, from a family still vilified as 'slaves.' I saw Freddie leave the room while we were talking but didn't perceive the reason why; it's his justified resentment. Perhaps he will survive, and I can do something for him. That slave legacy haunts us both. But for that you need to know the Khoin family's history."

Some time later, after learning that Freddie had succumbed, Anya, through angry tears, recalls that Spider alone refused to smile at jokes over anachronistic French texts tutoring the colonized about "our ancestors the Gauls." Freddie Khoin, like Antoine Karamau, descends from a far more ancient lineage than the European colonizers—older than the early settlers, now become elite families, who emerged out of the Indian Ocean to dominate AuxIndes.

Karamau cuts himself short by another wave of his arms, and, in parting, offers to shake hands once more. Roger is unable to take the gesture—from the same gloved hand that had seized Spider's gun.

"Sorry, Minister," he says. "We've already been cordial."

"And we will again, when this has quieted down," Karamau predicts. As he sweeps through the open gate into the winds of Babel, his coattails billow behind him like great black wings. Through that gate a hundred stunned students watch the bulk called Philosophe wedge into a police vehicle to follow a clamoring ambulance down the hill that Spider had only recently dominated on horseback.

Through the haze clouding his brain, Roger Masson recalls the shouted word "Ishmael." Looking up, he sees the warhorse Neptune appear to shift attitude, its head now pointing into the sky.

End of the 1996 Narrative

CHAPTER 2
THE REQUIEM CHORALE

My guests can labor through the translation without abandoning their own self-importance. Anya is now prime minister and Giselle the mayor, while Solange and Thérèse hold big-shot government jobs without needing the approval of men. Good for them.

As for me, Sophie Makoa, it's not enough that the author of *Vinaigrette's Fables* can keep Freddy Khoin alive at the source springs of liberation, in French. For her part, Cynthia Van Zan deserves to have Spider's story translated in English by her buddy Denis, under my byline.

Giselle changes the subject. "Is that fresh percolation I smell, Sophie?"

Yes, my place does smell of coffee. Why not? It's our national stimulus and we all depend on it. I have seventy-year-old parents who still pick beans off their own Robusta trees; they struggle to survive in a market hostile to hillside smallholders. The French poets called caffeine a writer's oxygen—or they should have—and Sophie Makoa has to write for a living. So her place naturally exhales coffee.

Visitors, my rare visitors, take it without cream or sugar. I always grind those beans; why weaken them any further? Just breathe it in—and by the way, don't accuse me of trying to play hostess. That's not Sophie's style.

But yes, the women are here—a few I can trust to testify to Spider's sacrifice, before I shoot the translation out to Cynthia Van Zan in her Nigerian refuge. She'll recall Thérèse Zaphyra who wrestled the military into submission until a few of them grabbed their guns and headed after softer targets; Solange Sériel who has never forgotten a statistic once she's audited it, least of all those pertaining to her male friends.

Above all, there's my beloved adopted daughter, bright-eyed Anya, defector from the haughty Wazimbwe dynasty. Now prime minister, at the top of her game, Anya dashes in late, shakes her hair loose, and struggles with the Spider episode from twenty years ago. "Do I *have* to go through this again, *Maman*?"

My Diva likes to play dissembler.

"I was in it deep, you know," she adds superfluously.

"You live in my chronicle, Anya," I respond more humbly than I intend.

"Your narrative does come very close, Maman," Anya observes. "How did you learn all this? Not from the monstrous Karamau?"

"You told me most of it yourself. Masson added the rest."

"How indiscreet of us," Anya answers. "I'll have to protest to Roger some day." She laughs quietly.

"It *is* pretty accurate, Sophie," approves Zaphyra. "You paid attention to all that while hobnobbing with our enemy, the obnoxious president."

"Not a bad spot to watch from," I retort, "even if it's only in your imagination."

Solange chimes in. "You seem to have held that old scoundrel back, Sophie. Tied the chief of state to your bedpost?"

"Stop that," I order. "Doménique knew to keep his distance from you amateurs."

True, they have me trapped between the president's boudoir and my Anya's insurrection. Two purposes in conflict, how I love that! Twenty years, and Spider still lives in our contradictions.

"Past becomes present?" muses Giselle, "Or is it vice versa?"

"Both," I assert.

"The wily Philosophe saw through that, didn't he?" suggests Giselle. "But doesn't your narrative give him too much credit, Sophie?"

"It doesn't," responds Anya Wazimbwe for me. "The brute was utterly clairvoyant; Incubus with the mind of Mammon. He was using his aides' research to cough up that preemptive roster of rewards for us, pretending to have a heart."

"No. Karamau sure knew what we wanted for ourselves," declares Thérèse, looking at the others. "Probably he was just sending us around the world, to dilute our bite."

"Fortunately," adds Solange, "most of us came back to reload."

"Right," says Anya Wazimbwe soberly, "but he bought a decade or more of time with all that. Well, I used it to adapt to Gandhian nonviolence."

"After I adopted you," I had to add to the metaphoric clutter. It's true that Anya did correct her adolescent naïveté when I took her under my wing. By then Doménique Bienportant was gone and Roger Masson was head of state. "Your commitment was always crucial, Anya. You didn't have to wait until you learned it from me—to reject your own family's corrupt authority."

"No, there were some belligerents left on that end," notes Thérèse who'd spent her ministry subduing unruly officers belonging to prestigious houses like the Wazimbwe. That may be why she begins every utterance with a negative.

"Violence was always a threat," interjects Giselle. "I had to keep my Roger from taking revenge against Spider's killers, or he would have never been elected president."

"No, is that why Masson didn't wear socks?" asks Thérèse.

As the others gesture incoherently, mention of Spider's sacrifice stirs Anya. "While willing to be amused," she says, "I was surprised that Spider Freddie showed no bitterness over being a pawn in that bizarre succession of contractors. Affluent men were exchanging commitments and switching people at will. They still are, just to enhance their own status, to boost their payoffs. Nobody's life is too precious to be safe from their expediency. Even languages get traded to rationalize the indefensible. Perhaps Spider was satisfied to remain an indigent student on a perpetual internship, the first of his family ever to get beyond elementary school. That's something, but not nearly enough."

This seems a word of advice from Wazimbwe to Van Zan, so I'll pass it on with this English version of my twenty-year-old story. Denis Guyane, her collaborator when they were here, called his translation of the piece a labor of love. If you knew us better, you'd know that sentiment was not meant for me.

"No, too bad Denis Guyane is back in New York," comments Thérèse Zaphyra. "That pensive Haitian was a life-saver for your thighs, Solange."

"Glad you noticed, love," says Solange Sériel. Nicknamed La Douce, she flashes her be-ringed fists into empty air.

I have to calm the tempers, so I resort to fact. "Only Denis's parents were Haitian," I say, "escaping the Duvaliers before he was born."

"So that their son could escort my Roger around the United States," proudly adds Giselle.

"No," says Thérèse with a cunning grin, "so he could introduce Cynthia to that lucky husband of yours, dear Giselle."

Her insinuation puzzles the mayor whose face clouds in embarrassment. That provokes a guffaw from Solange, glad to deflect attention away from her own dalliance with Guyane.

Giselle Masson returns to my article. "Your comments on wardrobe make us sound like slobs, Sophie," she objects. "As students, of course we dressed informally but decently, after all. You know, I think I will have another coffee."

Mayor or not, she waits in vain for it. I'm busy now.

Solange demurs. "If she publishes a tribute to adolescent uprisings, Cynthia will have to leave me out of it. They end in an oblivion that we can't even call history."

Anya refocuses us. "Cynthia Van Zan won't go off half-cocked. She's a disciplined fact-finder and balloon-buster, even when her drawings make us laugh. It's taken twenty years, but we're close to that future now," says Anya brightly.

I don't dare raise my eyebrows over that one.

Each in her own style, Cynthia Van Zan and Anya Wazimbwe once had differences, but they've made their peace. I'm proud of having brought them together—if I did. Even now, a continent apart, Cynthia admires the Diva's renunciation of family privilege, her authority as a radical, while, like me, Anya wishes that gifted American were here to interpret what the oceans and hills are buzzing about.

It's time we understood that Van Zan's work bears a foreshadowing of global catastrophe. She shows humans who suffer consequences from the same ingenuity that has exploited the oceanic and forest folk—digging out the earth, dumping our gas and plastic trash on the water, puffing carbon into bird land, "communicating socially" (meaning tribally)—without self-awareness. Unlike me, Cynthia won't wait for the Revolution to resolve anything.

Thérèse has a question.

"No, I admire Van Zan's art, but can we depend on her bubbling sea critters to display anything relevant to people? What do the fish know?"

"They know more about us than we know about them," retorts Wazimbwe, sounding more like me than I'd expected. "And they're in touch with the . . . the others."

Thérèse swallows the bait. "No. What others?"

"Animals, trees, birds," answers Anya. "Horses for instance. Have you noticed that statue lately?"

"You mean Neptune? No, sunk under the Governor to keep him from flying off somewhere? Old male tale that one. Don't you think so, Sophie?

I don't.

"All things considered," observes Solange Seriel, "you do seem to have given our translator some liberties with your original text. I recall that it opens with the French for 'a dark and stormy night,' although the whole drama operates in midday; what happened to that fiction?"

My reply was ready: "Dark and stormy was a setting for boys, for Spider's story, not for women like you, or girls like Cynthia was at the time. It's the climate for people who follow the Karamaus, who let Spider fall into the future."

"But that future has come. It's now," says Anya. "And Spider is still here, in spirit."

Maybe dark-and-stormy was not that bad for an opening line, although it sounds a little corny today—especially to an American ear, habitually tuned to corn.

Back in 1996, while still a young Vinaigrette, I chose to treat Spider's fall as an epic, not an accident. That does not condemn the veracity of the account, and it doesn't make me responsible for corn. Vinaigrette's *Fables* is Sophie Makoa's sheet, and I write what I choose.

I used that introductory formula back then to color the report, but do not mock me, good reader. Fine journalism attains the dignity of myth. If the lad called Spider fell to his death on Babel Hill during a "dark and stormy night," even though it happened in broad daylight, no reader thought they were looking at Sophie's weather report. My words invoked the *spirit* of the episode—a somber *night of the soul*.

Enlightened subscribers of the *Fables* (the only kind I have) readily grasped my conceit—probably including Van Zan's pretentious father in New Orleans. They knew that Spider was killed in a sunny afternoon, not in the dark or damp; that he was shot by cops doing their miserable duty to protect their chief; that the old Governor's statue would never trot eastward from AuxIndes, and his imperial shadow would hover ponderously over our island for decades.

As it still does.

Having emptied my coffee pot and exhausted my patience, the women take their leave, Anya as well. She doesn't need to reside here any longer.

So twenty years after the event, Van Zan's voice has risen across Africa to summon my narrative. Barely a teenager in New Orleans when the tragedy happened here, Cynthia suggests that I report it as it actually occurred. To prod me, she called one night from Nigeria, inviting me to "revisit" that fatal afternoon, when the student revolt collapsed, Anya Wazimbwe's leadership was aborted, and young Spider died.

He was hit by a bullet and fell into the future. That's the way it happened and how I saw it after filing the story in *Fables à la Vinaigrette*. When Van Zan saw the article as a kid twenty years ago, she couldn't handle the language. Even then her bully of a father pressed it on her. Now that she's Francophone, she considers my style a "caffeinated cliché." Is that a compliment?

Agreed that her new book requires the truth about that student uprising. She's getting it here personified through my Anya and Roger Masson in Denis Guyane's translation. Typically American, Cynthia suppresses her imagination at will and insists on "straight facts," even in the history that belongs to us, in all its complexity. Personally, I prefer myth, but Van Zan can bully gracefully to get what she wants. Despite her own West African roots Cynthia dares to trivialize "truth" as dependent on unadorned facts. Has Van Zan forgotten that she, too, is an artist, an essentially African one?

Gleaming brown Yankee, you pester me about the past when you too have risen above circumstances—in your narratives and parables, in graphic images, cartoons, blazing with intuition. You change a space by merely walking into it. For you and me, Cynthia, mere facts can only hint at truth.

Frankly, I'm reassured by Van Zan's prosaic summons. By insisting on "verifiable facts," an accommodation I seldom concede, she's showing confidence in us, that we can acknowledge and exploit the mundane, even when we prefer the enigmatic. Her trust evolved during five years at the job here. It surfaced after three long centuries of brutal servitude among alien cotton in America—bondage bequeathed through her mother's line. Now it's back in Nigeria, of all places.

Of course, slavery required dissembling the enigmatic as a survival strategy. We're still good at that. When Cynthia came this way as a young adult, reversing her slave-mother's trajectory to confront her ancestral continent, it was her dark energy that overcame self-doubt. She transcended her father's foolish admonition to play *la jeune fille* among us. Too strong for that game, she went for the jugular. In five years working here with her devoted Haitian-American sidekick, Van Zan learned to graft her people's survival to our buried roots. Now she's finishing her continental circuit in the very West Africa that had expelled her mother's people into bondage.

And still she demands "facts?"

At any rate, Cynthia's Anglo readers will finally learn what happened at Babel Mountain back in 1996: how the kid called Spider, born of enslaved ghosts, got shot off that imperialist statue and became a martyr to our island's freedom.

To our *struggle* for freedom, rather. Because it goes on. And on. Anya is right. By now, two decades after that boy's tragedy, the Republic has inched closer to the light. Still no revolution, not my kind of Revolution. Coffee persists, grinding away; Champagne hasn't popped, not yet.

As for the raw narrative of Babel Hill in 1996, Cynthia will have it—nearly shorn of myth, but still lively. In turn, Vinaigrette's fables continue, wafting on caffeine and the subtle energy of our women.

CHAPTER 3

BAIT AND TACKLE

New York, 2006: Denis Guyane with Masson

"Must I remind myself that I can't afford *not* to do this?" Guyane was musing half aloud while waiting for the Fisherman to rejoin him for dinner. "Nice spring weather in New York," he noted, "hotel lobby buzzing with prosperity, and I'm still spinning my wheels with no traction. To disappoint this visitor from AuxIndes will leave zero clients in Denis Guyane's pitiful portfolio. I'd better find ways to help Masson peddle his anchovies—or whatever he's trawling for in this country. Just wish I knew how to make it interesting."

That afternoon, on Roger Masson's arrival in New York, their conversation had been more tentative than purposeful. Denis did recognize the young fisheries tycoon from their introduction a year ago across lunch in Indesville. Their connection, the embassy's commercial attaché with no particular axe to grind, had identified Masson as an erstwhile student militant, now successful after a decade in seafood and related fields. He was said to be developing into a "person of caliber" in AuxIndes.

After exchanging cards at that lunch meeting, the Fisherman had apparently saved Denis's Agency address to seek guidance, "preferably in French," for a brief study tour of the American seafood industry. Now here he was.

Little from that initiative kindled any excitement in Denis Guyane. Fish weren't about to jump into his mind; mermaids didn't haunt his fugitive ambitions. Moreover, Masson had evidently been requesting service from the Agency in general, not from him specifically. Denis knew this when, earlier that day at Kennedy airport, the guest was surprised on arrival to find "Monsieur Guyane" also to be a Black person. Obviously, he'd failed to remember Denis personally from that Indesville handshake a year ago. So much for political-caliber recall.

In fact, it was only after Masson's open inquiry floated down the decision ladder that management assigned Guyane, their sole fulltime Africa hand, into what seemed a natural—and ominous—last chance.

Still, for better or worse, nearing thirty years of age, Denis couldn't reject the charge.

"Having regrettably almost no English," Masson explained in the cab from Kennedy, "I had asked your offices for a French speaker to accompany me on a tour. You do fill that role admirably. I expected a francophone escort to be hard enough to find here—let alone one who . . ." he left off tactfully.

"One who looks like you," Denis filled the pause, "our euphemism for racial affiliation. Although nobody does look exactly like anybody else."

"Look like me? Poor fellow," quipped Masson. Side by side, there was no likelihood that this sandy, slightly shaped Indian-Oceanite would be confused with Guyane's robust "African" physique. Were they off to a bad start? Was the client already disappointed in getting a Black companion? The Fisherman waved that cloud away.

"True, of course," Masson remarked, with a disarming chuckle. "We are not identical. You are much taller than I, and far better looking. We're both fairly young, though, another favorable sign. Your employers seem adept at accommodating their clients' needs. I'm pleased with my luck."

Roger Masson then fell silent, eyes closed, a habit he was inclined to inflict periodically on all interlocutors. It suggested that he was feeling something in the darkness—down the briny deep perhaps, among those sea urchins?

Eventually, Fisherman would learn that Denis Guyane's bilinguality had been bequeathed by Haitian-born parents and reinforced by a Peace Corps tour in Senegal. The client was not obliged to know that headquarters had assigned Denis to this fishing expedition to bail out his low-priority Africa project—improvised to extend the Agency's half-hearted "diversity mission." After three years of self-education and canvassing, little business had emerged, and Guyane's one-man shop quivered on the brink of collapse.

"So this trek could be my last," he repeated to himself, "a vicarious frolic in the tides of AuxIndes." He shivered momentarily, to shake off the spray.

Giving Masson time to shower and prepare for dinner, Denis quit the hotel lobby and circled several midtown blocks. Three years ago, back from Dakar, he had re-learned to navigate his native city, to absorb New York's confluence of incessant noise and tacit insouciance. Uproars of construction; traffic horns blown without purpose;

shouts across busy intersections to nobody in evidence. Too many people to be certifiably crazy, talking loudly into apparatuses, calling outer space—sometimes in English—without apparent effect.

So why was he out here, stalking around a hotel with little evident purpose? Feeling unhinged, Denis returned to await Roger Masson in the lobby and to initiate the Fisherman's American trek agreeably on this warm Manhattan evening. He'd already scheduled dinner for the occasion—conducive, he hoped, to AuxIndien taste: moderately haute cuisine without flagrant emphasis on seafood.

Masson seized the opportunity by ordering veal. "I appreciate your discretion," he told Denis. "Our island is not smothered in fish, as some might infer from my marketing strategy. You probably recall that it contains a staggeringly large herd of cattle, much of it edible, or otherwise exploited." He sniffed and sipped at a sedate Pinot Noir.

Accustomed by discipline to ignore appetite, Denis Guyane could always, or seldom, eat. Probing at a Dover sole, he summoned his research on AuxIndes culture. "I'm told the amputated cattle horns provide trumpet music or tomb decoration, and that the humps swell with saturated fat; ugh."

"Nonetheless, the live beast is real value on the hoof," Masson joined this ode to bovinity. "Cattle are our wealth, our savings banks, our discreet interlocutors. I have a modest herd of my own, and I occasionally discuss business matters with them; the cows never betray my confidence, even when they surrender to our pitiless greed. If it suits the schedule you are crafting for me, Mr. Guyane, I should be interested in seeing an American ranch. But if that complicates the tour unduly . . ."

"Not at all," Denis assured him, glad to have the opportunity to broach itinerary. "The Agency has contacts to accommodate your interests, maritime and terrestrial." At least he hoped that would be true. Continuing after a swig of Muscadet, "We might fit a visit to cattle country in Texas before you head for Southern California. Would, say, polled Herefords do?" How he came up with the French for that one he couldn't guess, but it worked.

"Oh, yes," replied the Fisherman with delight; his gray eyes brightened. "While we're on the westward route, awaited by fish, we'll be able to observe the excitement of what your cinema calls cow paunching. And, Denis, could we also pass through the Grand Cannon du Colodoreau, if that's the right term for it in English?"

So be it. The trip was informally invoked, and they had imperceptibly moved onto first-name basis *à l'Américaine.*

That exchange inaugurated two days of arrangements over maps, telephones, and transportation websites—too much for Guyane's forlorn office to manage by its single self. Fortunately, when he begged Personnel Services for staff assistance, he was rescued by the ageless and omnicompetent Irene Rodriguez, chief of that department, who appointed herself to act as his backstop. This volunteer demonstrated high proficiency in booking appointments as well as air passage ("Business class, of course, Mr. Guyane, right?"), plus vehicle rentals, private accommodations and hotel lodgings, tour guide services, and pauses for refreshment.

Without needing to know cumbersome details, Mrs. Rodriguez (she insisted on the title) deftly scheduled meetings around maritime and refrigeration practice, fish farming in California, even anti-piracy police work. She established lines of credit for the journey, channels for the invoices, and registers for the accounts to be covered by Masson's AuThon company at the close of what she labeled "the

Consultancy." During the men's month-long tour, Rodriguez field-ed calls for help, switching effortlessly into Spanish to underscore a point to patriots in the Southwest. She even managed to find "the perfect opera performance" as a diversion for the Fisherman in San Francisco.

A daughter of immigrants from the Dominican Republic, Irene Rodriguez claimed none of the university credentials that might have hoisted her to higher corporate summits. She acquitted her charge through skills learned while scaling the Agency's staff echelons one by one.

By now, bewildered senior management turned a blind eye ("one of many," she said) to her detour from regular duties in order to assist Guyane, the quixotic Haitian. She did it merely out of sympathy for a "fellow Hispaniolite." Advising Denis to "just call me your secretary, whenever you need to," Rodriquez bolstered his confidence in an assignment that she endowed with adroit management and rigorous accounting. All Denis had to do was to make everybody else happy.

Especially the Fisherman from AuxIndes. Participating actively in the process, Roger Masson gladly clarified his business priorities, his passion for pastries, distaste for socks in his footwear, and a suppressed inclination toward rough-house sports and gangster films.

In due course Guyane learned that an advantageous marriage underlay Roger's idiosyncrasies with patrician grace and forbearance. Licensed in pharmacy, Giselle Masson offered technical services to AuThon enterprises; but she kept an eye on public office for both of them once they found the appropriate opportunity. "She is far more adept at politics than I," Masson conceded, "and she should become mayor of Indesville, but has to be three times better than a male rival to get anywhere in our patriarchal morass."

Growing expansive as his confidence in the Consultancy strengthened, the Fisherman cheerfully described his own origins in AuxIndes. He was born into a mildly prosperous farming family that had sacrificed land, savings, "and even cattle" to provide for his needs. After taking pains to make friends and assert leadership at the University, Masson had abandoned his risk-prone student activism for the aggrandizements of commerce. Founding a fishery made him his own boss "and that pleased the elders," he admitted.

To make it happen, he had to thank, or to blame, the fellowship in Quebec procured for him by an avuncular cabinet minister in 1996 or '97.

"Our durable czar of the Interior and meta-police chief Antoine Karamau. I hope you have not had to encounter him in your own visits to the island."

"You're referring to that very large man also called Philosophe?" Masson nodded.

Having scored another point for research, Denis kept going. "Never had the pleasure, but I was wondering whether as a militant you were with him at that uprising around a statue about ten years ago—the one that ended with a student getting shot?"

The question may have unintentionally hit a nerve; Guyane had to watch the Fisherman grow taut in his chair. After another extended silence, eyes closed, sipping water, Masson replied gravely. "I was a principal in that protest. Freddie Khoin was my friend—the victim—and we had negotiated with Mr. Karamau that day on serious matters, like academic governance and online resources for the school we mocked as Facsimile-U. Understandably, all the subsequent media attention was devoted to Spider's ghastly execution by the police."

"I don't recall much about that," said Denis, as if to reassure his guest, "except that the minister seems to have been investigated for the incident. Yet he remains. Was he in fact innocent of the murder?"

"Oh, yes, Antoine has survived many inquiries and is invariably innocent." After a pause, "Have you had business with him?"

"With Karamau? I didn't know he was involved . . . in business."

"Well, perhaps not the kind you'd want to promote, Denis. But his position allowed, in fact still allows him after what—twelve, fifteen years—to do favors."

"Including for you, I believe. You mentioned the fellowship to Quebec," said Denis, trying to reassure while displaying his information. Masson seemed to have drifted away again, however, lost perhaps in grief for his role in the death of a friend. Guyane hesitated to pursue a subject that might end unfavorably. Still, he did not entirely regret his candor over a notorious police assassination on Masson's watch; it reinforced the impression Denis needed to make on his only client.

"Yes, I do owe that start to Karamau," said Masson, recovering his self-possession. "I admit that my friend Spider had been foolishly waving a pistol at the minister—unloaded but still threatening—before the police shot him. Philosophe had been masterful that day. He hacked our coalition into fragments. Study in Canada got me away from the island, and out of his hair, for a couple of years, while the police, his police, investigated the tragedy. Naturally, they too were exculpated. But that fisheries fellowship gave me my trade—and time to read, one of my passions; I learned that from the late

Spider. The extra brown bag you saw in my luggage is loaded with paperbacks, some of them from Freddie's collection."

"My parents would congratulate me on traveling with a literate businessman," Denis said, grinning. "They might even salute that big police chief for advancing your education."

"Ironically, Mr. Guyane—Denis—the AuThon company must thank him for its very existence. That Quebec course gave me a basic understanding of the industry, something sorely needed in my country of pirogues and smoke-huts on the beach. North Atlantic culture also introduced me to what I'm almost embarrassed to call the romance of the sea. I wish to learn what, if anything, we can give back to the waters we depend on."

"Nothing to be ashamed of in that romance; there is much great writing on it. All the books with you are in French?"

"Well, yes. Unfortunately, even after graduating from Babel Mountain, I don't have the brain space for another language beyond French and Creole; at most, I know only ten words of English. I never ventured out of Quebec into the United States during those two school years, not even to Ontario."

They were by then at lunch, picking salad combinations, preparing for the desserts that excited Masson most. "But in my free time at sea," he said, "I paddled through a translation of that great novel, *Moby Dick*. An extraordinary mind, your Melville, meticulous about the technology of whaling in those days, and even the business organization of the voyage. Giselle and I named our little dog *Moby*, but he declines to grow whaleish. I understand Melville wrote more about the sea, so I've brought the novella *Benito Cereno*, where African slaves adroitly overwhelm a European ship."

"That revolt is said to be a parable for my ancestors' Haitian revolution."

"So I've heard. The plot explores a remarkable reversal of stereotypes—and written by a white man! Freddie the Spider admired it, so I found a translation."

Masson chuckled, then paused again, and lifted his glass in a gesture toward Denis Guyane. "It's perhaps fortunate that I could not undertake Melville in his original language, for that weakness allows me to enjoy the privilege of falling into your very capable hands. Now," after glancing at the dessert menu, "I'll have the *crème brulée*."

Then, almost to himself, the Fisherman muttered: "Freddie was on *his* fourth language, or was it his fifth? Rest in peace, Spider."

❁ ❁ ❁

Thanks largely to Rodriguez, Roger Masson's southern and western itinerary took admirable shape during that two-day sequence at the Agency. On the second evening, Denis introduced the Fisherman to his parents over dinner at their apartment in Brooklyn.

Recalcitrant opponents of the Haitian dictatorship, Clotilde and Pierre-Louis Guyane had fled to the United States in the mid-1970s to avoid exposing their unborn son to threats from the *Macoute*. Unlike fellow migrants, they ignored the beckoning sunshine of South Florida in favor of "the real America"—in Flatbush. Calling themselves maroons, and with some exertion, the Guyanes earned a modest living there. Pierre-Louis functioned as a freelance accountant, able to read and write English without ever speaking it quite intelligibly. His wife Clotilde, claiming to have mastered only French and Spanish, taught them in a trilingual school. Together, they used French (and Creole) exclusively with their son.

When he was old enough to understand, Denis heard his father's grim summation: the family had escaped atavistic tyranny only to fall into the grip of industrial racism. "Being Black in Cap Haïtien used to be normal; white folks showed up only to push us around a bit. In Brooklyn, USA, just being light brown is a permanent handicap."

His mother added her voice: "Over there the spirits could function for you; here they run savage, with firearms." When the boy expressed eagerness for his parents' birth island, they both shook their heads. "Every visitor to Haiti senses there's too much that they are not allowed to see," his father said.

"And we can't be sure they'd let you out when you want to leave," added Mme. Guyane.

Clotilde Guyane nevertheless paid regular homage to Indigenous Haitian ritual, personified by the life-sized papier-mâché *Damballa* they had carried with them from Port-au-Prince. Her rationalist spouse complained: "Your mother made us take Papa Doc in disguise down the brain drain with us." He reluctantly indulged his wife's commitment to *Vodou* as far as enlightenment would permit.

In deference to what she called "Trickster statue Papa Legba," Clotilde wore no shoes indoors. She permitted students to call her the barefoot professor. Both elder Guyanes enjoyed acting as immigrant curiosities.

Even after he joined the Agency and was maintaining his own Soho apartment, Denis preferred to convene often with his parents, rather than become entangled in the usual coterie of Manhattan friends and lovers. During her son's visits, Clotilde Guyane would interrupt her life to sustain his. They talked, took walks together, read to each other; she also cooked copiously, compensating for what she regarded as his delinquent dietary habits.

Pierre-Louis joined them when he wished. Trained in mathematics, he was now in semi-retirement, but occupied in helping Haitians file their American tax returns. He insisted, said he, on a "scientific" approach to everything, from IRS ordinances to human relations. The arrival of an "African fisherman" in his son's orbit prompted the elder Guyane's interest in island republics, none of them so tragic or deserving, however, as his lost Haiti.

This evening, after serving her inimitable *céviche de conch* to an appreciative guest from the Indies, Denis's mother was bending down to retrieve a utensil when she remarked that this otherwise elegant entrepreneur was not wearing socks. "True," admitted Masson, "I learned to do without them years ago during months on swamped decks, where they're only a nuisance." Clotilde instantly perceived affinity: they were both maroons, with bare extremities probing for roots. Their insular homelands should become long-distance allies. To her regret, after some descriptive exchanges, they concluded that Indian Ocean Creole bore only fragmentary overlaps with Haitian *kreyol*.

To her son's amusement, dropping into the familiar *tutoyer* to address her new friend, Clotilde offered Masson a brief essay she had once published connecting Haitian and Bantu African religious symbolisms. Modestly, Masson declined qualification to comment on the thesis. Using formal address (to an older person) Roger remarked that Madam's scholarship could hardly have approached the excellence of her rice pudding. This lame compliment caused Denis

and his father to share an American grimace: the Fisherman was ste-
reotypically reducing a professional to wife and cook. Clotilde only
waved a hand dismissively, refusing to show offense. Pierre-Louis
returned to his habit of shelling and popping groundnuts—unsalted
and, if you believed the grocer—imported especially from Haiti.

"Admirable family," judged Masson as they returned to
Manhattan. "And from a valiant island country. Too bad Haitians
don't do enough fishing for their own good; they could benefit from
the abundance there of tuna, marlin, even sardines. As I ask my own
people, why depend on imported nutrition when you have protein
swimming all around you?"

On the third morning of his visit, their flight to New Orleans
allowed Roger Masson to survive the austerity of airline cuisine and
to admire the evanescent shapes and colors of the eastern American
landscape. From aloft, Fisherman pronounced the United States "a
handsome but dynamic patchwork with some unbridged chasms between the shapes. You'll never get it together," he predicted.

From his reading, the visitor showed lively interest in historical
identifications, looking for the Appalachian Trail, asking to be informed when the aircraft crossed the Mason-Dixon Line, and where
Jefferson's purchase of Louisiana began. Masson wondered what had
kept some border states ambivalent in the 1860s—sympathetic to rebellion, yet unable to join the Confederacy. He deplored the mid-At-
lantic electorate's hostility to Lincoln, an icon of universal respect, and
yet a victim of false consciousness in Baltimore and the Chesapeake.

In response, without mastering all the answers, Guyane recommended reading the quintessential abolitionist Frederick Douglass who escaped slavery to rank with Lincoln in American greatness— and to advocate for Haiti among his notable causes. As Masson took notes on Douglass, he might have been considering his own political future.

Not everything on the trip was so serious. In the aircraft during pre-takeoff security drill, the Fisherman admired an animated blond hostess who with a faux smirk dangled her oxygen-mask comically before him, pantomiming a sardonic streetwalker with her handbag. Joining the game, Masson took out his wallet and offered her a Euro; when she declined, he growled in mock-Creole disappointment and ordered a vermouth.

Once in New Orleans, Fisherman looked for more levity on the streets of the *Carré*, but in vain. The city appeared mired in segregation—and still stunned, he thought, from the rigors of Hurricane Katrina the year before. From his original vantage point, Masson had imagined Louisiana to be composed of several dozen gifted African Americans blowing exuberant music on homemade instruments. On site, he learned terms like "hip" and "square," and visited an exhibition of cotton cultivation, sensing sadder music in the wind.

After leaving New Orleans, Fisherman expanded his appreciation for the blues. In a small aircraft chartered by the Agency, Masson observed the lower Mississippi as an immense basin hedged by seawalls; the "earth" seemed composed of water, with sad fragments of land floating in it. These terrestrial flecks reminded him of the French nursery rhyme about "the wee ship that never went to sea." Anachronistically, fluid musical messages evoked Huck Finn's descent down the great river with the slave Jim; they, too, never reached ocean.

On southern shores, the winds delivered torrents from heaven, recalling the horror of Katrina that had recently descended like a homicidal plague. Inundated rice fields in Louisiana seemed just as vulnerable to climate as those his family maintained in their island. Not an obviously secure place for an orderly fisheries system, this was nonetheless a cornucopia of prawn gumbos and crawfish étouffée. Masson gladly realized how much he still had to learn.

On the ground, after a tour of seafood markets and provocative discussions of the perils of an overheating planet, their itinerary took them from New Orleans to the shrimp-infused Delta abutting the swamps south and west of the city. This sample of Louisiana provided evidence of heedless technology infused by corporate contempt for the natural and human biosphere. "Welcome to Cancer Alley," was the greeting from a faculty contact at a Black college near Lafayette. She explained that "we get contradictory results from our chlorine plants, refineries, and truck transportation. They assure jobs to able-bodied folk here, but underpaid workers rush home past polluted waters. They only hope the last storm hasn't carried off their trailers, or the next flood won't swallow their children."

Asked about government protection for their settlements, Professor Bechet pointed to ongoing irrigation projects, and groaned. "The environmental types come by. They prattle their premises, cluck their tongues, and go home, leaving us to handle dioxin in the soil and rust in the water. We're supposed to be reassured by 'reciprocity'—meaning that, since the country transfers energy from

Black folks to whites, we can now redirect its toxicity back from whites to Black. That's reciprocal, ain't it?"

Nearby, a shovel-bearing man from Lake Charles added, "All that taxpayer money comin' in again every time we flood. Fix up the houses, make the 'taters grow. But not for you this time, Rufus. You gotta know how to fill in the paperwork right." He went back to his job while Denis translated as well as he could.

Departing the area in profound sobriety, the Fisherman could still praise its local gumbos and catfish for their succulence and his Cajun hosts for their affectionate remnants of French. But the locals returned to particulars of the blues. "With our crawfish and fried pickles, we have to taste the spice of petro-chemicals," said another host, a Cajun newspaper editor.

"Ironically," replied Masson, "my own Black and brown country may be too poor to suffer from such blight. We couldn't even keep operating our one attempt at a petroleum refinery. Our main hope is that sun, wind, and waves will suffice for AuxIndes."

❈ ❈ ❈

After the visits to Lafayette and Lake Charles, Guyane became driver as well as interpreter. A rented vehicle brought them westward to look at port facilities and climate control technology around Houston. Then an interlude at a cattle ranch and tour resort that boasted prize-winning Herefords. Masson compared the cattle favorably with French Charolais, "except for the steaks," he confided quietly to Denis.

Later, wondering over the ethics of caloric consumption, Guyane asked whether his companion never suffered regrets over his own gainful dependence on "mining protein out of the ocean."

"Not regret," retorted Fisherman, "make it sheer remorse. Especially when I have to justify business prosperity to my closest colleague—a senior director whom I've known from student days. More or less vegan herself, Anya Wazimbwe looks for any opportunity to turn *AuThon* into a plant-based industry. So, while she remains loyal, this comrade exerts her subversive influence on my conscience from inside."

"She sounds very effective, but what about her own conscience?"

"Anya handles that contradiction adroitly," answered Masson with a smile. "Along with self-denial, she regularly condemns the whole land-based protein rage as a waste of the planet. She has paid for that, too, having alienated her very conservative family whose wealth depends on cattle. That rebellion against the plutocrat Wazimbwes has turned Anya seaward—to give the oceans a chance. So she dominates our industry from an inside position. She considers our enterprises capable of granting the high seas governance over their own productivity, sacrifice, and reproduction. At least the maritime world used to do so, until we became too numerous, too greedy, and . . ."

"And too efficient at destruction," Denis completed the indictment.

"So that humans now have to take responsibility for ocean mismanagement. But at least we AuxIndiens didn't contaminate your Gulf of Mexico. Indian Ocean industry still has an opportunity to convert to renewable energy sources. Our island must prevent the oil and gas vandals from infecting its coasts."

"They're on the verge of that, are they?"

"I hope not. Not yet. We listen to Anya's conservationist friends, and are trying to keep the unprincipled Bienportant government from selling out."

"Good," said Guyane. "If only more masters of capital and politics would do that."

"So just a few of us in our little oceanic niche won't suffice?"

"Not until you acquire more influence and more capital."

"Maybe that's why we're here," said Masson with a contagious grin. "Let's see whether we can impress our American interlocutors on this humble pilgrimage. But keep Anya Wazimbwe in mind. *La Diva*, who once led that student uprising, remains what you call cool. I seldom lose track of her."

A subsequent flight took them from Houston to Phoenix. Wondering at first why his itinerary deviated so far from the sea, Fisherman hoped at least to attend a gun fight outside Arizona's O.K. Corral. Instead, what Mrs. Rodriguez had in mind was a display of energy-saving refrigeration systems applicable to climates like AuxIndes in austral summer. "This Phoenix even welcomes fish out of water," explained Masson in his postcard home. "I expected a really hot town, but here you can walk into the Arctic."

After enjoying assiduously cooled facilities, the travelers took to the road again, for a survey of the Grand Canyon from its several observation points. The canyon geology resembled "an Olympian *mille-feuilles*," commented the Fisherman whose taste for sweetly layered French pastry was becoming sorely neglected. More pertinent to the journey, Rodriguez had found a government research facility on the Colorado River system that intrigued them, even while the supply of ground water underwent threat. "If AuxIndes could control its hydraulics, we'd lead the way," he said, "so why haven't humans learned to domesticate sudden storms into steady, predictable doses of rainfall?"

On this route, Masson also noted his first impressions of Indigenous America where lives resembled the plight of the AuxIndien poor. "You and we have the resources to remedy such misery," he growled as Denis drove through; "so why don't we do it?"

"The resources exist, but not the will to spend them on exploited communities."

"The will is always self-absorbed. It takes a combination of time, money, and literacy to enter the middle class, my spouse tells me," replied Fisherman. "With us, all three are in short supply, and I can only work on the money angle."

"That should take care of the other two, but, alas, it doesn't." Denis now found himself sounding like his companion.

After a night in the canyon park, Guyane drove them into Las Vegas for a visit that may have set a world's record for brevity. Denis was to keep the engine running at the curb on Fremont Street while Masson entered a modest casino. There the Fisherman dropped a single coin into a machine, cranked the arm as he had promised a nephew he would do, and, without waiting for the spin to conclude, returned to their automobile. As evidence for the nephew, Denis recorded this sporting sortie on video out the car window.

❀ ❀ ❀

The next stage, by air, was to Los Angeles where they expected instruction in anti-piracy technology, climate accommodation, and the Asian oligopoly of seafood farming, as such matters were understood in California. Masson looked forward to meeting "people who take fish seriously, even in the shadow of Alfred Hitchcock." Among other opportunities, he had his eye on prospects for marketing dry-iced *camarons* (Indian Ocean prawns) to the American west coast, that citadel of the modern appetite.

En route, Masson and Guyane spoke copiously and amicably—not only of fish and freezing, or hatcheries and climate devastation, but also of themselves in their respective worlds. As Roger warmed to the "laid-back" temper of the West, and to his American companion, he spoke more openly about political stagnation in AuxIndes, which occupied him nearly as much as his main business.

"You wonder how a potentate like Antoine Karamau can be satisfied with an unchanging portfolio in a parade of incompetent cabinets," said Masson one evening as if Denis had actually broached the subject. "Well, there's a live-and-let-live quality to Philosophe's arrangement with our venerable president. Thanks to the Interior Ministry's control over law enforcement and elections, Antoine is indispensable. So he is rewarded for loyalty by a guarantee that he can do anything he likes with the forces at his disposal. He's our version of your Edgar Hoover and Jack Palance combined. Of course, his cops were just doing their job when they murdered Spider.

"On the political level," he continued, "Philosophe's longevity is a precondition for any government, and our occasional reshufflings happen at his insistence. This dysfunctional collaboration started in the early nineties, and prevails today; no challenger has been able to outbid our feckless Domino's commitments to law and order. By the way, we call President Bienportant 'the Domino' because of the few white spots sprinkled on his dark soul."

"For his part Karamau was able to disarm our youth movement ten years ago, and we thought he was aiming for president sooner or later. But that's finished by now. He claims that his diabetes prevents him from tackling the top job; I salute that option by eating as much *patisserie* as I can. Actually, he probably just doesn't want his villainous record to face scrutiny in a national election."

"And no risk of a military coup?"

"There's no trust between the army and the constabulary. He'll have to buy his own battalion for that. One asset I must concede is that his supremacy over domestic security serves our business interests along with his own. It prevents our comatose generals from intervening in financial speculation as armies do practically everywhere else."

"That could change, however."

"Yes. Sooner or later," the Fisherman muttered as if speculating, "somebody with a boatload of funds will find a way into what substitutes for a heart (I didn't say conscience) of our inveterate Interior Minister. We live in a kleptocratic climate, so this somebody will have to make Karamau a very sweet deal—however that might affect his diabetes. AuxIndes's facsimile of corruption is still primitive, unlike the sophisticated versions of America and Europe. Our 'big crooks' are the old patriarchs—Anya's estranged Wazimbwe family for instance. They exercise their influence and take their profits discreetly—subtle ways to pick the shallow pockets of cops and clerks, minor agents and little fixers. In AuxIndes anybody with some leverage, whether financial or physical, can abuse it at will on everybody beneath them, especially through our deplorable biases of class and gender and age."

"We know something of those constraints, too," contributed Guyane.

"Eventually," Masson added, "protection of wealth will dominate petty self-serving, and we'll combine two classic levels of corruption—blunt muscular abuse and far more powerful leverage in favor of property. Then we'll have turned Euro-American."

"So who will make the deal with Philosophe, or without him, to replace the Domino? You, perhaps?"

Masson chuckled. "Me? I would welcome the chance to reform our system, to reward public service, but not to acquire political muscle or property. I don't really want to see our primitive corruption upgraded into your sophisticated style. But we tried during those student days to 'get them out of our way,' and Karamau simply picked us apart. Now ten years older and more prosperous, I'm suspect to young people. Anyway, who would give a mere fishmonger their vote? It would take a tsunami to make me seem larger and more crucial to the electorate, and nobody wills that on my poor compatriots."

"You might," speculated Denis, "figure out how to win, if you had the Philosophe, or others with muscle, on your side. Couldn't you expand your own instrumental range? Start with remote radio/TV stations for the provinces; donate food and other resources strategically; use social media to attract the adherence of townspeople and the literate classes. Ethically, of course; excite them, but tell them the truth. After that, build honest institutions nationally."

"Yes," answered the Fisherman, "I might become that noble when I've been able to export my *camarons* and take the business to a higher level."

"The very reason for your being here, right?"

Another of Masson's habitual periods of silence followed. It confirmed that at this stage in their odyssey, Masson and Guyane had come to an unspoken accord on the subject of AuxIndes—and, incidentally, to Los Angeles.

❈ ❈ ❈

West Coast hostess, Madeleine Lexus (no, Denis corrected himself: that's Ms. Luca's automobile, not her name) met their flight from Las Vegas and introduced elegance into their otherwise drab agenda. Sleek, observant, well briefed, Madeleine proposed a Saturday lunch-hour rendezvous, promising a weekend tour that only "special visitors" enjoy.

"We'll see," Denis observed skeptically; "Californian hyperbole, most likely. Chic sex, maybe, to top it off."

Fisherman kept silent this time.

The travelers spent that peaceful Friday night prowling their hotel neighborhood to generate appetite for life à la *Californie*. Sex was not on the agenda. Masson took advantage of the promenade to reconnoiter shops where on Monday he might replace a couple of ragged shirts ("thick neck, short arms, not easy to find"). He rejoiced at identifying a convenient Brooks Brothers for the purpose.

Madeleine Luca's limousine appeared promptly Saturday at noon. She counted on her Asian-American driver to know precisely the place for a lunch that would make an Indian Oceanite feel at home; it turned out to be a Burmese café. "Wrong side of your ocean," admitted the chauffeur who lunched with them, to prove his good faith. The café's curry had scarcely evolved from its pre-World War style—copious, variegated, and spicy enough for any exotic heritage. Even Masson approved, no sugary dessert needed. Madam Luca merely nibbled and signed the check.

Subsequently, as they circulated, Madeleine commented critically on the lives celebrated behind otherwise forbidding estate walls, especially those "in the Hills." Fisherman was impressed by how much she knew about underwater life, oceanic and domestic. He even quizzed her on his favorites in American film noir, wondering why California hadn't built a museum to honor the greatest of its sons, Humphrey Bogart. Madeleine only scoffed, à la Bacall.

No ordinary tour guide, she seasoned her discourse with intelligible French and even discussed the rigors of seafood refrigeration. This helped to prepare for useful exchanges on Monday afternoon when Masson hoped to explore access to an abundant import market for shellfish. That the session was to be chaired by Madeleine's husband, a successful importer, accounted for her assignment to the itinerant pair as more than a routine sightseeing escort.

When Saturday's promenade drew to an end, Ms. Luca proposed a leisurely Sunday in a shaded box with friends at their club's annual tennis tournament, followed by self-indulgence at its weekly seafood buffet. Seeing no inconvenience in this confluence of leisure and industry, Masson and Guyane concurred without hesitation; they were aware of social expectations to live up to advance billing from Mrs. Rodriguez in New York.

Tennis was underway as they took seats that Sunday afternoon. The matches featured amiable if not formidable talent seeking to qualify for subsequent rounds that would launch some toward coveted titles. Through a euphoric haze of gin and tonic (another deliberate Indian Ocean tribute), the visitors watched green balls waft hither and yon, over and into the net without much context. It didn't seem to matter to anyone who was scoring points against whom. The ardent players in this energetic ballet were virtually indistinguishable.

Except, perhaps, for one. It wasn't her artificial name or her prowess that attracted Denis's attention. It was, he admitted sheepishly to his companions, a rather inchoate yet familiar aura around her. "Yes, aura, not alcohol."

As Guyane viewed her at a distance, the player etched the dynamic space she inhabited. Lithe, bronze, but hardly overpowering, she seemed to float within her chalk-lined court, leaving imaginary lines after her, flicking a memory through his fuzzy consciousness. Her hair (presumably blonde like the others) was enveloped by a consummate cap, and her eyes took shelter behind crepuscular sunglasses that obscured her features. None of their companions recognized her, although one gentleman gallantly declared her more attractive than her game. She moved sporadically in fishtails of decidedly tanned limbs, beneath a skirt that flared persistently and nearly as erratically as the shots that left her racket.

Where had he seen the ambiance that framed those movements? He knew her, surely, yet could not identify how. In the end the bewildering sylph retired after a brisk two-set loss to her more athletically prepossessing opponent. She and her aura would not continue in this tournament.

Following the matches, diners at the club's seafood extravaganza feigned amusement over a welcoming speech by Madeleine's husband; Bill Luca regretted inability to offer any of Masson's "native dishes"—coelacanth filet, tortoise tongue, or thighs of giant squid. Fisherman merely winced at the translations. Shortly thereafter, leaving him in the hands of the French-speaking Luca family, Denis circulated with curiosity around the buffet. As usual, he was not hungry.

Luckily so, for the food counters were surrounded by layers of bodies, tall or squat, all sun-bronzed, in shorts and blouses, some in animated conversation. The women were conspicuously younger, blonder, less shorn than their male companions. They smiled distractedly, some greeting him in common French phrases as though that language would justify the presence of Black guests at the club. The comely tan fish-tailer from that afternoon's match was not to be seen.

As the diners chatted amiably, all seemed preoccupied with nourishment in the smallest doses obtainable. They served themselves, then turned their backs to the food tables to chat, blocking further access to their favorite dishes. A hungry intruder would have been out of luck.

What amused Denis most at this West Coast party was the popularity of platters holding lobster claws, haddock, cod, Hilton Head oysters, and striped bass—all conveyed to the buffet in dry ice from the opposite side of the continent. The local gourmets flocked to those exotic East Coast selections rather than to the succulent prawns, sea urchin, abalone, or Pacific tuna fresh from their own waters. When he mentioned this curiosity to Masson, the response was emphatic: "Why do you suppose I'm interested in placing my prawns out here? I sell tons of them to Europe while AuxIndiens pay outrageous prices for belons Atlantiques and turbot."

"Anyway," the Fisherman whispered, "the Grigio is still juvenile Californian. I'd have preferred a musty Chardonnet." In vain, Denis foraged the counters seeking to treat Fisherman to a genuine European sweet, finding only lemon meringue and fancy gelatins. Masson had to suppress his *patisserie* craving, as he had throughout much of the American trip.

Their return from club to hotel in a humid, alcoholic haze provided an excuse for a free Monday morning for broad-neck shirt procurement. They headed after breakfast to the Brooks Brothers which had just the collars needed, and Masson took advantage of the neighborhood to acquire Disney-print neckties, polka-dotted "papillons," and swash-buckled belts to bring home to his nephews. They meandered up a few side streets, seeking to absorb something characteristically Angelesian, but turned back in time to gear up for the afternoon's business session with Mr. Lexus—sorry, with Mr. Luca.

On the way to their hotel, however, Denis was astonished to hear his name called from a shop door to their right.

"Well!" cried a voice, "Is that Mr. Denis Guyane?"

Blinking in midmorning sunlight, he turned toward the doorway and blinked again. This chance salute came from none other than his abruptly departed and distinctly regretted ex-assistant at the Agency. Cynthia Van Zan was three thousand miles from the last time they had seen each other in New York, and he'd had no idea where she was heading when she left. He could never induce management to fund a replacement, even if he could locate anybody as qualified as she.

But this was indeed Cynthia, svelte as an exclamation point in flared trousers, her complexion radiating burnished silver, watching them from a shaded alcove that seemed arched just to fit her.

"So cool you're here!" she exclaimed as they neared. Turning Masson gently in her direction, Denis introduced them, alternating languages to describe his quest to her and praising Cynthia as a most creative designer in the tame wilderness of graphic art. She grasped the compliment without need of translation. Guyane had to ask what fate had posted her on this particular avenue.

"No purpose, really, just a distraction," she replied, touching her dark hair with its characteristic luminous streak running through it. "I'm living in Oakland, up the coast, but came down here for work; didn't find much, so had time on my hands."

"No work for you, with what you can do on a digital pad?"

"No, not that kind. Somebody talked me into taking . . . well, it was a screen test. But I'm heading back upstate."

"Screen test? For a movie? They still do that around here?"

Cynthia nodded ruefully.

"Now tell us that you've just scored a Hollywood breakthrough, right?" Her grimace disabused him. "Damn, I'm surprised. You would be perfect for the big flicks." He reported this to Masson who was grinning in assent. Then Denis realized something. "Did you also recently try your allure on the elusive sport of tennis?"

She just stared at him.

"Like maybe yesterday out at the Something Club tournament?"

Cynthia laughed. "Certainly not. No, Denis. You know I'm not up to country-clubbery. Anyway, I play like a perfect clod."

Denis gulped. Yesterday's faery shape may have lost her match, but she was anything but cloddish. The cap may have concealed Cynthia's dark hair, and inexperience alone could explain her defeat. He turned to Masson, who was unable to confirm a resemblance with yesterday's fish-tailer.

Time was pressing on them, so Denis gave up the chase, took down Cynthia's phone details in Oakland, and followed the Fisherman and packages to their hotel. He copied her coordinates for Masson who might be interested in Cynthia's flair for capturing essences in quick, incisive imagery—very mainstream for the California market.

"This Miss Van Zan who accosted us on the street," Masson said later. "You say she's from New Orleans, where we were flying when that stewardess dangled her oxygen mask like a hooker? A coincidence, I suppose?"

"Of course. Both women are perfectly serious in their work."

"So you regard her, this Van Zan, as a real asset to your profession?" Denis replied affirmatively, describing some of Cynthia's conversions of thought into pictures—like how artificial spray obliterates house dust ("Added strength: CLARIFY WITH CAPETOWN SUPERSPRITZ NOW!"); or the way a mass-produced *dashiki* can inspire a talking drum (silkscreen polyrhythms); or how CinderEffa's calabash turned into a Rolls Royce. These animations were ingenious, albeit too eccentric for the Agency's strategy toward prospective African clients. Her designs proved insufficiently bottom-lined for management. The Fisherman, now absorbed in fingering his new apparel, showed no further interest in the subject.

Monday afternoon, Bill Luca and a trio of colleagues proved as helpful as Madeleine had promised. At the top floor of an impressive building, the room was appropriately luxurious, with curated seascape prints from notable artists of the genre. Madeleine joined them there, and one of Luca's assistants, French-born, relieved Denis of half the translating burden, enabling the visitors to acquire data on America's insatiable appetite for seafood, even of doubtful quality. The United States, they were to understand, managed its own fisheries with attention to sanitation and sustainability—both at sea and in a still modest aquacultural industry.

Imports were another story.

The hosts deplored how South- and East-Asian fleets managed to subvert controls over "catch" requirements, application of antibiotics, and even forced labor. Anya Wazimbwe had urged Fisherman to challenge the Americans' own large-mesh gill nets drifting for swordfish off the West Coast; these snares are prohibited elsewhere for their entrapment of all kinds of sea creatures, including whales and turtles. Although reluctant to disappoint Anya, Masson thought better than to expose the iniquity too bluntly; he preferred to clarify his own less offensive market opportunities.

The outcome was promising. If Masson's AuThon proved well-managed and obedient to international norms (the Californians were sure it would, of course), and if price were not beyond reach, they might well find the American market open to penetration. All knew, but managed to ignore, AuxIndes's national reputation for official avarice. Not easy to do business with grasping AuxIndiens, although Masson's AuThon would of course be more amenable.

Encouraged by their meeting, Masson and Guyane invited the California team to dinner that evening at their hotel, knowing the overture would prove pro forma: American business people seemed invariably burdened by previous commitments. That was satisfactory to the Fisherman, who wanted to look up French language texts on local fisheries practice. They dined together, reviewing what they had learned that afternoon, and Masson retired to his laptop.

The encounter with Cynthia Van Zan continued to haunt Denis, however, as he sipped cognac in his room. Was yesterday's tournament loser with her own fishtail choreography a figment of his erotic imagination? Or was she a premonition of their impromptu encounter the next day with the real Van Zan on the street? Perhaps Cynthia had a tennis-playing sister? but that sounded wrong; if there was family in California, they'd probably be up in Oakland. The West Coast might abound in coincidences, but he must stay wary of meaningless portents while his career remained precarious.

He had to admit how little he actually knew about Cynthia, aside from her skill in translating a client's profit motive into market-savvy imagery. Yet what would a graphics talent like this be doing in tinsel-town with its philistine screen recruiters and sub-par tennis tournaments? There was something else he had watched on that sun-drenched court in his gin-induced fog.

That thought brought him vividly back to his first meeting with Cynthia Van Zan, three years earlier.

CHAPTER 4
FROM CARPET TO CONTRACT

Denis Guyane always despised wall-to-wall carpets. At best they function as common denominators between ornament and comfort; at worst, they are deliberate disguises for shoddy floors. Bland carpets are not to be confused with actual rugs that, whether posed or thrown, suggest an underlying spirit. Even Denis's mother, who traverses her house barefoot, never tolerates tufts, let alone plastic rag.

His first memorable disappointment at the Manhattan Agency occurred in 2003 when, already suffering in-house mockery for an ill-fated early promotion, Guyane entered his new office, and found it revolting underfoot. Hastily tacked down on buckling plywood in what had once served as a supply room, this thin, sour-green covering betrayed eruptions from below in a sea of treacherous wrinkles. "Satan tickling our hooves," he explained to his agnostic colleagues.

Later that day, as candidates appeared for the graphics job—his only budgeted staff—Denis repeatedly apologized for the uneven terrain they had to traverse before engaging his handshake. Not the most reassuring welcome from a still-unproven supervisor inhabiting an old broom closet. So far, for various reasons, all potential postulants had eased away from interest in the job. He didn't like any of them that much anyway.

This changed at five o'clock when someone named Van Zan came in; last of the candidates, a fugitive from the printing department. Trusting his courtly father's precept never to tolerate an artifact between himself and a guest, Denis circled around his desk in welcome; then, instantly, he had to blink in wonder. For as she crossed from the door, this slender woman seemed to be unconsciously smoothing his floor, leaving a silken surface in her wake, a pallid green surface actually turning verdant. Where had the color originated? Were the rough plywood eruptions gone? How did she manage to glide like that? Why did her shoes appear perfectly sensible?

Inarticulated by these questions, Guyane motioned his visitor toward one of three maple armchairs—also a paternal legacy, his best effort at decor. Rather than descend upon it, Cynthia Van Zan floated lightly into a seat that suited her like a fitted slipper. As he took a second chair, she had formed into a subtle crescent that redesigned the space around her; a silver streak divided her charcoal hair like an exclamation of light. Involuntarily, his mind shifted to Shakespeare's portrayal of the Queen of Egypt in her barge, "like a burnished throne [that] burnt on the water."

Then, Guyane noticed that this Cleopatra's hue even matched the chair's maple veneer. Was the candidate actually Black or could she turn color in any frame? what about white birch, or ebony?

Clearing his head briskly, Denis was about to formulate his usual opening gambit for candidates—welcoming, invitational; it was her voice, however, (although in his mind, it *might* have been the Egyptian queen's) that brought them gently to their business. He heard her ask, "What explains your commitment to Africa, Mr. Guyane? How did you induce management to let you extend the range that far out?"

This pacifier of wooden floors and furniture was already testing organizational policy. Who in fact was the candidate here?

That's the way it started, and how it would remain in his mind. Cynthia Van Zan, fleeing an unappreciative printing unit, commanded this scene as Denis knew she should through any episodes to come. For some reason she seemed interested enough in his marginal Africa-promotion office to present herself for this job. Already more at home in his new office than he would ever be, she resembled the proverbial house cat who rules uninvited. He did observe something feline in the way Cynthia determined comfort wherever she chose to rest, respect whenever provoked. The malicious flooring, a grisly carpet, that chair—his own father's legacy—greeted her presence as though fabricated for her purposes. Their impressions of Van Zan were indeed less confused than his own.

Through gentle probes, as though preparing to paint his portrait, Cynthia induced Denis to divulge the essentials—not so much about the job as his origins and family, education, and professional aspirations. Once reconciled to being reverse-interviewed by a candidate, he took the opportunity to explain his parents' immigration from Haiti to Brooklyn, away from the Duvaliers' paternal hand-off that they knew would sour; his bilinguality (with rudiments of *Kreyol* as *tertium quid*) that induced him to the Peace Corps in Senegal after NYU; a flair for communication strategy that attracted him to the public relations Agency; his impatience with business as usual, leading to his proposal of an extension to Africa. He found himself thinking in the third person, as Van Zan might write up the interview of him, or put it into her own digital imagery. She nodded indulgently at each point, showing interest without inquisitiveness.

About her, Guyane learned far less—only what she had already itemized in her job file: birth in New Orleans, early graduation from some place in the South so that, at twenty-one, she'd had three years of job experience with credentials in graphic design; her preference for freelance life and work; her attraction to the "continent of her ancestors"—all softly voiced without stress. At the close, he felt strongly in her favor, while ruminating on how she had caused him to reveal himself.

Inevitably, she got the job.

Guyane realized belatedly that his new assistant had failed to receive an adequate answer to her original question. He knew what he wished to do, but not precisely how to bring it about. He could never claim that his Haitian ancestry would qualify him to master the subtleties of African creativity, let alone generate production there for American markets. Of course he had done research to identify sources of commodities that could prospectively interest those markets. He knew the legislation through which Washington offered advantages to imports of certain products—textiles for instance—originating in Africa. He hoped to create landings for fine cloth from Ghana and Nigeria, and cashmeres by that niece of a former president, for authentic sculpture from Congo and Mozambique, even for coffee, cocoa, spices, and vanilla directed immediately to the States, bypassing post-colonial processing points.

The years as a PCV in Dakar and two trips along the continent's coasts had left Guyane with some rhetoric needed for marketing

Africana in the western hemisphere, if not the clues to successful staging of those exports. He could imagine preexisting obstacles posed by European and Chinese interlocutors more practiced than he in dialogue with solicitous African officials. Denis admitted that he hadn't found a way to open domestic markets for the genuine African product and he was not sure he wanted to sell bulk batiks and tie-dyes, unripened fruit in crates, or bundles of knockoff statuettes and thumb pianos. He wasn't "in production," only indirectly in sales, and he did not see himself as a lever to hoist genuine African artisanship into mass manufacturing for casual consumers.

And if he did, what would his own role be, actually? The Guyane skill world consisted of language, not marketing, and he wanted others to do the heavy lifting, while he proclaimed the cultural values of expanded exchange. His pitch had been persuasive enough to his superiors at the Agency, although not to himself or his African counterparts. That sufficed to support a couple years of probation and the budget for a handpicked, "preferably African American," designer for his pilot ventures. The context was serious—a logical extension of his education, his Haitian heritage, and its African origins. Hence this office, with its carpet and its mission, both appealing for redesign.

Was Cynthia Van Zan, artist-designer, going to fill the main job—visualizing the brands—as easily as she seemed to have leveled the floor?

This was a question Guyane asked himself during a subsequent visit to his family in Flatbush. He was surprised at how easily he found impersonal language to describe his new assistant—the French for "her surroundings suit themselves like a frame for whatever mood she's in"—while betraying no sign of his own self-doubt. His father, skeptical of other people's romanticisms, including his son's, glanced up from a pile of peanut shells spread across yesterday's *Times*. "You aren't in love with this person, are you?"

Surprised at the question, Denis considered it directly for the first time; that surprised him too. The answer had to come in a bewildered negative.

His mother came to the rescue. "I don't think she's after your affection. From what you say, she is approaching this job more spiritually than as a wife or girlfriend. She strikes me as a *sévitée*."

"A what? Oh, that Haitian thing—an emissary? From and for what?"

Clotilde had to wave off her husband's impulse to mockery. "Not only Haiti," she said. "In West Africa, sévitées serve the *orishas* as a *loa*, a kind of priestess."

"How do you see Van Zan in this role?" Denis asked, also ignoring his father's sneer.

"You didn't say so, but I perceive that she's a Black woman. Where do her people come from, this Cynthia?"

"Does it matter?" Denis countered. "She's just African American."

"So are you," she said, "and where do you come from?"

"From Flatbush, of course," Pierre-Louis interjected, hoping to divert the discussion.

"Where I come from is different, Mom. You know that."

"Yes, in the short-run," she admitted, "but she's from there, West Africa, long-term, like you."

"And a long time ago," threw Pierre-Louis over his shoulder as he left the dining room to empty shells off the newspaper. Clotilde pursued:

"Maybe she's a *loa* or *mambo*, maybe not. What do her parents do?"

"She didn't say. They're both dead, I think. Her mother's family was Louisianan. Her father seems to have immigrated from somewhere in the Caribbean."

"Her name, it's odd; like she's part Dutch. Still, could be Old Dahomey, a shortening of *Behanzin*, their last king before the French bundled him off to Martinique."

"'Old Dahomey' is Benin now, Mom, but I don't know. She's curious about Africa, in a way that Black Americans are without having been there."

"Hmm. Does she speak French? Did you test her?"

"I didn't ask, but her resume shows no languages except for computer speak."

"And there's a new medium for the old messenger class. I wish her well, especially if she can help you reconnect with the mother country."

"You don't mean with Haiti, Mom, I know. Should I send her off 'to Africa,' just like that?"

"She might end up there whether you direct her or not."

His father, back in the dining room, didn't have to intervene, but did: "Come on now. Who is the boss in that office of yours?"

"I'm not sure of the answer to that one, Dad."

Clotilde wasn't listening to the men. "If she's from the Benin, she'll find her place on some side of that border, Dahomey or Nigeria. They always went back and forth, friendly and otherwise. The *orishas* use highly attractive intermediaries—like dancers, or amazons, or artists. You didn't say this either: she is beautiful, too."

She returned to dishwashing, and Denis to stacking plates. Rising, Pierre-Louis had the last word: "That voodoo stuff might work in the old country, son, but it isn't going to get you anywhere in this materialist world. Better marry her than expect some sévitée to improve the balance sheet."

That was better advice than Denis had been prepared to take. Part of it, at any rate. The sprite Van Zan, despite her brilliance as an illustrator, proved of little value in resolving the contradictions of Denis's mission or improving receptivity to Africa in a tone-deaf management. They both heard in-house ridicule against their project, insinuations of flirtation with cannibals, tsetse flies big as frogs, and inveterate sloth. It was all racist, or worse, she would say in outrage, when projects turned to dust in the managerial grinder.

At times Cynthia condemned the mission directly, as if she lacked confidence in Guyane personally. She was prepared to devote her personal skills and vitality to the work, or to a fanciful conception of "Africa," but not to the organization or its clients. Or to him.

Aware of how vulnerable he was as a displaced marketer of ideas, Denis chose to think of himself as a misconstrued poet. He hadn't yet worked out a personal toolkit for retaliation, or even resistance, against bureaucratic skullduggery. Least of all did he contemplate instrumentalizing sex, which might have made a helpmate out of Cynthia, rather than a threat. He remained passive, and Van Zan showed no inclination toward intimacy. Just as well, perhaps; for Denis at 26, sexuality resembled a capricious weather system—dazzling, evasive, oppressive. Lightening sparked arbitrarily, never quite striking; thunder rumbled furiously overhead, across indifferent mountains. Van Zan might have fancied dalliance with a desolate Black guy who needed a permanent bed partner, but was it worth a try to test her? He thought not, and he imagined her to be equally incurious.

For Guyane, indeterminate identity devolved out of random "career" choices. He had considered, and discarded, options in teaching, diplomacy, even bohemian squalor as an East Village poet. Insertion into the public relations industry seemed at first a logical confluence of these vectors; hence his successful job search in Manhattan. This displaced Brooklyn boy with his Haitian background, NYU diploma, and African experience was to encounter a new reality as a New Yorker-in-training. He recalled some early incidents as parables of his reinitiation into the city.

One morning, shortly after his return from Dakar, while New York still convalesced from the horror perpetrated against its Trade Towers the year before, Denis was accosted by this very cool cat who rushed out of a shop carrying an open container of coffee. Dashing for a taxi, the man jostled him aggressively, spilling hot liquid on the sidewalk and on Denis's shoes. New shoes, acquired for job hunting. "Better watch where you're going!" the cat shouted back at him, and was in the cab before Denis could say a word in reply.

That three-year-old encounter would linger as emblematic of a city accustomed to all levels of terrorism, from impudence to atrocity, although it was followed by interviews that were to assure him a life. Even now, running an office on Seventh Avenue, Denis still found himself reviving his unspoken retort: "Hey! *You* bumped *me*, man!" instinctively casting furtive glances down at his footwear.

❁ ❁ ❁

During his first week at the Agency, Guyane sought a quick lunch at the *TieGuy* delicatessen, a tiny hole-in-the-wall just off Broadway. The place specialized in take-out sandwich combinations for theater companies in rehearsal. To comply with some rule mandating "indoors seating," the TieGuy contained three grease-stricken round-topped tables, about thirteen inches in diameter, each flanked by two tiny wooden folding chairs borrowed, apparently, from a kindergarten. Starting daily at 11:30, the deli counter was ringed elbow-to-elbow by messengers fetching lunch deliveries in cartons, so there was little time or tolerance for sit-down "diners."

Denis managed to order a sandwich, wipe off a chair at the least messy table, and wait. After ten minutes, somebody left the persistent telephone and circled around the assembly line with a plate holding one pastrami on rye, not divided in half, plus a paper cup of soda, and that was all. No bottle, no extra mustard, no napkin, fork, or spoon.

Ignoring the clamorous ringing, the cashier-cum-waiter hovered impatiently over Guyane's seat. Once Denis lifted his wobbly sandwich the man whisked his plate away and dropped a check into the space that had held the platter. Obviously, Denis had to cling to the sandwich. With his free hand he moved the cup away, reached for cash, and departed with whatever change he could collect from the inattentive cashier, to finish his lunch on the curb, just off Broadway, watching out for his shoes.

Later, after earning some of his keep at the Agency, Denis took out a loan to buy a used automobile. His visit to the car lot in Queens produced more urban imposition. He picked out his vehicle before addressing a salesperson who then joined him in a rapid ride around three city blocks. Guyane contracted for the car on the spot, but before taking it away for the holidays, proudly made the salesman await a brief inspection. Denis did know something about shock absorption, hose connections, brakes, and other mysteries of the automotive matrix. Satisfied so far, he ended the tour by opening the trunk; there he was surprised to find a scattering of several dozen small plastic fasteners, all the color of the vehicle, but none with an evident purpose. "So," Denis said, glaring at the salesman, "what the hell is all this?"

"Oh, them? Them, sir, are your spare parts," the man replied, cool as a rain shower, closing the trunk and walking away with his down payment.

Thus had professional life begun, spinning Denis Guyane awkwardly on his own in the city. By the time he was to encounter Roger Masson, he was an experienced New Yorker, for better or worse. Nonetheless, the urban dust continued to evoke sneezes, occasional reminders of the insistent horrors of September 11, and he saw himself personally and professionally afloat. "To make it in this town, you have to bring your A-Game," his first boss told him; he was still trying to find that game.

Seeing Cynthia off in a cab after her first meal in the Guyane apartment (his mother had insisted on the invitation), Denis took pride in how well the guest had responded to the food, the conversation, the Jacob Lawrence reproductions and Haitian "primitives" on the walls. Then, he returned to the kitchen to hear the verdict. Clotilde turned away from the running water, handed him the dish towel, and dried her hands on it. She spoke in a way he had never heard before about a person of interest.

"I admire your Cynthia's style," she said, "high-caste, carefully constructed, probably by her mulatto father. Clearly, her creamy shading, fine features, and body shape conform to white cultural norms. Yet, she carries that indelible slave mark on her—or in her mentally. You're surprised at the thought, but you know that her mother's family is deep Louisiana, back to old plantation hardscrabble. It comes out when you look for it—how she's had to fight to get free from that long root in American slavery."

"Sure, Momma, but we've had to do that too."

"A half century earlier, and we did it more decisively in Haiti. We expelled the slavers and the leftover masters."

Pierre-Louis, as always avoiding the dishwashing routine, interjected against his wife's triumphalism, "And we achieved all that *without* needing to rid ourselves of the slave mentality. We've hung onto that."

"But what about her?" Denis started to ask.

"Her people worked the slave stigma off, after a white man's army came down to subdue the old masters," answered his father. "But not for long; the tragedy of this country is that after twenty years the masters revived to dominate them (and us too here). Moreover, today the rest of the whites are allied, north and south—so now they can call it democracy."

"While in Haiti we only call ourselves underdeveloped," said Clotilde.

"You two got us away from that curse," Denis tossed out, grinning, as he piled saucers on one another.

His father only shrugged, "A curse we had to escape. We had the education to play elite in Haiti; that helped."

"And not here?" queried Denis.

"We are the color to be low-caste in Brooklyn, and there's a whole white race to corner us, now that we've adapted."

"So why stay here then?"

His father thought for an instant. "Maybe because of chinks in what they call democracy," he replied. "Look at you, with your double consciousness; you're educated out of Brooklyn, and now you run your own international office."

"Until I crash it," said Denis gloomily.

Clotilde returned to her original judgment. "We must see the Cynthias and her people in paradox. They carry the burden of the dominated together with the pride of a culture that originated in Africa and remains alive here."

"So you see American Black people as still somehow African, while we . . ."

"Oh we are that, too," said his mother, "but in Haiti we can't blame anybody else until we've confronted ourselves."

"And the mess we've made without the double consciousness excuse," added Pierre-Louis. "We have more earthquakes and hurricanes and gangs, more hungry kids than anybody, and even cholera today. Unfortunately, we can't just easily blame the white masters."

"That's too simple," objected Denis. "There's much holding Haiti back beside the weakness of Haitian culture."

"And there's much strength among Black Americans," said Clotilde, turning off the water with emphasis, "and that helps keep us here. The old resistance that still operates within them."

"But not in Cynthia?"

"Most certainly in Cynthia. In her spirit, her courage, her refusal to be ordinary."

Denis reflected for an instant. "Does she know that?"

"Oh, yes," responded Pierre-Louis, turning a page in the Financial section. "Doesn't she show it?"

"She does," agreed Clotilde, "but with you, Denis, a Haitian boss without that slave mark, she has to be very careful."

"And you be too," said his father, this time in English.

Returning to the office next day, he considered whether, and how, Ms. Van Zan was trying to "be very careful." If she were interested in advancement, she might have been able to circumvent him in the Agency without dislodging a hair. His self-doubt had devolved to that point by then, and he'd concluded that Cynthia could do a better job at commercial promotion than he. Then, before he could finish wondering if Van Zan might try to leapfrog him in rank and whether to craft a deterrent, she abruptly left the company and disappeared.

Cynthia's defection did involve ambition—as well as race and age. It began when a senior vice president had to leave the Agency abruptly, deftly extracting his fingers from the cash register on advice from legal counsel before anything could be proven. National search for a replacement turned up the expected list of white male MBAs, plus one "dark horse" technician—a 22-year-old graphics assistant named Cynthia Van Zan. Her candidacy struck the corporate world as a hoax: what right did she, of all people, claim to cynically overleap multiple echelons? Inevitably, her brazen application never passed the initial stages, not even to the courtesy of an in-house interview. Within a week, following consultation with a sympathetic but powerless Irene Rodriguez, the arrogant Van Zan had resigned from the Agency and left New York. Her presumption remained, however, to reflect poorly on Denis as a supervisor.

Now, nearly two years later, during the Guyane project's final fling, Cynthia has surfaced mysteriously in California; she is about to return to Oakland, to join whom? To do what? Denis finds himself intrigued.

The Fisherman's itinerary drew them back to the road in her direction, northward along the coast through Monterey, where Masson waxed ebullient over Steinbeck, sardine packing, and aquariums; then to San Francisco, where he breathed the sea air through special gills. At their industrial meetings, Masson's Indian Ocean gravity inspired collaboration, while his Asian-American interlocutors responded with useful instruction on aquaculture. Dining one night in a sushi bar, Fisherman probed the intricacies of shore-to-dumpster marketing with the restaurant's maître d'hôtel, using Denis as usual for translation (English/French, not Japanese) while he thought out his next questions.

"I'm beginning to learn what wrongs we have been inflicting on the oceans," he declared over breakfast the next day. "Without knowing it, our industry is interfering with interwoven circuits of communication through those waters. Life there uses the sea as a medium for its version of your profession, Denis, communication."

"Communication? But of what? It can't just be a process of random circulation."

"I think it can. You may communicate something, but for them, process is all."

"The sea creatures have no substance to communicate?"

"Very little if any. Substance in circulation turns into process; it's like being scared, or in love."

Denis chose to hear his father whisper skeptically; he rejoined, "But how do you get anything done?"

"You confuse getting things done with doing things. I'm more interested in doing than in finishing, maybe like life in the ocean. Remember your literature. Lear's Edgar said 'Ripeness is all.'"

"That sounds like something done," said Denis.

"Maybe but don't anticipate results, not yet." replied Masson, "I think Shakespeare meant ripening is all; it's everything."

Guyane sensed then that his companion was heading toward an outcome that he had yet to foresee. Somehow, he thought, Fisherman's cohort, the Wazimbwe woman, might provide that for him.

Before their first working day, Guyane had called Cynthia at her number in Oakland. The next evening, the trio gathered in San Francisco for Pacific comestibles followed by the Fisherman's first live taste of opera since his Quebec years. From New York, Irene Rodriguez had discovered a performance of *The Pearl Fishers*, a fortuitous subject for this expedition, thanks to Bizet. Now, she gladly added a third ticket for the lost Van Zan whom she had befriended at the Agency. The opera struck Denis curiously; he couldn't help identifying their own trio with the rapturous rivalry of tenor and baritone over the lovely Sri Lankan priestess. He thought it scarcely likely that he and Masson would compete for Cynthia—or anything else, for that matter; and they were certainly ill-equipped for Bizet's superb duet that displays masculine bonding in an ersatz Oriental setting. Still, he took whimsical courage from the climactic renunciation by the heroic baritone (surely the Fisherman) in favor of the flabby tenor (guess who).

Next morning began their free day before resuming discussions with the masters of sea harvests and aqua-farming. Still not quite distinguishing reality from illusion, Denis promised himself a promenade through San Francisco's galleries, while Masson assured that he would be "fine in my room working." He asked only that Guyane leave an order for his "favorite" lunch (anything but fish). And, casually, as Denis headed for the door, the Fisherman wondered if while fluttering among watercolors and Greek pots, Guyane might consider doing some work in AuxIndes. He thereupon subsided into his customary silence, allowing the question to dangle in Denis's head all day. Inspired by that baritone? the American wondered. Romantic opera gets into the least likely minds.

Later, over aperitifs, Guyane sought specifics. They were in what passed for a library off their Nob Hill lobby.

"I'm flattered, of course, by your interest," he began, then sipped his vermouth. "Actually, if what you have in mind is brand development in English-speaking markets, I might look forward to working on that. But before I modify my (ahem) flourishing function in the Agency, please tell me for whom I'd be working."

"Why, for me, of course," answered the Fisherman, "or are you asking whether I'm seeking to hire your whole corporation?"

"No, I was just wondering which brand I would be promoting— the fisheries enterprise or the presidential one."

Then came the pregnant silence that Denis had become accustomed to during this journey.

The Fisherman scratched at a bare ankle with one hand and drew a book off the shelf with the other; any book, it seemed, from the way he fingered it. Masson had dropped his lure into the depths and was awaiting a bite. Then he jerked the line.

"What do you know about the presidential part?"

Borrowing a leaf from the master, Denis let that one air out for a moment. After a long breath, "Only something about a certain 'philosophic' person who might have something to say about it."

"Ah," said the Fisherman. "I'm surprised that you're bothered by him."

"He's in it with you, then, and not with the Domino, or for himself?"

"Not for himself. Our Mr. Philosophe has barely emerged out of the myriad mediocrities that clutter our island regime. Sorry to mention class, but given his origins, Minister Karamau can only anticipate a role as broker for the next election—if, that is, he waits that long. He is available for rent, but not up for sale."

Evidently having exhausted what little interest he'd had in the randomly selected paperback, Masson discarded it roughly and looked up at Denis. "Why then should that have anything to do with . . . us?"

"Us, I don't know," answered Denis. "*You* certainly are talked about as his prize candidate."

"Interesting, this 'talking about.' Who is doing all that?"

This invited Guyane's turn for the evasive. "Oh, you can imagine how the diplomatic corps buzzes around."

"But why should the distinguished diplomats of New York or Washington bother about so obscure an item as the politics of AuxIndes?"

"Aah, that corps." Denis was beginning to enjoy the exchange. "Political buzz is their elixir; they imbibe and secrete it constantly."

"The African delegations, you mean. Charming. They have nothing else to do."

"Not much else, I suppose," admitted Guyane, "which explains why they're so much fun to be around. But, it's not just the Africans."

"No? Somebody else buzzes, too? Who? The imperious Europeans, I suppose. But why, I ask. Who cares what pops out to challenge our esteemed President Domino? Or if anybody does? Unless they worry about somebody trying to get rid of him?"

Denis left that question in the air, perhaps to insert itself into the notorious 'buzz.' He rose out of his chair as if weary of it all, drawing a grin from the suddenly inquisitive Fisherman.

"Pah! Perfect nonsense, Mr. Guyane. Tell your idle diplomatic chatterers that Antoine Karamau doesn't have an assassin's bone in his large, diabetic body. I know it."

"I'll take your word for it. But that doesn't make him any less effective as a kingmaker—or presidential patron. So that leaves open the question."

"Dear friend, you lose me. What question was that?"

"To rephrase, are you hiring an American to promote your brand of prawns or to serve your campaign for supreme leader?"

Again that typical pregnant pause. This time Denis decided to fill it. "Or is there really no significant difference in your thinking?"

"Meaning if I run for president, I'll also be netting, farming, freezing, and selling fish?"

Denis just grinned, waiting for the next non sequitur. It came.

"Or else, if people like my seafood they will buy my housing policies?"

"It's the same equation, sir, for you. For an aide, especially a foreigner, however, the distinction in purpose could excite conflict. So if I'm to spin out from my agency, would I be working for the fisheries king or a national kingfish?"

"The former, of course. Although I'm far from king of anything, and certainly farther from hiring presidential staff, especially ambitious expatriates."

"All right. And I have no ambitions worth considering. But you do have Philosophe to contend with. What will that be like?"

Another extended hiatus. Masson was evidently trying to determine whether he was already dealing, leveling with an advisor, or making a reassuring job offer. He decided to level. "When he stands up, Antoine is a peasant at heart. The top, toward the sun and the clouds, is political, thoughtful, albeit blunt and often menacing. The bottom is all earth, the kind that mixes cow dung with dandelions, and ends filling in graves. Your diplomatic friends may find him enigmatic, but he's really standing on hard ground. And he looks it; comes from a clan of massive men—some of them frighteningly big—and of impressive women. His father worked the fields with his fingers, to the bone, never able to get beyond a mere living, chafing at the markets, wearying under the sun. Even while mayor of the village, manager of the cow-and-cassava cooperative, he still couldn't get past the wealthy price riggers, the devious lenders, the cattle rustlers in business suits. So he sent his brightest son to school with the priests, sold off some land and even a good heifer to make sure the kid had the right clothes, and told him to get a government job, where he could take bribes and make the family comfortable. Antoine probably still has those clothes."

"He's a lawyer, though, isn't he?"

"That was the priests. They told him where to study—that place in Belgium—and I suspect they hoped to smother him in his cassock with a canon law dissertation under it. But he didn't go that way. His father and the holy soil won out."

"He didn't take to farming, though?"

"Surely not, but he never forgets anything. He even recalls 'slaving in the paddy fields' for my own father and grandfather; 'gentlemen farmers,' he calls them, with a smirk. It was during his Christian vacations in the highlands, five hundred kilometers from his maize-eating village. I was much younger, but at school in the capital. Still, he hangs with them."

"With the priests, you mean?"

"Oh, yes. Not strictly out of piety, I suspect. When and if you meet him he'll be eager to assess your French, but if you get his ego going you may find his English quite good. That comes from one of the fathers, a certain American named Andrew, I believe."

"A priest who teaches him English? Regularly?"

"Oh yes. Karamau is regular in everything; that's the peasant in him."

They let the interval extend a bit longer than necessary. Finally, the Fisherman ceded: "What do you say? Want to try your hand at a new industry? A wet one?"

Guyane had to calculate how to frame the response. He knew he was hooked, and he couldn't escape thinking that the lure concealed a trap in a third world political combat. He thought of asking New York for a leave of absence, pledging to return with all that experience in his toolbox. He doubted that the bosses would go for it, however, and the idea was unlikely to inspire confidence in the Fisherman. So he just held out his hand and smiled whimsically, adding: "I could hardly pass up the chance of testing Minister Philosophe's English."

"Right," answered Masson. "Of course." He smiled too, sipped his *pastis*, then let the usual pause take hold. He raised his eyes to meet Denis's, and held them.

"There is one more thing before we get to champagne and terms. I'd like Miss, eh, Van Zan to join us there, to work with you once more—if you have no objection, that is."

This caught Denis by surprise. He was about to ask if the Fisherman was sure who he meant, but he knew better: Masson depended on his hunches for his life. Denis had to hold back his disbelief. "What do you see as her role?" was the best he could interpose.

"Ah, I consulted her resume yesterday and had her work checked by the California people. She has a most attractive . . . style."

"Oh, I agree with that. Cynthia could have set fire to the Agency if she'd been given a better spot there. She'd be valuable for you in a business that begs for graphic promotion. But you've seen how hard she is to pin down. I doubt that I could persuade her to . . . "

"Don't worry about that, *old boy*," (apparently the Fisherman was quoting *The Great Gatsby*). "She's already agreed to join us . . . on one condition—that you'd be there as her boss."

That was skillful, Guyane had to admit to himself. The man had nerve to go along with his self-confidence. How, beside unearthing the *Gatsby* phrase, did he manage the language to make this pitch to

Cynthia in one day—or she to cope with him, in French? Was one or the other of them hiding linguistic fluency from him? Whichever it might be, Denis was caught. Already a formidable competitor in his industry, Roger Masson could be an effective champion for his own people in a political campaign. There was also the prospect of dealing with an oceanic economy needing expertise and with the peasant Philosophes—not to ignore the pleasure, he had to admit, of resuming close professional quarters with Cynthia Van Zan. These considerations precluded the doubts that would certainly come to hover over the entire enterprise.

The Fisherman appeared to have no such doubts. "The combination, the two of you," he said, nearly beaming, "will help us create the romance of the oceans out of a mere business of nets and hooks—pearls for the oysters of AuxIndes."

CHAPTER 5
FROM ANGLING TO ACTIVISM

Once he'd lodged Denis Guyane, with a comfortable work space at AuThon headquarters in late 2006, Roger Masson released the American to plot his own job—"for the time being."

Denis's office at The Fishery in downtown Indesville overlooked an impressive double row of imperial palms; they were deep inside the island with no water or sea creatures in sight. Pretty far to cast a net, Guyane thought, from the middle of a virtual continent.

Surprising his management team behind new horn-rimmed eyeglasses ("useful for scaling sea bass"), the Fisherman introduced Guyane in late 2006 as "deputy chief of staff for planning and public relations." Deputy to whom? since there was yet no actual chief of staff. "He's to develop the Brand, *la marque*—covering international relations and much more. Denis will also supervise the new graphic artist, Ms. Van Zan, when she arrives from Europe." Turning to Guyane with an impish smile, "I believe these reflect what you've expected to do."

Part of that introduction was true, although Denis may have been the only person in the room not to laugh. Surely, the incumbents were asking themselves whether a "brand" hadn't already evolved under their guidance without him. If not, how does a brand emerge and what assets could an expatriate neophyte bring to its fruition? Did he have some special talent, beyond bilinguality, to contribute to Masson's planning or to AuThon's relations with an expanding public?

Evidently, Fisherman intended the answers to expose themselves in time. All he assigned to Denis explicitly were to evaluate current marketing messages and an already doomed future "supervising" the mercurial Van Zan.

Guyane declined to overstate his qualifications as much as Masson might choose to exaggerate them. His three years in New York had proven unfruitful, although they showed ability to write coherently and some technical facility from broadband to social media. Agency work and Peace Corps service facilitated a wide, if not profound, acquaintance with African specificities—touching on markets, governance, and some of the chicaneries underneath them. This experience induced little more than an initial suspicion of the actors inside the Fisherman's strategic establishment. And of himself as, admittedly, a specialist in generalizations.

Beyond these mysteries, Denis wondered how service in a maritime business might interface with their boss's ineluctable political ambitions—and what did "interface" mean in the first place? He hoped that answer could wait.

After abolishing a disgusting gray carpet—unveiling a baobab-wooded floor in his office, the American began to study relations among upper management personalities. AuThon's directors composed a still youthful crew of Masson intimates some of whom Denis could identify from names dropped during the recent trip to

California. He'd perceived even then how deliberately Fisherman was reassembling the student team dispersed ten years earlier by a cabinet minister's wand.

For Masson, the elusive slogan "autonomy with compatibility" served as a staffing principle, aiming at performance by a "choir" of virtuosic cohorts. Most AuThon managers had graduated out of the dissonance of Babel Mountain to cultivate diverse forms of expertise and to mature on return into an ensemble of individuated voices. Their leader expected the principals to function self-reliantly within his organization; basses were not to try singing soprano, or vice versa, but to hear the other pitches in an effort toward harmony—for an ultimately sonorous world, so Roger wanted to believe.

Looking for clues to hierarchy among these soloists proved bewildering. The staff chart showed operational distinctions, but very little about rank. At best, status seemed to have cursory relevance to role. Only in practice did some stratification appear. The dazzling sprite Anya Wazimbwe and quiet, bearded Benjamin Bamiara functioned in closest proximity to Masson, as they had when students in 1996. One of them assertive, the other diplomatic, could they be front and back faces on the same coin? What interests motivated them predominantly? How about Bernard Neiru the engineer from a *Grande Ecole* in France? Or Ahmed Tabour, the sole practicing Muslim in the executive suite? What motivated the bespectacled Olivier Kolona who carried chapbooks of poetry to his marketing desk, or Solange Seriel who lived inside her ledgers and showed them to nobody except the Fisherman? Whom and what did they all serve most avidly, and which purposes would they endorse as "the Brand" evolved? Guyane knew he had to learn the way these and other trusted personalities functioned before postulating answers to any of his own questions.

Denis's respect for Fisherman intensified as he noted how over a decade Masson had persuaded the dispersed activists to turn back from their respective post-graduate careers and to join his nascent maritime enterprise. Confident in his objectives, the young entrepreneur revealed an exasperating flair for patience and flexibility. Once he felt on secure ground, Fisherman wore authority conspicuously but lightly. He was eager to hear others out, and firm when he needed to take charge. He relented rarely but decisively and amiably.

To sustain enthusiasm for the work, Masson turned marginal diversities into regularities—monthly culinary demonstrations, for instance (especially his own favorite patisseries), periodic fishing parties to freshwater sites, video interludes featuring marine oddities, scholarly explorations of the "blue revolution," open sessions for spouses and partners to criticize AuThon's performance.

As a ritual of professional passage, Fisherman required all managers to participate in a yellowfin trawler harvest. Getting wet on board baptized them into what he considered tangibles of the profession. When their turn came to join a forthcoming voyage, Guyane and Van Zan reflexively played "American"; Denis asked if he couldn't rather fish for his favorite, bonito; while Cynthia tried to hold out for a whaling expedition. Bluntly, Anya Wazimbwe declared that both would join whatever occupied the fleet in season: invariably, tuna. Her word ruled, and they passed their dampened ordeal in good spirits. Denis struggled to control his kinetic awkwardness at the ropes while watching Cynthia smooth the agitated seas and pacify the howling winds around their cruise.

These activities allowed Guyane to glimpse a complex world of agents, technicians, and seafaring personnel surrounding AuThon's managerial nucleus. Beyond the company were the usual clients, and further out, overseas marketplaces to be converted from producers and consumers of seafood into producers and customers of AuThon. As if schematized for him by Van Zan, these roughly concentric circles consisted of personalities, not just units in some digital alphabet or labels on seafood. The chain of values that linked them determined success or disaster for a brand's market. And they were largely unknown to the new deputy chief of staff who had to remind himself that they were the reason for his existence there.

Denis would eventually acquire a feel for the industry, and even for AuThon's burgeoning extensions into other sectors of food processing and distribution. Until then, he deliberately postponed consideration of the nameless throngs who, in time, were to become sponsors and constituents of a rising politician named Masson. Eventually, Fisherman would make them all decide how this industrial apparatus would link, if at all, with his political destiny. By then, Denis should have acquired familiarity with pertinent influentials—local officials, specialized ministries, a capricious legislature, media outlets, and the ubiquitous "police chief" Antoine Karamau, Interior Minister and Master of Everybody's Affairs. As for the spirited Van Zan, Denis was eager to resume their collaboration, but without expecting to capture her undivided attention. He knew that Cynthia's calling would put sea creatures at the center of those concentric stakeholder circles, but he did not embrace that way of configuring the world. Guyane would leave her to communicate autonomously with the blue economy.

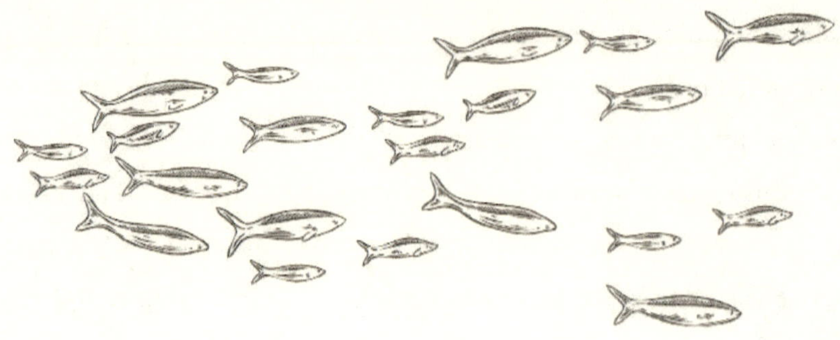

Nor did he foresee deep personal intimacy with his elusive colleague (sorry, Dad, she's not for me nor me for her). Still, once Cynthia appeared in Indesville, he felt protective enough to watch for any suspicious interest in her by their charismatic boss. Reassuringly, as time passed, he found none. Bizet's pearl-fishing trio entered Denis's mind only as an irelevant illusion. Oblivious to distraction, Cynthia invariably breathed cooler air, just as she walked on smooth surfaces, no matter what others were inhaling or treading. The Fisherman, for his part, candidly portrayed his own marriage as a convenient, if not unduly passionate commitment; and Mme. Giselle Masson appeared capable of enforcing the rules in that relationship, if she ever needed to do so.

Soon enough, Van Zan landed with flourish from her initiation in London and Paris, and began penetrating the local scene to an extent that belied her claim to language incompetence. She promptly forged contacts in the ruling party and familiarity with people called Vinaigrette and Angela, and a faculty don named Chaucret. Soon, this graphic artist had persuaded an entire network of well-placed, talented people to supply her needs for information, advice, explanations, warnings. Toward what end, Denis was never sure, but, like the Fisherman, he invariably appreciated her productions.

Under Cynthia's guidance, Denis gradually compiled a structure of portals into AuThon's particular cast of characters. They were identified by rhetorical idiosyncrasies—quirks of speaking or listening, ways of looking off, changes of posture. In her mind these traits were elements of personal "masks." Pondering this new metaphor for what he preferred to call personality, he remembered powerful masking performances in West Africa and thought he knew what to look for. Van Zan reached more deeply than that.

"Even you, Denis, if you weren't so tone-deaf, could identify people by their habitual sounds and gestures," she scolded him. "Masks prevail inside of what people wear; they show in typical behavior. For instance, the low growl and deep breath that Olivier uses to get your attention; how Bernard's Adam's-apple wobbles when he's stuck; the way Lucille interpolates 'un truc' where inarticulate Americans insert 'like' or 'you know'; how Georges claps his temples when he wants to find anything out, but not when he wants to make a point; that Solange opens all her responses with 'Non,' even when she's about to agree; or how well-bred Ahmed starts with some form of 'thanks,' then proceeds to send you over the cliff.

"Watch how aggressively Fisherman juggles his new glasses when he's unsure what he wants to say; that keeps his domestic life away from masculine violence.

"Or …" here Cynthia gazed up at the ceiling, "the way your Anya remarks on anything, including the weather, as a gift from first-person singular. Check her out when she's being most 'environmental'; it's not for nature's sake but for the human species that's put itself into her safekeeping. She protests against overfishing, mislabeling, dragging grill nets along the bottom, etcetera, because all that leads to shortages and higher prices, not because it injures the natural world. That's her pitch, and you get it from her. True, glamor helps, and she has a flair for décor, so when she confides in you, she flashes those eyes you like so much."

"Sure, but . . . come on!"

Overriding his stammering protests, Cynthia conceded reassuringly: "That strategy allows her to be more concise, more emphatic than others who have to stretch what they want to convey.

"And then there's the ineffable Philosophe, who waves his arms like an outraged football official without saying anything. It turns Anya livid, so for your libido's sake, try not to copy his signals."

Overlooking her insinuations, Guyane was willing to test Cynthia's technique, although mainly to prove to himself that she'd been wrong about his atonality. "I took piano lessons, you know, as a kid in Brooklyn, and learned harmony pretty well," he told her, without conviction.

"Maybe so," she retorted, "until you were hit on the head with The Rite of Spring."

Deferring to her last example, he asked how she already knew about the notorious Interior Minister whom neither of them had met. Van Zan smiled enigmatically and returned to her online sketch screen. "I watched Philosophe during the party congress at Angela's hotel. Also, in private your Diva does an imitation of Karamau— hilarious. I'll leave him for you to meet," she said while inking in a massive buzzard caricature, "but when you do, watch his wings."

To complete his research, Guyane spent a calculated fortnight visiting AuThon staff on their jobs; he listened intently, taking notes on preferences and ideas, and, indeed, registering their habits of listening and gesturing. He confirmed the resemblance of AuThon's inner circle to a choir of voices. Although not always in unison, they were far from a mere menagerie of flunkeys; rather more concerted, like a proverbial school of fish. This allowed him to attribute a signature to most principals, building on the prevailing examples of Fisherman, Philosophe, Diva, and the lamented Spider—as well as the esoteric Vinaigrette about whom he had heard from Cynthia. For subsequent cryptonyms (Lorgnon for Kolona, Robinet for Ahmed, La Douce for the tough financial mandarin Solange Seriel), he enlisted Van Zan to devise a logo for each "mask"; Anya's was the sole image to encroach into caricature. As his collection grew, the bewildered brand manager became more confident about his company's interactions within the fluid world of AuxIndes.

After observing everyone he could reach, from quiet minds in the cubicles to articulate hands out at the nets, Guyane proposed a compendium of objectives for "the Brand." It aimed at a dynamic pursuit of advantages offered in a confluence of systems—interlocking functions of research, production, markets; the security of community based on a partly understood model of oceanic intercourse; and the preparation of human institutions for impact by climatic forces. AuThon was to integrate disparate lines of activity without surrendering any assets in its existing escutcheon, even though Van Zan would readily depict departures from the "way things were done."

While accommodating salient values of Masson's inner circle, Guyane had to juggle insights, contradictions, and anomalies without consideration of rank or eloquence. He composed his draft cautiously, knowing that the national culture deplored overt assaults on sensibility; no idea, however unworthy, could be dismissed peremptorily without risking dishonor to its author and the company. To initiate debate, he proposed a role-playing exercise in which all ideas circulated among an enlarged choir of mandarin roles or "masks," without compromising any participant. Once the symposium concluded, an aggregate brand definition would go to the Fisherman by consensus, with all inconsistencies accommodated in footnotes.

Before exposing his ideas to the wider choir, Denis decided to try them out with a key soloist. He thought of Bamiara, the confidential operator, or Ahmed Tabour, an "outsider" voice, but, as Cynthia foretold, he was instinctively drawn to Anya Wazimbwe, Masson's most intimate comrade from student days. Smartly etched in discourse as well as appearance, categoric in her principles, Anya was then restoring her executive profile after a painful divorce from an abusive husband. She had already resumed the prominent name of Wazimbwe, a social distinction she had hitherto repressed. Small, fine-featured, she embodied aristocracy and punched above her weight. "You can't get cheekbones any higher if you were the Queen of Sweden," snapped Van Zan. "I'm told she's so blue-blooded that people actually see her as a blonde."

Unlike intimates who gladly used the nickname Diva, originally coined by Anya's nemesis, Karamau, Cynthia chose to refer to her as Medusa.

Wazimbwe's secret (hence widely discussed) objective was to revive an early romance with Masson. A decade ago, joined in militancy, the undergraduate pair had treated their partnership as a perpetual mechanism, wound up, ready to run. When their machine veered offtrack—through his effort to steer her into childbearing—they climbed out of separate windows and left it wrecked. Anya never forgave him for trying to pollinate her. "Please inject Masson with a case of measles!" she urged the University doctor. "That will sterilize him, won't it? Then I'll go to work on him."

It may have been the Diva's defection that impelled Roger to flee to Canada and cultivate his future on the seas. Separate nuptials and nearly a decade later, they had patiently restored their collaboration. By now she was in operational command at AuThon, about to be named vice-president of a "Brand." Anya had nonetheless to respect Masson's treatment of marriage to Giselle as a work in progress, requiring his steady loyalty. This commitment ruled out overt dalliance. Still, according to a fixed item in workplace lore, both their mobile phone batteries died whenever they were separated by more than a kilometer from each other. Denis Guyane scoffed at the meme; no relationship was worth such undivided attention.

Although Wazimbwe did not overstep the line, her Gorgon's curse prevailed: the Masson marriage remained childless.

Prudently, Denis resisted the temptation to ask Anya to join him in a private "branding" conversation over food and drink. "Too conspiratorial, once it's known. And I'm not, repeat NOT aiming at the thrill," he declared to himself, trying to be convinced. In any case, he was sure, even relieved, that this Diva would not flirt or respond to coquetry. Instead, he decided to consult her professionally, about "process," Masson's preferred term for strategy. Staging an ostensibly impromptu call at Wazimbwe's office, he arrived as if out of the blue, carrying a *New Yorker* article on climate change that he knew she would appreciate. Then, he "casually" sought her advice.

Anya seemed to welcome the intrusion. She listened sympathetically to the idea of a role-play simulation among "masks," a concept she already understood. (He recalled hearing something about her filial ties with the working-class activist known as Vinaigrette—an improbable relationship, in his mind.) Categorically aristocratic, the nymph Wazimbwe kept her hair styled and shoes chosen to remind island elites of their chic, unrepudiated Parisian heritage. She came to work in elegant print blouses, knit sweaters, sleek trousers. Every now and then a short skirt reminded observers of the fashion model that she might have become ten years earlier, before opting for grittier employments.

Given her status in the choir, Denis expected Wazimbwe to insist on clean processes, open books, assaults on corruption in the oceanic commons. Anya complied; she even endorsed the risks entailed by

Van Zan's cartoon conceits—including an exposé of pirates to be exposed in a series on foreign fleets. Responding to Guyane, the Diva looked forward to a "serious game." She foresaw her own role in promoting a robust social portfolio for AuThon, advising on nutrition, mother-child health services, and fisheries training for neglected youth (boys *and* girls). Denis conceded that such high-mindedness could prove instrumental for AuThon's evolving brand.

Wazimbwe needed, however, to doubt one element in the design. Her close friend, the "Peasant" Bamiara was to propose outright purchase of communally owned terrain on the West Coast. The company, he thought, had to control space to install its aquaculture farm, refrigeration plant, and storage facility, and to promote development of the hinterland. Skeptically, Anya wondered how she could display respect for Benjamin while warning that, even if the town should consent to sell, property ownership entailed profound social responsibilities. She worried over insidious effects on the mangrove shoreline, carbonization of wetlands, pollution of palm groves, ravages of a changing climate on the established settlements. Considering such industrial threats to human survival, Wazimbwe warned against risks of "climate racism," entailed by petrol spill, pollutant waste, and sundry other threats in a hitherto benign littoral environment.

Gasping for breath, Denis groped to accommodate Anya's polemics and still find a way to placate proud Bamiara—the antithesis of peasantry, as even Cynthia admitted. "Maybe I'm wrong about this," muttered Anya in mocking self-deprecation, lowering her glance modestly, testing Guyane.

"Hardly that," Denis countered. "I know you're right, but to save face for the Peasant, we have to be subtle."

"Just as he was," Wazimbwe gibed, "when he eased you into it."

"Off guard, was I?" Denis had to glance humbly down toward his shoes (New York calling?). He conjured an image of ravishing eyes beneath Medusa's venomous curls, but then came back with a solution. "What if you were to propose a feasibility study of the property acquisition, using an independent 'think tank' of Benjamin's own choice? You could ask them to calculate expenses on a long-term curve, counting jobs and health improvement as benefits to offset investment costs and environmental risks."

The Diva nodded, signifying survival of that test. She suggested that the contract project this study into offshore renewable energy and greening of the port town against storm impact in a deteriorating climate. Setting aside how "that catty genius" Van Zan might caricature such loftiness, Wazimbwe would argue for "decarbonizing and deoxidizing our maritime operations, and other acidification liabilities." Anya regarded this dimension of the project as a sobering reminder to the Fisherman of lessons from the past year's USA tour, which Masson had recounted to her. After his searing glimpse into the devastation of the Louisiana coast—"Ecocide!" she called it, "and your Cynthia comes right out of it!"—the boss would surely undertake any such operations cautiously. Benjamin's feasibility research would have to satisfy that precondition.

The land appropriation scheme nevertheless carried another implication that alerted the Diva: Bamiara had opted to locate the aquaculture plant at a particular harbor site across from the African continent. She saw that it lay within the political bailiwick of Interior Minister Karamau whose assent would be indispensable to their long-term strategy. The rapacious Philosophe would have to perceive advantages for himself in any major enterprise on "his" coast. Although Denis had yet to meet the man, he recalled that upon graduation Anya had worked in Antoine Karamau's office. She was not his constituent by origin or from his modest social niche; however, they clearly had little in common. But she knew the man's self-interest.

Wazimbwe admitted in confidence, her eyes indeed flashing, what everybody already understood—that after three years at the Interior Ministry, and while mired in her unwise marriage, she deemed Philosophe incurably interested in female companionship, especially her own. Hence she had resigned—"courteously," she insisted, "although Antoine never forgave me." While Diva considered an approach to Karamau indispensable to the aquaculture project, she was obviously not the person to broach the crucial connection. It would be best if Denis asked Fisherman to bring him to where he could brief the minister.

"In any case, you don't want to leapfrog the boss, not in something as political as this. Wait until Roger's back and we've executed the role-play successfully; then ask him to introduce you to Antoine. He'll probably take you to the Creole Club—as a guest, of course, since . . . well, you'll find out why."

Anya Wazimbwe proved crucial in maneuvering acceptance of Guyane's planning by the rest of the choir. Dressed "executively" for her role, she virtually dominated the proceedings, putting her principles of environmentalism to work toward company objectives. Bamiara and the others executed their respective parts admirably, even when nudged to modify a commitment. Before the day ended, Neiru had started designing facilities and Seriel began working on financial strategy. Cynthia Van Zan rendered the proceedings graphically with uncharacteristic approbation; to her it was a step forward, with many more remaining to be taken before the oceans approve.

Having returned with enthusiasm from his harbor tour, Masson watched the symposium play out to the satisfaction of nearly everybody's "core values." He even refrained from gesturing with his ferocious new eyeglasses.

Several weeks later, once the feasibility study had vindicated Bamiara's main ideas for the aquatic farm, Fisherman agreed on the timeliness of an approach to the Interior Minister. He introduced Denis at the exclusive monthly luncheon where spoken Creole was the rule. The wrong Creole, in Guyane's opinion, with their *Alo, ki mantu?* style of greeting, but this was no place to flourish Haitian correctives. Fortunately, the linguistic overlaps between "real" kreyòl and their Indian Ocean patois intrigued members sufficiently to accept Denis as a welcome intrusion. Until he could obtain competence in the vernacular, however, he could never qualify for club membership. Guyane was still unaware that his own assistant, Van Zan, was already acquiring conversational facility in the nation's lingua franca.

"Speaking of speaking," he said to the Philosophe in English after they shook hands, "Is it true that you now master my own native tongue?"

The big man only grinned, threw his arms up, then shook his massive head. By now, having reached full self-mastery, he seldom wasted a word. "English? too difficult! Stuck with two tongues, delinquent in both." Laconic but accurate?

"Oh? I've heard you have a demanding teacher. But none of us will ever satisfy the Jesuits. It's why we continue to frequent them."

"You 'ave been vell enformet, young American," mumbled Karamau, affecting a clumsy accent. Resuming in French, "I'm told you have an interesting proposal for me. Let's resume this, my office tomorrow." He flapped a hand at empty space behind Denis, to conclude the introduction.

Without knowing how much Philosophe had already learned of his intentions, Denis made the appointment and successfully pitched AuThon's aquaculture plan. Minister Karamau anticipated sufficient credit for himself in bringing jobs, investment, and development to a region heretofore over-reliant on touristic charm. That sounded too easy to Guyane's ear, but he opted to trust even an unreliable interlocutor whose acquiescence was essential to get the project on track.

Driving a company Jeep along trajectories of her own devising, Cynthia Van Zan forged regularly, alone and fearless, in search of intimacy with the sea. Gradually, she grasped how natural phenomena depended on associations. Even on shore, she perceived intrinsic rhythms of empathy or correspondence among species and their habitats—cliffs beckoning to soaring fowl and nimble goats; trees thrusting out of rocks to provide shelter and food; roots enlivening distant plant life. She noted the forms of "schooling" and protective changes of skin color among members of deep-sea species. And, thanks to Professor Chaucret, she learned how to use quotidian Creole, awkwardly but effectively.

Seeing linkages in natural communication permitted Cynthia to fill her professional role in AuxIndes. She invariably delivered visual facsimiles of what the Fisherman or his lieutenants would discover they needed to consider. Van Zan seldom had to confront Roger's otherwise uncomfortable questioning.

Van Zan did face persistent disagreement with Anya Wazimbwe, however. Their viewpoints clashed whenever either glimpsed an opening. Cynthia disdained Wazimbwe's "speciesism," perceived even when the Diva hurled a Medusan curse at flagrant miscreants. Anya responded by challenging Van Zan to focus her work more effectively, starting with a choice of prime target: "Would it be plastics congestion? Oil spills? Piracy? Climate change? Or something else—all are anthropomorphic threats to both the fish *and* the folks who consume them." To which Van Zan contended that oceanic life claimed as much help as humans to survive annihilation. "Let's try to prevent that *we* don't expire first," rejoined the Diva.

"There's a lesson there," Cynthia admitted. "Our mother, nature, seems bent on eradicating the human race, leaving more valuable species to pick up the pieces. We're not only devouring our vital surroundings, but ourselves as well. AuThon to the rescue?" The two could join for once in their apprehensions, and not for the last time.

Cynthia also had an axe to grind with Denis Guyane, who she accused of having over-sold Africa to her. Based on what he had recounted in New York, she expected to become inserted into a continental temple of *griots*—troubadour bards rapping heroic praises, of people who danced through ordinary life, and drums that "talked" in decipherable syllables. He offered her gratifying tales of natural polyrhythmic sounds, of gowns and head-wraps in vivid hues, of percussion that resounded through the night near places where strangers were lodging. "You can take it as a local folk welcome," he'd said, "but those drums may also intend warning against malevolent neighbors." Such colors typified the African tradition that excited her imagination and drew her toward the continent.

To her chagrin, Van Zan's forages around AuxIndes turned up nothing so creative as those picturesque tableaux. She traveled through scruffy villages flanked by fragile paddy rice or corn fields, roamed by twisted bodies clothed in patches. The scene was observed by self-absorbed humped cattle and animated by children who rushed up from ingeniously fabricated toys to hail any new arrival. Invariably, after leaving the city streets behind, she encountered no young men and few young women. Without work, they had no cause to remain in the countryside. Hunger and scarcity threatened; when rains failed or crops withered, those scourges prevailed. Finding words to press into action, Cynthia urged local authorities to summon a food truck or mobile kitchen from the AuThon extension service that made Roger Masson's name universally popular.

Her evenings fell on gatherings where tired women and their children held back while elderly men in plain robes outdid each other applying Creole proverbs to common complaints. Van Zan couldn't understand much of what they said, but she intuited enough to deplore morbidity in the island's culture. "They glorify 'life' in the world of the dead," she complained to Guyane: "stale male, and no music." It was more enlightening, she thought, to converse with the ocean itself. "I thought I was entering into a dynamic continent. Instead we just got dropped upon an island: bone-dry land. It's what surrounds it that matters."

Without hope, Guyane sought to disabuse Cynthia of the notion that "all Africa" should exhibit the cultural assets of one region. True diversity comes where you seek it. What intrigued her was found mainly on the continent's Atlantic side, he argued; there some languages were tonal and people less used to orate and more to dance.

"Like where my own family originated," rejoined Van Zan, "lots more interesting." She was satisfied, as always, to have had the last word. He left it there.

Once evolution of AuThon's "brand" took substance, the following months elapsed in deliberate progress and chaotic contingencies. Sea life continued to frequent the nets while aquatic farming was plotted along the littoral. From the island's center, the Fisherman's domain expanded cautiously into retail grocery and textile markets. Competitors and banks expressed obstacles, but they were contradicted by friendly multinational agencies and resisted through indomitable domestic leverage (some of it by clans affiliated with the Wazimbwe). Roger Masson threw inexhaustible energy into the uproar, carrying the organization over breaches and explosions, as well as through quieter ground. He paid attention to Benjamin's feasibility study, kept Denis close for solutions to perplexities, and depended on his Diva to hold the executive team together while allowing more peripheral staff to come and go.

Favored in its timing, Masson's financial model functioned successfully for AuThon's audacious expansion. The company maximized domestic sales, promoted by Peasant Bamiara's office; Denis and Olivier arranged overseas contracts; Western powers joined in combat against wildcat fleets and other invaders of the island's fisheries. Both the new farm venture and acquisition of under-capitalized businesses secured international finance thanks to the combined resourcefulness of Bamiara, Wazimbwe, and Papillon. Mentored meticulously by Seriel "La Douce," they took advantage of the company's distinction as the "multilaterals' darling" to locate capital at favorable interest rates, and to find sources of public invest-ment without recourse to expensive commercial debt.

Although conspicuous success was normally condemned as poor form in AuxIndes, the government saw no need to intervene. From his tower of immobility, President Bienportant understood the ad-vantages of favorable international opinion. Besides, he was already profiting from shady real estate deals in the central highlands, so that Masson's empire and a future fish farm in the West posed no threat to him. Moreover, the Philosophe's acceptance of a project that fa-vored his own interests enabled AuThon to count on key endorse-ments when it conveyed its proposals to local officials.

Tended by Bamiara the practical Peasant, facilities for fish-farm-ing began to implant on the West Coast. Soon the ponds and pools could be excavated, roads and port facilities extended, a work force trained and housed, the refrigeration plant constructed with access to hydro-power. Improved paddy fields and pasture surrounding the industrial site would provide for the needs of employees and their families. "Only don't let Fisherman think he's going to get the staff to *move* out there," warned the Fishery's labor union.

That preference was firmly seconded by Masson's wife, a cre-dentialed patriot for the capital city. Eventually, while these plans were evolving, Giselle revealed her particular motive for favoring the urban option: Indesville's mayoralty was to become vacant during the year coinciding with intense construction of the fish farm, and Mme. Masson had become determined to become the capital's first woman chief executive.

When she divulged this ambition to her husband, Roger hesitated, wary of a premature political campaign that could complicate his company's expansion. Eventually, however, he conceded that Giselle could claim the skills and insight to endow their venerable city with energy, and she certainly had the right to his complicity. Moreover, foreseeing business opportunities through having a spouse in charge of the capital, Fisherman pledged his support, supremely confident of Giselle's success, even before undertaking to survey any putative competition.

Then, after sounding out Vinaigrette, Masson learned that the indefatigable Karamau would probably be proposing a young "cousin or nephew" for the mayoral run; both the lad and Giselle were to seek nomination by the ruling National Party. Wary of conflict with the potent minister, Masson instructed Denis Guyane to negotiate the nephew's gracious removal from his wife's pathway.

Denis tried, directly at the source, in French and English, but in vain.

"Very unfortunate," Philosophe muttered, gesturing more aggressively than his voice suggested. "Kumar may be only a disc jockey, but he's bright, ambitious. And he's my brother's son. Loyalty to my family. Can't your boss dissuade *her*? Has he tried?"

"Very doubtful, both questions," admitted Denis. "Giselle is determined to take charge of the city; she's already recruiting a strong campaign team. It's about time for a woman mayor, you know. Would young Kumar be willing to accept an alternative job? Say at our new plant down in your neighborhood?"

Karamau hoisted his arms and snorted. "Far from it. That's what he's escaping—dreary family heritage, hole in the sticks. No room there for the New African sound, he says. And no tolerance for him as a gay man. I promised his father. The boy's worked five years in this city. He's entertained multitudes on Domino's radio station. This is what Kumar has chosen. He knows his mind."

"Yes, and I know Giselle's. We certainly don't want a fight with you or your family here or down on the coast. Does your Kumar have assurances of support from the Nationals?"

"Neither has your Giselle. Tell me why in hell you think the party would back a woman for so prominent an office?"

Suppressing his impulse to condemn that query from a personage already well-known for sexism, Guyane let the issue lie. He also knew better than to retort with reference to young Kumar's sexuality. Hence, he hoped that one or the other side would concede before the Masson family had to engage in intra-partisan battle with Karamau's, just as the new fish farm was nearing its genesis. When an amicable resolution failed, Bamiara took the pulse of the Nationals and reported to Masson that party leadership, all males, shared Philosophe's prejudice. Company staff, led by Anya Wazimbwe, vowed their loyalty to Giselle, even if it meant a campaign against the ruling party nominee. Instinctively, Cynthia Van Zan offered her services.

As the municipal confrontation evolved, Guyane's role stressed peacekeeping in behalf of the AuThon brand, its stakes in the fish farm, and prospects for further extension. At best, he succeeded only in temporarily keeping a wobbly lid on a simmering pot. As expected, the party executive conformed to Philosophe's preference, and nominated Kumar Karamau for mayor. They kept a discreet, but self-congratulatory silence over his sexual preference. The town would suffer nothing from it.

At once, Giselle refused to accept smoke-filled room misogyny. "I'll be damned before I allow that nepotistic puppet to waltz into city hall by default," she told her sponsors, "but I will not stoop to impugning his sexuality." She proclaimed her candidacy as an independent, and took her cause into the streets, protesting against reflex-action politics that endowed a single party with monopoly over access to high office—an advantage she had once been prepared to accept.

Thus did this cherubic, bespectacled woman earn the improbable nickname of *Siren*.

Masson had no alternative; he donated his prestige and delicate fortune to his wife's campaign, underwriting a succession of appearances by his spouse and her surrogates. Thanks to Wazimbwe and with back-door advice from la Vinaigrette, the rallies were skillfully organized, peaceful, and coherent. They were in vain, as it turned out, for, although Giselle worked vigorously, and with committed support, her forces could not overcome popular prejudice for the young entertainer—or against the Siren's presumptuousness, as so many citizens judged the matter.

While it played out, the contest proved increasingly raucous. Bodyguards had to accompany Giselle or her surrogates into rallies frought with pinching fingers and even ruder salutes. Tours of slums were disturbed by unexplained power outages and collapsing platforms; these accidents could occur even in the more affluent suburbs. The Diva Wazimbwe and Solange Seriel, although toughened long ago by repression against "radical" students, were now stigmatized as "uppity women," and taken by surprise over a recrudescence of adolescent terrorism.

The conflict inevitably veered into class antagonism. Siren's decorous followers would file quietly past half-built houses with ladders propped against the walls. When they neared, however, they saw those ladders occupied by youth shouting mockery of the candidate's cultivated manners and accents. Accurate French and polite convention became handicaps in a new generation of populist impropriety.

Although tempted, the campaign declined to reply in kind. Not only was homophobia off limits. Giselle's campaign also recruited gay men and women. But she firmly rejected recourse to another sure-fire card by forbidding mention of Kumar's low-caste origins in the urban districts most susceptible to snob appeals. "Win clean or lose," became the unexpressed mantra of a forlorn cause.

Elsewhere, the Siren's rallies were systematically drowned out by sound trucks broadcasting Kumar's own voice, his hip-hop message of "*Fraydome! Leebertay!*" conveyed through pulse, not logic. Invariably, when Masson or her surrogates succeeded in obtaining permits for a public rally (never a sure thing for Karamau protocol), they moved into a space already suffused by noise from platoons of mobile phones tuned in unison to the same wavelength, the same pounding sound, overwhelming the candidate's arguments with cacophony. The cell-phone squad, composed of subsidized youth, sang, shouted, and beat its meter throughout the city.

Masson's formal appeals to police met with cynical shrugs, no action. To Philosophe's counselors, loudspeakers perambulating on trucks were classified under free speech, streaming the latest "entertainment" for the crowds. It was all covered by the Kumar campaign's permits, protected by the constitution.

In their only debate, Giselle appealed to her opponent—whom Van Zan contrasted as *the Grim Rapper* (against the genuine *griot*): "Can't you see yourself trapped in this refusal circus that you are inflicting on the public? How can you pretend to transform a city, guarantee its progress, if you bury it in this filthy noise?"

Kumar had his uncle's height without his bulk, a ruff of black hair crowning a lively face seamed in smiles—to contrast with Antoine's impassivity. "What you call noise," he replied, "is the authentic sound of life in this town. It's our heritage and our future. Young people will assure its fruition. We'll build our dream out of your ruins. You can't get it to stop." Champion of his own callow ideology, this Karamau was nonetheless a chip off an old block.

"Your reliance on mainstream campaigning is old hat and ludicrous," boasted the Rapper. "Nobody reads the printed press; it has lost both its advertising and its influence; social media commands attention. Only phantoms take your newspapers; ancestors scan them in their tombs, to keep up with obituaries. You can't win elections with the dead. Real readers demand entertainment, not truth."

"You can't mean that," objected Siren. "We provide what our constituency seeks—reliable information."

"Your word," rapped Kumar. "Information is just as outmoded as truth."

Challenged to distinguish between Karamau's youth binge and their own student movement of the nineties, Wazimbwe and Roger Masson deplored the Rapper's delivery of illusions for a new generation "eager to be lied to." Anya half expected him to intone, "Get out of our way!" If he did, she vowed to sue him for plagiarism.

When the polls closed and Kumar was proclaimed mayor (God save the city!), Vinaigrette assured Giselle that she hadn't lost the election, "only the rhythm."

"The decibels, she means," cried Anya. "This is democracy?"

"You had the arguments," assented Vinaigrette, "sanitation, schools, health services, open contracts freely bid. But Kumar had the voice and the pace. The beats of some primitive tribal center inside a decaying city. Noise even captured the churches—the fringe ones, especially Samuel's."

She changed subject before having to answer the usual question about Samuel. "Did you notice by the way that some of those juvenile hecklers out there were off-duty cops? They're from Karamau's incubator, dressed like teenagers in torn jeans."

Cynthia Van Zan caught the glance Vinaigrette shot at her: as if to say "so much for *your* anti-establishment youth crusade."

Angoras

Through three office windows in the Fishery, Roger Masson could look into untamed secondary forest, exhorted to grow wild as if to erase memory of the axes and plows that had leveled the primeval bush. More dramatically, however, his view of the woods was partly obstructed by strange web patterns on the outside of the windows; to enhance this wilderness scene, Masson encouraged monstrous spiders to maintain their lair and conduct their lethal business silently across each exterior pane. Sustaining this grotesque decor, he prohibited intervention from cleaning squads or protectors of insects.

The resulting panorama often evoked gasps from visitors unable to explain the Fisherman's reasons for indulging such violence. Was it meant to simulate an open-air version of oceanic entrapment? Or to expose some latent menace in Masson's phlegmatic temper? Or was it all in homage to an outraged young martyr with a curious nickname? Even the boss usually sat with his back to the window scene, oblivious to the carnage.

Denis Guyane always entered that office obliquely, angling toward a neutral side wall, declining to tolerate the webs as a spectator sport. As usual, he drew a chair laterally toward one side of the desk, waiting for the boss to open a routine conversation. He was prepared for Fisherman's opening invitation: "Tell me, Denis," Masson said, "how our fish park is doing."

There wasn't that much to tell. Guyane had returned the night before from a bumpy tour of the coastal parcel that the company was to purchase for its farm site. Accompanied by Bernard Neiru (*Papillon*), his task was to assess local receptivity to land acquisition and, if necessary, to design an opinion campaign in favor of the fish farm. That morning, when the Fisherman's summons reached his phone, he was working confidently on the report. The communal terrain seemed bleak enough to allow development. Local elders posed no insuperable impediments to an AuThon project—even an artificial fish pond, provided of course that family tombs remained undisturbed.

The dead of this southwest town were lodged in a scattering of some two dozen rectangular grave structures, built up from the ground along the gentle slopes of an otherwise barren hill. Putatively Christian, the tombs differed from those of the central highlands by a profusion of robust wood sculptures planted across the top of each site. Most of the imagery was natural or of common subjects—cattle, motorcycles, athletes, firearms, lovers in tandem. Denis understood that these figures corresponded to qualities that the families wished to attribute to their interred forebears, and that the artists who rendered them kept in close touch with clan histories, the cohesive community, and one another. The tombs also assured interest in the area as a destination for cultural tours, embellished by glorifying narratives and photographic seduction. These assets provided some work for young men who could reside at home, rather than migrate to urban employment. Local families appeared all the healthier thanks to the tourist trade.

Below the hill was open pasture, not cropland; it abutted a delta with a diversity of salt marsh and river life—fresh-water fish, crustaceans, birds, crocodiles, insects, marsh grasses, trees, and shrubs. Neiru and Guyane regarded the spot as technically conducive to the fish farm. They conceded that Anya Wazimbwe would object to stocking tilapia—"a trash fish useful only to feed on insects in irrigated rice fields."

That's what he reported to the Fisherman in response to the question.

"Cattle, eh?" muttered Masson after a thoughtful pause, and ignoring the tilapia controversy; "no goats?"

"None that I could see," said Denis, "but there was some talk, if that's what you're asking about."

Masson nodded, and ominously began to clean his spectacles.

In fact, the local chatter had been freely offered. It depicted the visit a few weeks before by a half dozen men calling themselves farmers (although locals described them as stiffly garbed in new jeans); they were asking questions about land ownership and prospects for development. The visitors did not identify themselves explicitly, but told the elders of a recommendation from Minister Karamau, the region's favorite son. The men left some beautiful soft mohair weaves as gifts to the village ("We saw them in the town hall; they were startling, even if intended to be used as, ugh, carpets"). Having heard nothing from the visitors subsequently, the elders concluded that the project, whatever it was, would not materialize.

"Hence the cordial welcome we received. In fact, when they heard I was Haitian-American, they proclaimed that 'this country has gone global!'"

"Hm, funny no tip-off to us from Philosophe about that delegation," commented Masson, returning to the mohair purveyors. "Maybe he just resents what Giselle said about his nephew." He then grew silent, and Guyane knew the interview had ended.

That was it. Denis expected that repeated cross-purposes with plans by cronies of Philosophe's would require a Fisherman conversation with his ministerial acquaintance. So, with Papillon and Ahmed, he completed what he and Bamiara envisioned as a propitious argument to promote the fish farm to the region. Then he waited for further initiatives from Masson. By this time, Guyane had consulted on finances often enough with Solange to eventuate into a mutually felicitous dinner-and-bedroom relationship.

Word came within the week, and rather startlingly. Arriving that morning, Denis switched on his desk lamp (donated by Masson, in the sculptured shape of a wrestler grappling with an orca) and found an odd message on one of the Fisherman's own business cards: "How would you ok to work after all in a campaign of president?" An odd overture, first because Masson had written anything at all, and that he had tried to write it in English without using the electronic channels where such messages get translated into grammatical slush.

"He's put some sort of question to me. Can I see him?" Guyane asked Masson's secretary.

"Oh, yes," she replied, "He told me to cancel the usual morning rounds and to send you right in, chop-chop."

Chuckling at Mireille's antiquated slang, Denis tapped on the Fisherman's door and angled once more into the paneled office, eyes deflected from the webbed banquets hanging outside the picture windows. He waited until the boss looked up from the map on his desktop, finished his breakfast sweet bun, and adjusted his spectacles; then Guyane ventured to open the conversation.

"You talked to Minister Philosophe?"

"Oh, yes. Last night in fact."

"And he told you he's going to run for president?"

"Well, no, not exactly. Do YOU know that he is?"

This time Denis effected the conversational pause. "No, certainly not. But the note you sent me . . . Anyhow," after Masson extended the silence, "I can't see myself doing him any good."

"I'm glad to hear that. And I agree with you. Whether Antoine decides to try for advancement is his business, but that angora plantation and rug factory could get in *our* way."

"Right," said Guyane. "Glad you got to him about it. But this presidential campaign. If it's not Philosophe, then I suppose it's suddenly become . . ."

"My aspiration, indeed," broke in Masson uncharacteristically. "I've been contemplating it for some time."

"Although you've told me that you were not interested in becoming president."

"So long as I could do what I chose while somebody else had those political headaches, yes. Now . . ."

Then a characteristic Fisherman pause.

"Now, you foresee an obstacle to the fish farm, and because Philosophe seems to be behind that, you think you need to be chief of state to get his goats out of the way?"

Another long pause followed, giving Denis a chance to line up his objections.

"Putting it crudely like that," answered Masson, "I suppose that is what turned my mind. You don't seem enraptured by the idea. Why would you avoid a chance to help design a presidential run? Lots of your American colleagues must be eager to get that close to the White House. Is our country too small to tempt you?"

Guyane suppressed a derisive laugh. "No, your country deserves much more than my humble services. But it also deserves a chief of state who primarily seeks the national advantage, not his own commercial benefit."

"No doubt it does," argued the Fisherman, "And that's what it will obtain. But the two advantages must be integrated; otherwise the valiant chief of state will have little motivation to undertake the options he must confront."

"I certainly hope that's not true," blurted Denis, "And I trust that the farm venture was only a factor, and not the decisive one."

"Tell me, Denis," said Masson, rising from his chair and turning to look out a web-encrusted window at the suddenly dormant spider world, "what successful presidents do YOU know who did not join the national interest with their own advantage? Which ones have no ego, no ambition, no motives that serve their reputation, their legacy?"

"None, yet I hope that the most successful have been scrupulous enough to avoid conflicts of interest."

"Conflicts, certainly. We want none of those. It's compatibility of interests that I'm after. And you're the man to help me define how to join those interests—and to satisfy the world that they are indeed integrated."

In the aftermath of the municipal election, Giselle Masson and her partisans had been gathering periodically to discuss how to organize recovery from her defeat. This time, she prepared her friends to hear a crucial answer—the Massons' resolution of revenge. When Fisherman joined them, sliding a chair next to his wife's, he sought their advice on how to announce his own candidacy—for presidency in the election of 2010, two years hence. Following his spouse's example, he would run as an independent, challenging the perpetual ruling party whose incumbent, President Bienportant, would certainly seek a fourth five-year term. He humbly invited his wife's team to offer him their experience and judgment before opening the stops to a vigorous national campaign.

Surprised at the modesty, if not the substance of this initiative, Denis Guyane wondered how the decision would affect the fate of their various projects. Inevitably, Fisherman would be accused of a quest for power to advance his own business interests. This charge would carry him far from the ambition of decolonization celebrated during the student rebellion on Babel Mountain. By implication, how would others, especially the quintessential Philosophe, already in his own fourth round as minister, react to Masson's political venture? Would he greet it as an opportunity to break free of the cloying Domino, or rather, as a threat by hostile insurrectionaries with ambitions in his own fiefdom? How attractive could Karamau consider a mohair rug mill, compared to the aquacultural complex? Or was there another reason for excluding AuThon from that sea coast?

Suddenly, AuxIndes had become as embattled above ground as its marine dominion appeared to be below the surface. If American expats could appreciate that correspondence, how much deeper would these conflicts run for the islanders?

CHAPTER 6

CAMPAIGN: NETWORK & LABYRINTH

Once opened, the road to election appeared auspicious for Roger Masson. Campaign staff had learned lessons from the Rapper's victory over Giselle; at least they were licensed to make more noise. Television and radio outlets greeted prospects for lively competition, man to (ahem!) man. Domino's advanced age began to show, and his more ambitious henchmen appeared prepared to switch allegiances. Social media exploited boisterous angles with appeal to island youth. Masson's name had become identified with AuThon food donations among the rural poor, diverting nourishment that the elite would only discard. Campaign managers Wazimbwe and Bamiara raised funds and borrowed leverage discreetly, even inside ministries, without unduly provoking the presidency or its loyalist cohorts.

The expatriate team of Guyane and Van Zan confronted a complicated task. No longer were they merely a maritime enterprise's hired hands; now they could be suspected as alien intruders into domestic politics. To function without inviting opprobrium, their roles had to be worked into a national strategy that inevitably, but inconspicuously, included them.

Without much hope, the Americans expected Fisherman to articulate his expectations for their role in that enterprise. This proved elusive, for Masson had first to disentangle his own identities in the industrial, political, and social arenas. To make resources available to the campaign, all nonessential expansion, including the half-ready fish farm and the new textile plant, was suspended. Not much seemed to remain for Van Zan and Guyane to do. Dangling from this self-aborting structure, the expats had to ask what was expected of them, and their boss admitted some uncertainty over their pathway into the labyrinth.

"At first," he told them, "I had thought you might poke around the cesspools of Domino's corruption, get out of town and uncover useful intelligence in the hinterlands where you aren't recognized; where you might even pose as agents of, I don't know, Interpol? the FBI? But," he interjected promptly, seeing incredulity cloud Denis's countenance and sheer panic invade Cynthia's, "that's obviously insane. And yet your flair for discreet inquiry should be useful in some way that . . ."

"That doesn't contaminate your campaign," Guyane said.

"And get us thrown out of the country in the process," Van Zan completed the thought.

"Right." Then the customary pause. "So here's where I'd like you to start—to shift directions a tad. Not a real change of jobs, don't misunderstand. We'd have wanted this research to be done in any case to clear the markets for AuThon."

Noting persistence of disbelief in his interlocutors' attitude, Masson tried reassurance. "I want you to use the contacts you've already begun to be comfortable with—Sophie Nuru for one. And don't look at me like that," he shot into Cynthia's skepticism, and pushed his English. "She's prepared for this, and she is a mine, a gold mine of information; who do you think got me into the race to begin with?"

Van Zan had to nod half knowingly. Nothing about la Vinaigrette could take her by surprise. Yet she had her own suspicions over the distinction between a mine and a minefield; she wondered which it would be once she walked into it.

"You will, of course, continue to play *la jeune fille*, which Vinaigrette admires, even though she doesn't believe it. And record what you learn, using the magic of your visual imagination—which we'll be able to plant incognito through the popular media, as well as in our own."

"To start planting season, you might think about how a presidential contender ought to wear socks on full-screen TV," Cynthia responded. "You're going after the presidency now, not the white whale." Masson responded with a grin that did not clarify much for her. He turned to Denis.

As his departure point, Guyane was to undertake a field survey of food marketing in selected rural areas. He was to keep his eye out for the local consequences of illegal rake-offs and diversion of public contracts, artificial expense accounts, inflated bottom lines, kickbacks, bribes, sales of natural resources, and other self-dealing by officials, some of it traced in a running file kept by the encyclopedic Bamiara. Much of this intelligence came from central bank sources ("someone named Honoré" for instance), who were unwilling to risk their careers overtly by blowing whistles, especially in the direction of international patrons. "So they whisper the details to a religious sect that Benjamin frequents," he concluded.

"A sect that might be identified with a personage named Samuel?" Guyane guessed, eyebrows raised.

The Fisherman sank into one of his customary pauses, then merely shrugged his shoulders.

The interview was over.

As intended, it led to a heady rush of activity. Both Vinaigrette's memory and the Peasant's notes evoked court filings, ethics inquiries, and media reports of chicanery. Those accounts were often euphemized to shield the more notable antagonists in cases not yet—perhaps never to be—litigated. They would accumulate nonetheless into a stigma against the incumbent administration, demonstrating its nonchalance over deteriorating nutrition, housing, and public health in the republic. These conditions were especially severe in the arid South, suffocated by heat, abandoned by men, where women, children, and the aged chewed on prickly pear to fill their bellies. In truth, poverty reigned over the entire island countryside.

Guyane became habituated to suffering during several tours of problem localities. On these ventures into "the bush" with his driver, passing as an inspector of food stocks for AuThon, Denis surveyed villages consisting of thin lines of thatched huts frequented by exhausted people along dusty roads. Dwellings of any substance stood in various stages of construction or decay, depending on the fortunes of their owners. Cinder-block walls and roofs of thatch (rarely, corrugated metal) waited indefinitely to tighten against the austral rains and winds.

The habitable structures were populated by a few mothers and withered elders no longer distinguishable by gender. Their surroundings became animated by flocks of barely clothed children, birds, and livestock all chattering about local conditions.

Even migrating workers still called such places home, for a person's identity in AuxIndes invariably resided at a tomb outside the natal village. Those burial structures represented the family at its essence; protected against the encroaching bush, they remained in better condition than the ordinary domiciles.

As he drove through, Denis often paused so that hungry kids could dance around his car, eager for a distribution of crackers, but too polite to demand anything more. In the dry austral winter, children played upwind, to cough less. Their noses ran perpetually, until they were old enough to wipe them. Then they began school—usually on a long pathway to somewhere else, where people spoke French. They had to keep their khaki shorts and Tee-shirts clean enough through the week. When an adult neared, the driver, Patrice, would ask in Creole about daily life; the inevitable response was a prayer for better times.

There were opportunities, however, to collect information, or at least opinions, about matters reflecting obliquely on the efficacy of national leadership. The circumstances were various. Larger villages had edifices, built by republican or colonial authorities to house town meetings, elections, tax receipts, trials, certifications, and other formalities that left records of one sort or another. With their theoretically lockable doors, and with walls and roofs that resisted weather, these halls also offered shelter to travelers on foot, bicycle, donkey, or in vehicles. Pending dispersion of mobile phones, a typical town hall also offered the village's sole radio-telephone, an ancient device used for emergencies. Its messaging was usually superseded by flights of birds, clouds, or ominous swarms of locusts. By now, even adolescents could maintain better cellular communication for a few cents a day, if they had so much. Denis and Patrice bedded in such structures and could examine what passed for archives of the place.

Other affluent transients conveyed their own tents or trailers and were allowed to park at the village market, provided they cleared the space for commerce by early morning. Most merchants had time and inclination to try out their French for a foreigner's benefit. The atmosphere conveyed much for an astute listener, and Patrice translated what he heard in Creole. When rains did arrive, as in the austral summer, they could interrupt their "inspections" to avoid driving through floods and mud slides, allowing more extensive inquiry into local circumstances.

Whether peppered with usable intelligence or not, the tour itself proved educationally valuable to Guyane. Larger towns usually had something particular to offer at a market—sometimes a potter's or sculptor's wares, sturdy sandals, special cloth from goat- or sheep-raising regions, weaves of raffia or sisal fiber. Near the coasts, AuThon provided fresh or smoked fish trucked in by market day, although neither electricity nor ice was widely available for preservation. Cattle were ubiquitous. Slabs of beef hung at entrances to food stalls, usually as repositories for swarms of flies.

Foraging deeply into the South, or "famine land" as the unfunny quip called it, all bets were off. Nobody who stayed on that land survived past fifty years of age. Life depended on rare messages brought from wherever the clouds lived, conveyed by one or another wind; from far-off, that wind would come—one of them, each with its own name. All were known to the inhabitants who prayed for their arrival or departure in a different Creole that baffled even Patrice, forcing his use of primary school French to obtain directions. Unlike

Van Zan, Guyane himself never mastered the linguistic varieties that his intolerant father would have dismissed as "pidgin kreyòl." But he heard the elders quarrel over which of the hundred winds could be expected next, without ever agreeing on their memory. In any case, nobody, not even the ancestors, could reliably bring the necessary rains.

North of the desiccated cactus land, villages either drew water from a stream or maintained a communal well with its pump; when these became no longer functional, liquids arrived in containers—on trucks, the backs of animals, or the heads of women, and even children commuting on foot. Salubrity remained expensive, perpetually problematic.

No matter how pothole-pocked, dusty, and detoured its roadway, every hamlet on the island introduced itself on painted cement, stone, or wooden slab. These facsimiles of rural French signage carried the village name, sometimes followed by a brief boast, slogan, or claim to prominence. A similar device announced the end of town limits, often with the number of the putative roadway, and occasionally a note of farewell in French to the departing traveler. Near these signs, Guyane and Patrice often came upon a deposit of roadside plants or flowers, firewood, or bags of charcoal—all dropped off in heaps as though for random acquisition. Odors of mimosa and frangipani combatted valiantly against fugitive smoke from nearby dwellings.

Where clinics and churchyards existed, they were busy with food for distribution, some of it from overseas; these donations were always welcome, even if certain foreign grains had to be pestle-pounded. Every town had one or two church sites, each with its priest or pastor, in a nation divided by Christianities like a replica of 16th century Europe in miniature. Whichever their formal denomination however, all faithful respected the spirits of the earth. Funerals and sermons usually featured admixtures of Scripture with the wisdom of the ancestors—if not exactly specifying the benefits either of them brought to the inhabitants. "They both got us here," reminded the elders, unquestionably proud of that achievement.

In his random surveys of the countryside, Denis Guyane understood that religion and traditional lore ranked higher and prevailed more durably than government. One year after an election, few citizens recalled the name of their *député* (MP). "They're all the same," according to the residents, who nonetheless never failed to vote. Aside from local aristocracies that exerted practical influence throughout AuxInde's countryside, it was proverbial wisdom that decided the dates for weddings, festivals, and funereal commemoration. Women and girls shouldered virtually all the burdens of family life. Men reappeared from the towns when their families needed them for control of cattle, to till the warming land (sometimes with the same cattle), or to cement a new block or tile onto the house. After that, they vanished once more, in search of income to support the inevitable new baby eight or nine months hence, another weight on the women left behind.

Apart from outlets for resentment, these contacts provided usable evidence against a negligent administration that existed merely to serve its own purposes. Denis talked himself into believing that he was helping prepare for a more prosperous future.

Thanks to such intelligence, Roger Masson's campaign could explore several avenues for its assault on incumbent malfeasance. Some connected directly with Fisherman's own business preoccupations, and needed scrupulous treatment. For instance, foreign fleets, mostly Asian, habitually violated the island's territorial zone, but when observed would invariably claim license to fish inside the limited area. To display their disadvantages against such odds, local watermen explained the easy connections forged between alien trawler captains and underpaid coastal officials. Whether authorized or not, invader vessels could lease the necessary transponders to ward off satellite scrutiny and continue merrily fishing wherever they pleased. Thanks to Bamiara's contacts, Guyane was able to collect a few transponder sets from boatsmen, and Masson displayed them triumphantly from his TV platform as evidence of corruption in the house of the Domino. "How much money does a miserable local official get for delivering this little gadget," he would ask, "and where does the real payoff end?" he would pretend to wonder, innocently, pointing upward toward some Olympian, perhaps even presidential, empyrean.

From Wazimbwe's research, the campaign exposed ecologically destructive contracts to scrape manganese modules off the ocean floor, with payoffs to enrich cooperating bureaucrats. Ignoring scruples from Masson's legal counselors, Cynthia Van Zan played liberally with cartoons of this industrial version of pearl fishing.

Beneath the island's law-abiding pretensions lay spasms of insecurity that afflicted the entire population. Local press and media files revealed incidents of village devastation, property vandalism, and gang terrorism that raged more urgently as the election drew near. Law and order units deployed belatedly to besieged areas, invariably claimed efficacy in cleaning up after the damage was done, and sometimes even a "real kill."

Confidentially, disaffected functionaries exposed some usual typical "anti-terrorist" shams. Government minions would plant insecure cattle in the way of a greedy rustler gang, then pounce on the miscreants with an overpowering force of gendarmes. The press was invited to cover the capture of these desperadoes (most of whom escaped in clouds of dust). At times, however, reporters were treated to confessions by disgruntled bandits who complained with wounded pride that they had been hoodwinked into crime by the cops, and insufficiently paid for it. No news source could reveal such pranks explicitly without risk of retaliation by the Karamau ministry, but the graphic hints sufficed to arouse suspicion.

In another series based on international press reports, Van Zan depicted the surreptitious arrival of skillful poachers trapping and smuggling out exotic animals for sale to benefit global terrorist organizations. Money passes from criminal hands into the pockets of unnamed (of course) dignitaries in traditional AuxIndes apparel.

Even President Domino's chief of staff fell into a trap. For background: at a provincial party meeting years ago, Arnold Tsieroro sat humbly behind a table, his bald head cradled in his hands, his voice shaking with devotion to his benevolent superior. Recovering the power of speech, he opened his heart, expounding how President Domino had found him teaching in an obscure primary school and given him his chance. "It was like a rescue at sea in a raging storm," Tsieroro said, massaging the simile between hands that clutched his shaven skull. "I splashed and paddled until out of breath, trying in vain to impart history to a static tide of pupils. Until, like a glorious angel, he came upon me in that remote classroom."

At the time, Arnold's impassioned monologue stirred a hushed audience of elders, eager to have this fresh perspective on their head of state; it helped them adore Domino as a hero of simple, honest, marooned men. It happened, however, that one of those early listeners had captured the aide's rapture on video from the back of the room. Years later, a television host, planted there by Masson's campaign, asked the same question. Tsieroro responded, "It was like a rescue at sea . . ." reproducing the anecdote entirely, word for word, head in hands, half-triumphant, half-mournful, as if it were occurring to him in a sudden inspiration.

The video of the earlier monologue, shown on Masson's TV station along with the new simulation, exposed the chief of staff's improvisation as a performance. The Fisherman's campaign distributed both videos to various media outlets, suggesting times when they could play the tapes in a "wave."

Another spoof hit the regime in a hitherto sensitive spot—relations with the world's largest polity. It featured a Chinese energy company (with an artificial Anglo-Saxon name) that had obtained broad authorization to prospect along the sparsely populated eastern ridge. An obscure social medium reported the prospector's undisclosed discovery there—not of petroleum or natural gas, but of precious stones. Van Zan exploited this bonanza in a cartoon sequence portraying an investigation by the deceased inhabitants of local tombs. The enlightened dead mobilize patriotic young people to apply graffiti to the tomb walls warning the village against foreigners who steal their diamonds and bribe corrupt officials to escape. When the final cartoon shows the miscreants in prison garb and handcuffs, her audience can draw its own conclusions.

"Roger will have to make it up with Beijing for this once he's president," said Guyane to the triumphant artist.

"Then one or the other will need to acquire a sense of humor," replied Van Zan.

Putting such embarrassing accounts to political use for Masson's campaign proved relatively simple for his pen and her brush. Both flourished without byline although neither American could deny that they were "assisting the Fisherman's future." Cynthia invoked an assortment of genuine West African masks to sign her public releases instead of her customary logo, the stylized movie projector. Denis adapted names from Francophone journalism as pseudonyms for his own reportage.

Social media and the popular press consumed such messages with gusto, putting President Bienportant on the defensive against his inexperienced but ostensibly clean antagonist. Commentators portrayed Roger as the iconic honest businessman wryly exposing unscrupulous games by a malicious, self-serving, and incorrigibly incompetent regime.

"You never collected a penny of taxes from these culprits of yours," charged Masson in one of the campaign debates, "just siphoned off your chunk and left the thieves to fly away with their booty. Nothing for the people who own the wealth of the nation, according to their own Constitution. When I'm president, I'll tax those intruders when their acquisitions are legal, and jail them when they aren't."

"Maybe you should start with your own profits," was Domino's retort, inadvertently emphasizing the distinction between corruption and the comparatively honest marketplace.

In normal times, educated urban voters on the island are inclined to support opposition candidates while "provincials," with the most to lose, obediently follow the rascals in power. To help expose this paradox, Cynthia's China gambit focused credit onto the rurals, dead and quick. To offer compensation for urbanites, she produced comic videos, often on oceanic themes, with subtitles in English. Dolphins in revolt against killer sharks wearing "dominos;" the crippled sailboat *Dominant* threatened by fire from one shore, tidal wave from the other while its captain dozes; pirates burying treasure in the sands around "national" headquarters; animated swordfish wearing horn-rimmed eyeglasses who dig up the swag and donate it to feed the hungry.

"Shouldn't tell you this," admitted Karamau in one of his largely gestural discourses with Guyane, "but you 'ave caught the president in an uncomfortable corner; National Party too. Your girl's fishy stories, quite droll, make him look bad." He chuckled. "Election still not sewed up. Keep businessman's hands off public treasury; people don't trust him."

"Meaning they only trust generals, or bishops, or maybe policemen?"

"It's a habit, a tradition. Your man needs some disaster. Maybe contrive it; ask your beautiful environment lady. Otherwise you can't win—not against formidable machine."

"Which you helped Bienportant build over the last twenty years," added Denis. "But we'll find the crowning piece."

"The 'smoking gun,' your popular phrase? Where look for that, if I might ask?"

Guyane understood the signal. "Various places may turn it up," he replied, "maybe famine in the South, maybe the East Ridge, but not along the West Coast, if you're probing for that."

"Ah, yes, impoverished territory, charming burial sites, folkloric festivals, never a scandal. Unless it's also in diamonds."

"None found there, unfortunately. How about crooked disc-jockeying? Kumar territory."

"No. We appreciate your lady's good sense last election, not picking on low-status family; my people from wretched hinterland. Might have backfired on her to go after us."

That was about the longest commentary Guyane could recall Karamau using in recent conversations, so he took it as a veiled warning; he changed the subject. He would have preferred to discuss what he had been mentally replaying—the death of Masson's friend Spider on Babel Hill, and who gave the order to shoot. But this wasn't the moment; nor could he show the minister that he was interested in the shadowy prophet "Samuel." Instead, he asked for assurances that the permits sought by the Fisherman for peaceful rallies would be honored by police and judges without recourse to false pretexts. Karamau's assent—a mere nod—and his avoidance of any threat to expel the foreigners, signaled to Denis that the minister was weighing the possibility that Masson would win.

For his positive platform, the "incorruptible Fisherman" had only to divulge as much as he needed without legal jeopardy. He declared his intention to flatten the Domino's structure, replacing it with transparent government in the name of the Republic. His priorities would focus national resources on education, housing, and public health, conveying benefits to everybody, poor and . . . less poor. True to his vocation, Masson's aim was not to uproot the system entirely, or to imagine a new start for a still subordinate economy. He could not deny that AuxIndes lived in the sequel to colonization, a society of inherited classes and castes. But he argued that it must define itself as a nation among nations, in "a compromise with history," and a fulfillment of his late friend Spider's dream of autonomy in service.

At best, Masson's speeches avoided the usual patterns of cant—empty appeals to security and stability, unabated commitment to the hopes and aspirations of the populace, heartfelt pledges of service for social welfare. When accused of failing the test of patriotism, he would contrast the national benefits of a billion euro deposit of food against the extravagant waste of resources in palatial showcases for the island establishment.

The four other candidates—decent fellows all—were in the contest without hope of victory. Their object was to secure personal advantage toward a cabinet portfolio or other appointment, and/or to call public attention to their own local or professional constituencies. Expecting both Bienportant and Masson to fall short of the fifty-percent majority, they were ready to sell their respective voter fractions to the higher bidder in a second-round faceoff.

Frequently in their candidate debates, Domino had to extricate himself from public relations quandaries as all five opponents attacked from one angle or another. The Fisherman seemed to know exactly how much wealth each poached animal, gold or sapphire nugget, rosewood or mahogany log had brought the president in cash, trafficked by transnational smuggler organizations. The number was usually a guess, but Domino himself had never counted the pennies; the other candidates nodded as if they too had confirmed the improvised statistics.

Seeing so much rhetorical weight stacked against Bienportant, the technically independent media gradually abandoned their habitual

"Both-Sidesism." One outlet after another, they expounded on the antagonists' case, running risks of retaliation from Domino's vindictive party machinery—itself a sign of culpability.

Slight, blue-suited, with his lid of black hair above keen features and sharp eyes (with or without the hornrims), the Fisherman provided contrast to the incumbent's military, if no longer regal, bearing. He accused Bienportant of pandering to portly foreign cronies—although never by name; these "big bellies" were willing to accept Domino as a friend for their shell companies and properties, for laundering of reputations, and hiding of mistresses. Masson admitted he was having the time of his life.

What comes next, Masson asked—the bewitching stigma of terrorism or the perils of a changing climate? "Your gerontocracy is under the illusion that being an island assures the population that it's protected," he charged. "Face reality. Our shores want buttressing against the angry sea and our forests cringe before the torches of the peasantry in need of fresh turf for crops. You are unable to see how vulnerable we are to penetration, both physical and electronic. Some invaders reside here, some shoot from afar, most of them cross our territory between continents, but always at our expense."

"Our military are on the alert," answered the president. "They have training in identifying terrorists, even when the intruders are *your* friends."

"Your army calls everything terrorism when it's usually just somebody from somewhere else, or at worst primitive crime. What we need against the ominous climate is not an air force but a protected source of energy and sturdy housing. What we need against criminals is not a tank brigade, but a functional justice system. Give Minister

Karamau the tools you lavish on the army and demand decisive leadership from him and from the judges." (The gesture toward Philosophe was intentional.)

"What? Haven't we heard you complaining hysterically about police brutality?"

"Not me," said Fisherman with a grin. "I did not run for mayor. Still, in that case, we had a chance for a municipal government that reflected our values as a people, a culture. Now we have that chance for an entire nation."

"Your chance," retorted the Domino, "is to convert the entire nation into a mass of customers for your profits."

"Alas for my sake, that's not likely!" cried Masson, "but if it were, at least the nation would be exercising a choice—to buy or not to buy—not simply surrendering to official embezzlement. The people can reject victimization in this election."

"Yes, because this election will vindicate the benefits bestowed by my administration."

"Benefits? This is the first administration in national history," Masson charged, "where half the civil servants wished the other half weren't there. And it's reciprocal: the other half cancels what the first half does. The one is on the take and thrives while the other, in envy, can't get at it. Most of them never come to work anyway. Truth is that neither faction is paid enough to stay honest, let alone cooperate with one another. But maybe their polarized stalemate is the best we simple citizens can ask of you."

"You have invented all this in your sleazy business dealings," countered the president, stentorian in his rugged, bulky manliness. The Domino had turned gray, but his official bearing still conveyed masculinity. And he could assail crooked capitalism in general without offending the island's grand families whose respectability matched their wealth.

"What I've learned in business," answered the Fisherman, "is that you have to pay your people enough if you want them to produce. Otherwise those who can will steal from you, and the rest will just refuse to work. It's exactly that in your collapsing machinery."

"That's nonsense," replied the Domino. "You can't prove any of it."

"I can, but I won't have to," answered Masson. "I'll just promise a decent wage for honest work, with deference to their union (you might recall that they have one), and they will help vote you out."

"Then just see what a financial pickle you'll have put yourself into," tossed the incumbent, with a forced chuckle.

"If so, my pickle will have come too late for you to enjoy. Or for your few stragglers who will remain only to be able to steal from the rest of us."

"So, if they are loyal to me, they certainly won't vote for you."

"True, but I can run this apparatus with half of your gang against me. The other half is with the people, and that gives me a real majority."

At times, the incumbent accused AuThon of endangering coastal areas by building where ocean incursions and intense storms threaten livelihoods. President Domino had indeed discovered the phenomenon of climate change along with the seafood farm project; for him the two were synonymous.

As briefed by staff, Masson defended his farming and other projects, despite the financial losses he was incurring while they remained suspended for the election. When operating, he claimed, his enterprises were economically embedded in their natural environments, plunged into self-cleaning and nutritious waters, planned through consultation with residential communities eager for the employment and technology they bring. He repeated Anya Wazimbwe's lessons about care for the living shoreline, use of resilient construction materials, emergency and health services for staff and families, and adequate communication.

Without his usual pause, Fisherman sardonically offered his opponent a share of the collateral crop of kelp that the "ex-president" might put in his salads—"unless we need the seaweed to clean the waters after you've finished, or to provide fish feed for the farm."

General Bienportant changed the subject. Claiming credit for doubling the number of island youth, he predicted imminence of economic growth by natural pressures from a rising energetic population. The populace need only wait. Masson responded that growth was insufficient, that development did not depend on rising birth rates. "Rather, after neglect of education, health, and housing, even bright kids will be unable to get beyond semi-literate foraging at the bottom of an inert economy. You pretend that development can come naturally, because you are unwilling to invest in progressive commitments."

Responding as deftly as he could, the embattled Domino attacked Masson's business success, built on the sweat and pitiful savings of working and farming people. "You call for honest governance, without honoring that virtue. If you are not officially corrupt, at least you are commercially untrustworthy," he cried, "and now you are temporarily abusing your business, your money, to grab power."

"While you abuse power permanently to protect *your* money," the Fisherman retorted. "You have become so rich that you need only hope you last long enough to find some medical excuse to leave the country—and enjoy your illegal acquisitions in a comfortable climate. I'll help you do just that, if the tiger lets you off its back."

With that, the campaign prospered. The traces of incompetence and malfeasance were abundant enough for Cynthia to portray as a hierarchy of interlocking fiefdoms, each one linked to a presidential appointment and budget, all fed from the troughs of administrative largesse. The Fisherman's lectures on sleaze reached myriad ears. "Corruption," he would say, "is a mode of resource allocation in an unequal society, but it's another unjust mode of resource allocation, for the benefit of a few privileged takers. His government refuses to pay civil servants adequately, so that those who enjoy some form of leverage—policemen, tax collectors, permit agents, hospital officials—take what they can gouge from the vulnerable public, wherever they can lay hands on others' resources."

Here, as throughout the campaign, Van Zan could taste the savory combination of vinegar and oil. "Just hope it's not the wrong source for oil," she muttered to herself.

With support from Masson's dispersed business contacts, the campaign worked effectively in both towns and provinces, thus far without benefit of an organized political party. "No machine needed," Fisherman and his surrogates boasted. "Let the good news flow." Media attention sufficed. Merchants, labor unions, and teachers helped recruit advocates and poll-watchers in the election districts. Resident diplomatic missions kept an uneasy silence on the contest, in spite of appeals from cabinet ministries and government press for endorsements of the incumbency. The capital's grapevines interpreted ambassadorial reticence as a sign of international disdain for the notoriously acquisitive establishment.

Benjamin, Anya, Olivier, Solange, familiar with the industrial universe, took overt responsibility for the conflict, keeping the expatriates behind screens of their own design. Hitherto impassive youth devoured Van Zan's animated satires of a stolen birthright, signed with her "masks"; they flocked to Masson.

Some of their urban cousins whose misogyny had tormented Giselle Masson and her sisters two years before this, forgave their own errors, and joined the new opposition. From the challenger, they heard promises of honest budgeting for schools, technical training, scholarships, and health care; many now believed Masson capable of bringing these changes into reality. "Because he's male," said Anya Wazimbwe, quietly.

Not unexpectedly, there was resistance to the message. The National Party used its formidable organization, discipline, and resources to keep civil servants and law-and-order citizens in line. Adherents of the status quo feared both capitalist aggrandizement and political instability under the neophyte Fisherman. West coast students confronted Masson at a campus rally; they objected to his coastal development projects: "Must you industrialize this area? tear up and pollute the beautiful earth with no concern for sustainability?"

"I've visited southwestern Louisiana," replied Masson, "and seen what polluters and cynical exploiters do without effective government to control them. Here, the population grows and makes demands on the economy. The current masters of that economy respond not to you, but to their own interests without regard for you. Our national product goes to the powerful, not to the natural world or to those who share it. We take a different approach; we swim with the fish of the sea, breathe among the creatures of this island. We can listen to you, answer your needs, together with theirs."

Other students on Babel Hill above Indesville, knowing that he had once led a protest movement on that very campus, adhered to Masson's argument. Some even affirmed that they had witnessed Governor Charpentier's horse prancing with virtual delight under the legendary Spider on its back.

As the first-round election neared, opposition campaigns received a fortuitous boost—the break evoked whimsically by Philosophe in his dialogue with Guyane. It came through a widely publicized shipwreck off the island's eastern shore. The injured vessel had been chartered from a Bienportant sponsor by an affiliated export broker. The cargo included a wealth of legally protected timber as well as animal species, all meretriciously licensed for export without accurate inventory or other mandatory detail. Without risking specificity, even the pro-regime press had to acknowledge some irregularity in the incident, a deviant routing of permits and transportation, and some apparent fingerprints of authorizing officials. Cynthia's prompt cartoon reached a record number of respondents in the expanding media world of energized voters. Families in the less plugged-in hinterlands promptly learned of it ("birds digest well-informed earthworms and broadcast important news," explained Bamiara), and time ran out on the regime.

On election day, Van Zan and Guyane split up to avoid conspicuous presence at polling places, while eager to see how the process worked. Ahead of the seasonal rains, the polls proved accessible to virtually all constituencies, urban bus riders as well as rural trekkers on the dusty roadways. Some 18,000 polling sites provided access to the registered population, at an average rate of 500 voters per station. On this political holiday, with musicians to entertain them and cheap food and drink along the way, a majority of eligible citizens flooded polls in their districts.

The electoral process was devised under international scrutiny. On entering, each voter flourished an identification card to the local police officer assigned to maintain order at the poll; each had a stamp imposed on one hand to prevent the "frequent franchise" tacitly recommended by some campaigns.

In this unitary election, voting was simple, without requiring literacy. Holding a colored ballot bearing the photograph and logo of all six candidates, the voter moved behind a dark curtain to mark one box on the paper, then deposited it into a slot that closed immediately after swallowing the ballot. The slot reopened once for each subsequent voter. Polls closed only after all had passed through the process. Then the receptacle was opened, unmarked or multiple-marked ballots put into a rejection pile, and the remaining votes counted by a trio of officials in the presence of a delegate from each campaign. The local electoral count was efficient, without claiming to be high tech: the presiding official chose one ballot at a time, flourished it for others to see, and announced the voter's selection aloud; a second agent added a mark beside that candidate's name on a white board in plain sight; the third officer entered the vote in a digital file. After all ballots had been tallied, the marks were counted and each campaign's representative signed the digital tally. These local packets were then sealed and conveyed to Interior for tabulation.

A labor-intensive process, but it worked, observed Cynthia when she and Denis met late that night to exchange impressions. She had chosen to witness the vote at a station in a notoriously pro-Domino district. Her sketchbook was filled with illustrations of the lineup, a confusion of elderly or bewildered voters, and the accounting process surrounded by avid campaign workers. Denis attended proceedings at a trio of more pluralistic sites where pollworkers spent the day anxiously, albeit without disruption of a remarkably serious ritual. He almost became disappointed over the day's tranquility.

The plurality of candidates in the lists seemed to preclude an absolute majority for any of them. Incumbent Bienportant expected to finish first, or as a close second with, if necessary, a runoff election within two weeks. Domino counted on that second round to apply administrative leverage on a reduced number of co-opted voters. That had worked before, but it took money and other risks. Then, despite the informality of Masson's campaign, without organized party or coalition allies, when the final tallies came in, Fisherman maintained an official plurality "dangerously close" to 50 percent. Yet he was not quite there, according to Karamau's ministry: what about 48.5? Bienportant came in a distinct second.

After announcing the date for a runoff between the president and his leading antagonist, Philosophe excluded himself from further contact with the political scene. He did not respond to Masson's demand for an independent recount of votes, a clear indication to those who sought one, that the original election had delivered a decisive majority for the challenger.

That was when the Fisherman made his second existential decision without consultation: flourishing his eyeglasses on television, he refused to participate in a superfluous second campaign, called for a general strike in the towns, and summoned his partisans into the streets. Bureaucratic Indesville was to model "democracy" as though a Masson were indeed at City Hall. While Mayor Karamau blustered in rappese, his uncle declined to mobilize the police force against legal demonstrations, a hint that Philosophe was indeed hedging his bets.

For its part the army, sworn to shun "politics," remained steadfastly in its barracks. The generals would intervene only if national security were in jeopardy; it wasn't. One by one, ministries and agencies closed doors and released their civil servants to join the protests renouncing a runoff election. At the end of a week, the administration began to reopen, but under surrogate authority—not by ministers or party managers, but by hitherto under-rewarded surrogates.

Some of their former superiors rushed northward to join the beleaguered Domino in his rural refuge. There they were protected by special police units, commanded by none other than Antoine Karamau.

"The juggler king, showing his true colors," commented Wazimbwe, unaware that Philosophe had retained contact with Masson through his confidant and confessor, Father Robinette. Together they agreed on a way to break the stalemate without recourse to violence. To ensure domestic tranquillity, Karamau asked the High Court to preside over a recount of ballots as demanded by the challenger, but this time under scrutiny by denominational leaders and the diplomatic corps. To defend AuxIndes' international reputation (and to avoid responsibility for the consequences), the justices, all Domino appointees, approved the presence of embassy dignitaries and clergy as observers. The Interior Ministry was to supervise the laborious recount of precinct talleys; all sides placed trust in its indispensable minister.

"Philosophe on top," muttered Benjamin Bamiara, "where he's always been. Somebody ought to go up the hill to see if he's started riding Spider's horse."

"Poor beast," said Waimbwe; "the man's awfully stout."

When the recount emerged, it conveyed a clear majority for Masson, even in regions hitherto dominated by the National Party's champion. Diplomatic observers and clergy ignored the incumbent's apologists, demanding further review of the global talley. Faced by this consensus, Karamau arranged for an accommodating embassy to invite outgoing President Bienportant to a medical "vacation," in consideration of his extended age and diligent service. Days before his inauguration, Fisherman instructed Bamiara to issue a pledge of unfettered passage to all who wished to use the Republic's passport for immediate departure. They were entitled to retain AuxIndes citizenship and its privileges while in exile, but without immunity from prosecution for any illegalities committed during their term of service.

Some recalcitrant loyalists organized militias and vowed to restore the Bienportant apparatus, but they had to defend him in his absence. While they gathered behind barricades in their redoubts, Domino and several ministers quietly dismounted from the proverbial tiger without feeling its bite. A hired aircraft lifted the ousted leaders to safe haven.

Philosophe was not among either the rejectionists or the self-expatriates. He had decided that he could survive any circumstance, and thus would offer his services loyally to the new chief of state. "Where does he think he's sitting now," asked Olivier Kolona of nobody in particular, "on his helicopter or the General's iron horse?"

"Horse? tiger? pussycat? what's the difference?" responded Wazimbwe. "He'll ride his way out no matter what's under him." Then the Diva offered her services to Viviane Zaphyra, Masson's designated Minister of Defense. "Fisherman needs an army to clean up the bush resistance, and if he doesn't get regular troops now, it'll have to be with amazons," she exclaimed. "Just the battle Sophie has been wishing for!"

Cynthia Van Zan blinked in astonishment at this war cry from an unexpected voice: was it Anya's bravado or her echo of a call to arms from Vinaigrette?

CHAPTER 7

ACTIVISM AND ITS ANGLES

Driving a company 4x4 along her own trajectories, Cynthia Van Zan crossed AuxIndes alone and determined, in search of intimacy with the sea. Once there, scuba-garbed with camera, she swam, snorkeled, paddled—and sought how to befriend the aquatic spirit. She tried speaking her thoughts to the waters and occasionally heard back. Gradually, her mind began to grasp how natural creatures contrive their vital associations within deep webbings.

Moreover, as water warmed under a perilous calendar, she felt the southward polar defection of migrating species. Not much time remained, she knew, before humans lost contact with them.

Encountering people along her itineraries, Cynthia learned whatever she could derive from exchanges in quotidian Creole. She progressed awkwardly in the national language under Professor Ommaney's guidance. By contrast, nature's discourse proved fluent. At sea and on land, Van Zan perceived intrinsic rhythms of correspondence among species and their empathic habitats. Across the bright edges of her imagination, land creatures became amphibious, the sea grounded into offshore ponds, trees advertised hostelry for wanderers on the wing. Overhead, cliffs beckoned to soaring fowl and nimble goats; foliage thrust out of rocks to offer shelter and food; roots extended under deep distances to quicken life.

Van Zan also lingered at times to observe work by laboratories researching the procreation, migration, nourishment, and collective security of sea creatures. Funded by combinations of overseas donor agencies and scrawny support services, these valiant installations remained perpetually underbudgeted, short of resources. Yet they plodded diligently to clarify the readjusting relations between the island and its volatile oceanic environment. She understood that AuThon's business fortunes lay in their microscopes.

On these visits, teams of national and expatriate specialists tested Van Zan's eager assumptions and corrected her intuited fantasies. But she held firmly to the conviction that life had a purpose beyond survival—namely, to form alliances, adapt, flourish, and grow. She wondered that this amity could prosper without claiming humanoid sympathies.

Technicians at the isolated labs enjoyed Cynthia's energy and curiosity, her ability to learn. Their isolation permitted some to wonder at her supple frame and its powers in land and sea, to regard her movements as if they demonstrated sheer invulnerability. Attractive as she was to men and women, her brown sleek body bore the unapproachability of a goddess. "She doesn't have to say no," commented one woman, "or emit some deterrent odor; just a smile stops both male and female advances in their tracks."

To compensate for what she learned at these stations, Van Zan donated packets of edibles from AuThon. Lab staff responded with cooked meals that supplemented the fruit and bread, rice and beans that enabled Cynthia to survive during her solitary treks. Her health depended in part on simple meals served off the Bunsen burners. "Scientific nourishment," she called it. Although tempted, she had been warned from the start to avoid the ubiquitous roadside fritter stands lest she engender a "tapeworm long as your arm."

To satisfy company expectations, Van Zan dutifully delivered commercially viable designs to the Indesville staff; they included illustrated forms of collaboration or "schooling" and protective changes of color among members of deep-sea species. Her graphic renderings of natural affinities were adapted by the Fisherman's staff into AuThon's production, marketing, and public discourse. Thus the company could benefit from Cynthia's enthusiasms without having to live them.

In their tandem office, Denis Guyane registered Van Zan's exploits and managed her accounts. Against challenges, he defended her notorious privileges by itemizing their advantages for the enterprise, even if questioned "upstairs" by the boss. When she returned to base with photographs and sketches, Cynthia seldom encountered Roger's otherwise uncomfortable inquisitions . . . or his pregnant silences.

Van Zan did face occasional discord from Anya Wazimbwe. Their viewpoints clashed wherever either glimpsed an opening. The Diva barely tolerated the blank check that Cynthia seemed to have acquired from Fisherman. "You seem to have no trouble navigating this island that you find so tedious," remarked Wazimbwe in one of her patriotic moments. How is that?"

"I could answer that better," replied Van Zan, "if I could understand how you can claim to treat exploited species humanely. How do you do it?"

"Do what? Go ask the exploiters. You know I'm a vegan."

"More or less, Anya. You earn your loaf by filling others' craving for consumption of animals."

"Including your own appetite, my artist friend. You surely don't try to deceive those cute underwater wards of yours about making them off-limits to human consumption."

"No. Of course they identify me as an honest member of the predatory class. We're ubiquitous for them. But they realize that my way of exploitation is merely paradoxical, whereas yours is purely hypocritical—selling what you don't consume to others for a profit, like some pseudo-vegetarian cattle-rancher in the lowlands."

Playing with a paper clip caught in a rubber band, Anya said only, "Ho-hum, you've suddenly found the human condition, to dominate and consume, for the sake of the species."

As always, Cynthia descried Wazimbwe's "speciesism"—treating the seas as a reserve for human needs—even when the Diva hurled her Medusan curse at modern pirates and other mutually abominated miscreants. Anya responded by challenging Van Zan to aim her work categorically, starting with a choice of targets: "Would it be plastics congestion? Oil spills? Neo-colonialism? Climate change? Or something else? All are anthropomorphic threats to both the fish and the folks who consume them."

To which Van Zan contended that to survive annihilation, oceanic life deserved help, with or without humans.

"Let's just prevent that we don't expire first," rejoined the Diva.

"There's lessons to be learned for that," Cynthia answered. "Nature, our beloved mother, seems bent on eradicating her human line, leaving more reliable critters, or distant planets, to pick up the pieces. We're not only devouring our vital surroundings, but ourselves as well. What can we do? AuThon to the rescue?"

"And why not?" retorted Wazimbwe. The two women could join here in their apprehensions—and not for the last time.

Van Zan also had an axe to grind with Denis Guyane, whom she accused of having oversold "Africa" to her. What he had recounted back in New York stimulated Cynthia to expect insertion into a continent-wide temple of *griots*—troubadour bards rapping heroic praises—attended by earthlings who danced through ordinary life, and drums that "talked" in decipherable syllables. He offered tales of natural polyrhythmic movement, of vivid gowns and head-wraps, and percussion that resounded through the night where strangers were lodging.

She had cheered when he added, "You can take it as a local folk's welcome, but those drums may also intend warning against malevolent neighbors." Van Zan's mind associated these demonstrations with the more ominous "minstrelsy" of her native New Orleans.

Such imagery had excited her to anticipate romance with Africa, the ancestral birth ground. But this island would not confirm these conceptions. And her lab friends only laughed at such Gothic fantasies.

To her chagrin, Van Zan's forages around AuxIndes turned up little that was so creative or picturesque. She motored through scruffy villages flanked by fragile paddy rice or desiccated corn fields, roamed by twisted bodies clothed in patches. Tempting odors of town life changed gradually into trails of smoke from burning trash, then floral airs of pungent plants like the ylang ylang and patchouli or even bananas, occasionally medicinal ambergris. Rivers conveyed the speech of lateritic soils downstream, and human aspirations with them.

The scene was observed by self-absorbed cattle and animated by children who rushed away from ingeniously fabricated playthings to petition any new arrival. Compensated with sweet handouts, they returned to enliven the dust.

While the smaller children eagerly accepted biscuits and chocolates, they also welcomed pencils, crayons, note-pads, toys and tools, as well as used postage stamps, most of which they traded to older kids for biscuits. So as she increased her mileage, Cynthia expanded her supplies of wafers.

Throughout the "bush," hunger and scarcity prevailed. When rains failed or crops withered, those scourges inhabited all she could see. Able-bodied youth were obliged to migrate; for in cities there was work, even if merely work: anything that kept the body functioning in an urban environment. After leaving city streets behind, only rarely did Cynthia encounter young men or childless women.

Dispersed in larger villages and towns, she absorbed folk music fused with "high-life," watched boys parading in basketball shorts (the virile mask?), and girls in uniforms parading single file on their way to somewhere. When Van Zan tracked these school groups, she usually ended up at a male football or wrestling match in the ineluctable dust.

Finding words to mobilize against mass deprivation, Cynthia listened to rural officials who proved to be well aware of what was needed. They longed for useful resources that failed to reach them, except for some donations sifted through the offices of bishops and priests who exacted canonical homage for the favor. But who could bring the timely rains? Van Zan had nothing new to offer on the ground, except pledges to alert marginal, distant, but sympathetic entrepreneurs. When conditions permitted she urged local authorities to summon a food truck or mobile kitchen from the AuThon extension service that had begun to popularize Roger Masson's name. At sea coasts and river banks, she applauded vigorous but "humane" pursuit of seafood and helped extend AuThon's purchasing network into local markets.

That offered some scattered relief without precipitating celebration.

In isolated places, Van Zan's evenings fell on weary women and their children holding back while elderly men in faded robes outdid each other applying Creole proverbs to common complaints. Cynthia could not understand all they said, but she intuited enough to deplore morbidity in the island's culture. "They glorify 'life' in the world of the dead," she complained to Guyane: "stale male, and no music. It's more enlightening to converse with the ocean itself. I once thought Fisherman was introducing us to a dynamic continent. Instead, we just got dropped on a bone-dry island. It's only what surrounds it that matters."

Without hope, Guyane sought to disabuse Cynthia of the notion that "all Africa" should exhibit the cultural assets of any region. True creativity comes where you seek it. Here, he insisted, it's in poetry, the heritage of myth and reflection. What had intrigued her in his New York tales, he argued, was found mainly on the continent's Atlantic side. There much discourse was essentially tonal, verging on song; people were less used to orate and more to dance.

"Like where my own family originated," rejoined Van Zan. "Lots more interesting." She was satisfied as usual to have had the last word. He left it there, as usual.

❀ ❀ ❀

Work in the Lyrical Mode

As if in response, AuThon's staff was soon to be entertained theatrically, courtesy of an enterprising band of university players improvising in song and dance on an ostensibly mundane subject—the evolution of the job in AuxIndes.

"A masquerade about what? Toil? What's so theatrical about toil?" asks Denis Guyane, as they squeezed out of the taxi; he was inviting more than he imagined for a standard answer.

"My students posed that very question," says Professor Chaucret, as he swings the theater door open for the American guests. "As you would expect, they have an existential interest in employment suited to their assumed talents."

"Once you're done with those talents, Professor," appends Cynthia. "But Denis has intended a more academic question."

"Namely?"

"Namely, how do AuxIndiens assess opportunities to work, for what, and through whom does that contact operate?"

"Precisely what we propose to show you, Ms. Van Zan."

"Cool, Professor. And while you're at it, can you or your students explain why women get so tangled when they knock on the door of a job?"

"Possibly. There's no denying the gender schism. You do have La Vinagrette's answer—bourgeois oppression breeds its own reactionary impulses—that may be a bit too ideological for you. Hence Sophie urged us to explore further, to provide grist for her *Fables* mill."

"But did she request a staged pageant—like what we're about to see?"

"There's no better way to explore the world of work than through a work in progress. This one is indeed theatrical, so we've taken over the City Theater for a few days. Our review joins a number of vignettes that can be performed in specified language, with music, and graphic exposition. They touch on historical change, gender differences, social status."

"Controlled by what? Aah, faculty lecturing?"

"No, by how the students see these conditions. The vignettes flow chronologically through generalities—a bit tedious, but they use slide projections, costume changes—well, hat-off/hat-on switches, you know—a touch of music, and some dialogue. I think my kids did well to craft work locations, openings and closings, rewards and punishment."

"For their own interests, I see," interjected Denis Guyane. "Grades. An admirable motivator for any lesson."

"Yes. Well, once you've seen it, we'd like to have your help in the language (much of it tries to be in English), and in graphic illustration, costumery, music—whatever especially highlights the factors bearing on AuxIndiennes' emergence in the workforce."

"You'll have it, of course," replies Van Zan, "provided our complicity doesn't disturb Mr. Masson or (ahem) Ms. Wazimbwe. We still have to 'work' for them."

"They are invited, of course, and may be already here. It's about curtain time. La Vinaigrette signals that we're set to go."

Cynthia squinted backstage. "A drumroll I hear. Meaning Vinaigrette has arrived?"

"Not only she," tossed Chaucret. "Not only she. Take your seats, please. For here come our Alpha actors. Lights!"

A dozen students, well-rehearsed in English, French, and Creole, enact their panorama, *A Century Quest for Work in AuxIndes* through six *tableaux*, each with its own vocabulary, musical accompaniment, and screened projections. The actors change roles rapidly in full view, as they navigate male and female employment experience.

"Preliminary, hence arbitrary," interjects the Professor to discourage unfavorable skepticism. He distributes printed scenarios with this sequence summary:

I. Colonial period: in French, music from Offenbach's "Orpheus"; projections à la Toulouse-Lautrec, action by pith-helmeted Europeans brandishing control over semi-naked natives. In colonial times, race determines career prospects, education conditions opportunity for males, domestic security absorbs the females. Work functions are transmitted through hereditary roles, rewarded through family status. No need to apply: one is chosen (plucked) or ignored, conveyed to the site or left to scrounge. Garments are rude, of course. Women actors are fully wrapped in cloth except for two who loll lasciviously, bare-legged—the lost ones (a "slight satire," admits Chaucret, "to set foot lightly into the subject").

II. Late Colonial (from post-World War I): in Creole; musical mix of Debussy's *La Mer* and imported 1920s jazz; *Fauve* and Surrealist projections of cattle herding by boys; urban migration by men in overhauls; sisterhood bonds develop among village women in scarves. The dance exemplifies loose nomadic energy for young AuxIndiens. Social needs determine prospects for advancement and adaptation to educational targets. War experience reshapes young men here; employment appends a fluid cosmopolitan sense of social echelon. Select males enjoy postwar opportunity in expanding small-sale industries and international trade. Wartime also allows some women to break away from convention, with better or worse results. This interwar period witnesses a demand surge by young women for university study, internal migration, and rudimentary individualism, but the disappointed majority faces subordinate roles alone. World War II imposes subsistence hardships on the entire population, as the economy sinks into a grappling for subsistence, the outside world becomes more remote, and opportunity shrinks. Postwar AuxIndes enters a fluctuating determinism of opportunity, success, and failure.

III. Independence 1960s: in French, celebratory anthems fill the air against vigorous drumming. Social class becomes conspicuous: urban bureaucracy of men in shirtsleeves; other men circulate in rags. Secretarial and counter service open to women in skirts as male-monopolized hierarchies grant or deny opportunity. The urban/rural split widens; agriculture remains stagnant under internal migrations, requiring heavy doses of consumer imports. Males turn away from pastoral supervision to serve as cheap labor in estates under overseas proprietors of export crops, in tourism, and light industry. Rural and older women remain mired in domestic subsistence while younger, schooled sisters get rudimentary clerical training in towns; shopwork and retail marketing rub against "European" expectations. External currency controls govern price inflation and wages, facilitating or hampering employment. AuxIndes has indeed joined "the West" in aspirations, although not entirely to its benefit.

IV. Autarchic Governance 1970s to 1990s: in Creole; Music: *Giants* theme from Wagner's *Rheingold*; centralization of economic control; pantomimes of gradual exodus by foreign bureaucracy, police enforcement of mores, rampant government corruption. A select few migrate for schooling (female and male); men find jobs overseas and in domestic industry, delivery, and construction; remittance finance expands from employed expatriates. Burdens of agricultural self-sufficiency and public health are imposed on women, with more young females seeking domestic service and other employment at home and abroad. Public programs succumb to apathy, cupidity, and incompetence, precipitating resentment against government. Family overflow aggravates urban unemployment, the informal economy, moral untidiness.

V. Twenty-First Century: in language mix; to make a point, Creole yields to French and English. Music is strongly influenced by West African high-life and jazz, mixing with folk themes. Economic blight forces emigration, both male and female; women in the island's towns become cheap labor for foreign-organized shopwork (textiles, food processing, exportable household utensils, health services), while males compete for specialized training, government jobs. Male control over family weakens.

VI. Entrepreneurial Innovation: in French and English; a random sequence of international musical influences. Class structures become firmly pronounced: job opportunities remain largely dependent on diplomas, manipulated by elites; basic schooling languishes. Family units are fragmented by labor mobility under expansion of entrepreneurial energies in mining, agricultural processing, fisheries. Women claim equality of opportunity, referring to international trends; they often settle for symbolism, imitative fashion, quiescence. Despite rapid urbanization, the rural/agricultural economy remains virtually unchanged from pre-World War II. Higher education takes hold on the privileged postwar population, male and female, engendering breakthroughs in commerce and public works, as well as international exchanges with Europe, African neighbors, and so-called Great Powers.

Ability to migrate, to sacrifice freedom, strengthen male and female employability, urban mobility in factories and sweatshops, and consumer advantages; educated women obtain opportunities for self-employment (especially in textiles and garment manufacturing), while less schooled young women become susceptible to offers of domestic employment overseas, including Arab countries. The "loose" female remains an object of moral suspicion while her comparable male counterpart enjoys the prestige of individualism. Without job skills, males become labor pawns in the postwar economy, often with great risks in health and security, while women obtain flexibility in occupation, consumption, and domesticity.

"There you have it," proclaims Chaucret. "What do you think?"

Guyane and Van Zan find grounds for compliment. Reflection on national history is inevitably productive of . . . something, if only grist for the mills of Vinaigrette. Sophie is beaming at the end, considering how she can turn the sequence of vicissitudes into a sociological lesson. "The student creators will never forget this," muses Denis, "and they should have the chance of playing it to dispersed audiences, schools, and community audiences. That should prove healthy as national self-awareness grows." Van Zan only nods in silent agreement. What strength has the mask if it cannot effect a critical turn of events?

❊ ❊ ❊

Domestic Progress and Reversal

Once AuThon's "brand" takes shape, months elapse paradoxically—in deliberate contingencies and chaotic progress. Sea life continues to frequent the nets while plans for aquatic farming promise to enliven the littoral. Starting in the island's center, the Fisherman's domain is extending into retail grocery and textile markets. Competitors and banks interpose resistance, but are contradicted by multinational agencies and through indomitable domestic leverage from clans like the Wazimbwe.

Letting his moments of silence speak for him, Roger Masson throws energy into the uproar, carrying the organization through breaches and explosions, as well as over quieter ground. He implements Benjamin's feasibility study, sends Cynthia's artwork through the press, and keeps Denis close to treat perplexities. Fisherman depends on his loyal Diva, Anya, to hold the executive team together while more peripheral staff might come and go.

Favored in its timing, Masson's financial model functions successfully for AuThon's audacious initiatives. The company has maximized domestic sales, promoted by Bamiara's team; Denis and Olivier arrange overseas contracts. Both the new farm venture and acquisition of under-capitalized businesses secure international favor thanks to a resourceful executive staff. External powers join Anya in combat against wildcat fleets that intrude on the island's fisheries. They exact concessions—pier extension and longshore facilities—for indulging the insatiable Japanese appetite for whale meat.

In effect, without fully earning it, the company is acquiring a reputation as the "multilaterals' darling." That distinction allows them to locate capital at favorable interest rates, and to find sources of public investment without recourse to foreign commercial debt. In this effort, Guyane is mentored by the formidable *La Douce,* Solange Seriel, who guides him in financial strategy while they both entertain themselves corporeally.

Although conspicuous success is normally condemned as poor form in AuxIndes culture, the national establishment sees no need to object to AuThon's expansion. Wealthy families tolerate bold business ventures provided they respect precedent and preclude new taxes. From his tower of immobility, President Bienportant appreciates the advantages of favorable international opinion. Besides, he is already profiting from real estate deals in the central highlands, so that Masson's commercial empire and a future fish farm in the West pose no threat to him. Significantly, Interior Minister Karamau's approval of a project that favors his own interests enables AuThon to count on key endorsements when it conveys proposals to local officials.

Tended by Bamiara the practical Peasant, facilities for fish farming begin to implant on the coast. Soon the ponds and pools could be excavated, roads and port facilities extended, a work force trained and housed, the refrigeration plant constructed with access to hydropower. Improved paddy fields and pasture surrounding the industrial site will provide for the needs of employees and their families. A new phase in the national pageantry of labor is dawning.

One note rings sourly and from an unaccustomed source. "Just don't let Fisherman think he's going to get the staff to *move* out there," warns the industry's labor union. "Our fisherfolk won't leave; they are staying home, here in the city."

That preference is firmly seconded by the pharmacist Giselle Masson, a credentialed patriot for the nation's capital. Eventually, while plans are maturing on the coast, she reveals her motive for rejecting displacement: Indeville's mayoralty becomes vacant during the year, and Giselle is determined to become the municipality's first woman chief executive. She could scarcely undertake that challenge from a bungalow surrounded by a fish farm.

When his spouse appeals for support, Roger hesitates at first, wary of a premature political campaign that could tarnish the company's reputation. On second thought, he concedes that Giselle could claim the skills and insight needed to enrich their venerable city, and she certainly has a right to her husband's complicity. Moreover, foreseeing business opportunities if he were to have a spouse in charge of the capital, Fisherman becomes confident of Giselle's advantage— even before assessing any putative competition.

Eventually, after sounding out Vinaigrette, Masson learns that the indefatigable Karamau would probably be proposing some own young "cousin or nephew" for the mayoral run. Both the lad and Giselle intend to seek nomination by the ruling National Party. Wary of any conflict with the potent minister, Masson instructs Denis Guyane to negotiate the nephew's gracious removal from his wife's pathway to City Hall.

Denis tries, directly at the source in French and English, but in vain. "Very unfortunate," Philosophe mutters, gesturing more aggressively than his voice suggested. "Hannibal may be only a disc jockey now, but he's ambitious. And he's my brother's son. Loyalty to my family first, you know. Can't your boss dissuade *her?* Has he tried?"

"Very doubtful, both questions," admits Denis. "Giselle is determined to take charge of the city; she's already recruiting a strong campaign team. It's about time for a female mayor, you know. Would young Hannibal conceivably accept some alternative job? Say at our new plant over in your home neighborhood?"

Karamau hoists his arms and snorts. "Far from it! That's what he's escaping—dreary family heritage, hole in the sticks. No place there for the New African sound, he says. And no tolerance for him as a gay man. I promised his father. The boy's worked five years in this city. He entertains multitudes on Domino's radio station. This is what Hannibal has chosen. He knows his mind."

"Yes, and I know Giselle's. We certainly don't want a fight with you and your people here or down on the coast. Does your Hannibal have assurances of support from the Nationals?"

"Neither has your Giselle." Karamau pauses for an instant, then pursues. "Tell me, Guyane, why in hell you think the party would ever back a woman for so prominent an office?"

Suppressing his impulse to denounce this query from a source renowned for sexism, Guyane lets the issue lie. He also knows better than to impugn young Hannibal's sexuality. At least, he hopes that one or the other side would concede before the Masson family has to engage in partisan battle with Karamau's, just as the new fish farm is nearing its genesis. When an amicable resolution fails, Bamiara takes the pulse of the Nationals and reports to Masson that the party leadership, all males, shares Philosophe's prejudice.

At AuThon, company staff led by Anya Wazimbwe vow their loyalty to Giselle, accepting the risk of a campaign against the ruling party nominee. Eager for battle, Cynthia Van Zan offers her services promptly. Time for a new phase in the sequence of AuxIndes labor relations.

As the municipal confrontation opens, Denis Guyane's role stresses peacekeeping on behalf of the AuThon brand, its stakes in the fish farm, and the company's extended prospects. At best, he manages only to temporarily hold a wobbly lid on a simmering pot. The party executive, as expected, adheres to Philosophe's preference, nominating Hannibal Karamau for mayor. Maintaining a discreet, self-congratulatory silence over his homo-eroticism, they expect the town to tolerate a chief executive who is gay—but a *woman* mayor . . . ?

In disgust, Giselle refuses to accept smoke-filled misogyny. "I'll be damned before I allow that nepotistic puppet to waltz into city hall by default," she tells her partisans. "I will beat him on the merits, party complicity be damned, and without stooping to discuss his sexuality." She declares her candidacy as an independent and takes her rebellion into the streets, denouncing reflexive politics that endow a single party with monopoly over access to high office (an advantage she would have accepted if it had been offered her). Her cause resounds like insurrection against the peacefully established order.

Thus did this cherubic, bespectacled woman earn the improbable nickname of *Siren*.

By now, Masson has no alternative. He donates his prestige and fortune to Giselle's campaign, underwriting a succession of appearances by his spouse and her surrogates and sacrificing a regrettable quantity of cattle to her rallies in Indesville's suburbs. Thanks to Anya Wazimbwe and with backdoor advice from la Vinaigrette, these events are skillfully organized, coherent, and peaceful. They are in vain, as it turns out, for, although Giselle works vigorously, and with committed support, she is unable to deflect suspicions against the Siren's song. Her arguments fail to overcome popular prejudice for the young entertainer—and against a woman's presumption, as Indeville's citizens judge the matter.

While it plays out, the contest becomes increasingly raucous. Bodyguards have to accompany Giselle or her surrogates into scenes fraught with pinching fingers and even ruder salutes. Tours of slums are disturbed by unexplained power outages and collapsing platforms; such accidents occur even in the more affluent suburbs. Anya Wazimbwe and Thérèse Zaphyra—previously toughened by repression against them while "radical" students—are now stigmatized as "uppity women," and vilified in a recrudescence of adolescent terrorism.

The conflict inevitably veers into reverse class antagonism. Giselle's decorous followers would file quietly past half-built houses with ladders propped against the walls. When they near, however, those perches spawn youth in mockery of the candidate's cultivated accents. Accurate French and polite manners become ladylike handicaps in a new generation of populist impropriety.

Although tempted, the Siren declines to reply in kind to such provocations. Not only is homophobia off limits; Giselle's campaign deliberately recruits gay men and women, and her lieutenant Thérèse (*La Brise*) is unabashedly bisexual. The candidate firmly rejects recourse to another surefire card by forbidding mention of Hannibal's low-caste origins in the urban districts most susceptible to snob appeals. "Win clean or lose," becomes the accepted mantra of a forlorn cause.

Elsewhere, Giselle's declarations are systematically drowned out by sound trucks broadcasting Hannibal's voice, his hip-hop message of "*Fraydome! Leebertay!*" conveyed through pulse, not logic. Invariably, when Masson or her surrogates obtain permits for a public rally (never a sure bet from Karamau protocol), they move into a space already suffused by noise from platoons of mobile phones tuned in unison to the same wavelength, the same pounding sound. Overwhelming the opponent's arguments with cacophony, cellphone squads of subsidized youth sings, shouts, and drums their way through the city.

Cynthia Van Zan despairs of this setback against her faith in autonomous youth. To her, a school of mackerel seems far more enlightened. Her cartoons caricature Hannibal as *the Grim Rapper* impersonating the contemporary *griot*.

Formal appeals to police meet with cynical shrugs, little action. Philosophe's agents readily classify truck-borne loudspeakers as a form of free speech, streaming the latest "entertainment" for city crowds. It is all covered by the Hannibal campaign's permits, protected by the constitution according to Uncle Philosophe.

In their only debate, Giselle appeals to her opponent. "Can't you see yourself trapped in this refusal circus that you are inflicting on the public?" Giselle cries. "How can you pretend to transform a city, guarantee its progress, if you bury it in this shameful noise?"

Hannibal has his uncle's height without his bulk, a ruff of black hair crowning a face seamed in smiles—to contrast with Antoine's impassivity. "What you call noise," he replies, "is the authentic sound of life in this town. It's our heritage and our future. Young people will assure its fruition. We'll build our dream out of your ruins. You can't get it to stop." Champion of his own callow ideology, this Karamau is nonetheless a chip off an old block.

He claims as well to be up to date. "Nowadays only social media commands attention," he declares during the (televised) debate. "Your reliance on mainstream palaver is old hat and ludicrous," boasts the Rapper. "People don't listen to dumb speeches. Nobody reads the printed press; it has lost both its advertising and its influence. Only phantoms take your newspapers; ancestors scan them in their tombs, to keep up with obituaries. You can't win elections with the dead. Live readers and listeners demand entertainment, not truth."

"You can't mean that," objects Giselle. "The truth should be unassailable. We must provide what our constituency seeks—reliable information."

"That's only your word," raps Hannibal. "Information is just as outmoded as truth."

Challenged to distinguish between Karamau's youth binge and their own student movement of the nineties, Wazimbwe and Roger Masson deplore the Rapper's delivery of illusions for a new generation eager to be lied to. Anya half expects Hannibal to intone, "Get out of our way!" If he did, she vows to sue him for plagiarism.

When the polls had closed, and after Hannibal is pronounced mayor, the losing team regroups for its postmortem (under a banner appealing to God to save the city). Working out her report for the next *Fables* issue, Sophie Makoa assures Giselle that she hadn't lost the election, "only the rhythm."

"The decibels, you mean," responds the candidate. "This is democracy?"

"You had the arguments and the swing," assents Vinaigrette. "Sanitation, schools, health services, open contracts freely bid. But Hannibal had the voice and the pace. He caught the beats of some primitive tribal center inside a decadent society. Noise even captured the churches—the fringe ones, especially Ishmael's."

She invariably changes subject before having to answer the usual question about Ishmael. "Did you notice by the way that some of those juvenile hecklers out there were off-duty cops? They're from Karamau's incubator, dressed like teenagers in carefully torn jeans."

Cynthia Van Zan caught the glance Vinaigrette shot at her—as if to say, "So much for *your* antiestablishment youth crusade.“

To shake off the stigma of her "Siren" mask, Giselle has begun regular attendance at Indesville's Anglican church, with its fervent Indigenous pastor. When asked about her apparent conversion, she recalls the social platform that she'd thought to carry into the mayoralty—municipal sanitation, safe housing, inspired education, protection against climatic disaster. "Not here to save my soul, or anybody else's for that matter," she explains; "the personal is for Pastor Jatoma to secure; my burden remains with the collective."

Shortly after the campaign, Cynthia is surprised to encounter the defiant defeated candidate at, of all places, a funeral service for one of the city's renowned pagans; the deceased was a follower of Ishmael who carries to his grave the heretical vocabulary of invective, Ishmael's stock in trade. Asked how she could reconcile her newfound piety with this violation of the genteel Church's embargo, Giselle admits obtaining Pastor Jatoma's consent for her to attend the funeral precisely in order to serve Cynthia's own need for translation of the Creole proceedings. "The Reverend knows you are a distinguished foreigner, of some importance to our business, and that you were a friend of the deceased so he released me to attend this travesty—my first such pleasure in a long time."

"Although I appreciate your and his concern," responds Van Zan dryly, "I think I've learned enough Creole to understand the proceedings at this funeral without needing an interpreter, even so distinguished a one as you."

"Shush there," whispers Giselle. "Don't blow my cover. Your presumed ignorance of the language has given me my first chance in years at such fun. Just let me seem to be translating for you."

As they watch the elaborate burial proceedings, Cynthia confirms her intuition of the cultural life that she sensed AuxIndiens yearned to have but could seldom risk . . . until the end nears.

The Angora Angle

Through his office windows in the rear of the Fishery, Roger Masson admires an acre of untamed secondary forest. He has exhorted these woods to grow wild as if to erase a memory of the axes and plows that had once leveled the primeval bush. On the exterior, the windows are obstructed by dense web patterns; there, to reenforce the wilderness image, Fisherman seems to be encouraging gigantic spiders to conduct their lethal business silently across each pane.

To protect the grotesque decor, Masson prohibits all attempts at interference from cleaning squads or protectors of insects caught in the spiders' lair.

This raw exhibition delights Cynthia Van Zan, whose tattooed shoulder twitches in affinity. Here truly she prceives Indesville's world of work. Inevitably, however, the spectacle evokes gasps from visitors unable to justify the Fisherman's reasons for indulging such carnage. Even the boss usually sits with his back to the brutality outside his windows. Did he mean the webbing to simulate an open-air version of *oceanic* entrapment? Was it there as homage to an outraged young martyr with an arachnid nickname? Or did the choice of scenery expose some latent menace in Masson's temper?

Denis Guyane declines to tolerate the webs as a spectator sport. He always enters the chief's office obliquely, angling toward a neutral side wall. This time, he draws a chair laterally toward one side of the desk, waiting for the boss to open a routine conversation. He is prepared for Fisherman's invitation: "Tell me straight, Denis," Masson asks, "how is our fish park doing?"

There isn't that much to tell. Guyane has returned from a bumpy tour of the coastal parcel that the company seeks to purchase. Accompanied by Bernard Nairay (*Papillon*), his task was to assess local receptivity to land acquisition and if necessary to design an opinion campaign in favor of the fish farm. That morning, when Masson's summons reached his phone, he had been working confidently on his report. The West coast communal terrain seemed bleak enough to crave development. Local elders posed no insuperable impediments to AuThon's project—not even to an artificial pond, provided that family tombs remained undisturbed.

No problem there. The region's venerated dead are lodged in a scattering of some two dozen rectangular structures, built up from the ground along the slopes of an otherwise barren hill. Putatively

Christian, the tombs differ from those of the central highlands; they sport a profusion of realistic wood sculptures planted across the top of each mound. Most of the imagery is of natural or common subjects—cattle, motorcycles, athletes, firearms, birds in flight, lovers in tandem. No fish, though, not yet; Cynthia Van Zan works elsewhere.

Denis understands how these robust tomb figures correspond to qualities that the families attribute to their interred forebears. The artists who rendered them keep in touch with clan histories and the community, as with one another. The unique grave sites attract interest in the area as a destination for cultural tours, embellished with glorifying narratives and photographic appeal. Working these assets permits some young men and women to reside at home, rather than migrate away to urban employment. Hence, tourist curiosity over the dead could take credit for enhancing the fecundity of local families.

Below cemetery hill is open pasture, not cropland; it abuts a delta with a diversity of salt marsh and river life—fresh-water fish, crustaceans, birds, crocodiles, insects, marsh grasses, trees, and shrubs. Nairay and Guyane agreed that most marketable species would survive in those conditions, while conceding to Anya Wazimbwe's objection against the idea of stocking tilapia—a trash fish in her opinion, useful exclusively to feed on insects in irrigated rice fields.

"Local agents urged us only to assure space and sustenance for local cattle," answers Guyane. That would be elaborated in what he reported to the Fisherman.

"Cattle, eh?" mutters Masson after a thoughtful pause, ignoring the tilapia dispute; "no goats?"

"None that I could see," says Denis, "but there was some talk, if that's what you're asking about."

Masson nods, and begins ominously cleaning his spectacles.

The local chatter had been casually offered. It depicted the visit a few weeks earlier by a half dozen men calling themselves farmers (although local elders mocked them as stiffly garbed in new jeans). Asking questions about land ownership and prospects for pasture, those visitors did not identify themselves explicitly, but referred to a recommendation from Minister Karamau, the region's favorite son. The men left some soft mohair weaves as gifts to the village ("We saw them in the town hall; they were startling—genuine rugs—not, you know, mere carpeting."). Having heard nothing from the visitors subsequently, the elders concluded that the project, whatever it was, would not materialize. They kept the rugs.

"Hence the cordial welcome we received. In fact, when they heard that Nairay was half-Indian and I was Haitian-American, they proclaimed 'this country had gone global!'"

"Hm," muses Masson, flashing the novel he has been reading, "it's oddly Balzacien to get no tip-off from Philosophe about that mohair delegation. Could be he still resents what Giselle said about his nephew." He then grows silent, and the interview has ended.

Guyane expects that cross-purposes with cronies of Philosophe would require a Fisherman conversation with his ministerial interlocutor. So, with Papillon and Ahmed, he completes a propitious argument to justify the fish farm in the region. Then he waits for further initiatives from Masson.

Word comes within the week, and rather startlingly. Arriving that morning, Denis switches on his office desk lamp (a gift from Masson, representing a wrestler grappling with an orca) and finds an odd message on one of the Fisherman's own business cards: "How would you ok to work after all in a CAMPAIGN OF PRESIDENT?" An odd overture, first because Masson had written anything at all, and that he offered so portentous an invitation in English without using the electronic apps that translate such messages into impersonal slush.

"Can I see him?" Guyane asks Masson's secretary. "He's put some sort of question to me."

"Oh, yes," Valona replies, "He told me to cancel the usual morning rounds and to send you right in, chop-chop."

Chuckling at Valona's attempt at slang, Denis taps on the Fisherman's door and angles once more into the paneled office, eyes deflected from the webbed banquets hanging outside the windows. He waits until the boss looks up from the map on his desktop, finishes his sweet-bun, and adjusts his spectacles. Finally, Guyane ventures to open the conversation.

"You talked to Minister Karamau?"

"Oh, yes. Last night in fact."

"And he told you he's going to run for president?"

"Not exactly. Do YOU know that he is?"

This time it's Denis who affects the conversational pause.

"No, certainly not," he replies in time. "But the note you sent me . . . Anyhow," after Masson extends the silence, "I can't see myself doing him any good."

"I'm glad to hear that, Denis. And I agree with you. Whether Antoine decides to try for advancement is his business, but that angora ranch and rug factory could get in *our* way."

"Right," says Guyane. "Glad you got to him about it. Perhaps we can talk him, or them, out of it. But this presidential campaign. If it's not Philosophe, then I suppose it's suddenly become . . ."

"My aspiration, indeed," breaks in Masson uncharacteristically. "I've been contemplating it for some time."

"Although you've told me that you were eager not to go for that job."

"So long as I could do what I chose while somebody else had the political headaches, yes. Now . . ."

Then a characteristic Fisherman pause. Guyane supplies the sequel. "Now, you foresee an obstacle to the fish farm, and because Philosophe seems to be behind that, you think you need to be chief of state to get his goats out of the way?"

Another long pause follows, giving Denis a chance to line up his objections.

"Putting it crudely like that," answers Masson with a slight smile, "I suppose that is what turned my mind. You don't seem enraptured by the idea. Why would you avoid a chance to help design a presidential run? Lots of your American colleagues must be eager to get that close to the White House. Or is our country too small to tempt you?"

Guyane suppresses a derisive snort. "No, your country deserves much more than my humble services. But it also deserves a chief of state who primarily seeks the national advantage, not his own commercial benefit."

"No doubt it does," argues the Fisherman, "And that's what it will obtain. But the two advantages must be integrated. Otherwise the valiant chief of state will have little motivation to undertake the options he must confront."

"I certainly hope that's not true," blurts Denis, "And I trust that the goat ranch was only one factor, and not the decisive one."

"Tell me, Denis," says Masson, rising from his chair and turning to look out a web-encrusted window, "you've read biographies. What successful presidents do YOU know who did not join the national interest with their own advantage? Which ones have no ego, no ambition, no motives that serve their reputation, their legacy?"

"None, if you insist. Yet I hope that the most successful have been scrupulous enough to avoid conflicts of interest."

"Conflicts, certainly. We want none of those. It's compatibility of interests that I'm after. And you're the man to help me define how to join those interests—to satisfy the world that they are indeed correlated."

Denis swallows hard, and asks for "time to think." But he already knows where they were headed.

In the aftermath of the municipal election, Giselle Masson and her partisans have been gathering periodically to discuss recovery from her defeat. This time, she prepares her friends to hear a crucial answer—the Revenge of the Masson Clan. When Fisherman joins them, sliding a chair next to his wife's, he seeks their consent to his own candidacy—for president in the election of 2010, two years hence. Following his spouse's example, Roger will run as an independent, challenging the perpetual ruling party whose incumbent, General Bienportant, would certainly seek another five-year term, his fourth. Masson humbly invites the Siren's team to offer him their experience and judgment before opening the stops to a vigorous national campaign.

Surprised at the modesty, if not the substance of this initiative, Guyane wonders how the decision is to affect the fate of their various projects. Inevitably, Fisherman would be accused of a quest for power to advance his own business interests. This charge would carry him far from the decolonization motif of student rebellion on Babel Mountain, or the illusory quest for the white whale. By implication, how would others, especially the quintessential Philosophe—anticipating his own fourth round as minister—react to Masson's political adventure?

Denis hopes the minister would greet an opportunity to break free of the cloying Domino, that he could see Masson's candidacy as an opportunity—rather than as a threat by insurrectionaries with ambitions in his own fiefdom. How attractive could Karamau consider a mohair rug mill, compared to the aquacultural complex? Or was there another reason for excluding AuThon from that seacoast?

Eventually, AuxIndes would become as embattled above ground as the shark-infested dominion imagined by romantics beyond its shores. If American expats could appreciate that correspondence, how much deeper would these conflicts run for the islanders? Eventually, Guyane expects Cynthia Van Zan to angle out the answers, and that he and Fisherman will buy them hook, line, and undertow. Eventually.

CHAPTER 8
CAMPAIGN: NETWORK & LABYRINTH
PART 2

From reading Renaissance history, Roger Masson imagined himself a modern Henry the Navigator commanding caravels into ports eager for sustenance from afar. Consequently, on staff advice, candidate Masson readily likened his presidential quest to "a peaceable fleet sailing toward election in 2010."

While critical of Denis Guyane and other teammates for encouraging grandiose maritime comparisons, Cynthia Van Zan used it in a series of tongue-in-cheek cartoons; the caravels dock gently, and populations dine humanely on their cargos. When prompted, Anya Wazimbwe tolerated Fisherman's princely fantasy "so long as the return voyage is not intended to carry slaves somewhere." Her advice to Masson: "Suppose you've disembarked, Roger, barefoot as always, but you're talking to real earth-bound people." That seems to have settled the waters for a time.

On drier ground, political lanes auspiciously channeled Fisherman's ambition; "the fleet" soon became a key metaphor for reformation of the island. Something new was happening. No previous government had been overturned by election; predecessors either expired in exhaustion or were dumped by an impatient military. But this time, national stagnation had finally aroused public attention, and policy was to blame. The popular mood should welcome relief from the weight of another intractable half decade under Doménique Bienportant.

So thought the challengers at Masson's Fishery, especially Benjamin Bamiara. AuThon's paradoxically dubbed "Peasant" had developed the Princely Navigator conceit to enforce his prediction—that youthful spirits would respond to a dynamic, socially progressive entrepreneur freshly emergent out of the high seas. He anticipated defectors to the Fisherman's cause, even from inside the desiccated administration, for the Domino's more ambitious crew must be eager to board a new and modern vessel where their service would reach some objective.

Two years before, in Indesville, the Masson team learned sobering lessons from Giselle's defeat by young Hannibal the Karamau Rapper. At least, they realized that a political campaign was entitled to make more noise than sense. Hence, stressing the island's maritime position and the candidate's exploits in overseas trade, the Fisherman's deckhands inundated television and radio outlets with alarums of lively competition, vessel to vessel, man to (ahem!) man.

Alerted by warnings from the ubiquitous Vinaigrette, the campaign eventually perceived satirical reverberations emanating from Nationalist Party sources. Showing unanticipated signs of life, Government press and TV commercials prefigured explosions onboard tuna trawlers, shipwrecks by barefoot politicians in marine garb, and disasters for "Massoneers" skirmishing against triumphant Bienportants. The Thons-of-state, they taunted, would never sail.

When political stigma began to affect business operations, Fisherman's crew turned to less swaggering similes. Eventually, the body politic assumed a quieter complexion. Masson declared his personal and financial interests in full, revealing no trace of piracy. Homes and villages absorbed his calming radio voice bearing the promise of tangible change in a poverty-stricken land. There, more than on the high seas, the Fisherman could speak with credibility. Not only had his international prominence become standard knowledge. His name was soon identified with AuThon donations to the rural poor, credited with diverting nourishment to them that the "National" elite would only discard.

While sober folk downhill mused dubiously about "a business person booting the generals out of government," academic faculties above Indesville fulminated with fanfares of reform. Boisterous memes in social media recalled the heady time of student activism when Masson had helped lead the indomiable Wazimbwe's protest movement on Babel Hill. They revived the 1996 slogan "Get Out of Our Way," animated in new designs by Cynthia Van Zan. Some even claimed to have witnessed Governor Charpentier's horse navigating skyward from campus, the legendary Spider on its back.

Fisherman and entourage shaped his agenda with dexterity. Health, housing, education, roadways called urgently for new investment apart from the usual streams of patronage. Campaign co-managers Wazimbwe and Bamiara raised funds discreetly, leveraging international channels without flagrantly alarming the Presidency or its loyalist cohorts. From market grounds and fishing ports trickled donations of resources for campaign expenses. The movement pledged businesslike austerity, however that was to be understood.

Caught in this tide, the expatriate team of Guyane and Van Zan confronted a clouded horizon. No longer were they merely a maritime industry's hired hands. At the outset, the Americans anticipated an anonymous function in Fisherman's camaign voyage. If they ventured conspicuously into the campaign, they could be stigmatized as alien intruders in domestic politics. To function without inviting opprobrium, their roles had to be worked into a national strategy that inevitably, but inconspicuously, included them.

This proved elusive, for Masson had to dismantle some exposure to industrial, political, and social arenas while sustaining his distinction as a cosmopolitan prodigy. To make resources available to the campaign, all non-essential business expansion was suspended, including the half-ready fish farm and the proposed textile plant. Even the angora goat ranchers seemed to be minding their own business. After assisting in this disengagement, not much seemed to remain for Van Zan and Guyane to initiate. The expats had to ask what awaited them—and their boss admitted some uncertainty.

"At first," he tells them with a grin, "I thought you might poke around the cesspools of Domino's corruption. Get out of town and uncover useful intelligence in the hinterlands where you could pose as agents of, I don't know, Interpol? the FBI? But," he interjects hastily, seeing incredulity cloud Denis's countenance and sheer panic invade Cynthia's, "that's obviously inappropriate. And yet your flair for discreet inquiry should be useful in some way that . . ."

"That doesn't contaminate your campaign," Guyane says.

"And get us thrown out of the country in the process," Van Zan completes the thought.

"Right." Then the customary Fisherman pause.

The Americans wait, beginning to calculate how quickly they might pack their bags and leave town. "So I'd like you to start," he resumes, "just by looking at what people outside the city need from a serious administration—to shift directions a tad. Not a real change of jobs, don't misunderstand. You're still promoting a brand, only somewhat enlarged."

"And a trifle grandiloquent," interjects Guyane.

"Whatever that means," says Masson. "We'd have wanted this research to be done in any case—to clarify the markets for AuThon, of course. And you'll continue on the fishery payroll. Cynthia resumes creative travel, using her knack for new information. Denis will report on market conditions to Seriel in Finance; you'll find Solange less formidable than she seems, albeit not as "Douce" as she's labeled."

At this point, Guyane senses a shift in Van Zan's posture, as if her chair had become an impediment. He looks over and she shakes her head slowly.

Noting persistent skepticism in his interlocutors' attitude, Masson tries reassurance. "You should be able to take the economic pulse using the contacts you're already comfortable with: local business folk and journalists, university faculty, independent-minded officials—bankers who talk to Bamiara, or Sophie Makoa's underground sources. And don't look at me like that," he barks into Cynthia's skepticism. "Sophie is prepared for this, and she is a mine, a gold mine of intelligence; who do you think got me into the race to begin with?"

Van Zan shrugs in recognition. Nothing about la Vinaigrette could take her by surprise. Yet she has her own doubts over the distinction between a gold mine and a mine field; she wonders which it would be once she walked into it.

Fisherman is prepared for Cynthia's mood. "You will of course continue to play *la jeune fille*, which Vinaigrette tolerates, even though nobody believes it. You're still free to roam, to wade in the water, but wherever you are, record what people need from their leadership. Convey it through your visual imagination, as you do brilliantly. We'll be able to plant your products incognito through the popular media, as well as on our own channels. It's a voyage of discovery."

Cynthia tries to toy with the metaphor. "As for discovering, you might imagine a presidential contender who wears socks on full-screen TV. You're going after the presidency now, not the white whale."

Masson responds with a smile that does not clarify much for her. He returns to Denis.

As AuThon's agent, Guyane is to undertake a field survey of food access in politically sensitive rural areas. With that as a formal point of departure, he will keep an eye out for the local consequences of illegal rake-offs and diversion of public contracts, artificial expense accounts, inflated bottom lines, kickbacks, bribes, irregular sales of natural resources, and other self-amusement by officials. Much of this lore is buried in obscure communal and church collections. Useful intelligence comes from central bank sources ("someone named Honoré" for instance), who hesitate to risk their careers by blowing whistles in the direction of international patrons. "So they whisper the details to a sect that Benjamin frequents."

"A cult that might be identified with a personage named Ishmael?" Guyane guesses, eyebrows raised.

The Fisherman sinks into one of his customary pauses, then takes a deep breath, signalling that the interview is over.

As intended, it leads to a heady rush of activity. Both Vinaigrette's memory and the Peasant's notes contain evidence of official chicanery—unrequited petitions, court filings, ethics inquiries, media reports. "Excavating dry turf," Anya Wazimbwe calls the Americans' mission. Understandably, public disclosures are often euphemized to shield notable antagonists in cases not yet—perhaps never to be— litigated. They will accumulate suggestively against the incumbent administration, however, indicting its nonchalance over deteriorating levels of nutrition, housing, and transportation.

These conditions are especially severe in the arid South, suffocated by heat, abandoned by men, where women, children, and aged stragglers chew on prickly pear to fill their bellies.

In truth, as Van Zan has personally observed, while misery reigns throughout the countryside, it is flagrantly defied by criminal privilege. Among the Wazimbwe, for instance, who treat local farmers as dependents. Curiously, Anya fails to flinch over her repudiated genealogy. "It's that easy to be free of guilt," Cynthia concludes.

"No, not easy," cautions Bamiara, "for sooner or later you'll see Anya turn that key to our advantage. And nourish the people."

Denis stays reticent, while he too witnesses scarcity in his exploration through "the bush." On these ventures, posing as an inspector of food stocks for AuThon, Guyane surveys thin lines of huts along dusty roads frequented by exhausted shadows. Houses of any substance stand in various stages of construction or decay, depending on the fortunes of their owners. Each sub-region has at least one sturdy "manor house," inhabited by its fortunate proprietors during a few favored weeks of the year. Everywhere else, straw frames pose no resistance to weather, while cinder-block walls and roofs of thatch (rarely, corrugated metal) wait indefinitely to tighten against vicious seasonal rains and winds.

When habitable, these forlorn structures are populated by a few mothers and withered elders not readily distinguishable by gender. Their landscape acquires animation from flocks of barely clothed children, birds, and livestock, all chattering about local conditions.

Yet even such barrens are home to its own emigrants, for in AuxIndes personal identity invariably resides at a tomb in one's natal village. To them, burial structures represent the family essence. Shielded against encroaching bush by faithful guardians, the tombs remain in better condition than the ordinary domiciles of the still living. "A death culture," Van Zan calls it, "waiting to live."

As they pass through, Denis and his driver/interpreter pause regularly so that hungry kids can gather around their car, eager for a distribution of crackers, too shy to demand anything more. In the dry austral winter, children play upwind, to cough less. Their noses run perpetually, until they are old enough to wipe them. That's also when they begin school—on a rugged pathway toward somewhere else— to towns where people speak French. While struggling upward, they have to keep their khaki shorts and Tee-shirts clean enough through the week; spares are too expensive.

When an adult resident nears, the driver, Patrice, asks in Creole about daily life. The inevitable response is a prayer for better times.

AuThon's researchers find abundant opportunities, however, to collect intelligence reflecting on the effects of national leadership. Larger villages have edifices built by republican or colonial authorities to house records of town meetings, elections, trials, tax collection, certifications, and other formalities that leave traces of one sort or another. With their theoretically lockable doors, and with walls and roofs that resist weather, these halls also offer shelter to visitors on foot, bicycle, donkey, or in vehicles. When Denis and Patrice bunk in such structures, they can examine what passes for archives of the place.

In the most forlorn circumstances, where mobile phones have only begun to proliferate, a typical town hall might offer the village's sole radio-telephone, an ancient device used for emergencies only. Even then its messaging is usually superseded by flights of birds, clouds, or ominous swarms of locusts. Clearly, adolescents could maintain better cellular communication for a few cents a day, if they had so much.

True, rural AuxIndes also transcends its squalor. Towns and larger villages usually have something particular to offer at a market—a potter's or sculptor's creations, special cloth from goatherds or sheep flocks, weaves of raffia or sisal fiber, leather sandals. Mayors and government agents live under intact roofs, while village councilors commute from their farms. Near the coasts, AuThon provides fresh or smoked fish trucked in by market day—or every day when neither electricity nor ice is available for preservation. Cattle and goats stray ubiquitously. Slabs of beef hang at entrances to food stalls, usually as repositories for swarms of flies. When in need or doubt, travelers subsist on rice or boiled cassava and canned provisions, usually impregnated by local spices.

Some centers of activity attract affluent transients who arrive with their own tents or trailers. Allowed to park at the village market provided they clear the space by early morning, they speak openly about conditions observed en route. Most merchants have time and inclination to try out their French for a foreigner's benefit. The atmosphere itself conveys much to an astute listener, and Patrice translates what he hears in Creole. When rains arrive, as in the austral summer, they must interrupt their "inspections" to avoid floods and mud slides, deflecting their extensive inquiry into accessible dry land; to show sympathy, they offer small monetary donations for winter repairs.

Foraging deeply into the South, or "famine zone" as the unfunny quip calls it, all bets are off. Few who stay on that land survive into middle age. Life depends on rare precipitation brought from wherever the clouds live, conveyed by one or another wind. From far off, those winds come—one of them at a time, each with its own name. All breezes are known to the inhabitants who pray for their arrival or departure in a recondite Creole that occasionally baffles even Patrice, forcing recourse to his primary school French even to obtain directions.

Unlike Van Zan, Guyane himself never learned the linguistic varieties that his intolerant father would have dismissed as "pidgin kreyòl." But he hears the elders quarrel over which of the hundred winds had last come, without ever agreeing in their recollections. In any case, nobody, not even ancestors, could reliably command the capricious rains.

North of this desiccated cactus land, villagers either draw water from a stream or maintain a communal well with its pump. When these are no longer functional, liquids arrive in containers—on trucks, the backs of animals, or the heads of women and children commuting on foot. Odors of mimosa and frangipani combat valiantly against fugitive smoke from nearby dwellings. Salubrity remains perpetually problematic, always expensive.

No matter how pothole-pocked, dusty, and detoured its roadway, nearly every hamlet introduces itself by name on painted cement or wooden slab. These facsimiles of rural French signage sometimes carry a brief boast, motto, or claim to prominence—as in "Home of Champion Wrestler Komo." A similar device announces the end of town limits, often with the number of a main roadway, and occasionally a note of farewell to the departing traveler. Next to these signs, Guyane and Patrice often come upon a deposit of roadside plants or flowers, firewood, or bags of charcoal—all dropped off in heaps as though for random acquisition.

Women shoulder virtually all the burdens of rural life. Men reappear from the towns when their families need them for control of cattle, to till the softening land with the same cattle, or to cement a new block or tile onto the house. After that, they vanish once more, in search of income to support the inevitable new baby due eight or nine months hence—another weight on the women left behind.

Where clinics and churchyards exist, their personnel collect food for distribution, some of it from overseas; these donations are always welcome, even when imported grains need to be pestle-pounded. Every substantial town contains one or two church sites, each with its priest or pastor, in a nation as speckled by Christianities as 17th century Europe. Mosques and temples show in some regions, but not all. Whichever their formal denomination, however, all faithful respect the spirits of the earth. Funerals and sermons usually feature admixtures of Scripture with the wisdom of the ancestors—without specifying the exact benefits either of them confer on the inhabitants.

"They got us here," remind the elders, unquestionably proud of where they fit into that achievement.

In his random surveys of the countryside, Denis Guyane understands that religion and traditional lore rank higher and prevail more durably than government enterprise. Few citizens recall the name of their *député* (MP) for more than a few weeks following an election. They're all the same, according to the residents, who nonetheless never fail to vote. In addition to the influence exerted by local aristocracies throughout AuxIndes's countryside, it is proverbial wisdom that decides the dates for weddings, festivals, and funereal commemoration. The elders know who to consult on such matters. The pundits rarely bother to hold public office.

These contacts and records provide usable evidence against a negligent administration that exists mainly to serve its own purposes. In an atmosphere of deprivation and resentment, Denis has talked himself into believing that he is helping prepare a more prosperous future for the island. Whether peppered with politically usable intelligence or not, the research itself proves instructional. Guyane's more sophisticated business occupations could seldom unlock as much basic reality. He begins to sense a deeper purpose in himself, but characteristically postpones the impulse to define it. Whatever Denis's boss has chosen for life's metaphor, swashbuckling is not for him.

On return to town, he says as much to Solange Seriel, the corporate treasurer to whom he reports findings. These debriefings legitimize occasions for animated contact with the well-endowed "La Douce" who discards severity and welcomes their personal interaction as much as she does his research. When they remark a general brightening in Seriel's demeanor, colleagues confidently attribute it to dalliance with her new "field hand."

Thanks to the travelers' reports, Roger Masson's campaign can explore several avenues for its assault on incumbent malfeasance. Some connect directly with Fisherman's own business preoccupations and need Anya Wazimbwe's treatment. For instance, foreign fleets, mostly Asian, habitually violate the island's territorial zone, but when observed would invariably claim license to fish inside the restricted area. Invited by Van Zan to describe their disadvantages against such odds, local watermen exposeu the easy connections forged between alien trawler captains and otherwise underpaid coastal officials. Whether authorized or not, invader vessels can lease the necessary equipment to ward off satellite scrutiny and continue merrily fishing wherever they choose.

On occasion, Cynthia is able to collect a transponder set from a boatsman and convey it to Anya Wazimbwe, enabling Masson to display such items triumphantly from his TV platform as evidence of corruption in the house of the Domino. "How much money does a miserable local official get for delivering this little gadget," he asks the screen, "and where does the real payoff end," he would pretend to wonder, innocently, pointing upward toward some Olympian, perhaps even presidential, empyrean.

The Fisherman's campaign also exposes ecologically destructive contracts to harvest mineral modules off the ocean floor, with payoffs to cooperating bureaucrats. It's obvious who pockets the benefits. Ignoring warnings from Masson's legal counselors, Van Zan sends cartoons of water spiders to assault this industrial invasion of honest pearl fisheries, festooned by notes from Bizet.

Beneath the island's law-abiding pretensions are spasms of insecurity that afflict the entire population. Local press and media explore incidents of village devastation, property vandalism, and gang terrorism that rage even more urgently as the September election draws near. Law and order units are deployed belatedly to besieged areas; they invariably claim efficacy in cleaning up—after the damage is done.

On Masson's behalf, Bamiara is able to expose false claims of police "kills" without laying blame on the untouchable Minister who rules that roost. Disaffected functionaries, speaking in confidence, expose typical "anti-terrorist" scams. In one sequence, Government minions plant a few insecure cattle in the way of some greedy rustler gang, then pounce on the miscreants with an overpowering force of gendarmes. The press is invited to cover the capture of these desperadoes most of whom escape in clouds of dust. Afterward, reporters are treated to confessions by disgruntled bandits; some complain with wounded pride that they had been hoodwinked into crime by the cops and insufficiently paid for it. No news source dares reveal such pranks explicitly without risk of retaliation by the Karamau ministry; covered hints in social media suffice to arouse suspicion.

In another sequence based on international press reports, Van Zan depicts the surreptitious arrival of poachers who trap exotic animals and smuggle them out for sale to global terrorist organizations. Money passes from criminal hands into the pockets of unnamed (of course) dignitaries in traditional business apparel.

"You're looking for more than the fancy-dress ball," Vinaigrette said to her. "It's fulfillment of Spider's revolution that works on you. Well, Spider knew that all revolutions start with bread, not meat."

"But they end with blood," retorted Van Zan.

"Mostly," admitted Sophie, "blood or blood and oil. For now, Masson's example only continues our uprising with tuna fish, in tins. That's an improvement. Still, I always prefer coffee."

Even President Domino's chief of staff stumbles into a trap of his own devising. Years ago, invited to speak at a provincial meeting, The Honorable Arnaut Tsieroro sat humbly behind a table and delivered his "confession" to an admiring audience. Bald head cradled in his hands, voice shaking, he intoned devotion to his benevolent superior. With opened heart, he expounded how President Bienportant found him teaching in an obscure primary school and given him his chance. "It was like a rescue at sea in a raging storm," Tsieroro proclaimed, massaging the simile between hands that clutched his shaven skull. "I splashed and paddled out of breath, trying in vain to impress a static tide of pupils. Until, like a glorious angel, Doménique Bienportant came upon me in that remote classroom."

At the time, Arnaut's impassioned monologue so deeply stirred its hushed audience, that the organizers eagerly invited him to return during the next presidential campaign. What they heard was identical to his previous tribute to their head of state—Domino as hero of simple, honest, marooned men. "It was like a rescue at sea . . ." reproducing the anecdote entirely, word for memorized word, head in hands, half-triumphant, half-mournful, as if it were occurring to him in a momentary inspiration.

Then, displayed on Masson's TV station, the Tsieroro's "new" improvisation emerges as a performance. "A stump speech, learned by heart." comments Bamiara. "He never changes a word of it."

To recover from such body blows, the Bienportant machine must find ingenious vehicles of counterattack, improving on its hitherto wobbly strategy. It commissions several professionally produced TV commercials—attributable to La Vinaigrette herself (she'd never reveal whose side she was on—both of them evidently). One ad shows a faintly disguised Fisherman suffering from sea-sickness on board a tiny dinghy ("the fleet") while free ocean creatures leap in glee.

A nastier video focuses on a sequence of attractive young women each surprised in some innocent domestic occupation—toasting a bun, opening a car door, hanging wash, pouring milk. Each actor responds with precisely the same line: glaring at the camera she repeats, "Roger Masson? The Fisherman's wife? I didn't know Roger was married!" Since TV viewers understand that Masson does have a spouse—once herself a notable mayoral aspirant—the cumulative effect is to expose the candidate as a philandering adulterer.

The Domino commercials require counterattack, and Van Zan is there to stage it. In a new video, Giselle herself rises up from her modestly set dinner table to steer a ship while praising her husband for his faithful support, so that "together we will serve and win." Dominoes tumble off the sea-borne table while fish and shrimp dance merrily.

In another simulation, Cynthia hits the regime in a sensitive spot—relations with a proud polity. This strip features a fictitious "Chinese" energy company bearing an artificial Anglo-Saxon name with authorization to prospect along the sparsely populated eastern ridge. An obscure social medium reports their discovery—not of petroleum or natural gas, but of precious stones, exported eastward without appropriate declaration. In Van Zan's treatment, digging noises awaken the deceased inhabitants of local tombs. The enlightened dead mobilize patriotic young people, inciting them to post graffiti onto the tomb walls warning the village against foreigners who steal their diamonds and bribe corrupt officials to escape with the swag. When the final cartoon shows the miscreants in prison garb and handcuffs, her audience draws its own conclusions.

"Roger will have to make up with Beijing for this once he's president," Guyane remarks to the artist.

"Then one or the other had better acquire a sense of humor," replies Van Zan.

His pen and her brush contribute to Masson's campaign without byline although neither American could plausibly deny that they were "assisting the Fisherman's future." To replace her customary logo—the stylized movie projector—Cynthia signs her releases with one or another West African mask image. Denis adapts pen names from Francophone journalism as pseudonyms for his own reportage.

Social media and the popular press consume such messages with gusto, putting President Bienportant on the defensive against his inexperienced but ostensibly honest antagonist. Prevailing comment portrays Roger as the iconic businessman wryly exposing unscrupulous games by a malicious, self-serving, and incorrigibly incompetent regime. The Fisherman's rhetoric conforms to the noble Navigator icon, and his style becomes all the more aggressive.

"You never collected a penny of taxes from these culprits of yours," charges Masson in one of the campaign debates. "You just siphon off your chunk and leave the thieves to fly away with their booty. Nothing for the people who own the wealth of the nation, according to our constitution. When I'm president, I'll tax those intruders when their acquisitions are legal, and jail them when they aren't."

"Maybe you should start with your own profits," is Domino's retort, inadvertently emphasizing the distinction between corruption and the putatively honest marketplace. Ignoring Vinaigrette's advice, the veteran president stops short of anti-capitalist invective, but he is far from comfortable against pointed challenges.

Paradoxically, in normal times, educated voters in urban milieux habitually support opposition candidates while "provincials," with the most to lose, obediently follow any rascals in power. To reverse this impression, Cynthia's "Chinese" diamond gambit gives credit to the rurals, dead and quick. Then to compensate urbanites, she produces comic videos, often on oceanic themes, with subtitles in English: dolphins in revolt against killer sharks wearing "dominos;" the crippled sailboat *Dominant* whose captain dozes while it is threatened by fire and tidal wave. Another depicts pirates burying treasure in the sands around "National" headquarters; animated swordfish wearing horn-rimmed eyeglasses dig up the swag and donate it to feed the hungry.

Thus has the nautical strategy some sort of rebirth, in satire.

CHAPTER 9

SONGBIRDS AND SHADOWS

Scene. **Vault of the Khoin Clan,** outside Indesville

Freddy Khoin, aka Spider, joins his elders

SETH. Listen closely, Freddy. Ishmael will be calling them out soon.

SPIDER. Oh! So are we . . . ?

RAINA. Let's hope this time it's only for prayer, not to fight.

SPIDER. Good. How do you know that?

RAINA. For one, he's having them set up chairs.

SETH. Lots of chairs.

SPIDER. Yes, but *how* do you know that, or anything at all? Anything that happens outside?

SETH. Outside where?

SPIDER. Outside this . . . wherever we are?

RAINA. We're here, of course.

SPIDER. I mean, we can't *see* Ishmael, can we?

RAINA. Well, not exactly.

SPIDER. Uh huh.

RAINA. You'll learn soon enough. Anyway, welcome, Freddy. Incidentally, where have you been?

SPIDER. I don't know. . . Flying, I guess.

SETH. Excuse me, Raina; the men . . . *those* men . . . are they showing up?

RAINA. I don't think so.

SETH. Maybe it's still too early out there?

RAINA. Perhaps. In any case, the bird is still chattering.

SPIDER. The bird? What bird?

RAINA. Actually, it's a flock of birds; ghastly, like having tinnitus.

SETH. That's how she knows the men haven't come out yet.

RAINA. When those men come out, the birds shut up. No more tinnitus.

SPIDER. So we . . . you can hear the birds? Now?

RAINA. Of course, but not exactly.

SETH. Just think about it, Spider-lad.

[Pause]

SETH. Raina, what do you suppose Ishmael will say to the men— when they come out?

SPIDER. IF they come out? Must they?

RAINA. He will preach against the government. What he always does. Boring.

SETH. It is what he's paid to do.

RAINA. It's what men do. Very tedious. Women, on the other hand . . .

SPIDER. Wait, this Ishmael. I've heard of him, his name anyway. You mean he's actually paid by them, by "the men?"

SETH. Oh, IS he, really?

[Pause]

RAINA. He says he's a prophet . . . rewarded by the Lord. Provided we recommend it.

SPIDER. We? The Lord listens to us?

SETH. He listens to everybody . . . everybody who comes in truth.

RAINA. In *search* of truth. That's why He mainly hears women. [Pause]

SPIDER. So, again, how do we know?

RAINA. We know. [pause] Wait. Ah. A few have come out.

SPIDER. Out? To hear Ishmael?

RAINA. Yes. The birds are quiet.

SETH: Why did they stop? They're supposed to be messengers!

RAINA: Nasty men on the way. Ishmael never feeds them, the birds. They refuse to repeat his blather.

SPIDER: So they fly away?

RAINA: They fly up, of course, but not away. Birds always return . . . with messages.

SETH. And the chairs have moved now. Some chairs have people in them.

SPIDER. Enough for a . . . a service?

SETH. Not that many. But Ishmael wants to start anyhow, doesn't he?

RAINA. Maybe not. No men yet. It's just the people.

SPIDER. What people? Ishmael's congregation?

RAINA. Yes.

SPIDER. Why aren't they enough for him?

RAINA. Because they are assumed.

SETH. Just people, you know. They don't count.

RAINA. Like us, when we were . . . when we resided out there.

SETH. They come with Ishmael. Always. Anyhow.

RAINA. But this time the birds are gone already. They must expect a sermon.

SETH. Or a conflict, God forbid. Whenever the men come out, it all goes *poom*!

SPIDER. Poom?

RAINA. Ah.

SPIDER. So this is actually . . . not religion? It's all political?

RAINA. What can be "not religion?" Can you think of anything?

SPIDER. Yes, I can think of some things.

RAINA. That's because you're still young . . . were young.

SPIDER. True, I guess. I'm 18, or was 18 before they shot at me.

SETH. Twenty, according to La Vinaigrette. And before they *shot* you, not just "at" you.

SPIDER. I don't know that. Not for sure. I did have to fall. Subject to the Law of Gravitation. But I ended up here—wherever we are—so I guess you're right.

RAINA. And you think that's not religion?

SPIDER. All right. So the men coming out. They may do something risky—even during prayers? As I did when I got shot at . . .

RAINA. . . . .

SPIDER. . . . got shot?

SETH. Especially if they have a gun, like you had.

SPIDER: Unloaded. No ammo, just a gun.

SETH. Too expensive, bullets. Which explains why there aren't more men out there.

RAINA. But if they have a gun, they might know how to use it. Not like Freddy.

SPIDER. Bull! But wait. There *are* more. How can I know that? Those cow horns on top of here—where we are: antenna? I can sense people coming up the hill, from another direction.

SETH. You're beginning to get the idea.

RAINA. Beginning to listen.

SPIDER. Whatever. Anyhow, those word clouds that I can't really see are following people up the hill.

RAINA. And those people, what you call people—are they men, too?

SPIDER. Yes, all men. But where are *we*?

SETH. And they are armed? the men?

SPIDER. Oh, mainly clubs, axes.

SETH. Fools. Like your friends. And look where you ended up.

SPIDER. Yes. So where *is* that?

RAINA. Aha! Now Ishmael's coming.

SETH. He's in the middle, right?

SPIDER. Middle? Middle of what? Nobody, practically nobody, is coming along with him.

RAINA. Poor Ishmael.

[Long pause.]

RAINA. We don't want another battle, not today. Does anybody here have contact with the other groups?

SETH. The others? The ones with guns?

RAINA. Maybe.

SETH. I don't.

SPIDER. No, I don't either, obviously.

SETH. Could be that you do. Try. Somebody shot . . . shot at . . . you.

SPIDER. Sure. Several. The whole police force. But it's not obvious. They came in cars, from Karamau's place, the big stone house. Does that make a difference?

RAINA. For Ishmael it certainly does. His church is open-air.

SETH. Not funny. Try anyhow, Freddy.

SPIDER. I understand, even though I don't, really. Your birds are quiet. Or they only echo through the clouds, and it's foggy.

RAINA. Try some other way. Forget the birds; they're all Protestants, or something worse. Tune into those cattle horns again, or trees maybe.

SPIDER. We have a link with trees?

RAINA. Could be.

SPIDER. Francis of Assisi, he spoke with birds. Was he a . . . a Protestant?

SETH. Uh-uh. Too early for that.

RAINA. Right. Don't be anachronistic; didn't you study history?

SPIDER. A while ago. Mainly English; no religion. [Pause] The horns on this place are glum; even they aren't saying anything about Ishmael.

RAINA. Look up. Try the trees.

SETH. Or down. Earthworms, a last recourse; they don't sing, and scarcely dance. But they dig the roots. Ha-ha.

RAINA. And sometimes the worm turns. . . . Just kidding.

SPIDER. Got it! Trees moving under the clouds. They're calling Ishmael a rebel.

SETH. Oh! Oh!

RAINA. Poor Ishmael. He was a silly man as a drunk. Now he's a silly sober man.

SETH. A clown, a prating clown. Not trusted to be around guns and clubs.

SPIDER. Maybe. But I had heard about Ishmael, before . . . Tell me, did he really take the money?

RAINA. What does it matter if he took the money? They all do. Whether he did it or not, everybody thinks he did.

SETH. They recall him as a self-serving, inebriated preacher.

RAINA. They had it better when he was a wild prophet. Now he's only sober.

SPIDER. So what did Ishmael do with the money?

RAINA. Exactly what? Probably spent it on that church.

SETH. The open-air church. His church.

RAINA. Yes. Not ours, obviously.

SPIDER. So the cops were right to . . . shoot at . . . *him*?

RAINA. They might have been right. But they only hit you. Obviously the wrong target.

SPIDER. Oh. I thought they'd got Ishmael too. Of course he wasn't there, with me, at the time.

[Short pause]

SETH. The Big Man was there. What's he supposed to have done with the money?

RAINA. Who? Ishmael? What money?

SETH. No, the police minister. What's his name?

RAINA. His name is Karamau; Spider told you that. Some call him Philosophe. Funny name.

SPIDER. Yes, for a policeman.

SETH. Probably just a paradox, to amuse the educated.

SPIDER. So what *did* he do with it?

RAINA. With his name? Nothing. He kept it.

SPIDER. No, with the money . . . that he got from the President.

SETH. From the *former* President.

SPIDER. I guess so. It's complicated.

RAINA. I don't know. New uniforms maybe. He's a police chief. They like uniforms.

SPIDER. Whew! Twenty thousand dollars for uniforms? That buys a lot of brass. How much is that in real money?

SETH. You mean in *our* money? About four million, maybe.

RAINA. If it *was* twenty thousand. Nobody knows.

SPIDER. Still, was it worth killing an innocent civilian—me, it seems?

RAINA. Not just a civilian; you were high up there on horseback, and you had friends with their sticks and clubs.

SETH. And stones. Big stones. One of their guys got it too—a cop, hit by a rock.

SPIDER. He did? So do we have company? Here?

SETH. Yes, but that was in revenge for your . . . loss. He's in another sepulcher.

SPIDER. Hey, that doubles the death count!

RAINA. Big deal. In our country, armies can spend a whole day firing at each other and by the end they have only two bodies to show for it. Hardly a day's work.

SPIDER. One body is too many, if it's mine.

SETH. That's to our credit, Raina, low mortality rates. Why would you want more dead?

RAINA. Why indeed? We're ancestors, after all. We advocate nonviolent conflict. At least I think we did. It's the waste that bothers me.

SPIDER. Yeah. All that ammunition for only two bodies—and the other one only got it with a rock.

SETH. Plus the holes in the buildings, the collapsed tent. Or was that a different battle?

SPIDER. Maybe I'm not worth all that expense, even with company from the other side. So Philosophe gets a twenty thousand dollar uniform to show for it?

RAINA. I don't know. What of it? And it's not for him; he only wears that black cloak—a vulture trying to look like a raven. Most likely his senior officers got the new clothes.

SETH. Fancy threads to impress their women!

RAINA. Huh! It's about time they had something that worked.

[Pause]

SETH. Wait. Here they come—lots of them.

RAINA. Carrying weapons?

SETH. Some.

SPIDER. Scary. Where are WE?

RAINA. Don't worry. You're already shot.

SPIDER. Guess so. Does that make me—us . . . safe?

RAINA. Of course.

SETH. Listen. It's quiet now. The birds are all gone.

SPIDER. *They* aren't safe, right?

RAINA. Right. They've heard of bird shot.

[Silence]

RAINA. That was a joke, you know.

[Pause]

SPIDER. But these guns going off. The President—not the new one who was my college friend. . . . The old one called Domino, he's still blaring orders, right?

SETH. It seems so, from some hiding place.

RAINA. A sanctuary, so he thinks. They say he's on the tiger's back, can't risk getting off. Must be a mother tiger, very vindictive.

SETH. He ought to die and get to his own place, like this one.

SPIDER. This one what? [Pause] All right. And Ishmael wants to bring on the revolt? To stop him? With a sermon?

SETH. Him *and* the new President, your friend. They're both infidels, according to Ishmael.

RAINA. Poor Ishmael, sober and confused.

SPIDER. Poor all of them, but still I'm the one who's been shot . . . at; me and that other guy who got in the way of the rock.

SETH. An ex-cop, so he must have friends and relatives with weapons; maybe they even know how to use them.

RAINA. Bad news if they do.

SPIDER. Because of the firing? This is a battle now? Can't Ishmael stop all that?

SETH. Ishmael will take care of himself. He always does.

RAINA. Still, the whole world is jittery.

SETH. Maybe the earthworms are safe, but the rest of the network has gone silent.

SPIDER. Dead?

RAINA. I wouldn't put it that way.

SETH. We might as well close down, until the firing stops.

SPIDER. Can't we do anything like now, to stop this, before it turns violent and becomes . . . whatever got me?

RAINA. We might, but we're just ancestors. We can influence only by example, and yours is no help here, not at this point.

SPIDER. Our example? To whom? Who are we ancestors for?

SETH: We never know after the first batch, and even then . . .

SPIDER: I do recall some of that ancestor stuff, though—about how grandfathers . . .

RAINA. Grand *parents*, please.

SPIDER. Yeah, well, how they "got us here." And how we must respect them for that.

RAINA: Meaning, respect *us*. Especially women, straight or gay, bulwarks of family. Real ancestors.

SPIDER. So when might we express this brilliant message—our example of *avoiding* violence?

[Long pause]

SETH. Maybe when the earth links are back. The world is complex.

RAINA. But not at this moment, Spider boy. They are going to slaughter each other now. Birds, clouds, trees, worms, even water, all taking cover. We're the lucky ones; we can be eternally patient.

SPIDER: When I was . . . travelling, before I got here, wherever we are. Met this young woman from America, called *Loved One* or some such name. Killed while still a baby. Put here, or somewhere, by her mother—to protect her. She was still figuring it out, angry too.

RAINA: We heard about her. From a great writer.

SETH: The mother sacrificed her child to prevent her from being returned to slavery.

RAINA: That's what I mean. Something more important than just living.

SPIDER: But does it do any good, ancestoring like this?

SETH. Of course it does, if it's phrased better than "they got us here." Learn from the woman who recounted that story. Eloquence, poetry, oratory, pithy proverbs.

RAINA. Music always helps.

SPIDER. There has to be a better way—to get to peace. Maybe my horse statue could help take us there. With music? Maybe not. I see you don't think so.

[Interlude to let the battle transpire. It doesn't matter for how long; the dead listen in perpetuity.]

Shadows Over The State

Prophet Ishmael's dissidence knows no pause, respite, or reset. His followers carry chairs into the streets to defy whoever profanes the Lord's chosen island. Their militant wing confronts secular authority in all its forms. For the moment, their target is Roger Masson, the latest pretender to dominion. As witnessed in spirit by the late Spider, this urban confrontation erupts even while armed forces are subduing the final twitches of unreconciled Bienportantism in the northern countryside.

Despite efforts to reverse his predecessor's iniquities, the new president remains an imposter in Ishmael's book. Although he's done little to invite reproach, Fisherman's benign promises sound blasphemous to the pious. Their battle against godless despotism goes on.

Virtue will not be entangled among the nets of worldly power. The Prophet has webbing of his own; those nets can even ensnare spiders.

(Another poor joke, thinks Seth.)

Once installed at his precarious summit, Masson has limited room for maneuver. He must endorse his Interior Minister's pacification of the urban landscape, defied by Ishmael. Simultaneously, AuxIndes's army mobilizes against resistance in the north by partisans of the absent Domino. Both tasks require diplomacy, for the operational commanders are reluctant to assault religious and civic establishments. Thérèse Zaphyra gets it done by announcing that if one force doesn't do its job, the other (hers) will. She takes advantage of Philosophe's hostility toward military intrusion into domestic security; just as she exploits her generals' fear of Karamau's gendarmes on the battlefront.

The Fisherman's legitimacy has depended from the outset on an unstable marriage of violence and civility. While aggressively securing his authority, the new president must labor peacefully to sustain it. This objective requires some rapid changes in operations. He reminds his triumphant partisans that only a credible governance—hard work in any case—will keep the lights on. He'll also need to schedule parliamentary and local elections to ratify his transitional ordinances and legitimize future acts. To manage this institutional cascade, Masson's team has to convert their improvised movement into a political apparatus. He calls it the BeauxIndes Party (BIP).

Any reform-minded administration needs to turn new leaves, especially after decades of withering, self-serving bureaucracy. Fervently, the BeauxIndes leadership scours hinterlands and civil society, seeking to recruit people of talent dedicated to public service.

It occasionally succeeds. Appealing to local patriots, academics, and businessfolk, Masson's party also seeks managers and technicians from a widely flung overseas diaspora. This expatriate elite claims to be awaiting opportunities for honorably remunerated service at home; they had fled abroad to escape the Philistine vulgarity of the ousted regime. "Poor Domino financed their careers, but they saw only how he was offending their feelings," quips la Vinaigrette.

To abandon posts in multilateral institutions, specialists like economist Régine Zolytra and planner Daoud Tabour (Ahmed's brother) need assurances that the new system aims beyond protection of somebody's fishing business. They already blame Masson for failing to complete the revolution that had collapsed fifteen years ago on Babel Mountain.

Inevitably, recruitment must contend with a plethora of unwelcome advice from one self-styled patron or another. While all purport to sponsor a new "meritocracy," such language frequently camouflages a predilection for ethical compromise. In particular, hints of loyalty toward the Interior Minister—or his nephew, the exuberant Mayor Hannibal—prove easy to spot, albeit difficult to ignore. Forced to reappoint Philosophe to his accustomed post, Fisherman finds himself on the wrong foot. He must protect positions of influence against the ambitions of Karamau's acolytes, but cannot then accept his staff's recommendation of Anya Wazimbwe for prime minister, lest the entire edifice collapse in partisan strife.

"She's too close to the business, and likely too hostile toward Karamau to join the cabinet," concedes Giselle.

"Plus oversexed, both of them," adds Van Zan. Consequently, for several weeks following inauguration, there is no premier.

It's Guyane who helps Fisherman mobilize Wazimbwe's assets. After placing the fishery business in trust to Bamiara, Masson enlists the Diva to lead a new public-private authority over environmental and maritime protection. Ambitiously, they envision the project as an autonomous crossroad for the so-called blue and green economies, "where natural values can inform human agency." It is to assure sponsorship for harbors, park reserves, seed banks, cold storage facilities, as well as security and insurance safeguards, professional training, academic research—however Anya wishes to attack those challenges.

Progressive ideas will inevitably confront vested preferences in agriculture, forestry, land management, and urban development, portending conflict with Anya Wazimbwe's own kinsfolk. In other respects, her appointment is defensible to objective observers, few though they be. Beyond evident glamor, the new commissioner's professional record qualifies her to combat the perils that threaten a sea-locked polity, even against the privileged within it.

Fisherman announces the commissioner's assignment with pride. He may even expect the enterprise to succeed, since, for her rhetoric alone, Anya is nothing if not credible. At AuThon Wazimbwe has vigorously attacked what multilateral protocol terms "illegal, unreported, and unregulated" violations of the island's maritime zone. She has negotiated for best managerial practices within international fishery organizations and for an Indian Ocean Tuna Commission. "All she does is look at them, and the toughest waterman forgives her landed birthright," remarks Guyane.

"And the squirearchy rushes to its yachts," comments the inverately skeptical Van Zan.

Her omnibus charge requires Wazimbwe to leave AuThon and to keep her distance from the omnivorous Interior Ministry. The appointment energizes malicious critics nonetheless. Ignoring the commissioner's efficacy and dedication to principle, they rage against flagrant favoritism for the president's business tribe and/or his imputed amorous urges. Letting tongues inevitably cluck over her presumed loyalty to AuThon, Anya pledges that all enterprises are to benefit from protection of a million square kilometers of oceanic commons surrounding 5,000 kilometers of coastline. To reach nationwide development, she expects to incorporate the island's unrealized potentials in crop and livestock improvement as well.

After Anya's transfer, tempting as it is to raid the AuThon brain trust to fill official vacancies, Masson hesitates to weaken his corporate apparatus any further. Cynics are already stigmatizing the presidential office as "AuThon's aquarium." Bamiara, like the American duo, must work under two hats; they participate informally as occasional presidential counselors while drawing their paychecks from the Fishery. There, the Peasant continues to organize solutions to his own passions—the ubiquitous climate revolution and its implications for nutrition, landholding, energy, and migration.

These priorities inevitably carry Bamiara toward interaction with his former team leader, even though he and the Diva must negotiate them from alternative viewpoints. Wazimbwe's new public-private commission welcomes Benjamin in combat against the inevitable onslaught of a changing climate upon the fragile biosphere. Nevertheless, as AuThon's acting CEO, Bamiara's perseverance in harvesting the warming oceans entails conflict with Anya, his alter ego.

Moreover, the Peasant keeps an undisclosed holiday retreat on the East Coast and he understands landowner distrust of wind farms and their retention of counter-conservationist bio-fuels. All part of a day at the business.

To answer speculation over personnel, the president completes a compact, technocratic team by designating his family's physician, Pierre Chameau, to double as Prime Minister and Minister of Health. Inevitably, a blogger wag perceives the appointment as "two fat humps atop a *Dromedary*"—one economizing on salaries, the other underwriting Masson's health insurance.

Wherever he isn't already popular, the Fisherman's idiosyncrasies evoke speculation. His childless marriage suggests impotence, and his avoidance of hosiery arouses suspicion over jungle-rot. Even Roger's love of poetry is ridiculed as somehow unmanly. Yet he attracts reproach for approving Philosophe's ruthless deployment of the security apparatus against maverick churches and domestic outlaws. "Always a victim of my own virtues," groans Masson, with a self-mocking smile as he wipes his eyeglasses.

The president's most troubling waves of dissent emerge, however, from a more martial sector. Once the pro-Domino vestiges have been routed, the island's army has little to do outside its immaculate barracks. To sustain focus, AuxIndes military tradition resents imposition of Masson's choice for Defense Minister—the brawny physicist, Zaphyra; her very name evokes its own pseudonym, *La Brise* (breeze, also breakup), that filters satirically through the camps. The general staff only grudgingly acknowledges Thérèse's descent from a decorated military lineage, her honorable background in UN peacekeeping, and an efficient mop up of the Bienportantist militias.

She also invariably defeats her officers in arm wrestling.

Upper echelon critics contrive grievances to lob over Zaphyra's head to the president. Some sanctimonious patriots blame her appointment on surreptitious influence by La Vinaigrette, a notorious opponent of military interests, even (or especially) while sharing General Domino's bed. Others resent the new minister's approval for Bienportant loyalists to deposit military pensions into their overseas bank accounts. La Brise's magnanimity prompts the current officers to protest in defense of their own financial security.

During a lengthy audience with Masson, the generals focus not on Tory corruption (who, after all, will cast the first grenade?), or on the minister's gender that nonetheless disturbs military discipline. Rather, the officers assail Zaphyra's familiarity with the institutions of Southern and East Africa where the president intends to cultivate new security relations. Inevitably, this "Africa option" arouses suspicion of a conspiracy to promote AuThon's business on the continent.

The most earnest resentment comes from a patriotic faction that understands the Zaphyra appointment in terms of a strategic revolution. The specter of a woman reorienting the nation's warrior soul toward certain "Anglophone" continentals has offended the heritage of AuxIndes's officer corps. It provokes the military establishment to charge Fisherman with insensitivity to warfare as "a form of civilization." They contend that his ignorance of martial culture exposes him to illusory feminism, favoring superstitious African strutter. The president's futile and obsolete anti-colonialism is an affront to decades of cordial European stewardship. "Our entire vocabulary descends from Napoleon!" cries a prominent general to a TV reporter. "Must we now learn how to salute in Afrikaans? or Swahili?"

By instinct, President Masson dismisses what he regards as the military's snobbish, sexist sentimentality. He persistently defends his African policy affinities as in AuxIndes's deeper interest. As the complaints persist, he juggles procurement budgets, brandishes the right of reprisal when promotion lists emerge, and threatens to replace the Republic's dysfunctional navy by "contracting out" surveillance of the coastal waters. As Guyane warns him, none of Masson's pugnacity helps resolve the hostility, and nothing he does can pacify the offended warriors. Upon resumption of domestic tranquility, the military institution has little else to do. The island faces no overt antagonist and the combat against cattle rustlers and meddlesome civilians falls within Philosophe's jealously guarded domain. Fisherman feels secure while those two missions remain distinct and mutually suspicious.

Nevertheless, any departure from custom provokes all manner of doubt about the presumptuous Fisherman—even extending to his choice of headquarters. Rather than follow his predecessor into the pretentious Art Nouveau "palace" bequeathed by the old governors, President Masson has installed his chancery in a modest two-story apartment building. He pays to transfer dispossessed occupants to alternative quarters and to convert condominium units into functioning administrative bureaus—plumbing and all. The new Presidency soon bears the nickname *Aquarium Lite*.

When they are not strictly promoting fisheries, the American expats frequent a lounge in the rear of the Presidency's second floor. Their windows give onto a building site owned by an amiable landlord who has interrupted construction at that site in deference to presidential proximity. At night the deserted work terrain is guarded by an ageless watchman swathed in tatters. This security agent's self-designed occupation is to manage a motley assortment of plastic wrappings that he collects in daylight from urban dumpsters and trash cans. When his watch begins at twilight, he rinses these bags under a water tap on the aborted construction site and pins them to dry on the bare rafters. Then he goes to sleep. By day, the guardian carries his dried sacks for sale to households and businesses. As he goes, he liberates new batches of soiled plastic from trash cans for the next night's round.

Weekends this same entrepreneur rents out a dozen *bidets*—portable versions of the basins used for intimate ablution.

Viewing such industry as a backyard lesson for their own mission, Cynthia Van Zan has inked a portrayal of Commissioner Wazimbwe reacting in pristine horror at its toxic implications. It amuses staff but fails to provoke action; free enterprise still commands respect in the AuxIndes establishment. Denis Guyane draws his own conclusions from this dubious operation in the presidential neighborhood. Presuming that the plastics recycler never bothers to pay taxes on his revenue, Guyane leaves a hint with the man's employer. The enterprising watchman is eventually dismissed, or probably reassigned, to conduct his trade less conspicuously.

On the Aquarium's other side, lies the main reason for Masson's choice of headquarters site—a wooded remnant dominated by tree-dwelling bats. Fisherman delights in functioning next to the town's final forest. The bats help console him for missing the voracious spiders adorning the windows outside his AuThon office. "High and dry where we are," he once remarked, "those great webs have become oceans of silk." While she shudders at the contradiction, Cynthia Van Zan understands the sentiment.

Now in his new office, the president speculates that his private messages might be conveyed at night by bat folk to the sea creatures he cultivates—and still exploits. "Not your business," he snaps when Denis Guyane questions this improbable claim. "Bats enjoy special powers, beyond your mundane imagination. Your literal-minded culture might benefit from reading our poets, as Olivier does. Even chiroptera know more about life than you've been taught."

Guyane has to gasp at the unaccustomed vehemence of Masson's reproach. He makes a mental note to consult the scholarly Kolona on reading AuxIndes poetry for clues into the chief executive's occult thinking. Then, embarking on one of his habitual pauses, Fisherman removes his horn-rims and gestures casually with them toward the office window. He appears to reassure his winged protégés that, like the web-queens outside his AuThon suite, their secrets remain safe with him.

As he grows into the job, the new president enlarges his dimensions of self-confidence. "Politics, like business, is essentially a zero-sum game," Masson professes to the Americans, "but governance relies on illusion. It must assure perception of advancement by all. Not easy to do, but I rely on your expertise in this as I did in the fisheries affair and our election campaign." As he speaks, he crosses his legs to show that even a head of state may still go without socks.

Fisherman proceeds, practicing for a new radio speech, which needs their advice. "We must hope to rebuild out from the vestiges of Bienportant's disastrous decades. Those remnants are poisonous, vicious. After so long in power, the Domino expected loyalty from townspeople and peasantry without realizing that his administration had forfeited its claim on them. Government had become the hostile, menacing stranger, worse than any exploitative corporation. Now we must build consensus, we transients in a resentful land. The sun shines on Africa but not on African government. I don't deny the legacy of African darkness; but we need to shed light on it."

"Oh?" probes Van Zan, "When was it ever dark?"

"Figure that out for yourself, or at least read Conrad. I'm only responsible for this island and for correcting the retrograde influence of my predecessor's fifteen years. That's what AuxIndiens can recall: deep, murky problems, in need of light. You two know how to focus, so you must help us communicate that we're here to satisfy their needs."

"Sure," responds Denis, "but they're going to demand more than a light bulb, even if it glances on some fresh filets in their kitchen."

"True, they need assurance that much else will arrive, and that a healthy community generates its own energy. Remember, I came out of the landed peasantry of this country. Cattle-raising got me more votes than the business pretensions that meant so much to the gentry."

"Okay," Cynthia says, switching to English when she needs to, "we used those identities for all they were worth in the election campaign. But having farmer forebears isn't going to pile meat and potatoes on every proverbial plate. What is it that we're supposed to light up?"

Here Masson pauses, translates in his head, then removes a shoe and looks inside it, as if in search of a reply. It comes as an oracular lecture. "National progress requires three assets: capital, technology, and markets; we have to find and aim them. So we begin with public health," he says to the bare foot. "Nutrition, sanitation, medical facilities, training are our first commitments, even if we have to borrow resources and services over some transitional period to supply our market. I have Daoud working with Dr. Chameau and university scientists on that combination—technology first, then the capital. After a few years, for one example, we should be able to turn the island's unique endowments into exportable medications."

"Fish oil, for instance?" suggests Guyane, almost facetiously.

"Why not? Nutrition must be coupled with diligent education. Once a new generation of healthy young people matures, they will be the engine of progress; then much else falls into place and budget resources can be siphoned into new sectors. A sustained, healthy population will demand investment in other basic needs—housing, transportation, clean water and air—even if we have to work patiently for them to show up. Beyond that there's transmissible solar, wind, and tidal energy—abundant here, exportable around the global South, given substantial time and technology. You know that's Bamiara's passion. And mine."

Then, Masson slips a shoe back onto his bare foot, adjourning the conference.

"So speaks the flying Fisherman," comments Denis to Cynthia as they leave the office, more or less aware of the inadequacy of their roles in an ambitious national process. "You and I come from a country endowed with capital, technology, and markets, and still we don't see the fruits distributed to everybody. Here, our patient angler hovers over the deep, waiting for the nets to fill."

"I see the hooks," she replies, "but not the bait."

CHAPTER 10

THE FLEET IN HARBOR

"Shouldn't tell you this," says Karamau in one of his large-ly gestural discourses with Guyane, "but you 'ave caught the president in an uncomfortable corner. Your girl's fishy stories, quite droll, make him look bad." He chuckles while ominously revealing awareness of the Americans' politicking. "But election's still not sewed up. Keep businessman's hands off public treasury; people don't trust traders."

"Meaning they only trust generals, or bishops, or maybe policemen?"

"It's a habit, tradition. Business is selfish. Politics not supposed to be. Your man needs something. Some disaster to fall his way. Maybe contrive it; ask your environment lady, the Diva. Otherwise you can't win—not against Nationals' formidable machine."

"Which you helped Bienportant build over the last twenty years," adds Denis. "The campaign is not my affair but I wander around and suspect they will find that crowning piece and use it against the incumbent."

"The 'smoking gun,' your popular phrase? Where look for that, if I might ask?"

Guyane understands the signal. "Various places may turn it up," he replies, "maybe famine in the South, maybe corruption along the East Ridge, but not on the West Coast, if you're probing for that."

"Ah, the West, impoverished province, charming burial sites, folkloric festivals, never a scandal. Unless it's also in diamonds."

"None found there, unfortunately," Denis says. "How about a goat scandal? Or maybe crooked disc-jockeying—Hannibal territory?"

"No. It's still clean. We appreciate the Masson lady's good sense; during municipal election; not picking on low-status family—my people from wretched hinterland. Might have backfired on her to go after us."

That was about the longest commentary Guyane can recall Karamau using in recent conversations, so he takes it as a veiled warning and changes the subject. He would prefer to discuss what he had been mentally replaying—the death of Masson's friend Spider on Babel Hill, and who gave the order to shoot. But this isn't the moment; nor could he show interest in the sinister prophet "Ishmael," Philosophe's nemesis. Instead, he asks whether permits sought by the Fisherman for peaceful rallies would be honored by police and judges without recourse to false pretexts. Karamau's assent—a mere nod—and his avoidance of any threat to expel the foreigners offer hope to Denis that the minister was weighing the possibility that Masson might win.

Bamiara advises the "incorruptible Fisherman" to clarify his platform, divulging as much as he needs without specificity that could incur legal jeopardy. Masson declares his intention to flatten the Domino's structure, replacing it with transparent government in the name of the Republic. His priorities will direct both national and "informal" resources to education, housing, and public health, conveying benefits to everybody, poor and . . . less poor.

True to his vocation, Masson's aim is not to uproot systems, or to imagine an artificial freedom for a still subordinate economy. He could not deny that AuxIndes is traversing a sequel to colonization, retaining a society of inherited classes and castes. But he argues that it must find its way as a nation among nations, in "a compromise with history," and a fulfillment of his late friend Spider's dream of autonomy in service. Explicitly how will have to be forged in social interaction.

At best, Masson's speeches avoid the usual pathways of cant—empty appeals to security and stability, rhetorical commitment to the hopes and aspirations of the populace, heartfelt pledges of service for social welfare. When accused of failing the test of patriotism, he contrasts the benefits of a billion-euro donation of food against the regime's waste of resources in palatial showcases for the island establishment.

The four other candidates—decent fellows all—are in the contest without expectation of victory. If both Bienportant and Masson should fall short of the fifty-percent majority, they are ready nonetheless to sell their respective voter fractions to the higher bidder in a second-round faceoff. Their object is to secure personal advantage toward a cabinet portfolio or other appointment, and/or to deflect public attention toward their own local constituencies.

Frequently in candidate debates, Domino has to extricate himself from public relations quandaries as all five opponents attack from one angle or another. The Fisherman claims to know exactly how much wealth every poached animal, gold or sapphire nugget, or mahogany log has brought the president in cash when trafficked through transnational smugglers. The number is usually a guess, but Domino himself has never counted the pennies; the other candidates nod as if they too had confirmed the improvised statistics.

"Men, all men," comments Solange Seriel. "Cram one woman candidate into the mash and you'd see the flesh fly." Anya Wazimbwe nods in rueful assent.

As it is, so much rhetorical weight has been stacked against Bienportant that the relatively independent media gradually abandon their habitual "both-sidesism." One outlet after another expounds on the antagonists' case, running risks of retaliation from Domino's vindictive party machinery—itself a sign of culpability.

Slight, blue-suited, with his lid of black hair above keen features and sharp eyes (with or without the horn-rims), Fisherman provides contrast to the incumbent's military—if no longer regal—bearing. He accuses Bienportant of pandering to foreign cronies, many of them also in uniform. These never-named "big bellies" are glad to accept Domino as a host for their shell companies and properties, for laundering reputations, and sheltering mistresses. National brass commit the same improprieties, Masson asserts, only more discreetly.

While the island's generals rage among themselves, he seems to enjoy exposure of their complicity. They would not forget.

What comes next, Fisherman in a debate asks Bienportant—the bewitching stigma of terrorism or the perils of a changing climate? "Your gerontocracy is under the illusion that being an island assures the population that it's protected," he charges. "Face reality. Our shores want buttressing against the angry sea. Our forests cringe before the torches of the peasantry seeking fresh turf for crops. A military man like you should see how vulnerable we are to foreign penetration, both physical and electronic. Some invaders reside here, some shoot from afar, most of them cross our territory between continents, but always at our expense."

"AuxIndes's forces are ever on the alert," answers the president. "They are trained to identify terrorists, even when the intruders are *your* foreign friends."

"Your army calls everything terrorism when it's usually just somebody from somewhere else—or at worst, primitive crime. What we need against the ominous climate is not an air force but a protected source of energy and sturdy housing. What we need against criminals is not a tank brigade, but a functional justice system. Give Minister Karamau the tools you lavish on the army and demand decisive leadership from him and from the judges."

The gesture toward Philosophe is intentional; but disrespect for the military would come home to roost.

"What?" Domino turns the tables. "Haven't we heard you complaining hysterically about police brutality?"

"Not me," says Fisherman innocently. "I did not run for mayor. Still, in that case, we had a chance for a municipal government that reflected our values as a people, a culture. We lost. Now we have that chance for an entire nation."

"Your chance," retorts the Domino, "is to convert the entire nation into a mass of customers for your profits."

"Alas for my sake, that's not likely!" cries Masson, "but if it were, at least the nation would be exercising a choice—to buy or not to buy—not simply surrendering to official embezzlement. The people can reject victimization only through this election."

"Yes, because this election will vindicate the benefits bestowed by my administration."

"What benefits? This is the first government in national history," Masson charges, "where half the civil servants wish the other half weren't there. And it's reciprocal: the other half cancels what the first half does. The one is on the take and thrives while the other, in envy, can't get at it. Most of them never come to work anyway. Truth is that neither faction is paid enough to stay honest, let alone cooperate with one another. But maybe their polarized stalemate is the best we simple citizens can ask of you."

"You have invented all this to promote your sleazy business dealings, you and your nostalgic band of stragglers," countered the incumbent, stentorian in his rugged, bulky manliness. The Domino has turned gray, but his official bearing remains gladiatorial. His coaching from Vinaigrette allows him to assail AuThon as exemplary of crooked capitalism without offending the island's grand families whose respectability depends on their wealth. "Your greedy affairs have taught you nothing about governance."

"What I've learned about governance in business," answers the Fisherman, "is that you have to pay your people enough if you want them to produce. Otherwise those who can will steal from you, and the rest will just refuse to work. It's exactly that in your collapsing machinery."

"That's nonsense," replies the president. "You can't prove any of it."

"I can, but I won't have to," answers Masson. "I'll just promise civil servants a decent wage for honest work, with deference to their union (you might recall that they have one), and they will help vote you out. They might even walk out on you before they vote."

"Then just see what a financial pickle you'll have put yourself into," tosses the Domino, with a forced chuckle.

"If so, my pickle will have come too late for you to nibble. Or for your few stragglers who will remain only to be able to steal from the rest of us."

"So, if those subordinates are loyal to me, they certainly won't vote for you."

"True, but I can run this apparatus with half of your gang against me. The other half is with the people, and that gives me a real majority."

At times, the incumbent party accuses AuThon of endangering coastal areas by building where ocean incursions and intense storms threaten livelihoods. President Bienportant has indeed discovered the phenomenon of climate change, along with the seafood farm project; for him the two are now synonymous.

In campaign declarations, Masson's staff defends his farming and other projects, despite the financial losses he is incurring while they remain suspended for the election. When operating, they claim, his enterprises were economically embedded in their natural environments, plunged into self-cleaning and nutritious waters, planned through consultation with residential communities eager for the employment and technology they bring. The campaign repeats Anya Wazimbwe's lessons about care for the living shoreline, use of resilient construction materials, emergency and health services for staff and families, and adequate communication with the public.

Engaged in debate without his habitual pause, Fisherman sardonically offers his opponent a share of the collateral crop of kelp that the "ex-president" might put in his salads. "Have your fill unless we need the seaweed to clean the waters, or to provide fish feed for the farm. You can have what's left."

General Bienportant habitually changes the subject. Claiming credit for doubling the number of island youth, he predicts the imminence of economic success by natural pressures from a rising energetic population. The populace need only wait for growth to assert its demands on the economy. Masson nevertheless considers growth as insufficient, contending that development does not depend on rising birth rates. "Rather, after neglect of their education, health, and housing, even bright kids will be unable to get beyond semi-literate foraging at the bottom of an inert labor market. You pretend that prosperity can come naturally, because you are unwilling to invest in progressive commitments. So after all these years, where can anyone find that development?"

Responding as deftly as he could, the embattled Domino attacks Masson's business success—built, he charges, on the sweat and savings of working people. "You call for honest governance, without honoring that virtue. If you are not officially corrupt, at least you are commercially untrustworthy," he argues, "and now you are temporarily abusing your business, your money, to grab power."

"While you abuse power permanently to protect *your* money," the Fisherman retorts. "You have become so rich that you need only hope to last long enough to find some medical excuse for leaving the country—to enjoy your illegal acquisitions in a comfortable climate. I'll help you do just that, if the tiger lets you off its back."

With that, the peaceable fleet sails in. The campaign prospers, denouncing various traces of incompetence and malfeasance. Fisherman's lectures on sleaze reach myriad ears in the electorate.

"Corruption," he contends, "is a mode of resource allocation in an unequal society, but it's an *unjust* mode of resource allocation, for the benefit of a few privileged takers. This administration refuses to pay civil servants adequately, so that those who enjoy some form of leverage—policemen, tax collectors, permit agents, hospital officials—take what they can gouge from the vulnerable public, wherever they can lay hands on others' resources."

Masson's dispersed business contacts allow the campaign to function in both towns and provinces without benefit of an organized political party. "No machine needed," Fisherman and his surrogates boast, "Let the good news flow." Media attention suffices. Merchants, labor unions, and teachers help recruit advocates and poll watchers in the election districts. Resident diplomatic missions keep an uneasy silence on the contest, in spite of appeals from cabinet ministries and spokespeople for endorsement of the incumbency. The capital's grapevine interprets ambassadorial reticence as a sign of international disdain for the notoriously acquisitive establishment.

Throughout the campaign, Van Zan could taste the savory combination of vinegar and oil. "Just hope it's not the wrong source for oil," she mutters to herself.

Young AuxIndiens who vote in their provinces also turn in Fisherman's direction. Some of the urban bands whose misogyny had recently tormented Giselle Masson and her sisters eventually forgive their own errors and join the new opposition. From the challenger, they hear promises of honest budgeting for schools, technical training, scholarships, and health care; many believe Masson capable of bringing these changes into reality. "Because he's male," says Anya Wazimbwe, quietly.

Not unexpectedly, there is resistance to the Fisherman's message. The National Party uses its formidable organization, discipline, and resources to keep bureaucrats and law-and-order citizens in line against the neophyte. Adherents of the status quo, including the military establishment, fear both capitalist aggrandizement and political instability at the hands of an entrepreneur. West Coast students confront Masson at a campus rally; they object to his coastal development projects: "Must you industrialize this area? Tear up and pollute the beautiful earth with no concern for sustainability?"

"In America I visited southwestern Louisiana," replies Masson, "and saw what harm polluters and cynical exploiters do without effective government to control them. In AuxIndes, the population grows and makes demands on the economy. The current masters of that economy respond not to you, but to their own interests without regard for you. Our national product goes to the powerful, not to the natural world or to those who share it. We are taking a different approach; we swim with the fish of the sea, breathe among the creatures of this island. We can listen to you, answer your needs, together with theirs."

As the first-round election nears, the opposition campaigns receive a fortuitous boost—perhaps the very break whimsied by Philosophe in his conversation with Guyane. It comes in a widely publicized shipwreck off the island's eastern shore. The injured vessel has been chartered from a Bienportant sponsor by a friendly export broker. Its cargo includes a wealth of legally protected timber as well as animal species, all meretriciously licensed for export without accurate inventory or other mandatory detail. Police search the grounded ship's manifests and their findings leak through the wreckage.

Without risking specific accusations, even the pro-regime press has to acknowledge some irregularity in the incident—a deviant routing of permits and transportation, and some apparent fingerprints of authorizing officials.

Cynthia's cartoon of the scandal reaches a record number of respondents in the expanding media world of energized voters. Even in the less plugged-in hinterlands people promptly learn of it ("birds digest well-informed sardines and broadcast important news," she observes), and time runs out on the regime.

On election day, well ahead of the seasonal rains, the polls open to virtually all constituencies, urban bus riders as well as rural trekkers on the dusty roadways. Some 18,000 polling sites provide access to the registered population, at an average rate of 500 voters per station. On this holiday, with musicians to entertain them and cheap food and drink along the way, citizens flood neighborhood political centers.

The electoral process is conducted under international scrutiny. On entering, voters flourish an identification card to the police officer assigned to maintain order at the poll; each voter has a stamp imposed on one hand to prevent the "frequent franchise" tacitly recommended by some campaigns. Vote-casting is simple, without requiring literacy. Holding a colored ballot bearing the photograph and logo of all six presidential candidates, the voter moves behind a dark curtain to mark one box on the ballot, then deposits it into a slot that closes immediately thereafter. The slot reopens once for each subsequent voter.

Polls close only after all have passed through the process. Then the ballot receptacle is opened, unmarked or multiple-marked ballots move into a rejection pile, and the remaining votes are counted by a trio of officials in the presence of a delegate from each campaign.

The electoral count is efficient, without claiming to be high tech; the presiding official chooses one ballot at a time, flourishes it for others to see, and announces the anonymous voter's choice aloud; a second agent adds a checkmark beside the candidate's name on a white board in plain sight; a third officer enters the vote in a digital file. After all ballots have been tallied, the marks are counted and each campaign's representative signs the digital tally. These local packets are then sealed and conveyed to Interior for tabulation.

To observe the process, Van Zan and Guyane split up discreetly, avoiding conspicuous presence at polling places. A labor-intensive enterprise, but it functions, observes Cynthia when she and Denis meet late that night to exchange impressions. She had chosen to witness the vote at a station in a notoriously pro-Domino district. Her sketchbook is filled with illustrations of the lineup, a confusion of elderly or bewildered voters, and the accounting ritual surrounded by avid campaign workers. Denis took notes at a trio of more pluralistic sites where pollworkers watched the clock anxiously, albeit without disruption of a remarkably serious ceremony. He is almost disappointed over the day's tranquility.

The plurality of candidates in the lists virtually preclude an absolute majority for any of them. Incumbent Bienportant had expected to finish first; he is prepared for a runoff election within two weeks against any second-place candidate. Domino counts on that second round to apply administrative leverage on a limited number of coopted voters. That has worked before, but it took money and entailed other risks.

This time, it doesn't suffice. Despite the informality of Masson's campaign, without organized party or coalition allies, when the final tallies come in, Fisherman maintains an official plurality "dangerously close" to 50 percent. Yet he is not quite there, according to Karamau's ministry: what about 48.5%? Bienportant comes in second with less than 40 percent.

After announcing the date for a runoff between the president and his leading antagonist, Philosophe excludes himself from further participation in the public scene. He does not respond to Masson's demand for an independent recount of votes—a clear indication to those who sought one that the original election had in fact delivered a decisive majority for the challenger; that Karamau was hedging his bets.

Then the Fisherman makes his second existential decision without consultation; flourishing his eyeglasses on television, he declares himself a majority winner, refuses to participate in a superfluous second campaign, calls for a general strike in the towns, and summons his partisans into the streets. Bureaucratic Indesville is to model "democracy" as though a Masson were indeed at City Hall.

For its part the army, sworn to shun "politics," remains nervously in its barracks. Confused generals agree to intervene only if national security were in jeopardy; it isn't, yet. But an urban concentration of civil servants heeds the strike call. One by one, ministries and agencies close doors as their staff vows to boycott a runoff election. At the end of a week, the administration begins to reopen, but under surrogate authority—not by ministers or party managers, but by hitherto under-rewarded surrogates.

While Mayor Karamau blusters in rappese, his uncle agrees to a compromise: Philosophe orders a recount. Moreover, the minister declines to unleash his police force against legal demonstrations. Some incumbent functionaries rush northward to join the beleaguered Domino in his distant refuge. There they are protected by special police units, commanded by none other than the same Antoine Karamau.

"The juggler king, showing his true mix of colors," comments Wazimbwe. Philosophe is not among either the rejectionists or the self-expatriates. He has decided that he will survive any circumstance, and thus offers his services loyally to the new chief of state. "Scientists tell us," comments Anya, "that every action must beget a reaction, which explains why every initiative of ours evokes an emission of flatulence from Antoine."

"But where does he think he's sitting now," asks Olivier Kolona, "on his helicopter or the General's iron horse?"

"Horse? tiger? pussycat? what's the difference?" responds Wazimbwe. "He'll fart his way out no matter what's under him." Even she is unaware that the resilient Philosophe has been retaining contact with Masson through his confidant and confessor, Father Robinette. Together they agree on a way to break the stalemate without recourse to violence. "To ensure domestic tranquillity," Karamau asks the High Court to preside over a recount of ballots as demanded by the challenger, but this time under joint scrutiny by a select forum of denominational leaders and the diplomatic corps. To defend AuxIndes's international reputation (and to avoid responsibility for the consequences), the justices, all Domino appointees, approve the supervision of willing ambassadors and clergy over the Interior Ministry's laborious review of precinct talleys.

"Philosophe on top," mutters Benjamin Bamiara, "where he's always been. Somebody ought to go up the hill to see if he's riding Spider's horse."

"Poor beast," says Wazimbwe, "underneath Antoine the cow-herd."

When the recount emerges, it conveys a clear majority for Masson, including regions hitherto dominated by the National Party's champion. The diplomatic and clerical observers ignore the incumbent's demand for supplemental recounts. Faced by this consensus, Karamau arranges for an accommodating embassy to invite outgoing President Bienportant to a medical "vacation," in consideration of his extended age and diligent service.

Several days before his inauguration, Fisherman pledges unfettered passage to all who wish to use the Republic's passport for immediate departure. Philosophe complies. Political emigrants are entitled to retain AuxIndes citizenship and its privileges while in exile, but without immunity from prosecution for any illegalities committed during their term of service.

Nonetheless, the deposed Chief of Staff Tsieroro urges recalcitrant loyalists to organize militias and strive to restore Bienportant's apparatus. While these tories are gathering behind barricades in their redoubts, Domino and several officials quietly dismount from the proverbial tiger at a military airfield; they never feel its bite. A hired aircraft lifts the ousted leaders and families to safety in absentia. From there they disburse, and the former president cheers his partisans onward.

Philosophe is not among either the rejectionists or the self-expatriates. He has decided that he will survive any circumstance, and thus offers his services loyally to the new chief of state. "Scientists tell us," comments Anya, "that every action must beget a reaction, which explains why every initiative of ours evokes an emission of flatulence from Antoine."

"But where does he think he's sitting now," asks Olivier Kolona, "on his helicopter or the General's iron horse?"

"Horse? tiger? pussycat? what's the difference?" responds Wazimbwe. "He'll fart his way out no matter what's under him." Then the Diva offers her services to the mercurial Zaphyra, Masson's designated Minister of Defense. "Fisherman needs an army to clean up the bush resistance, and if he doesn't get regular troops now, it'll have to be with amazons," she exclaims. "Wield your black belt, Thérèse. Just the battle *Maman* Sophie has been expecting!"

Cynthia Van Zan blinks in astonishment at this war cry from an unexpected voice; was it mere bravado from Anya or her echo of a call to arms from Vinaigrette?

Discomfited by such belligerence, Denis Guyane urges more peaceful resolution, taking advantage of Karamau's unexpected good offices. But women cohorts have their own answer—as he learns directly from Thérèse Zaphyra. As he opens his apartment door that evening, he is tackled from behind by this habitually quiet martial artist; with a python's grip she drags him against a sofa. "Now it's on," mutters La Brise in his ear, "Figure how it feels when BullyBoy goes after Little Bo-Peep. We need your undivided attention. How's this for a start?"

Even before he could decide to surrender, Thérèse has pressed her tunic firmly over his astonishment and held his shoulders under control. An irresistible force pries his trousers down and joins herself onto his body.

After releasing him, La Brise removes keys from his pocket, locks the apartment door, returns the keys, and hands him his trousers with a radiant smile. "Just don't tell Solange," Thérèse whispers, as she clamps on him again, more tenderly. "She'd bill me for this. I know you've done wonders for her thighs."

"Uh huh," Denis grunts in assent. Never before, not even in Brooklyn, had he enjoyed such violence.

CHAPTER 11

SILHOUETTES IN THE NIGHT

Claude De Justesse's family did not own the entire mini-island off AuxIndes's north coast; they merely behaved as if they did. Theirs was the last property remaining on it.

Since before living memory, the tiny exclave had been attached by land bridge to Grande Plage peninsula, which has recently grown into AuxIndes's most fashionable vacation resort. As hotels proliferated on Grande Plage, with its harbor, airport, and football stadium, the Bienportant government decided to eliminate the bridge to its islet appendage, now called Plage Mineure. Dredging that channel had allowed close passage around the cape by pleasure boats and small freighters using the harbor.

"This cut will also promote the interest of your seafood industry," Roger Masson was mendaciously assured when he first visited Grande Plage. He promptly calculated the toll to be taken by erosion: disappearance of farming and fishing on both sides of the strait.

Emergence of Grande Plage as a Mecca for foreign vacationers also made its native forest superfluous. Old shade-giving mangoes yielded to an invasion of decorative palms that provide more picturesque, if less practical, coverage. Soon, most of the peninsula's human residents followed suit. Rather than modernize their way of life on Grande Plage, watermen and farmers gradually vanished, yielding place to hospitality and commercial staff whose main business was to welcome tourists.

The ancient forests surrendered stubbornly; however, they maintained a literally underground root communication system, so the remaining old folks said, that would eventually conspire in revenge.

While development ensured the destiny of Grande Plage through hotels, piers, and open-air festivities, the amputated islet, Plage Mineure, was left with no economy. Its Indigenous people withdrew their anachronistic selves entirely, to languish elsewhere and perhaps, like the mangoes, to prepare their own vengeance.

The alienated little exclave remained forlorn until its final proprietor, the Frenchman Claude De Justesse, finished appropriating what was left of it. An established Indesville entrepreneur, De Justesse had kept a beach cottage on the islet for weekends during earlier times while Grande Plage (where he also owned property) was growing into a paradise for visitors. After the land bridge disappeared, but before all of Plage Mineure would succumb to erosion, De Justesse seized his opportunity to become the islet's suzerain. He paid pittances for sites whose flimsy dwellings, left to the mercy of waves and wind, were falling seriatim into the sea.

A backer of Bienportant and Karamau, the islet proprietor obtained government help to secure his dominion through heavy deposits of riprap and bulkhead that protected its sandy littoral. He installed a formidable seawall along Plage Mineure's shore facing Grande Plage to shield his landing pier—and his privacy—against intrusions from vacationers. To develop this domain, De Justesse dug for fresh water and contracted electric power from the mainland; he installed modern radio and mobile-phone networks to defy a climate periodically punctuated by cyclones.

To accommodate his selected guests, De Justesse's construction firm built facilities on tracts well back from the raging ocean. At the center of the islet, it erected a wooden castle for him, encased by veranda and fringed by a new skirt of eucalyptus—reminding the land sarcastically of its vanishing forest endowment.

In time, behind the jetty and its gate lay a principality, *La Justesse*, financed by Claude's entertainment business and its lucrative spin-off into the construction trade.

Well before his presidential election, Fisherman Masson visited Grande Plage as Claude De Justesse's guest. He had been invited to consider mounting a refrigeration plant within the Frenchman's complex on the main peninsula. There the De Justesse property already included a pleasure-boat wharf adjoining a floating bandstand that featured, among other acts, the jazz quartet, *Les Silhouettes*, especially its piano prodigy, Marty Bondoo.

After a brief inspection, Roger Masson decided against trying to pack shrimp in that percolating atmosphere.

By the time Fisherman assumed the national presidency, De Justesse Senior was in sedate retirement. His enterprises were managed by his sons, Claude Jr. and Jean-Michel, both of them Silhouette musicians, both diligent stewards of their father's estate. When Plage Mineure was ready, the family plane began ferrying guests and supplies from Indesville into Grande Plage airport, from where they were shuttled by cart and launch to accommodations on Plage Mineure, now a private islet. Weekends brought to this satellite a diverse coterie of couples and solitaries—colleagues, compatriots, AuxIndiens as well as international personalities. They came to frolic in private sands, bounce through animated waves, flick missiles on tennis and badminton courts, buzz through jazz concerts, and enjoy a plethora of lobster tails, spiced legumes, and chardonnays on the porches of La Justesse.

Most guests paid the owner for their sojourn; others shared expenses or performed for their overnights; some came for the presumed pleasure of their company. The social temperature was relaxed. Much intimacy found its way to the spare, airy bedrooms. A tiny private zoo was regularly tended by a French veterinarian named Andrej Sokolsky, who also performed on drums with the Silhouettes. The estate's meals, maintenance, housekeeping, and transportation—by boat, van, and golf cart—were diligently managed by Abdou and Aïsa Mahmoud and their extended family; they were the islet's sole year-round residents. All visitors, AuxIndiens and foreigners alike, compensated the Mahmouds liberally.

She feels him watch inquisitively as she enters the office that initial Monday morning. Late, not her habit. Her right hand rises to touch her hair, feeling the bright streak. Yes, she could tell him.

"They have this place on an island," Cynthia says, booting up her screens. "De Justesse, I mean. You know them, Denis; that downtown music shop? They flew me out there and back for the weekend. Big house, swimming pool, zoo. Private retreat. Tiny bit of land, though. They bring people through the beach town, Grande Plage. Don't seem to be married. No wife in sight. Just local staff."

Preoccupied with the keyboard, Van Zan speaks in sporadic verbal bites, to ward off interruptions. She retouches her hair nervously. That's not her habit, either; Cynthia Van Zan's presence usually defines the environment. This time something was working on her.

Juggling her cursor, Cynthia resumes. "Now where's that darned island?"

"Where? Underneath us, maybe? We live on an island here."

"Not this one."

"What is this one? Did he give it a name, De Justesse? Called it after himself?"

"No, it's kind of a satellite to Grande Plage," she says. "I never heard it explained clearly. They speak so fast, and I don't always listen."

"Yeah, they do," he scoffed. "You'll catch on. *Plage* is French for beach. You're sure they were talking to you in French?"

"Of course. And you don't have to be so . . . *mesquin*."

"Right word. Sorry. Did you have a good time on Little Plage?"

"Fine time, less stress than around here. Okay, it's called Plage Mineure. They leave me alone to work, as a real *artiste*."

Guyane does know Cynthia's weekend hosts, casually—not the father, but the sons. The younger De Justesse, Jean-Michel, runs the construction company but prefers to think of himself as Miles Davis's successor on the horn. His older brother, saxophonist Claude, Jr., is an exporter of traditional instruments, wool rugs, decorative paper, and other crafts. All three De Justesses frequent obscure edges of the political class like other resident expatriates, but are not known as activists for or against the Fisherman president.

A big house on the small island, a private airplane, a swimming pool (why need that when you're on a beach?) betoken considerable success for that family. But what, Denis wonders, explains the invitation to Cynthia? Although she invariably attracts attention, the laconic Van Zan doesn't flaunt her exotic gifts openly. She shuns sporting life, doesn't "join in," and is unlikely to encourage weekend carnality. Moreover, her evolving language capacity hardly promises much conversational glitter to sophisticated Frenchmen.

Given these constraints, Denis decides not to expect many repetitions of Cynthia's weekend hospitality at Plage Mineure.

He is surprised at how relieved that conclusion makes him. Guyane quietly supposes that only he and Masson recognize Van Zan's obsession with the sea. Cynthia's positive response to a retreat on Plage Mineure suggests a breakthrough in mood, an avenue of diversion that she seemed to need, so distant from the blare of New York and the doldrums of Indesville. "I do enjoy the weekends," she admits after returning from her third, or perhaps fourth sojourn. "Very comfortable, good food, but mainly because they consult me about music for the quartet and they respect my need to work whenever I want to."

"Aw . . ."

"You think I'm just saying that to throw you off, but when they aren't trying out new jazz licks—and Marty is pretty good at his keyboard—I have time for myself in my own cabana on the beach."

"Jazz, is it? Doesn't he—*they* want you . . . to maybe dance for them, or some such practical function?"

"Stop being nasty, Denis Guyane. You're glaring at me because you know I'm missing some sleep, but not . . ."

"I wasn't glaring, Cynthia. Anyway, it's none of my business, unless of course you got inspired enough on that beach to neglect the health animation project."

"Almost finished it, actually. I got the fish-oil message into it with a logo that Mr. Masson should appreciate." Instinctively, Guyane knew that would be true.

So, during Roger Masson's inaugural year as president, Van Zan becomes an accustomed visitor to La Justesse. She is flown in privately on Fridays and returned to the city on Monday mornings. The setting works for her; she has the ocean for intimacy, pronouncing its slow-paced lessons in resilience. She poses no bother for the human habitués, most of them professionals adept at dancing, music, sports, and attractive companions; she can avoid those who use the beach for fancy business deals or, with more proficiency, for trysts in the tides of Justesse.

Despite her linguistic imperfection, Cynthia is readily accepted by the widower host and especially by his musician sons. She provides American authenticity for the Indigenous pianist Bondoo, with his swing-to-bop flair reminiscent of Erroll Garner's *Concert by the Sea*. But her most zealous admirer is the fourth Silhouette—the Franco-Polish animal doctor who keeps both the menagerie and his drum set at Plage Mineure. When he has an opportunity, Andrej Sokolsky's courtly accents spiral into Cynthia's ear like the hum of a soft seashell.

She is nonetheless an odd choice, thinks old Claude, for this extended sequence of weekends. The senior De Justesse has no objection to Cynthia's race or nationality. Once an avid musician himself, he enjoys listening to her voice and admires her rare, dazzling smile.

The islet tends to take on a new ambient glow when she appears for a weekend there. The girl evidently enjoys La Justesse, a platform to show her café-au-lait complexion at its most admirable. And the ocean responds, seeming to stoke her flair for graphic figuration—innocent enough, in Claude's opinion.

Yet, Van Zan is a curious regular, considering how other women behave toward his sons—one unmarried, the other enjoying separation from his Parisian wife. True, the musicians gain when she adapts local idioms into American jazz beats. They protect her privacy and respect her style, and Dr. Sokolsky swears love for her. Still, thinks Claude, speaking little English, and needing less, they perhaps tend to over-rely on Cynthia's charm and the quality of her French.

More intriguing to the old man is Van Zan's relationship with the current national leadership. She still works within the president's industries, alongside the discreet Benjamin Bamiara and the formidable Wazimbwe. Does she also frequent the president now that he's theoretically separated from the business? Claude had hoped to learn the answer by evoking current politics with her, but Cynthia shows little interest in such matters.

"Knowing your tendency to intrusive buggery," Van Zan says to Guyane after the first month of weekends, "I've brought some studies on what surrounds me out there. The screen doesn't do complete justice to that white beach, rocky outcrops, a seething volcano, pirogues decorated for battle against the demons of the deep . . ."

"I get it," he remarks while several dozen images follow on Cynthia's monitor, most of them in fresh flashes of style. "And I can see how you came to terms with the health promotion project. Did you bring the originals for us?"

Van Zan admits with a touch of embarrassment that the renderings had been borrowed for his own pleasure by the drummer-veterinarian who failed to return them in time. "Andrej admires my work," she adds, "claims to have seen a lot of good drawing in his college years; always preferred the women artists in France. Said he wants to marry me. But I don't think he was serious." She again touches her hair and returns to the screen that lights up for her.

"Ah, a veterinarian lover of the arts!" chants Guyane. "I hear the drumbeat already. champagne and pigs' knuckles, seagulls singing, codfish dell'arte will do it every time. Up with public health! Next you'll produce a rhythmic portfolio on cows and chickens and have your percussive vet right where he wants to be."

Van Zan merely sneers. Actually, she fears Dr. Sokolsky is quite earnest. It was he who had insisted on including Cynthia in successive weekend parties at La Justesse, and to try her out as a singer with the quartet.

"It's goats, actually," she mutters as she emphatically closes her monitor. "Not cattle. That's what they are really into—angoras."

She waves Denis out of her office before he could try mixing the metaphor. But he suspects where that datum will lead.

Late one Monday morning, the unraveling begins. Van Zan looks no worse (or better) than on previous Mondays after her private weekends on the islet. The bold streak in her hair luminous as always, Cynthia wafts into his office, a mild breeze at her back. "Know you were at Saturday night's concert downtown," she says, with a tinge of weariness in her voice. "Thanks for coming. So what did you think of the Silhouettes?"

He reflects for a moment. "Well, the art critic in me thought everybody looked good—well outlined, etched in chiaroscuro, very theatrical your Silhouettes. I suspect you had a say about that backlighting."

Cynthia shrugs. "It goes with the name," she says dryly. "But I'm really asking about the music."

"Ah, that. Don't you still consider me tone-deaf? In any case, the visuals are easier to praise. All right. The sound came off as a bit . . . derivative; too much listening to the standards, except for those sudden keyboard riffs. But how did you know I was there? With all that glare, I doubt much of the audience could have been visible."

"Doubt not," she replies. "Vinaigrette saw you from backstage. She sees in the dark."

"Oh, and she recognized me, although we've never met?"

"That wouldn't deter Sophie."

"And yourself? The lighting didn't reveal your profile. Where were you exactly? Backstage? Or curled seductively inside Sokolsky's snare drum?"

"No, silly, but you're close. I was not supposed to be seen, so they sat me behind Marty's piano. I sang on mike since Norinne was sick and couldn't utter a note. She mouthed while I voiced her songs."

"Oh, I knew that piano was sounding pretty warm. Now I see why. The best piece was the "Summertime" rendition of that French Christmas carol."

"Yeah, "Oh Holy Night." Hard to bring off in mid-July here; especially with lyrics in Creole."

"Creole! That's what you were singing? How . . . ?"

"Not so easy, but with Marty's guidance and Norinne to correct me, I couldn't do much worse than those opera stars handling Dvorak or Mussorgsky in original languages."

Denis has a sudden image of Cynthia as the mercurial Cleopatra pledging love to Marc Antony in Latin, not her own language. "Actually, Bondoo shows himself the real musician in the bunch. Without him . . ."

"I know," she admits. "In reality, four Silhouettes are there to surround Marty's keyboard; an AuxIndien with ten fingers born into jazz, plus three Europeans and an American trying to fit in."

"Norinne is American?" he asks with mock incredulity.

"No," she counters soberly. "It's me. That's why I'm asking you. Listen now. The De Justesses and Marty—and Andrej—want me to join their upcoming Paris tour."

"Oh ho! Paris, is it? I'm impressed. So you have to come out from behind Bondoo's admirable piano and . . ."

"And what?"

"And show what you've got, of course. It's about time. If you had done that in L.A. you'd have nailed your screen test and we'd never have come out here to win elections."

"That's pushing it, Denis, but you're on track. I need your help with Bamiara and Fisherman. Before he switched to being president, Roger did promise us some vacation time; do you recall that?"

"Vaguely." It was true. The past five years have diverted and absorbed them so copiously that they hadn't thought of asking for much release from service to the fisheries or the campaign. Her weekends at La Justesse serve mainly to recharge professional batteries—as well as a veterinarian's libido in the bargain, he thinks, without uttering a word.

"Well," she continues, "the Silhouette's Paris gig comes up in six weeks, and we're going to rehearse with Angela down at her hotel to get in the groove, if we can find one. I need you to persuade the Peasant and the president to let me off for a while."

"Benjamin's no obstacle, but Fisherman? He's never let anybody out for so long since I've known him," admits Guyane. "Couldn't you promise him some sort of diplomatic project to work on in France—while you're conquering St. Germain des Près on the side?"

"Sure," says Cynthia, with a dazzling smile. "I could, like, get UNESCO to register those tombs around the fish farm as historical sites, or some such thing."

"Superb! Plus maybe seduce the French defense establishment on the side; they're famous for marching to American jazz singers who come with their own drummers."

"It'll be good to get away from you for a while," she says, no longer smiling, "while you still have sex in the head. Please work on Fisherman and Benjamin. Tell them I'll be back in two months."

Masson does not exactly embrace the idea. While still anchoring his administration, Fisherman needs, or thinks he does, illustrative proofs of its virtues, and she's the best illustrator for those assets. But he relents in order to be fair to Cynthia. Moreover, perhaps the Silhouettes' Paris concert will help promote AuxIndes tourism. Even the idea that Van Zan might get international recognition for the West Coast tombs appeals to him—as a gesture to Philosophe who, despite his renewal as Interior Minister, is being anything but cooperative in the new administration.

"His birthright," comments Anya Wazimbwe, still shuddering whenever she refers to the insidious Karamau. "Conceived under a truculent rock. If he can't play president, nobody can."

❀ ❀ ❀

The Paris concerts came and went, with some favorable attention to Marty Bondoo's piano, nothing more than that for the Silhouettes. Then a month or more passes, the European musicians have returned to serenade the island, but with no sign of Cynthia—except for a few cryptic postcards addressed to "President M. and Team" at the Fishery. Then even they stop coming. Guyane has no answer to inquiries about the artist who had proposed a mere two-month leave. Paris working a spell, even on the invulnerable Van Zan?

One evening, at an otherwise tedious reception for lower-rung dignitaries, the veterinarian Sokolsky approaches him with a conspiratorial air. He towers gauntly above the drinkers, casting shade downward on Denis's awkward juggle of an anchovy wrap.

"Monsieur Guyane," he begins, "What should we do without . . . without *Saintée*?"

"Saintée? You're asking me about holiness? Or the *Santé hospital? or the prison*? Something to do with your job?"

"Of course not," says Sokolsky with impatience. "You know who I mean. Please don't shrug it off. I'm in love with that woman, and besides we—the Justesses that is—don't know how to keep contact with your boss while she's not here to transmit their messages."

"Wait, Doctor!" Denis interjects. "If you're referring to my colleague Ms. Van Zan, whom we call CYN-THI-A, she never pretended to be a saint, and I don't recall that she reported to Mr. Masson for your friends. All I know is that she went to France with the band. As you say, she hasn't returned."

"Right," says Sokolsky. "Too bad. Painful. And dangerous for your president. We thought she was interceding for us with him. That mohair mill? And then the break with Karamau and his mercenaries."

"What break?" Guyane waits, but receives no answer. He has heard rumors of Philosophe's alleged courtship of certain military personalities, but nothing explicit. The veterinarian returns to his subject.

"I feel partly responsible for her . . . her delay in returning. You see I asked her, several times in Europe, to marry me. She refused—gently, but devastatingly for me."

"Sorry about that."

"I think she may be waiting for you, Guyane, wherever she is. Don't laugh, please. You are important to her. And because there is that other thing. Things that you and your boss may not know enough about. The De Justesses wanted Masson to be informed, but without an official channel, they . . . well, they told Saintée—*Sainthi-ah*—about it when she visited Plage Mineure. She seemed to be writing it down, in English. Now . . ."

"Really?" interjects Denis, truly bewildered. "Perhaps she was telling the president whatever your friends wanted him to know. I've not been involved, I can assure you, and . . ."

"Well, your CIA should find somebody else, then, and soon," urges the veterinarian, "because he is in danger, your boss, if he has not yet heard from well-informed sources. And I think you and I, we'd both like to see her back, Saintée."

Guyane nods as though he understands—including the reference to US intelligence, which, so far as he knows, has not been in touch with the Fisherman. Still, he considers the conversation disturbing enough to ask to see President Masson the next day. Of course Guyane wishes to have Cynthia back in Indesville, and he certainly wants her identity (and his own) cleansed of any clandestine implications. Fisherman concurs in both motives, and seems as unaware of his own putative jeopardy as was Denis. They both infer that the lovesick Pole had been overplaying Cynthia's presence on the islet for his own purposes.

To seek greater clarity, however, Masson calls La Vinaigrette directly and arranges a conversation with her for Denis Guyane "as soon as convenient."

"Since she doesn't know you yet, she'll put it off for a few days—research, you know." He smiles, then continues. "In the meantime, Denis—unless Benjamin needs you urgently—could you fit in a quick visit to Angela Dumesnil at Indes-les-Bains? Her hotel—you've been there, right?"

Now Guyane has to grin: Masson was playing him as a rookie. So he waits for the wipe of presidential eyeglasses.

"You know, Denis, that BIP is considering a spot to stage the party's first national convention, in September. I have nothing against the Grand Hotel, even if there is no ocean nearby."

"*Especially* if there's no ocean. You don't want to make the connection all that obvious, do you?"

"No. You're right, although fishermen wade in quiet trout streams too."

"Not barefoot, I hope."

"No. Now, for this convention, I'd rather not simulate Domino's narcissistic ceremonials. See if Angela can offer something original, more republican, than the Nationals' worn-out boilerplate."

"Sure. With or without the Vinegar lady as headline crowd pleaser?"

Fisherman sighed. "Much as I love, honor, and obey Sophie, maybe Angela could persuade her to be a bit more upbeat for us this time. They're friends. Sound her out."

Assenting to the assignment, and while waiting for Vinaigrette to issue her summons, Denis reminds himself that Angela Dumesnil had been one of the last islanders to spend time with Cynthia before her departure with the Silhouettes. During those rehearsal sessions at the hotel, the innkeeper might have detected some clue to Van Zan's subsequent itinerary.

"Not sure I can be any help," says la Patronne, sharing a half bottle of local *mousseux* across the bar, and looking him over approvingly. No, she realizes with disappointment, *his* appearance does not alter the Acajou's color scheme; only one American could do that, and they both miss her. But his presence does give Angela a chance to exercise her English.

"Your Van Zan lands here for the first time as Little Bo-Peep," she says, "and manages to leave as *la grande jeune fille*, even after a lecture from Sophie. Then she comes back this year for singing lessons, frequents the fishmongers in the market, and leaves again. Now she's Billie Holiday. And gets lost in Paris. Helluva leap for that tawny cat of yours!"

"Yes, I've put up with Cynthia's tone shifting for years. But did she show anything during her time here, especially those rehearsal weeks, that might betray her subsequent intentions or commitments? Something we ought to know?"

"Van Zan came here rarely, on her way into or out of the deep blue sea. Actually, Marty and the boys originally wanted to work me into the gig. You know that he used to back me up on song nights here. The thought of Paris was freaking them out, those amateurs, and they hoped I'd offer some sort of 'class' if I joined up. Class indeed! One look at this old has-been and the Left Bank would have consigned our Silhouettes to the compost bins. Why should anybody be snatching this wobbly cadaver out of her grave? No, I graciously declined the humiliation, but thought your Van Zan could vocalize what they needed and that she would look delicious on a cabaret stage. So Marty decided to work with her, and the Justesses had no choice. The reviews from France imply that she helped Marty come off authentically."

"I see. But you did work with them here. How did they sound to you?"

"Have you come to spend the night? I can get a room ready for you. No? So in short, I didn't exactly turn the jeune fille into Lady Day at Angela's bar. Her style rang *zydeco* rather than swing; she'd have been more at home with a squeeze-box and washboard than a grand piano. But everybody played behind Marty, a modest version of Basie or Ellington's international period. Her role was as a backup instrument who . . ." Angela sighs, sips and inhales. "Call it envy, but I've never seen a woman look so good with so little cover. No makeup to speak of, just her own subtle shading, the flash down her hair, that lithe outline, the lift in those breasts, not a muscle out of place. How do you guys do it?"

He guffaws. "She's only one person, alas, not a national figurehead. I'm not included. But you mention Marty, his importance. Did Cynthia appear to be . . . I hesitate to ask it, knowing her as well as I do."

"Did she 'come onto' him, or anybody here? I don't think so. Of course she spent time with Marty. She had to do that, and she improved his flair. That veterinarian hung around, too, looking jealous most of the time, but for God's sake, he's just a drummer. It comes with the territory."

"And the brothers in Justice?"

"Ah, they worked on their horns, mainly let Marty figure out the charts, and they kept the drummer from going off his nut. Old Claude showed up, too, from his wee island fiefdom. Good for us, because he paid their bills here and kept André, my soggy husband, happy."

"I see," says Guyane, distractedly. "Do you know what happened to them later? Marty Bondoo, I believe, is still in Europe, but . . ."

"Yeah. He has concerts and club gigs everywhere these days, and I'm told he flips his crowds with African polyrhythms, solo. Way beyond the Silhouettes who can barely keep three beats on three, let alone four on six. But if you're asking about Van Zan, so far as I know, Marty travels by himself. No backup, no . . . women. I really don't know where she went. Why don't you ask Sophie?"

Denis doesn't need to pursue the Silhouette trail any further with Angela. Time to talk political party convention. Here, the innkeeper gladly accommodates presidential inclinations; she even promises to persuade Vinaigrette to feed the party more honey, less bile in her lecture. "I don't think she'd mind changing the liturgy, although your party might have to prepare for a mainline Marxist harangue."

"I'm told Mme. Nuru may be itching to deliver that message. All right with me."

"Although it won't be easy for your party's well-heeled magnates to swallow. Like the fat cats who dig your man Benjamin. He came by a while ago, looking at soil erosion and all such stuff that I suppose goes with hawking fish. He's very ingratiating, by the way, that Bamiara. Rugged finesse. The rich barflies order our best whisky to pick his brains, but he drinks only Perrier water. We bill them for the twelve-year single malt anyhow. That should ensure his future. Want another shot of bubbly?"

Denis gets the point and thanks Angela for the offer and for her time. Then he motors back to Indesville, still in bewildered search of a trail toward Cynthia Van Zan.

CHAPTER 12

SPREADING THE NETS

The Polish Quest

Decades ago, when he was six or seven, Andrej Sokolsky sat for the first time at his grandfather's massive dinner table in the Pas de Calais and shared snuff with the old man. Grandfather Benyowsky had come upon his daughter's boy at midnight still awake, in the bed shared that night with cousin Les; he invited Andrej downstairs for a glass of water and to get acquainted. The bearded patriarch perched on his straight-backed chair, inhaled snuff, and handed an occasional pinch to the dazzled child's nose. Neither the boy's parents nor anybody he knew in Paris used such volatile powder.

For a half hour, conversation at that table consisted of quiet questions, even more quietly answered, about Andrej's school, his friends, his pride as a French person of Polish descent. This catechism was punctuated by an extended duet of sneezes followed by solo prayers: the old man sniffed tobacco, sneezed, and Andrej reacted, "Bless you, Grandfather." Then he sniffed, sneezed, and responded, "Bless me, Grandfather."

Reciprocal sniffing, sneezing, and benediction concluded only when, fighting somnolence, the boy looked up at the portrait on the wall behind the old man and wondered, "Who is that soldier, Grandpapa?"

"Ah," breathed the old man. "Something I've wanted to tell you. That officer with his gold braid and no beard yet is your grandfather, when he was much younger."

"That's you? You were in the French Army, then, Grandpa?"

"No, not the French. I was a major in the army of Poland . . . or what used to be Poland."

"Isn't Poland still there, Grandpa?"

"Poland is a very weak country now, suffocated by its enemy, but she was not always so."

"Did you fight that enemy?"

"In a way, I did. Yes, in fact I really did."

Then, closing his snuffbox, the old man spun a tale that the excited boy would never challenge, never expunge from his emergent, outrageous sense of himself.

It told of a horse trainer born near Cracow in 1915, schooled in French and the sciences. At age 23, Benyowsky was commissioned in the cavalry of an army pitifully unready to confront a modern enemy—let alone two. As German and Soviet divisions ploughed into Poland from opposite directions, Ernest Benyowsky's regiment sat paralyzed between them. He was one of six young officers, skilled horsemen who spent restless nights in their mess with no deployment against either invader. To pass the time, they swore oaths and swilled vodka or cognac, whatever they could fetch, until one night, foreswearing indolence, they decided on their own to launch a crucial assault. After a debate over which way to direct their attack—but attack they must for honor and country—they swore to first destroy the enemy to the east, Poland's inveterate nemesis. They would beat the Soviets back into the steppes, or wherever they came from, and then turn against the monstrous Germans. After a few more rounds of vodka they would be ready at sunrise to inspire their regiment into action.

Except that, thanks to the vodka, the officers neglected to rouse that regiment. So, hurling themselves at dawn upon their steeds, a half dozen unaccompanied cavaliers advanced headlong into the embrace of an astonished Red Army patrol. Hastily immobilized after a futile swishing of sabers, the Polish patriots then languished in a makeshift military prison. When their captors decided not to resist the Wehrmacht's eastward momentum, they loosened their captives and dispatched them into the mercies of No Person's Land. From there the Poles could try to get home.

By the time he reached Cracow on foot, Benyowsky learned of his sister's successful arrival in France before the opening of hostilities. Among her possessions, Maria had carried her brother's officer portrait with her to confirm their social position while she sought suitable work among the Polish expatriate community. After several months, Maria married a shopkeeper in Pas de Calais, proudly mounting the martial brother's image in her parlor.

The subject of that portrait, still unaware that World War II had frozen all of Europe, set out to rejoin his sister in France. He headed north, where he had trained for the cavalry and knew people who could provide shelter; there he could steal a horse when he needed one and get to the Baltic. In early 1940, Ernest Benyowsky found a stranded French fishing vessel looking for crew to skirt the Wehrmacht and reach Boulogne "in time." The boat did get nearly there, but too late. By then, France was scarcely more free than Poland.

Once across the Channel to Dover, Benyowsky spent the war as turbulently as he could. He volunteered with the Gaullist liberators to redeem a France that he had just dimly seen. After the war ended, he joined Maria's household in Pas de Calais, married a family friend, Brigitte Taragon, and worked a variety of trades, until becoming a teamster/truck driver. A generation later, their daughter Thérèse wed a young history teacher, Pierre Sokolsky; she moved with him to Paris where Andrej was born. When he was old enough, they took him to Pas de Calais to meet his bearded, snuff-taking maternal grandfather.

On that visit, Andrej excitedly exhibited the portrait to his own father. The similarity of name reminded historian Pierre Sokolsky of the picaresque career of one Maurice Beniowski, an 18th century nobleman-adventurer, cousin of General Casimir Pulaski and an acquaintance of Franklin's in Paris. In his action-packed memoirs, known in France since 1791, Count Beniowski audaciously escapes from a Tsarist prison, battles through Siberia to the Pacific, swashbuckles his westward return by sea, and fights his way into the major capitals of Europe.

Despite the skepticism of his scholarly son-in-law, Andrej's grandfather adopted the Beniowski heritage as confirmation of his ancestry, recommending the animated narrative to any stultified young patriot. He assured little Andrej that the heroic horseman and corsair would have ruled the Indian Ocean's greatest island if the American Congress or the French Crown had only appreciated the opportunity. Instead, just as Poland was repeatedly betrayed, Beniowski's exploits ended in assassination by jealous Gallic rivals from Mauritius.

Indeed, after that snuff-inspired night in Pas de Calais, Andrej Sokolsky's head buzzed with two epic marches—the global adventures of an embattled "Emperor" as well as Grandfather Benyowsky's northward passage and warrior exploits two centuries afterward. They spoke to Andrej of headlong rides, hillside burrows, treacherous traps, quick escapes, and violent skirmishes on land, sea, and horseback.

A decade later, Europe had reopened from west to east for Andrej Sokolsky. On vacation after completing veterinary studies in Toulouse, a lofty and towhead Dr. Sokolsky (nicknamed *Ski*) decided to trace his late grandfather's steps through a rejuvenated Poland from Cracow to the sea. A dedicated romantic like the old man, a percussion player in amateur musicales, he stopped for a week of opera performances in Poznan. Leaving the theater after the final night of Wagner's *Ring*— inspired by the heroine's leap on horseback into her lover's funerary fire—Ski glanced up at the sculpture of the winged horse Pegasus.

Stopped in his tracks, Andrej heard what he could at first not believe. The building was replaying Wagner's "immolation" music, this time from the rooftop through the equine messenger of Olympus. It was as if Brünnhilde's faithful steed *Grane* had risen from the pyre in white marble, beating its wings to drum a message, a call that penetrated him like a transfusion. As he thought it out, Sokolsky understood: he was to take his career to the ocean where his ancestor Beniowski had once reigned, fought on horseback, and died by an act of treachery. Horses would be there to assure his welcome.

Once his romantic fervor had subsided into professional research, Dr. Sokolsky came upon a genuine opportunity. It was in a republic called AuxIndes. There he could help domesticate a wild equine strain, remnants of a breed brought to the island by early Arab colonists. Through urbanization, descendants of the settlers had wearied of their herds and let them run free in the highlands. Surviving on fresh grass in the aftermath of periodic brush fires, the animals became nuisances to cattle herders who appealed to the authorities for relief. A military expedition corralled them into an abandoned mission courtyard where they were offered for donation by the Church, albeit with few takers.

The most domesticable specimens went to an ambitious tour operator who was developing a public recreation park outside Indesville. Preparing to offer cross-country rides, hunting parties, and dressage training, the agent broadcast an urgent need to France for veterinary assistance in training and breeding the animals. He would find plenty to occupy his time and skills; work was also to be done on angora goats being raised somewhere by the entrepreneur's French associates, named De Justesse.

In the year 2000, the bachelor Andrej Sokolsky came to AuxIndes with a drum set, a scientific mission, and a faith that his ancestral roots lay imbedded in the island culture.

Now, ten years later, had he also just met his own Brünnhilde in a tawny graphic artist from Louisiana?

Vinaigrette: the Prophecy

President Masson was not used to frustration, but he had to swallow an exception for the sibylline Sophie Nuru. Calling more frequently than his dignity allowed, he was unable to make contact with La Vinaigrette for months after Guyane's disturbing encounter with Sokolsky. What should he have learned from De Justesse that they dared not reveal to him directly? Why, after Van Zan's absence would Sophie also disappear? A bewildered Anya Wazimbwe proved of no help in locating either of the unreachable women. Cabinet officers, staff, even the omni-wired Philosophe, all merely shrugged when asked. Then—was it already a year?—Vinaigrette replied to an ancient voicemail message and called Fisherman as though no time had elapsed at all.

Although he knew Cynthia's admiration for Nuru, Denis Guyane had yet to meet that vinegary sage. He had noted her radio voice—hoarse, whispering until she wished to emphasize some political, often unpleasant, theme suitable to her popular name. Odd that Van Zan had never shown him a sketch of La Vinaigrette, except in that idealized amazon guise; nor could he recall anybody describing her physically—only her stiletto mind and verbal dexterity. Hence, when

Guyane arrived at her lodgings, he expected to encounter the usual middle-aged AuxIndienne—white-draped, matronly, self-consciously overweight.

For a moment after the door opened, he thought he was being admitted by a perhaps familiar domestic. The woman was slight, black-sweatered, in tight slacks, quick in gesture, underfed perhaps from birth, dark (so probably low-caste). She recalled descriptions of the young "Spider" who had been shot off the Governor's statue twenty years before. The woman's acerbic welcome revealed her, however, as in fact mistress of the house. This Vinaigrette seemed composed entirely of points and edges. She rapidly sized him up, then repeated her greeting with a nod rather than a word, and guided him into a room where she evidently performed her work. Whatever it was she did.

The "it" was anything but dusting and vacuuming; clearly, La Vinaigrette had little inclination toward decorum. Spidery as she seemed, her web was almost a deliberate mess, offering no comfort to intruders. Dust covered the shelves, crumbs the carpets. Books lay strewn over her tables and rugs, some of them lying open, or weighted down to some presumably selected passage. Coffee mugs littered most of the remaining surfaces, surmounting dark rings and puddles of *crème*. "I don't entertain often," explained Mme. Nuru unnecessarily, "especially not foreign gentlemen like yourself."

Without rising to the bait, Guyane moved to a large table pleasantly redolent of steamed vetiver oil. He lifted an open volume of a deceased local bard's poetry, a Masson favorite recommended to him by Kolona. "I know this one," he said, after turning pages, feeling her gaze on his back. "Grief for his dead daughter," he added. "Stunning metaphor of an extinguished song. Do you read him often?"

Vinaigrette only grunted, and took the book gently from his hands. Motioning him into a soft chair, as though he had just failed some test, she perfunctorily offered coffee, more out of island patriotism than from hospitality. He knew enough to decline, and opened the conversation by asking whether Cynthia had visited the house. If so, she had never revealed its chaos to him.

"She's been here," replied La Vinaigrette, "although not since she took up with those self-indulgent musicians."

"Well, they've been back in the country for some time. Without her. Do you have an idea where she is now?"

Vinaigrette thought for a moment, then shook her head. "Why do you think I should? She works for you . . . and for your bigshot boss, not for me."

"Worked, yes, but not lately. Sounds like you lost sympathy for her." Then, after waiting through silence, "Can you tell me why?"

"Not what you call sympathy, you Americans; you flourish sentiment as another pretext to show power. Van Zan is a gifted woman, still in the struggle, only not in ways that involve me."

"Those 'ways' suggest you know something about Cynthia that might help us."

"Help YOU? To do what? Find her? Retrieve her for some bullies? Or so she can marry that Slavic drummer boy? Leave her wherever she is."

The bitterness of this last shot seemed to escape from Sophie Nuru inadvertently. He followed the clue. "Of course, but *where* do we leave her? Cynthia parted from the Silhouettes nearly two years ago. I sense that she wouldn't stay in Paris unless she had to."

"You're right, young man. She'd be afraid that they, or your Masson, would find her there."

"Wherever she is, I'm willing—the president is willing—to leave her undisturbed. But if she consents, she might be useful . . . "

"In his show down with Philosophe?"

"Yes. You know about that, of course." Denis only wished that he himself were better informed. "So give me a clue and I promise."

"You can't promise anything that she would wish, except to let her do as she pleases. And to keep that horse doctor away from her."

"It's not horses anymore, Madam Nuru. It's goats, angoras."

"Whatever they are. Tell Masson to feed them to his fish—or vice versa so far as I'm concerned. You men care only about how you use property. And Cynthia" (she pronounced the name carefully, evading Sokolsky's 'Saintée' distortion), "Cynthia is no doubt where she functions satisfactorily without your permission."

"And where would that be?" he asked, as mildly as his voice would allow.

She nearly smiled at him. "You need her of course; she enlivens the air you breathe." The woman paused, then moved on, more softly. "Nonetheless, Monsieur, you are Haitian, so you are a talent looking for a purpose, which is why Haitians emigrate so much."

"My parents, perhaps, but . . ."

"And you might be good for her, if and when you grow up. Even though you are both in love with the same . . . person."

This caught him off guard. "In love? Who are we supposed to . . ."

"To what? I leave that to you."

"It's absurd," he blurted, "Cynthia has never . . ."

"No, and don't imagine that she resents your fancy for my Anya, either. Wazimbwe is one talent who's found a purpose, and you're not it. Cynthia Van Zan is beyond all that; she doesn't just want to be good at the game, like Anya, but to create the game herself. Give her time. Cynthia IS purpose; she could make or break an empire if she concentrates on it."

"And you? You seem so protective of both women." He was becoming very uncomfortable.

Vinaigrette laughed quietly. "Me? I'm only envious of them, their freedom to search. I'm bound to the reverse purpose, a search for freedom; born and bred for it, like a Japanese wrestler—only a rather little one."

"Yet you claimed that Cynthia and I were . . ."

"Yes, you two, craving the affection of a man who's already married and isn't considering . . ."

"A man? Surely you're not . . ." He couldn't complete that thought.

"Of course. Why else would you both come all this way to work for a . . . a little gay or maybe bisexual Fisherman?"

"Well, if any of that's correct, it's a new notion to me. Still, you're suggesting that Cynthia is looking for a cause, not a mate. So she needs somewhere to find it. Where is that?"

A brief smile took over the gray eyes; he had refused to be distracted. "I don't know exactly; she seems to have done well enough to get away from him, and them, and you."

"She'll need money, Madam. So, by this time she should be at work, presumably in her own field. But to help we'll have to find her."

"You know your way in that profession. Go look for clues, for her style."

"I will try. But not in Paris, right? Her field, graphics, would be difficult to break into there."

"Yes. She would choose somewhere that needs her skills." She paused deliberately, then as though guessing, "Maybe, I don't know. Try Africa."

"Africa! The whole continent? Or do you mean the west, about which she's heard . . . things . . . that struck her fancy?"

"Perhaps. She's a Behanzin, deformed to Van Zan, so why not there?"

He recalled his mother's intuition. "I know Dahomey—Benin; Behanzin. But it would be hard for her to function in that country; you have to carry auspicious contacts. And they'll want stronger French than she has."

"True," admitted Vinaigrette "She could do better in a more open environment—like across the border that those quarreling Europeans made."

"In Nigeria? The Yoruba bridge, you think?"

She shrugged. "Maybe, but watch out; nothing in Africa is as primitive—in need of you, or of her—as Americans think."

He swallowed his objection. Vinagrette was obviously willing to help, albeit in her own Delphic way. She noticed his perplexity.

"So here's another clue—it's all you get today, young man, not even coffee."

Guyane waited, turning pages in the poetry book.

"Remember the last rejection Cynthia received in your damned patriarchal universe? Some time ago—and not in this country. You know how she makes white bodies nervous, then bad things happen—to her. That time, back in America, after New York, Hollywood . . . When she knew you'd be there. She never tried to win that tennis match."

"You know about that? It really *was* her?"

"Oh, yes. But not as a contestant. She only wanted to get your attention."

"*My* attention? Or Roger's?"

Vinaigrette shrugged. "What's the difference? In any case, the rejections she received in New York and Los Angeles prey on her like an obsession; she converts them visually into her work. You must have noticed. Find where and how she exploits that humiliation today."

Then Sophie Nuru stood up, turned toward the door, and gestured him out.

"I like you better than that horse doctor," she said on the door sill, "but don't be too eager to capture Cynthia Van Zan. Men broke her heart before, and she's quite capable of torturing a prisoner if she feels cornered."

Unmatched as they were, Vinaigrette and Guyane's father struck the same ominous key: they stressed Van Zan's search for retaliatory leverage against the men who deny dignity to others. It was indeed a theme in Cynthia's choice of imagery. But more precisely, how was she supposed to be exploiting her rejection by the American "patriarchy?" Of what relevance was the putative legacy of Behanzin, the dethroned shark-king of old Dahomey? Denis would rather not see her entangled in recrimination against some historical injury; but could he impute more affirmative motives to whatever she was currently undertaking? He only hoped so, but that did not get him very far.

As for the "love triangle" insinuation, Guyane postponed thinking about Vinaigrette's meaning until a period of greater tranquility, if that should ever arrive. And he adhered to Pierre-Louis's assumption of his son's heterosexuality, unconsummated as it remained.

At the Presidency, Guyane found Masson and his intimates poring over documents, maps, and aerial photographs. They showed him permits issued for the angora goat farm and rug factory in Philosophe's bailiwick. The terrain abutted, as if deliberately, the very shore that had to be kept free of contamination to allow pristine seafood production. They believed that this husbandry project betrayed the crafty minister's hand, joining with the Europeans De Justesse against the Fisherman and the oceanic commons. One reason, perhaps, for Cynthia's defection.

Anya Wazimbwe was there. She explained why the project appalled her, evoking anthropocentric contingencies, not, as Cynthia would have insisted, the broader planetary perils. But she was sufficiently persuasive. "Shifting this mohair industry up the coast will impoverish the herds people and weavers in the South. Few of them will be invited to move and even fewer willing to accept displacement; it will aggravate desertification down there while polluting the entire area around the western port."

Listening to Anya's denunciation of what she called a deliberate invasion, Denis could sense the president developing eagerness for a showdown with his Philosophic nemesis. The bellicose atmosphere discouraged him from reporting on his gleanings from the ambiguous Vinaigrette conversation. He couldn't help considering poor Olivier, AuThon's marketing manager who regularly carried an adorable brown dwarf goat to work, kept her quietly browsing potted ferns, and diapered to protect the floors from her "pebbles." How could the president declare war on caprines as a corporate and environmental threat? Surely something other than angora goats had to become the regime's main conflict of interest.

After that session ended, Guyane went to the Fishery, letting himself into Cynthia's studio to gather examples of what Vinaigrette might consider to be sublimated clues for his quest. Access to Van Zan's files posed little obstacle. Her desktop was easily dissected—or at least that part of it available to his eye. This was not the first time he had searched her office; Cynthia knew he would comb for hints and had probably left false leads for him. Now he was looking hard at choices of imagery, on paper and online. These were familiar for the most part, illustrating primarily what the two of them worked on together. The remainder, without clear context, could be divided roughly into clusters—any of which might provide a clue to where she had gone and what she was doing—or to nowhere and nothing at all.

One group of sketches brought him to the places where Dr. Sokolsky worked. Discarding doodles of Ski combing through goat hair, he found nothing in this collection to betray any existential obsession, although it contained a conspicuous theme of horses in motion. Denis decided to call the veterinarian's office to ask whether Cynthia had taken on equestrian interests.

"Yes, but not exactly as you might think," answered Sokolsky. Glad to know that Denis was actively hunting, he recalled Van Zan's admiration of the ways animals communicated across and within spaces beyond our immediate apprehension—in the oceans, for instance, or underground and in the air. As for horses, she was particularly impressed, he said, by the legendary choreography of the white Lipizzaner breed, which he had studied at the Riding Academy in

Vienna. She perceived the genius of those animals as transcending what mere humans could impart. After the concerts in Paris, she had agreed to accompany him there to sketch, then to his family home in Cracow, and later, to Poznan where, among other sights, she copied the Pegasus statue prancing on the crest of the municipal opera house. The very image that had compelled him to come work in AuxIndes.

"We had a grand time in both countries," he said. "She seemed to be firmly grounded, as she is everywhere, and at the same time floating, soaring up there, joining the flight of Pegasus, but . . ." Sokolsky's voice trailed off.

"But she didn't stay, choose to stay—is that what you were about to tell me?"

"That's the last place I saw her—not on my own account. I loved, still love, her so much I would climb that theater roof for her if she wanted to remain in Poland, or Vienna, or any other place. But after one day in Poznan, she made me drop her at the airport and . . ."

"And you haven't heard from her since then." Without awaiting a reply, Denis went on: "Is there something else? When she left, after those days together, do you think she might have already been . . . pregnant?"

The call ended in silence. And so did that research path.

A second group of images seemed to fall even farther from actuality. They reflected an interest in, of all things, classical European music. Ski hadn't mentioned an actual concert in Vienna or at Poznan.

Broadening the subject, Guyane uncovered a series of illustrations of comparative symbiosis—an orchestra's strings, winds, percussion, and operatic voices likened to intercommunication of sea creatures and root systems; still, this observation seemed to lead nowhere except into a suggested theme for AuThon's promotional strategy.

The orderly compilation and her underscoring of these fragments did suggest that Cynthia was leaving hints about herself for someone to find—for himself he hoped, although he could never be sure about his elusive accomplice. White stallions in Poznan or Vienna could mischievously refer to Sokolsky and his Silhouette jazz buddies, but to what end? Romantic music recalled for Denis the occasion when Van Zan had joined him and Masson for the *Pearl Fishers;* that shadow—of an imagined competition for her between himself and the Fisherman—had vanished from his healthier consciousness, only to be invoked now, and suppressed once more. Could she be distorting the conventional love triangle—two male adversaries for a female— toward Vinaigrette's insinuation that he and Cynthia competed for the affections of the Fisherman? Once again, he put this unwelcome thought aside.

And where in all this was the traumatic "rejection" that Vinaigrette had prepared him to find? The stallions of Vienna, the mythical steed atop Poznan Opera, and the communal messaging of orchestras, singers, and natural species failed to locate Cynthia Van Zan in the present, let alone to shed light on what she was doing.

Before sifting through the remaining materials with even less hope of discovery, he recalled Vinaigrette's nonexistent hospitality and found that even he—the ever-sated Denis Guyane—could become hungry. Awkwardly stalking the halls, he discovered no one to share a late meal with, so he descended to AuThon's basement where off-duty security guards regularly watched television and raided the Fishery's refrigerators. He greeted both men by name and, as something about their mood troubled him, casually added that he was merely working late that night. What was it that their unresponsiveness suggested? Surely they couldn't suspect him of any sort of surveillance mission. That would be far from his line of duty—and from his personality. Yet they didn't smile, wouldn't wave or speak to him, and it appeared that he was intruding on something they wished to keep to themselves.

Rummaging in the kitchen, he left rice packets undisturbed, found bottled water and enough bread and cheese for an admissible sandwich. On his way out he passed the pair of guards, now with a trio of women employees, watching an old French portside drama infused in fog and beset with gloom. He waved at them and found his way upstairs with his repast.

Back with Cynthia's visual files, his mind returned to the movie that he had just brushed past, but without immediately understanding why. The third collection of images did indeed cohere around an austere motif that, with stretching and turning, could be combined with the others. The common figure consisted of a three-dimensional shape—a box or an animal's head supporting two elongated extensions, like exaggerated ears, or antennas, or horns emerging from a helmet; or even—and here his mind stopped whizzing—the armatures of an ancient cinema projector like the one downstairs—extensions that support the feed-in and take-up reels of film.

"Or," he said to himself aloud, "a screen test fed back to the humiliated Black girl?" An untypical "hopeful" already scornfully rejected by a corporate search committee in New York?

Gradually, he became aware of having frequently encountered Cynthia's use of the proverbial shape with protruding armatures—as a horse's or dog's head with extended ears, an archaic television apparatus with antennas, a backpack with two loose shoulder straps, a house with two chimney pipes, a caricature of a horned Valkyrie's helmet, or a cuckold's sprouts—especially, a long-gilled fish or school thereof. Such images abounded in Van Zan's graphics—subliminally joined yet not explicitly highlighted—ever since she began working in AuxIndes. If the film projector served as prototype, the signatures would link up with her Hollywood "failure," a lucky defeat from his and the Fisherman's standpoint. Leafing through the mass of cartoons, articles, sketches, and doodles compiled on Cynthia's shelves and computer desktop, he rarely saw a scene without some reference to this rough cinema-projector shape; all animal heads had a related template; all sopranos wore Brünnhilde's helmet; the logo appeared even when she signed her own initials in the lower right corner of a piece.

Now came the obvious questions: how to pursue this visual clue to track the real Cynthia Van Zan to her current place, to determine what she was doing there, and how she would react to being "found." If Vinaigrette was right that West Africa, perhaps Nigeria, was a source for Cynthia's identity, would it produce a home and a professional role for her? Assuming that all three image clusters were intended for him, where in that huge expanse of continent could he find a town or country associated with horses, music, *and* cinema? Why not more apt alternatives—Japan? Spain? Argentina? The three frames seemed unlikely to combine in any country on AuxIndes's neighboring continent, unless perhaps they fit into modern South Africa or some cosmopolitan site north of the Sahara. He preferred to give Vinaigrette benefit of the doubt. Besides, a West Africa location reinforced his mother's intuition of Van Zan's descent from an African dynasty celebrated and feared for its women warriors, helmeted or otherwise.

Truly, amazon references abounded in Van Zan's selection of mythical characters in her second cluster of images. "Women heroes through great music," Denis said to himself. "Just like Cynthia to elbow her way into the noble art of opera."

While the cameras grind on without her.

Now, where precisely could Cynthia Van Zan position herself? Guyane had traveled through Africa's western regions without identifying equine, operatic, and cinematic themes in any one country, not even in the otherwise rich cultures of Ghana, Senegal, or Mali. Could he depend on Vinaigrette's hint about Southwest Nigeria, old Dahomey's neighbor and traditional rival? The valiant, lost Dahomey of Behanzin, the shark king, had shrunk into a small modern state, borrowing its name, *Benin*, from a southern Nigerian kingdom with a shared turbulent history. One slim bridge across the Yoruba divide.

Old Benin's bronze treasures were stolen, and the kingdom emasculated, when British troops invaded in 1897. Could this be the place for the shark to surface as Van Zan? What if Cynthia had chosen that matrix to work her trade? Was it to be some kind of revenge for the genocidal wickedness of slavery in her mother's Louisiana? Revenge for West Africans' own responsibility in facilitating that iniquitous trade along the Slave Coast? This indicted Behanzin's (hence her own) rapacious forefathers who captured and condemned other Africans (her mother's people) into that ghastly destiny. Both Fon and Nago, Cynthia's DNA could merge only in mythical hostility.

Guyane preferred not to see Van Zan trying to work through this historical paradox. He understood more readily how Nigeria's contemporary vitality could exert existential attraction on her. The robust charms of a theatrically musical, dance-inspired West Africa would appeal to her tastes more fully than AuxIndes's overly verbal culture.

One buttressing line of inquiry popped into his consciousness. To grasp it he had to solicit items addressed to and (hopefully) retained by the boss and other staff. Roaming the offices next day he stumbled on several examples of Van Zan's touristy photographs and postcards from Paris, and there it was. The Silhouettes had performed that year in a "third world" festival conspicuously dominated by music and dance troupes from two or three nationalities, including Nigeria. One stage photograph, enclosed with a "having good time" message and signed with Cynthia's cinema-projector logo, even featured Afrobeat highlife musicians from Yoruba country. Unless Van Zan was deliberately throwing colleagues off her track, western and southern Nigeria became the place to look for her.

Working out this conundrum required greater understanding of a most complex environment, and especially how the mercurial Van Zan might operate within it. Seeking help, Guyane scanned his memory for someone in Nigeria who might locate examples of graphic production that would reflect Cynthia's pictorial talent. As his leaves of recollection turned, they stopped at one person— Ededayo ("call me Eddie") Oyelemo, an oversized Puck, collector of Nigerian sculpture and proprietor of a formidable consultative business in Lagos. This larger-than-life Yoruba man, who swept along corridors of power in his embroidered *agbada* and pearled sandals, had once encouraged Denis's desultory efforts to promote trade in textiles.

Eddie might recall the evening when, over fountains of bubbly, they talked intimately of his short-lived marriage. Years before, after transacting his way into an exclusive club, Oyelemo taught his country-bred wife to hit tennis balls so that she could accompany him into the sporty Anglophile set. Equipoised, bronzed from birth, with hair billowing in ringlets, Sabrina Oyelemo quickly learned to hammer winners with her left-handed twist-serve and unerring two-fisted backhand. She habitually beat not only Eddie but all the other men at the club. Sabrina's proficiency nearly provided a pretext for blackballing Oyelemo himself, with disturbing consequences for his business. To avoid expulsion, the pair separated amicably, and Sabrina left for Kenya as a safari guide. For Eddie, ambition had prevailed over love.

Now Eddie Oyelemo was dividing a self-indulgent bachelorhood between commercial trading and evening imbibing. He became legendary for champagne consumption and high-life parties, and for responsiveness to handsome women. But it's widely believed that he was looking for Sabrina ever since—around his sailboat, in the airwaves over Nairobi, or within his sparkling wine glass.

A late morning call, bouncing off Paris and London, confirmed Oyelemo's congenial recollection of Guyane from five years back. He expressed unawareness of, but curiosity about, the possibility of Cynthia Van Zan's professional activity in Nigeria. This was a man who could be expected to take interest in a new and (Denis assured him) talented and attractive presence in the profession. Oyelemo could also be expected to accommodate the needs of a confidential counselor to a head of state, as Denis described his current status. The call ended with Guyane's commitment to fly out to Lagos carrying materials for an intriguing research project.

Now it was time to report to that chief of state. Masson invited him to share sandwiches at the "palace" (a word he used with some sarcasm). The neighbor bats were sound asleep. He welcomed brief accounts of Guyane's dialogues with La Vinaigrette and the lovesick veterinarian. Excluding some content that still bewildered him and would most likely confuse the president too, Denis summarized the results of his almost sleepless night among Cynthia's materials, and his hunch that Lagos might be an auspicious starting point. He posed his request in the metaphoric form that he hoped Masson would appreciate: "Do you think this worth a few days out of here, combing a Nigerian haystack for an elusive stylus?"

After one of his stock pauses, Fisherman expanded the question. Yes, such a quest might be worth the effort, not merely in tracking the missing artist, but for a new and immanent purpose. He told Denis in confidence that Minister Karamau was no longer in collusion with De Justesse and his Silhouette team of angora raisers and rug manufacturers; De Justesse and sons, as well as the angora magnates, were out of the way, under investigation for attempted bribery. Philosophe had turned to backstairs negotiations with their competitors—oil companies interested in the sands, shoals, and offshore depths of that same coastal region. Masson appeared to have become aware of that conspiracy belatedly, without contact from De Justesse. His likely source would be the astute Vinaigrette, recently recovered from her holiday on somebody's boat. His own Gulf of Mexico visit vividly in mind, the president understood that oil/gas prospection offshore could endanger a vast neighborhood for fishing, indeed for life culture of any kind. It happened that one of Philosophe's interlocutor companies had been mining for decades in Southeastern Nigeria, with ecologically devastating results. "I understand," Masson said, "that the oil maelstrom has swallowed up that region's entire economy, farming and fishing included, and not for Nigerians' better digestion." Hence, while in West Africa, Denis might keep his eye open for anything that would enlighten AuxIndes about the implications of an intrusion by these exploiters—even provide grounds for heading them off.

While this last note opened an unfamiliar chapter for him, Guyane looked forward to the break away from Indesville. He would be glad to learn what might be of interest to the state, not to mention its environmental counselor, the beguiling Diva Wazimbwe.

The president did not mention, if he knew of it, Minister Karamau's putative relationship with certain disgruntled military, another subject of what Ski and his friends had proposed to provide to AuxIndes intelligence through "Saintée" Van Zan. Already informed of the oil/gas initiative, Masson must have been aware of the military side of Philosophe's treachery. So, while wondering why Fisherman did not summon Karamau to an accounting for such apparent skullduggery, Guyane withheld comment on treatment of that volatile loose cannon.

He was equally glad to have kept silent on Vinaigrette's obscure allusions to romantic conflicts, and to have neglected his shiver of unease over last night's behavior by AuThon's security contingent. A jaunt to the other side of Africa now looked even more inviting to him.

CHAPTER 13

NIGERIA–SHARK LANDING

Visa acquisition and air passage to Lagos via Nairobi consumed most of a day for Guyane. He traveled on his AuxIndes credentials and with a briefcase full of materials, including his United States passport and analyses of oil/gas exploration that might threaten the island's shores. For his arrival in Lagos, the Oyelemo Company sent a car to help him survive the rigors of Muhammad Airport and the proverbial recalcitrance of Nigeria's roadways. After a shower at his downtown hotel, Denis walked to Eddie's office where he found his host ready for a working dinner, just the two of them, a first bottle already effervescent.

Their conversation started with ebullient reminiscences, then proceeded to an exhibit of photographs of Cynthia and illustrations from her work; these pleased Eddie vividly, although he had no recollection of so impressive a personage anywhere around Lagos during the past year. As anticipated, calls the next day to the Immigration Service and the American consulate elicited no trace of her arrival. Of the imagery framed in the Van Zan portfolio, however, Oyelemo offered a more encouraging response than Guyane had expected.

"First of all, we still have an equine tradition in the Nigerian military, low as that institution may have otherwise fallen. Polo players don't get very far stampeding against night raiders and rapists; yet they maintain discipline, and the horses are quite beautiful. Now, classical music, if it means European productions, would be hard to discover around here, although schools occasionally present such stuff. Jazz lies buried in Afro-dance pop, so you have to dig it out. Our Yoruba musical productions have operatic structure and the music is complex in its own way; great drumming especially. I really miss the masterful Duro Ladipo, but he has his successors—even if the women don't wear horned helmets."

Third but not least, Oyelemo waxed proud over the national cinema industry, which he vigorously supported, both in theater and for TV. He wondered if a comely American Black woman might be seen in the cast lists of "Nollywood," or in the art credits. They could check for that.

Eddie concluded, "I see why your Van Zan might have set up these clusters for an inquiring eye. Since she is a recent arrival if she's here at all, and you say she'll need a job, we might find leads around the horsy world, or if she's been a singer . . . well, not really."

"That sounds logical enough for the moment," Denis replied. "We're best advised to examine graphic work in your press, cinema, social media, and such modalities."

"Right, and it's my business to know what's going on there."

For that purpose, Oyelemo proposed to bring in a bright intern with "an eye for content analysis." She would scan for the appearance of prominent symbols derived from the portfolio brought from Indesville, especially the signature "movie projector" and its avatars.

Once found, such an image could be traced back to the source. Hoping the research could be accomplished in the next three or four days, Eddie suggested that Denis could spend that much time "getting re-acquainted with Nigeria."

Although he'd preferred to engage personally in the research project, Guyane agreed to let it proceed without his intervention. Instead, he grasped the opportunity to study petroleum extraction eastward of Lagos. While playing innocent tourist, he might uncover useful intelligence without divulging Masson's strategic purpose for sanctioning the visit, not even to Eddie.

His host declined Denis's proposal to pay for the time and expenses incurred by Bisi Ibukun, the intern. Eddie intended to supervise her work himself, predicting that his own business would inevitably benefit from the effort.

Denis did not bother to ask what business that might be.

Oyelemo also insisted on assigning a company driver to conduct Denis in his visit around the country. When Guyane hesitated over being "accompanied," Eddie reminded him that negotiations at police check points and other aggravations could cost an inexperienced motorist precious time, money, and even worse inconvenience. They agreed to keep in touch as intern Ibukun did her survey; her name, she explained, meant blessing.

Next morning, in his identity as a vacationing American fisheries executive, Guyane, joined by Monday Amos, his chauffeur, started a four-day road tour of southern Nigeria. He aimed it toward the Niger delta's oil hub, Port Harcourt. Before arriving at that strategic location, however, he expected to disarm curiosity through conventional visits to several historically notable places that a tourist wouldn't want to miss.

Short-sleeved, baseball-capped, Denis was merely a Black foreigner in the passenger seat of a mid-range Subaru next to a hired Nigerian driver. Off they went, first for Ibadan and its renowned university, then for the night in Oshogbo. There Denis replenished his admiration for the creative movement known as *Mbari Mbayo* and the region's veneration for its water divinity, the heroic Yoruba spirit *Osun*.

"Ife next," he instructed Amos, "but we want to make Onitsha and Benin City by nightfall." He saw doubt on the driver's face, for they had already been interrupted for several impromptu inspections. "They have to film us with their new toys, just for the record," Monday said. "That'll delay us, but we'll be okay. Just to talk naturally, smile a lot; don't watch them or show them how tall you are, and don't display your big wad of dollars."

"I don't have a big wad of dollars," Guyane demurred.

"Fine, don't show that either," answered Monday with a grin.

Short and chunky, contrasted with his passenger, the driver sported a brush cut with a thin ruff on top, his clean-shaven almond cheeks spread in a knowing smile. Like most contemporary Nigerian men, he bore no facial scars. Monday knew his way around the coasts and found the clearest roads to avoid checkpoints. While driving, he carried pumpkin seeds at his side—"to keep awake," he explained; "salty ones if you let me stop to drink and pee." He was surprised that Denis chose the front passenger seat. Mr. Eddie always rode in back, for rear seats implied "status." Once, Monday recounted with a laugh, Mrs. Sabrina Oyelemo had sent him to fetch an African ambassador's family; five children piled upon the diplomat's ample wife, all in the back seat, because only low-castes would ride in front with the driver.

As they whisked through sites of interest, Denis had to apologize for this philistine-like rush; his time was short and he had to return to Lagos promptly. That was as much as Monday would learn for the moment, but Guyane needed to find alternative explanations if he intended to dwell for two days of research in Port Harcourt, an oil-boom city of less historic or aesthetic significance. By this time, Monday and Denis had developed cordial boyish relations, so the driver allowed himself to speculate whether the American might have "an old flame" in Harcourt; the answer was a smile and a shrug. "Just business," said Guyane. The city was after all a major port with a rich fishing tradition, although by this time that occupation had become virtually extinct.

While scanning oil industry reports on his lap—in French, which he hoped would preclude curiosity from the clever Monday—he could absorb the immensity of the Nigerian scene in both admiration and horror. "You have a monstrous country," he reported to Oyelemo by phone after their second day on the road, "a sea crammed with humans, all going in different directions as though somebody was busy stirring them with a huge paddle. But you don't need to hear that from me. How is Bisi doing?"

So far nothing explicit, admitted Eddie, but she was busy analyzing content, and following traces assiduously. He promised more in due course, and urged Denis on with the "sight-seeing."

Guyane noted vestiges of a publishing tradition in Onitsha; then contemporary bronze-casters, heirs to centuries of the art in Benin City; he gathered samples of newspaper and advertising media wherever he could find them but saw nothing that would suggest participation by Cynthia Van Zan in any of these arenas. During the third day, they arrived at the lodgings booked for them in Port Harcourt. Monday invariably declined such accommodations, preferring, he said, to be put up by relatives whom he claimed to have in every town on any itinerary.

Giving Monday a free day and some spare cash, Guyane recovered his distaste for the congested, refinery-dominated city, plagued by both coal and petroleum processing. Although it was January, Port Harcourt was hot and sooty, an atmosphere bathed in stagnation. He could understand the residents' nostalgia over the loss of the Niger delta's deeper traditions of farming, tree culture, and fishing. Nevertheless, Denis's inquiries produced information, both published and online, about the precarious oil economy, the predations of pirates and kidnappers, and the inevitability of sea-level rise against the low-lying harbor zone.

In this morass, local and federal agencies struggled to stabilize institutions, combat lawlessness and corruption, and improve an increasingly hostile environment. In conversations with the American tourist, young frequenters of Port Harcourt's nightlife deplored the sterilization of the place they preferred to call by its Igbo name, Igwuocha. Little of their love was wasted on the ill-fated Biafra rebellion that had proposed to capture Nigeria's petroleum destiny entirely for that territory. "Our luck to lose the war in 1970," said one beer drinker. "It brought the oil curse down on the Hausas and Yorubas."

Another interlocutor compared government programs to feeble nets tossed into oceans of evil, hauled up with most of the catch spilling out through gaps in the webbing.

That was language Guyane could readily understand.

After two days in Nigeria's petrochemical capital, it was time to turn directly back to Lagos. Heading into the eroded and polluted landscape bequeathed by the proverbial oil "boom," they had to expect a sequence of police controls on the highways. When he opened the Subaru boot to load his bag, the American was surprised to discover a half dozen Christmas-wrapped packages lying there, late by more than a month for that holiday. "What's this stuff you're bringing back?" he asked the driver.

Monday shrugged, and passed him what looked like a receipt.

"Wine, eh? Cabernet from Algeria! Why such luxury now? Christmas is already over."

"It's not me, boss. Mr. Eddie said you'll pay him back, in champagne." He pointed the car into the northwest thoroughfare.

"Me? Who's supposed to drink this wine?"

"You'll see," Monday replied, chuckling.

The 700-kilometer road ahead carried them through special blockades and military checkpoints; officials who scolded them for traversing perilous terrain were tacitly reconciled by donations of cabernet; calls to Eddie solved problems when the wine ran out. They drove all day and most of the night, obliged to push because, as Eddie tersely explained, Bisi had "found some things." Besides, somebody had tried to call Guyane from Indesville but was cut off and not subsequently reachable.

After a few hours of sleep in Lagos, Denis entered the Oyelemo office well before Eddie showed up. Bisi Ibukun, her long braids escaping under a bright headscarf, was waiting for him with a file of graphic findings. Some of them turned out to be dead ends, she admitted, but were kept there for context—backpack ads, photographers buried behind long-eared apparatuses, social media posts of jerricans with extended spouts ("those oil companies!" Bisi interjected bitterly). Some advertising samples, however, seemed to show an emphasis on the film-projector shape, unless it was his imagination looking for vindication of a trip that had thus far documented only contamination of a hopeless landscape.

Few horses, little music, not even a statuesque soprano wielding her spear.

But there was one genuine lead, found by accident, saved for last so that Eddie could be there to watch Denis's reaction.

Bisi's mother, a diabetes sufferer in Lagos, had showed her daughter a get-well card from a friend in the national capital, Abuja; playing on idiosyncrasies of farm animals, the card was so attractive that the mother (was her name really Ellavunky, or did Denis mis-hear?) had saved it on her refrigerator for six months. What caught the intern's eye was a stylized imprint at the bottom of the card's reverse—a fantasy sea creature, its head a letter C with V and Z as elongated gills. Bisi saw no other product by this hand on social media or in open sources, and nothing else to compare with the originality of the style. A moment after his arrival, Oyelemo pronounced it crucial.

Inquiries by telephone in Abuja revealed that an animal-rescue agency disseminated such cards along with cover letters and envelopes seeking contributions. Other charitable organizations had contracted with the same studio for similar purposes, but could not provide more than a URL for it—*Kondographics*. Bisi tried through the website to obtain a street location and/or telephone number, but found none. When she sought to place an order for Easter cards with an accommodating stationer (needed promptly and real cheap), she was directed to inquire through a private press run "by a Dahomean couple." Bisi noted the printer's address and obtained instructions from Eddie to accompany Mr. Guyane to Abuja on a next-day flight. They were to be seeking original "summer solstice cards, or whatever," but crafted by that particular designer. As Denis left the office to recover more lost sleep, Eddie escorted him to the door with a firm hand.

"Have a successful trip tomorrow but be gentle," he whispered, "the girl is a virgin. They do still exist."

You should know, thought Denis, very much to himself.

The following morning, Monday Amos steered them to the airport through Lagos's version of a European metropolis—skyscraper wealth hovering over misery and deceit. Guyane and Ibukun talked about cultures of Nigeria during their flight, until they landed uneventfully in the capital. Starting from their hotel in Abuja's center, Denis asked the intern to look around bookstores, gift shops, and other places that might carry examples of Kondo Graphics's style while he called at the Dahomean stationers' shop in hope of meeting the designer. After a search along real sidewalks that distinguished downtown Abuja from the teeming foot traffic of old Lagos, he found himself in a cramped facility, crowded with much press operation and a display room but no evident creative activity. He sought out the owners and met Mr. Atayi—"an ancient Dahomean name," the elderly man explained, glad to be speaking French, even to an American.

Guyane took the opportunity to express appreciation for the rich heritage of old Dahomey. He learned that the Atayi family had immigrated to Nigeria in the 1980s to escape the chaos of an all too crude revolution. Things are better in Cotonou now, the stationer admitted, but Abuja, once it got started as a capital, has been friendly to them and their business. "Here they know better than our people how to keep their city fine."

"A propos," Denis turned the conversation, "my company in Lagos has been attracted by the fine work of a studio called Kondo Graphics. We understand that you do their productions, and we'd like to see whether we might contract with them—through your auspices, of course."

For an instant, Atayi's countenance sombered, as if he suspected these Lagotians of an intent to kidnap his prize artist. He recovered, however, and replied cordially enough. "Kondo is one person, and we handle all Madam Kondo's work exclusively."

"The name Kondo invokes Dahomean history, does it not?" Denis asked, in an appeal to Atayi's patriotism. "Is this woman also from Benin? And can I meet her while I'm briefly in Abuja?"

"No, she is American," Atayi confided to a suddenly trembling customer, "but claims our heritage, as her name suggests. However," he quickly appended, "she's very busy now; has a young daughter and is working with us on a graphic novel in English, a major attraction for Nigerian kids."

"That's fine. We wouldn't want to interrupt her—your—work schedule. And my company could make it worth her while, and yours." He let this sink in. "Can you show me how to find Madam Kondo?"

"Not easily. She works out of her domicile in the suburbs and prefers to meet clients here at the press. We're set up for that. Like all Americans, she drives her own automobile, and being in this setting gives her a business touch, you see."

"Yes, of course. Could you arrange a meeting here for us?"

After a moment's hesitation, Atayi did just that for mid-morning the next day. He dispatched a bicycle messenger to the designer's studio with instructions. "Tell Madam Kondo it's an associate of Eddie Oyelemo."

"Two associates," Denis appended. "I have a Nigerian assistant with me. She knows the business well." Somehow, that did not seem to have reassured Mr. Atayi.

Night was falling on Abuja, and Denis spent the evening in shivers. Poor company for Bisi, he was glad to see her invited to dinner with her mother's friends—people who had already sent out one card by Kondo Graphics and who might have others to show. Bisi had learned that Kondo's products were largely contracted with non-profit organizations and at least one hospital, but there was this graphic novel that Denis had already heard mentioned, and some "3D work" in the offing.

For his part, tingling nerves came from two different sources: first, the prospect of rejoining what he fondly called "his professional other half," even under her improvised identity. The other reason for anxiety developed when his attempts to report progress by long-distance to Masson's office kept coming back as undeliverable. "Stupid country," he muttered as he tried various numbers and addresses for telephone, texts, and email, in both French and English. "Nigeria will never get anything right," he concluded unfairly. Then he forgot to eat and went to dream-filled sleep.

Arriving at Atayi Press next morning, Guyane looked around the installation eagerly waiting for "Madam Kondo" to join them. To pass the time he admired the apparatus, praised the products on display, and quietly asked Bisi to examine samples for further evidence of the "projector" motif. She found several, mainly in the Kondo's signature at the base of greeting cards; she purchased samples and photographed others casually. "Big gills on that shark," he observed, "or are they rabbit ears on a lobster?"

"A shark would never be caught with ears like that," corrected Ibukun. "This fish probably had legs, too, but the lettering makes the point—your Miss Van Zan is no rabbit."

Fifteen minutes after the time scheduled for their meeting, Denis sought Mr. Atayi to ask if the artist had forgotten their date, or should he just wait and listen for her?

Atayi chuckled. "It doesn't do any good. Madam Kondo invariably comes in without making a sound. I can't say how she does it, but the door won't click when she enters, and you don't know she's there until she 'unmutes' herself."

"Striking how that suits the legend of Dahomey's shark king."

"In fact, Atayi continued, "she may be here already. We have much for her to look over. I'll go see."

"Good, Mr. Atayi, thank you."

He knew, of course. Like the submarine predator that King Behanzin took as his *mask*, "Madam Kondo" had been watching him wade around the shop for some time. He considered diving more deeply to catch the light, but the shark struck peremptorily.

"I don't know whether to laugh or to cry." Cynthia whispered urgently from behind, then gripped him and held on for minutes. Atayi and Bisi entered promptly, but backed away, differently astonished.

Finally, Van Zan explained to the printer that she and Mr. Guyane were old friends from New York. Denis nodded silently, then turned. Although impelled to hug Bisi too, he could only toss a warm glance toward the girl.

For the intern this meant success. For him it was an epiphany.

Bisi Ibukun returned on the afternoon flight to Lagos, with Denis's note of appreciation for Eddie and a promise to report in detail, settle accounts, and see to a proper reward for the diligent intern. Obviously, he needed time with the Kondo artist, to meet her child, and be sure of their security. And he did want to order something of value from the accommodating Atayi Press. So he naturally lingered in Abuja—"a nice town, compared to Lagos," Cynthia assured him, "even without an ocean front." To calm down, he spent the afternoon writing up the horror of a "Port Harcourtization" of western AuxIndes if Karamau's petroleum project should arrive there. He used language that he expected Anya Wazimbwe to appreciate.

Allowing Cynthia time to get her work done, he met her for dinner while two year-old *Ocean* was entertained by a neighbor. Over Peking duck, Van Zan heard him describe his mission and promise to respect her free wishes. She made clear what those options were. She was not to return to AuxIndes, or to resume her employment with the Fishery or the administration, and never to see Ocean's self-designated father again. If he wished, Denis could maintain personal contact with her in Abuja, where she and the child were happy, but (brandishing a pointed duck bone over his wrist) he was to vow silence about her exact coordinates. While she might take on a project or two for him online, President Masson needed to know only that Van Zan was "out of the way" in Nigeria. And if the Fisherman sought to dislodge her, he would have to answer . . . to Vinaigrette. "He's scared to death of her, you know."

Denis agreed to the terms, as if he had a choice, aware of how malignly he had been played by the wily Nuru. As if to compensate for his trouble, Cynthia let him pick up the check and offered him most of the next day.

Back in his room, Guyane envisaged the continued tribulations of a Fishery and Presidency forever bereft of their skilled animator. But he was still unable to call or text any kind of message to Indesville. Apparently, the game was changing for the Fisherman anyway, and they might have to accommodate new circumstances regardless of Van Zan's defection.

Denis hadn't realized how much had changed until he was jostled that evening by a cryptic telephone call from Oyelemo. Everything, in fact. Can't talk now. More when he returned. Denis asked Eddie to book his flight back to Lagos for the following afternoon.

Next morning, Cynthia drove Denis through the Federal Capital Territory in her Morris Minor. They admired the massive Aso Rock around which Abuja was growing into a metropolis of five million, and glanced at the government and multilateral office buildings, banks, and diplomatic nests crowding the business district. Guyane took it all in, absorbing Cynthia's descriptions of misplaced juxtapositions—lion sculptures flanking pacifist organizations, flagrant graffiti splashed on walls of Bauhaus sterility, and refugee settlements without public transportation to places of employment.

"It's not as lively here as I'd expected of Nigeria," she said, "after swallowing your West Africa homages and knowing the Nigerians in Paris. But if you just ignore the politicians—they all sound like Domino in jerrybuilt English—this culture is less puffed up than AuxIndes; less verbal wind."

"How about security, though? Do women shudder when they go out of the house?"

It's safe enough here," she said, "until the climate carries the seashore 500 kilometers northward; then this will become another Port Harcourt. There are squatter camps in the area, but we live poor and look it. Oh, kidnapping and other nastiness come and go. Nigeria is as crowded with greed as any other place—only more notorious."

Soon they both wanted Denis to meet Ocean, a new edition of the inimitable Van Zan. Fetching the child at noon from daycare, Cynthia drove them to a small, rectangular zinc-roofed cottage near a private school and its clinic. The cabin sat in a landscape that seemed ephemeral, waiting for the developer's cosmopolitan axe. Yet, it rose transcendent out of a green savanna, reflecting light in shimmers, as did Van Zan whenever she stood up.

Cynthia's house fit her aura like the barge and the maple chair in his indelible early recollections. Large enough for a bedroom, studio, and kitchen, skirted by an ample garden, the structure once had a hayloft, now remodeled into a nursery for Ocean. The staircase leading up to it was lined with reproductions of Picasso ceramics, an inimitable bird printed on each colored plate: "Wake-up birdies," Ocean called them, and each had a name that she pronounced as her mother carried her up to the nursery.

"She's not afraid to go to bed at night with those birds there to keep her safe."

Cynthia set out a lunch of fruit and nuts, brown bread, cheese, honey, some melon soup for the three of them, and a liter of local beer for two.

Ocean chewed and watched the strange man in indifferent silence. After finishing her lunch, the child sat on the wooden floor merrily shuffling a pile of pots and lids. ("No carpets here, I'm glad to see" remarked Denis.) She was a creamy waif of a creature, with sparkling blue eyes and the constant promise of laughter that rarely sounded. He thought about an appropriate gift for her before he left town.

IF he left town.

Van Zan interrupted his revery.

"I've been reading about admirable older women of the world, most of them yearning, in torment for never getting what they deserve, always expecting some sort of fulfillment—I used to envy them for what they did have. Then . . ."

"Then this child?"

"She is already a fulfillment, and I was unprepared. I now need to be worthy of her."

"How? Through Christmas jingles and get-well cards?"

"Not only, although they're a step above cartoons of babbling prawns and mendacious politicians. That's no longer my mask today. Now it's books that I'm doing, and soon dramatized narratives of the real world in 3D—educational nutrition, the way poetry and song used to be, or theater, cinema, opera . . ."

"Ah yes," muttered Denis. "Thanks for the opera."

"I knew you needed to wake up to what those sopranos had to tell you about the decline and fall of authority. All those who died for love of men."

"Not for humanity?"

"They didn't get that chance. Men popped in first, bloody handed, with their needs and their constraints."

He needed to change the subject. "So tell me how you managed to . . ."

"To get out here?"

"Yes, into business with the Dahomeans, and," (gesturing toward the preoccupied child) "with her."

"She did it, didn't you, noisy little Ocean? She and the Nigerians—and Paris."

"Yes, how did that combination happen—and to you?"

"To me, of all people? Of course, where else does a floundering fish go to reach an ocean?"

"To Paris? You found Paris on the high seas? And now Abuja, halfway inside this big country?"

"Sure. You only have to imagine yourself on the way, from the headwaters, down a great river . . ."

"On the way, 'AuxIndes,' as it were?"

"Right. I'm still swimming down."

"How did that happen? You needed money, work, medical care in Paris. Did you have a job or something?"

"Sure I did. Got it all, all I needed. First from the Nigerians. We just joined their music. I arrived there as a singer, after all—not a good one, but I faked being good, joined their beat. They knew me as a returning captive from West Africa, via a long, tortured interval in the USA and a warm-up in the fisheries of AuxIndes." He noticed again how the streak in her hair glowed brightest when she became excited.

As Cynthia explained her last two-plus years, she had befriended the Nigerian musicians in Paris's polyglot Clichy, eliciting curiosity from the start about a café-au-lait American woman singing to hybrid music out of the eastern sea. "Those Nigerians were displaced, too, like us Yankees in Indesville. Open-ended France kept them busy as beavers, and as destructive. But they took us in—me and then Ocean. I really thank Marty's piano for their interest; they heard him at the stadium where we were all playing, à la festival mode. He was on the cool wave-lengths of those islands, blended with jazz originality and swing. The French heard that, and the Vietnamese, also the Arabs, the Hausa and Ibos from this country. After they listened to Marty backed up by the Silhouettes, they had me write songs for them. I even sang some."

"They paid you for that?"

"More or less. And stop being so haughty, Mister Critical. They were more than just exotics. This was part of a close-knit enclave imbedded in third-world Paris. So I also got some illustrative work and digital messaging—designs, photographs, advertising, some stuff I'm not proud to own and didn't sign with the long ears. They made sure I was getting on."

"Even in Paris?"

"Especially in Paris."

"And her, the baby, her too?"

"She was crucial. She proved that I could start again, learning how to learn, to grow, to be human."

"Yeah, you and a father."

"No, she's fatherless. By the way, my AuxIndes passport got us the Nigeria visa, and kept me away from the US Embassy, but one day I'll have to register Ocean as an American born 'out of wedlock,' ugh. Please don't speculate, Denis. The guy who thinks he's it? He only wants to own a child, MY child. After all those years helping large mammals push out kids for themselves."

"How did he fix on you, then?"

"You really want to know? Ski is really very sweet, but he's obsessed with that great-great-great something or other of his, the one who claimed to be a Hungarian or Polish nobleman; who galloped through Europe to the end of Siberia—on a white stallion of course, it has to be a white stallion—and claiming to become the ruler, the legitimate king, of a south sea island eerily similar to AuxIndes."

"You mean Ski identified with some old psychedelic lunacy?"

"After a second vodka, he never stopped raving about it, and how he would resume the conquest some day. When we were in Poznan he even fixated on mounting that flamboyant horse on top of the Opera House, and flying off into outer space, and landing as emperor of the Indies. He imagined breeding Pegasus with that mare in the old governor's statue, if it is a mare. I'm supposed to be there, his brown amazon, to film the whole thing. He loved that awful monument, his fetish. Masson should have pulled it down when he could."

"I think I see why you decided to leave Poznan."

"So you've heard that story?"

"Some of it. Not the aeronautical fantasy part. And for your information, I've not heard him claim paternity over your . . . pregnancy; I'm not sure he knows about Ocean."

"So much the better, Denis."

True, Guyane thought. Ocean did not betray her origins—creamy beige color with blue eyes and fine hair; she could be sired by Ski, or the younger De Justesse, or Marty, or . . . Masson? At least not by Guyane. But somehow he couldn't banish the mental image of a cuckold's horns sprouting on his own head. Did that malicious Vinaigrette lady plant the Valkyrie's hat on him?

Van Zan penetrated his delusion. "Wake up, Denis. It's not for you to worry about."

He groaned. "Right. But you also had to get out of Clichy; no place to bring up a child." He looked around at the cabin fitted to herself from some sort of shed offered by the clinic or school, with electricity, plumbing, her studio, expressionist abstractions on the walls, and Ocean's stairway through birdland.

"How did you get here?"

"Here and not elsewhere? Not even Lagos by the sea? It was the midwife, the one who coaxed Ocean out of me into Paris." She beamed at the child. "Turns out that nurse was unlicensed. But she had the touch, old Sola, and Ocean forgives her, right, love? Anyway, Sola was deported back to Nigeria. The French honor the diploma more than they do professional efficacy. Since she's from the central region, Sola headed back into her own family in this fast-growing town that needs expertise, with or without diplomas. With or without the sea, so we brought our own Ocean out here. This became what Baldwin called 'Elsewhere,' our refuge, now our incubator."

"So your musician friends let you go."

"Reluctantly, yes. They miss Sola more than me. She has a job here with the hospital, and the children's clinic is part of a school, private but very non-profit. The staff invited me to join them on campus, at least until the squatter town disappears and our prairie comes up next for construction. They found guys to redo the cabin. I contribute my rent by photo-ing the patients, teaching the kids how to draw birds and mice, filming the school families—free for them. Their stories are treasure troves. Nigeria is full of stories."

"Including yours, Cynthia my friend."

"Yes." Then she sighed. "But mine has just hit a bump—pleasant but troublesome, like a snow drift. For you show up here waving some sort of printing contract from Big Eddie in Lagos. AND anything else?"

"Nothing else. Not even sure about that contract, although you deserve one, you and your Dahomean Atayis. Just a vague hello from the Fisherman and the rest of us over there. Unless *you* want something more than that."

"You know already. Nothing, except your silence. I'm happy here. Ocean is joyous; she has friends and can play concertos on her pots and pans while I work. She could become a triumphant young person in Abuja. And if you divulge where we are, we'll have to leave. I'm sick of having to dance on the treadmills of identity."

"I understand, but don't try to make me regret that I found you."

"No, I'm thrilled that you did. But I don't want to risk all this . . . this freedom. Who else beside you and your girl Friday knows where we are?"

He had to think for a moment about the answer. "Others know that I came to Nigeria looking for you on a hunch. But actually, only Eddie and Bisi know you're here."

"Not the Fisherman or anybody else in the pool?"

"Not even Vinaigrette, assuming I can take her literally. She'd never betray you if she did know." Here he paused. "But if you're not yet outed, it's just my dumb luck. I did try to report—not to expose you, just to tell the boss where I was. Tried to email, to text, phone, but haven't been able to get a word through to Indesville, not even to Bamiara. They know I've come to Nigeria, but that's all. It's strange."

Cynthia, smiling: "Very strange. Rather lucky."

"Eddie knows something that seems to have happened there. Possibly serious misfortune on the island. Somebody may have died; or a bad cyclone, with all power lines down. Not the first time. Yet, he'd have specified anything like that in detail. And there's no word from anybody there. Eddie didn't want to discuss it on the phone, wary of blowing my 'cover.' So I need to get back to Lagos and at least learn what it's all about."

They looked at each other, shook their heads in unison.

Van Zan stood up. "Better go," she said finally, then stooped to hoist Ocean, who was still flourishing a saucepan. "Let's hope your flight's not full. Or rather, hopefully it is full. We really don't want you to leave. I love your visit, want to continue talking to you. But this may be more important. I'll drive you to the hotel and the airport."

Guyane insisted on stopping to bring Ocean into a toy store and purchase whatever she wanted, which turned out to be a miniature forest full of painted birds and squirrels to attach to tree limbs and a few worms to burrow underneath. "Real wood?" Denis asked hopefully. The clerk shook her head.

"Plastic."

He let the child carry her box of plastics back to the car.

Once he'd registered for his flight he texted Eddie.

After Van Zan parked, they both emerged for a long silent hug that Denis knew he would remember for the rest of his life—his body joined to Cynthia's lithe, glowing vitality. "I hope you don't have compunctions about embracing a shark," she said with a rare grin.

"Not if we're both under water . . . Adieu, Madam Kondo," he growled. Peeking into the rear seat, he saw Ocean scanning images on her unopened carton of forest life. She appeared to be reading them—a two-year-old studying the natural world through plastic images. He realized how blessed Ocean's father had been, for one moment at least, and how lucky any successor would be, knowing Cynthia's potency.

As the plane was taxiing into its berth, Guyane received a text from Oyelemo: "I'm here. Don't show other passport. Use American one." Himself had indeed come. In the arrival area, Eddie towered imperiously over the crowd. Enclosed in his voluminous *agbada* and crowned with a bright head-scarf, he seemed a gowned obelisk claiming the land for terra cotta. Approaching the gate, Denis waved a greeting that froze in the air when he noted his host's expression.

CHAPTER 14

EMBARKATIONS

The deposed chief of state, 2015, on an African beach:

What! growling again, *Moby*? Every morning brings out your snarl of the day. Are you rehearsing a role in Speranza's annual Zoo Story or trying to teach me some new invective? Kindly quiet down and give the ocean a chance. Bulldogs aren't supposed to get jittery. And there's no use barking at waves; they break but don't speak canine.

Believe me, exile isn't all that painful, not while we still have one another. The Massons—Giselle and you and I—are welcome in Speranza indefinitely—or as long as our funds hold out. Here I can plod along a shore barefoot, you paddle against the surf, and we no longer worry if the fish will forgive us for what we've done to them.

Freed from cares of state and industry, let's anticipate a more promising future. I'm growing a beard, you draw crowds gossiping in your global language, we eat fruit galettes until the honey oozes out, and there's plenty of poetry to bark and read. Being here improves my English without betraying our sacred Francophone heritage, yours or mine. We count on sympathy from our host, Speranza's president who perpetually fears a coup d'état under his own nose. If that happens, he'll know where to seek shelter—assuming I can offer it by then.

FYI: that's a principle called reciprocity among nations.

Admittedly, temporary exile from our island has some disadvantages. I miss conversing with my bats and spiders, for instance, and with your big buddies the Charolais. Worse, on this continent, we have to watch out for lions and snakes. AuxIndes doesn't have such predators; only its humans get that malicious. Worst of all, people tell me that as a guest here, I may have to start wearing socks to formal events. You don't think that's necessary, do you? I'll forgive you for not answering that one.

On our morning walks, Moby, you're good at playing president, so that I don't have to do that any longer. I'm pleased when you tug me to your favorite places and toward your friends. When dogs walk their people (some think it's the reverse, but we know better), I perceive how a canine uses humans to carry messages to and from other dogs. Consultation gives you a reason for keeping us around. As the Americans say (or they should), there's more than one way to pick up poop.

If it's true that you guys practice systematic communication on land, we might accept Van Zan's argument that sea creatures also have comparable powers in their own world. Perhaps their languages provide ways of taking care of their interests, without conflict.

Then, however, Anya Wazimbwe's anthropocentrism makes less sense. (By the way, where is the regal Diva now?)

But even if ocean folk manage the world better than we landlubbers, what good does that do on land? Can they be of use to us? Could whales have protected me from the striped weasels who now presume to govern AuxIndes? Could I have finished off Karamau with a poisoned prawn?

Frivolous, trivial thought, that one; it reminds me of the plight of exile. (Sigh.) So go ahead, Moby, growl all you please.

You must have been glad, though, to see your friend Guyane join us—temporarily at least. I owe Denis a great deal from the day when we started together at Kennedy Airport. How can I repay him for such service? Perhaps Giselle and I could learn to play card games and pay him off with our deracinated aces and kings. Would you like us to do that, Moby, while you bark in spades?

Not today, though, for we have matters of pith and moment to consider. There is this afternoon's broadcast to my partisans back in Indesville—the telephone harangue that Speranzans call my "pep talks." Once a week, I say something positive to the party—to buttress fragile trust in my faithful BeauxIndiens. Remarkably, the less believable I am, the more trustworthy I become. Fortunately, the Karamaus have been clumsier communicators than I. We're both unable to mobilize Samuel's birds or Vinaigrette's masks or Cynthia's schools of porpoises. At least my message is honest, while the usurpers trip over themselves trying to pitch their fabricated illusions to "the masses." Eyewash! all those pretenders know is to keep shooting Spiders off the old Governor's horse.

And since the spiders creep back, what do I say to the loyalists today? Perhaps I could explain how, like the lugubrious Philosophe, I foresaw everything happening, placed it in a context, and believed I could impose my will. That might ring true, although, unlike Karamau, I couldn't make it work. I lacked his guile. I had no desire to trick anybody. *My* "everything" just fell apart by itself. Useless to say that to the partisans.

Or maybe admit that I counted too heavily on our business success, my place in the larger world, access to international funding agencies, respect for universal standards of governance. Those are assets, too, but I failed to understand that political affairs, like industrial progress, demanded results, not just convenient affiliations or mere good faith. No, too confessional. The BeauxIndes party doesn't need reminders.

When they think about it, my people should grant me credit for refusing to depend on old colonialists with ulterior designs. Moreover, I created the party out of whole cloth, so that we could recruit the Bernards and Benjamins and Solanges back into the public orbit; even the African-American duo, Cynthia and Guyane who initially came out just to help me sell fish. And then did so much more.

Strange that Karamau's usurpers slander that American pair as "Black mercenaries," while popular opinion considers them to be white.

Better to leave that part out, too. Where were we, Moby?

Yes, Denis Guyane. After finding the enigmatic Van Zan in Nigeria, he's had to join me directly here in Speranza. He's forced into our exile with what he believes to be his own secret—even after meeting Vinaigrette. Hah! I know you are fond of Denis, Moby. He's been the most transparent of them all, polychrome yet shadowless, unaware of himself. Sadly for you and me, Vinaigrette thinks he'll be leaving us soon, to return home, if New York is indeed where he belongs. Of course he won't want to stay indefinitely in our Speranzan refuge—a *triple* exile for Guyane, if you start him off as a Haitian maroon in Brooklyn who defected to AuxIndes with me, and then perforce to this place where you bark at breakers.

Back to today's weekly sermon from our refuge. It's fortunate that Bamiara can broadcast my voice around our shuttered supermarket in Indesville. Benjamin has only limited scope to act, though, for Philosophe's people are constantly watching and listening. In their mendacious theory, I voluntarily resigned as chief of state and chose exile to escape impeachment. Our agile Peasant has to accommodate that lie in order to assure my chance—as a failed politician, to speak long-distance today into the AuSecours parking lot.

Failed? At least Roger Masson is not an enemy of the people chased by the hounds of justice. Not yet. You will alert me when you hear it from those dogs, right?

Assuming I can get it past Karamau's censors, our listeners might appreciate a Victor Hugo lesson. They would learn how a ruthless Interior Minister could steadily exploit what I'd failed to see—that his motivating factor in public life was pure self-service; that a hypocrite can be competing while ostensibly cooperating. It was not merely my own mistake: the Wazimbwes and our other entitled families allowed that vicious trickster to seduce them too, by accepting his pretense as defender of their property rights as grounds for his insurgency.

You may growl at that, Moby; blindness got us all into real trouble.

To give Karamau due credit, I now perceive how shallow was the public support for what I wanted to accomplish. While I deluded myself into expecting appreciation for our compassionate policies, it was easy for him to distort my motives, to denounce my crucial decisions as originating in business greed. Moreover, I calculated only in terms of my five-year mandate while Antoine managed for a quarter century to guarantee his own survival across changes of policy and administration.

Able to bide his time, harmonizing hypocritically with the logic in my options, he waited for circumstances to combine in his interest.

Combine they did for him last year, just in time to head off my inevitable reelection. Philosophe could exploit his prerogative to investigate corruption, falsely impugning my governance reforms as "power grabs." He denounced our commodity boards as subsidiaries to unnamed foreign firms. He fabricated fictitious abuses by us against urban real estate, making me appear to be (hah!) anti-business, so that his nephew could win cheers for expropriating our urban property just to build a bus depot—they even named it Karamau Station! When such misinformation was challenged, he evaded lawsuits by intimidating the feeble magistrates who he had recruited after amputating their backbones.

I could explain how Antoine needed to keep La Vinaigrette's caustic pen out of the country; that he concocted that "mercy mission" for Sophie to sit at the moribund Domino's bedside in Europe. For all I know, he might have been slowly poisoning old Bienportant all the time. While courting the oil companies for his finances and the Silhouettes for distraction, he even diverted the tipsy prophet Ishmael by branding me an atheist and a patron of pederasts.

Most crucially, my partisans should realize that the Army would ignore Karamau's conspiracy when the time came. Of course, our fastidious troops would never intervene in "politics"—certainly not to save an unreliable incumbent like me. Not while Thérèse Zaphyra was there to defend me and antagonize the true believers. I handed Antoine that one. Was I wrong to let her "breeze" into bed with anybody she could overpower—meaning the whole officer corps? They knew how to retaliate.

The climax came when I dispatched Zaphyra to Pretoria and then North Carolina in our effort at modernizing the armed forces. Allowing my brawny pacifist Defense Minister to stay away for so long enabled Karamau to subvert the one battalion that he needed to invade the "palace" and disarm my faithless guards. With nobody around to muscle their quiescence, they swallowed Philosophe's solemn pledge that he and Kumar would pick up where Bienportant left off. They would revive the National Party and restore Napoleonic discipline. That lie kept the remaining troops in their barracks toying with their telephones.

After evicting us, Moby, Antoine's police militias took over from the Army. They besieged my ministries, occupying them under a sham state of emergency, and never looked back. That maneuver shadowed what I had done to the Domino five years earlier through the labor unions—while Karamau watched and took notes. When time came to sabotage me, he just stood there waving his arms, "conducting" an operation that would hoist me on my own petard.

I was not Hamlet enough for that emergency. The outcome might have been even worse if I had followed my instincts and vigorously resisted expulsion. Don't look up quizzically like that, Moby; you know you were barking me on. There we were, we two, a humiliated forty-year-old statesman and his dog, both raging in impotence at an armed squadron. It took a trio of women—Giselle, Anya, Solange Seriel, to calm us down—prompted by a strategic call from Vinaigrette in Europe, forcing me to face inevitability with some dignity intact.

Unfortunately, I can't divulge all that in public now without giving my enemies a pretext to cancel my chances for restoration. After such useless speculations, here I stroll, leashed to you, my grumbling Moby. So let the oceans roar with reassurance to the (ahem!) multitudes at home that I shall return, bringing redemption to AuxIndes.

Or some such message.

Too bad Philosophe's puppet, Kumar, has authorized only one entry visa thus far—for Guyane. You were looking for him, but Denis is going there today on his American passport, ostensibly to pack up his own and Cynthia's affairs, and get out of the country. That's hardly a triumphant avenue of repatriation for me, the legitimate chief of state. Naturally, he'll try to negotiate more on the spot. I wish Anya were in Indesville to add leverage—and glamor—to that petition.

Or that they all were *here*, where we are now. That I could reassemble our crew of thinkers and technicians, using Speranza's advanced media facilities. From this beach a government in exile could launch Van Zan's billboards into orbit.

That's a sandcastle, I know, daydreaming. But we'll see what Denis can accomplish if he manages a conversation with Karamau.

For now, old Moby, we're reduced to barking over a telephone hookup into an unseen crowd at the mercy of Antoine's Gendarmerie. Getting down to today's message: I'll tell them that emissaries will arrive to arrange my return under honorable circumstances, whatever they might be; that international pressure is on our side; that all Africa, the Great Powers, the United Nations, everybody condemns that despicable putsch. I know they do. You do too, so remind your friends. They will listen to you.

Think about it. Can a stranded kingfish devour an aberrant philosopher? You seem dubious, but never underestimate the ferocity of a hungry tuna.

If you agree, Moby, wag your stump of a tail. Good job. When our walk is over, I'll rehearse my speech to you.

❊ ❊ ❊

Into the Net, and Then?

Early that morning, while Masson and Moby were exploring destiny on the beach, Denis Guyane left Speranza. He reached Indesville as the police were digesting Fisherman's exhortation to his partisans. On arrival, Bamiara told him that the speech had landed favorably among an "audience of dozens." No reaction yet from the Ministry whose agents had listened from dispersed positions in the parking lot. "Easy enough to spot," Benjamin said, "even without the obvious recording devices under their sweatshirts. They'll take a while to decipher the monologue he delivered today—trying to figure out who this 'Moby' is and then why Roger would harangue a dog!"

To facilitate the visit, the Peasant expected that Denis could collect his and Cynthia's keys from the police at "Interior" without incident. "Karamau ardently wants to wipe you out," he said, "and especially Van Zan."

Bamiara urged him nonetheless to wheedle a conversation on the spot with the traitorous Philosophe, favoring Masson's repatriation. "Let's hope he'll want to practice his *Hinglish*."

So it went. As he was about to exit the Ministry with their keys, Guyane encountered the great man's personal secretary who drew him to a corner of the lobby with a message from her boss. "The Minister will meet you tomorrow morning at 8:15 on University Hill by the equestrian monument. He assumes you know how to find the site. Please don't be late. Mr. Karamau has little time, but it's a place that he visits with respect. I hope I can tell him that you will be there."

Repressing his surprise at the location and immediacy of the appointment, Guyane assented. He then went to his own and Cynthia's flats. Indeed all their personal and business effects had been stored in those domiciles—after the obligatory fumbling and sifting, no doubt. Benjamin had authority to pay rent and shipping costs out of residual funds in AuThon's accounts—the ones not yet confiscated.

Once inside the apartments, Denis found the contents disposed in a semblance of order. Little if anything was missing; they had even left printouts of Van Zan's most trenchant cartoons and digitalized parodies. He began packing, took possession of the most valuable personal items, threw out nonessentials, and called a forwarding agency to bundle and ship the rest to his parents in Brooklyn. If he remained overseas, the elder Guyanes would have to resend Cynthia's property wherever she directed. Soon Denis could stare along the blank vectors of his own future.

He packed vigorously for several hours, then neglected to have dinner.

Next morning, Guyane perched by the Governor General's pedestal, his feet on the grass border. He watched University staff and students surge out of their buses and trickle into the campus buildings, most of them late for their 8 a.m. class or office hours. That was probably why Philosophe had decided on this time, he mused; it was typical of the man to watch from inside an animated throng. At an earlier or later hour he would have been conspicuous.

On the dot at 8:15, the minister's shadow hovered over him. As usual, Karamau was shrouded in his black redingote, and as always, he gestured with his hands before speaking. "I should be insincere if I regretted your having to depart so abruptly," were Philosophe's first words after waving off the handshake that Denis had not proffered. Seated on the pedestal rim, he waited for Guyane to resume his place and looked around at the setting. "I come here at times," Karamau said, "to rejoin the kid who was killed before he could shoot at me. Or pretend to shoot. You've heard that story, I'm sure. Freddy Khoin, the Spider, still inhabits this site. It's supposed to be a listening post for messages from the prophet Ishmael."

Then a dismissive arm movement, as if to add I don't suppose you know much about all that foolishness.

"I've heard some of that," Denis replied, "and I can see the situation still has power. But that you . . ."

"That I would take the time and trouble?"

Philosophe's face nearly came to a smile, but it resisted. "We have common origins, Spider and I—and probably Ishmael, too." He dropped both arms to his sides. "Inherited low caste, Africa-shaded, nappy hair. Not like your elegant boss. I don't hold that against Masson, not personally. He probably doesn't even recall this, but once, when he was home from school, his honorable father told Roger that 'some slave kid' had come to kick footballs with him. That kid was me."

"Hmm," mused Denis, "I'd never impute that kind of prejudice to the man I know."

"Not to your decent Fisherman, perhaps. But note that I'm ten years older than he; do you think the story explains something about his origins—and about me?"

"Never crossed my mind," Guyane answered quietly, wondering why Philosophe had suddenly become long-winded. "But you did arrange Roger's Quebec fellowship, setting him up for business and for what evolved. Unless that only gives you reasons for . . ."

"For overthrowing him?" Karamau grunted deeply in his throat. "No need of that. He expelled himself. True to his class, Masson confuses status with power, illusion with reality. He couldn't understand the hypocrisy of the great clans, the networks. They called him brother, when they fully intended to uproot his authority if ever it challenged them. Them and their military." He waved up to the statue. "Although your man Bamiara knew this—that crafty fake Peasant—still Masson could never understand it."

"Meaning," Denis interpreted, "that the Fisherman President was too much the gentleman . . ."

"No, too much the reformer, the superior patrician allowed to pry our culture loose. He thought he could show where the money comes from before it's laundered; that he could ignore the prerogatives that men—always the same men and their sons—that these men hold over our institutions. He thought himself into that class. And he even tried to get his own wife elected mayor!"

"I understand that part of it, Minister. You saw Giselle as a destabilizing threat. Like Anya, both Massons were trying to correct the unstable rhythms that come from suppression of women in this society."

"What suppression, may I ask?"

"Aborted education of girls, abusive bride prices and dowries, toleration of domestic violence, unbalanced divorce and property laws, interference with women's authority over their own bodies . . ." He watched Karamau raise his great hands over his head, thumbs furled. "I see, Minister, that you've heard the melody."

"Yes, my American moralist. And I'll skip the obvious retort about your own country's flaws; those you already know too well. I concede, however, that it's actually a strength that your national brand of feminism has aimed at parity—a homage to men—rather than at emasculation." He enacted the snapping of a branch over his massive knee.

"Now that we're in charge here," Philosophe continued, "I no longer deplore the buxom Giselle or her aggressive suite. La Vinaigrette has got too old to be anything more than an occult nuisance. Even your compatriot artist-lady and her doodlings seem well away—and good riddance to her trouble. As for the sublime Wazimbwe, like you I'm so enamored that I'd follow her into ecological Nirvana if she invited me; but she too has gone off. And you had already taken refuge with the charming accountant Seriel, while I . . ."

He paused, and Denis waited.

"Actually the last straw," Karamau said blithely to reinforce his reputation, "was Masson's insufferable Defense Minister. Think of it, a poly-sexual female in charge of the Army! You should have heard my police officers discuss your Ms. Zaphyra. Muscling into the military establishment, taking our command staff out to South Africa for retraining. *Re*-training, mind you, after generations faithfully formed in the schools that their titles and language come from— from Napoleon, from *him* . . ." He gestured up to the prancing

Governor. "General Charpentier is probably returning Thérèse's sa-lute in mockery from his grave. Some of those officers composed a malicious song, in English: 'No beer, Zapheer,' it starts."

He stopped again, a bit out of breath.

Declining to acknowledge such perverse misogyny, his interlocu-tor said nothing. Denis still felt La Brise's loving assault on him dur-ing the election campaign. He knew the Karamaus to be immune to sexual or cultural subtlety; they would always think in bimodalities.

Philosophe changed the subject. "By the way, we have proposed to pry this monument off its hill and put it downtown at the mu-seum. The French didn't object, but University faculty wanted to keep him here. The faculty, mind you: Liberals! Perhaps because they so rarely show up to work, they never have to see the statue anyway."

"Any way indeed," Denis echoed; then impatiently, "I suppose you agreed to this chat, Minister, with an object in mind. What do you want me to convey back to President Masson?"

Karamau glanced skyward as if awaiting authorization from the statue. "*The* president, President Hannibal Karamau, has listened to his advisors and will not be unreasonable. Mr. Masson retains his passport and will be permitted to return to the country after the lapse of enough time for popular outrage to subside and support for our current program to consolidate. Say after one more year, but the timing will be subject to negotiation here with Mr. Bamiara. As will the consignment of Masson's industrial interests—those that don't infringe on the justifiable rights of other businesses, or on the state.

"To protect domestic security," he continued, "Mr. Masson will be precluded from competing in the next election and from any sub-sequent access to national office. That's the message, very gracious,

I assure you, requesting that you convey it to Citizen Masson. President Karamau's offer will not be put into writing or made public until we have heard acceptance through Bamiara. Now forgive me if my time has expired."

He turned away, pausing at the spot where Spider had fallen nineteen years before. "And if I lack the courtesy of offering you a ride back to town. Better we had not, you understand."

"I do," Denis assured him. "But you will of course anticipate some objection to the preconditions you've just enunciated. Including the rights of property and some international concerns due to a duly elected chief of state."

Karamau nodded slowly, taking a deep breath. "Negotiation! Humbug!" He stressed the words in English with a contemptuous gesture, then strode through the gate to his staff car.

As he watched this exit, Guyane thought: so that's what they call a strongman. Someone who apprehends threats from women, who now talks too much, and who leaves principles of rights and comity up to conflict among unequals.

Speaking later with Bamiara, Denis learned that Karamau's dalliance with the oil companies had induced him to forsake the De Justesses, that he threw some sort of bribery laws at them. They were languishing in jail awaiting a trial that might never come. How could the man be trusted to keep even his own self-serving bargain?

Sensing that he was being watched by the martyred Spider atop the horse's great mid-morning shadow, Guyane walked forlornly downhill to the apartment. He was eager to talk with Vinaigrette and with Benjamin, and to prepare the uncomfortable conversation he would have next day in Speranza with the Fisherman.

On his way to the flat he replenished his coffee provisions and, after starting a cup, tried to reach Sophie Makoa, to invite her to talk that evening. Vinaigrette didn't answer, but left a message in response. She was not interested in a meeting. She hoped he would remember her to Cynthia if he ever saw her again. Van Zan had a touch that could enliven so many spirits. "But it's all over out here," Makoa concluded, "except for your beloved Masson's agony once he comes back. A changed mask for him. But for now, keep his hopes alive. The struggle continues. Goodbye and bon voyage."

For some reason, he chose to see this dismissal as a release.

At lunch hour he went to meet Bamiara at a café to discuss the weekly telephone broadcasts from Speranza and prospects for Masson's repatriation. The Peasant listed attentively to Guyane's account of the exchange with Philosophe, if only to infer what it meant to the business he maintained for AuThon. Yet he seemed especially curious about the decision to leave the equestrian Governor deployed on University Hill. Benjamin had, after all, participated in the campus demonstration that ended in Spider's demise, so it was odd that he now approved leaving the statue in place.

"It keeps the image of the foreign conqueror presiding over Babel," Bamiara said by way of explanation. "And thus justifies our recovery of integrity. Despite inherited differences between classes and gender, this island has achieved what your greater polities still struggle to do: under Masson we incorporated a heterogenous population into a functioning democracy—interrupted by the current temporary setback, of course, but we'll have it back again shortly."

Guyane wondered at such confidence, but Benjamin went on. "We've done it through having a common enemy—namely, the colonizers. Of course the historical record is always ambiguous. Up there on Babel Hill, that statue stands for the hated model, for 'benevolent oppression.' If that were to get transplanted downhill, our own demons would be rising to take its place. We'd be at war with ourselves. Iconoclasm has no legitimate role in enlightened democracy."

"Yet monument removal is just what Americans are undertaking today," replied Denis, "as Haitians did over 200 years ago."

"I don't care much for Haitian iconoclasm either. But you Americans think you can legislate your inequities away—that you can smooth out a twisted culture through the rule of law. Those laws can be flipped on their back like a beached turtle; they turn into mere 'law-and-order,' kicking legs aimlessly in the air. You aren't going to unify a country peacefully by ordering people together who don't want to be together. You need an enemy, and there are times when you must create one from within. Having rehabilitated the old British colonizer you Americans fling yourselves on your despicable slavemongers—the lost cause that now rears up as the 'white man's mission.' Just beware the repercussions when you demolish the monuments of the conflicts you've won."

So, thought Denis, the proud island republic had found a reason, even for the once rebellious Benjamin, to retain an imperious governor at the top of its mountain. The enemy, on horseback, going nowhere—just where it belongs.

But if Spider takes the saddle, then what to expect? The proverbial Peasant seemed immune to the question.

On Denis's departure morning, Benjamin had a surprise for him. After stowing Guyane's bags, Bamiara opened the rear door of his

Renault, keeping its windows black-shaded. At first the American was surprised by the oddity of being ushered into a back seat, then by the discreet presence of another passenger already there. There was no mistaking the luster that emanated through the veil. The Diva beckoned Denis in beside her and took his hand.

"I'm not really here," Anya said in the softer voice that she reserved for confidences. "So far as anybody knows I'm out on the high seas, still helping attack the enemies of peace. Actually I've been sheltered by somebody you've met. When the old woman realized that I didn't need protection from you, she deputized me to come with Benjamin, to say goodbye for her and deliver her regrets over not taking your phone call more graciously. That gives me the chance to tell you that I have begun to understand Cynthia—her principles and her style, if not her tone. And specially to express my own appreciation for all you've done for us, Denis, and how rewarding it's been to work with you."

Barely able to breathe, conscious for the first time of having a chest cavity, Guyane closed his eyes and nodded for nearly ten seconds, as Benjamin's vehicle careened the chaotic streets. Then Denis rejoined the world. "This means very much to me, Anya. Thank you."

After another long pause, he added, "While we're here, please help me understand something. On the phone yesterday, Sophie warned me that Masson would be unhappy once he returned. She advised me not to break it to him, but can you at least explain that for me?"

The answer came in Wazimbwe's crisp professional voice. "She's right, and I think you have an inkling already. The usurpers have been coerced by the multilateral agencies and African presidents to schedule an election in a year or two. Karamau agreed to make it happen, Satanically obtaining a condition that Roger be prohibited from resuming office—from taking the revenge that he deserves. Don't warn Fisherman or put anything in writing, but the internationals agreed."

"That's unreasonable interference, Anya. You know that Masson would never resort to vengeance. It's not in his repertoire."

"Perhaps, but Antoine thinks differently; he thinks if somebody can retaliate, they'll do it. Moreover, with Roger out, Karamau could have a pretext to withdraw himself from the race."

"Out of an abundance of reciprocity? Him?" Denis nearly guffawed.

"No. He'd never risk election, but he can pretend self-denial as a gracious price to keep Roger away from the Presidency."

"So who will actually show up in the lists? The Rapper on that side, maybe; and who against him? Not Giselle if her husband is rudely excluded. You, perhaps?"

From the driver's seat, Bamiara hoisted an approving fist in the air. The Diva pulled Benjamin's arm back down and shook her head emphatically. "In this automobile," she answered quietly, "I can only assure you that Masson's legacy won't disappear. The candidate will have adequate resources and endorsements. But please don't prepare Fisherman; he'd rush in and jeopardize it."

The Peasant continued to drive, but Guyane watched his countenance darken in the rearview mirror. Denis nodded, and turned to the Diva. "I'm impressed, Anya. Living with Madam Makoa has given you a sibylline flair. And since you're there, I'll bet you've taught Vinaigrette to use the vacuum cleaner."

She laughed and squeezed his hand, while Bamiara clucked his tongue and pulled up to the terminal. For security, the Peasant let Guyane retrieve his bags alone, keeping the doors closed and shaded against any curiosity. Then Benjamin drove off into a future that might some day clear those windows.

In the cottage placed at his disposal by their Speranzan hosts, ex-President Masson welcomed Denis back from Indesville, eager to learn how near, if at all, he had brought repatriation. Cheered by his reception at the rally in the AuSecours parking lot, he did not appear overly dismayed by Karamau's preconditions. The report offered by Guyane put him a step closer to his own country, his surviving enterprises, and a future for Giselle. He applauded Wazimbwe's clandestine repatriation, and noted Denis's admiration for Bamiara as his political emissary (if not as an authority on American social justice).

Modest improvement in the Fisherman's prospects gave Denis an opportunity to broach his own return to homeland and family. He sensed, however, that he was contradicting both Masson's and his father's thinking. Like Roger, Pierre-Louis had encouraged him to retain work in Africa, because, his father wrote, "you transmit the best that white culture can offer to the colored islands and continents. Africans appreciate you better than the USA ever will, and they will reciprocate. For Americans it's that you don't have a white body and aren't protected by white institutions and property."

Masson, concurring, added that "Americans with grievances will still blame you, the 'minorities,' for what elites and property-grabbers have done to them. In Africa you can claim acceptance as an honorary Black." This was a fiction that Fisherman and the elder Guyane favored over a forlorn trek through the obstacle course of American racism which would never accept him as an "honorary white."

By now, however, the son preferred to follow his mother's advice, and to avoid both shams. He had decided on an attempt to compose his own "*mask*"—Vinaigrette's way of specifying character. "My experiment in ambiguity is complete," Guyane told the Fisherman, "and you've been the main reason for its achievement. Cynthia and I have tried to assist a microcosm of this world, your republic, to help you adjust its trajectory, while the entire planet is becoming unrecognizable. Van Zan saw that already, back in California."

"Yes, Denis, and now I suffer for it in exile."

"By the way, Fisherman, speaking of that time in 'Frisco, how did you decide so spontaneously to bring Cynthia on board with us?"

"It wasn't all that abrupt," replied Masson, leafing through a book on his lap. "We got to know each other through a common medium."

"Surely not through the language—English or French?"

"Not quite, but Ms. Van Zan and I shared an ocean from long ago, a sea of enslavement that taught both of us to hate ourselves, separately, until . . ."

"Until what, Roger?"

"Until you showed up. We both needed you, and you needed her before we even met."

"Sure. But for business only."

"Of course, Cynthia embodied what you call your 'A-Game.' But your whole Agency staff, the women anyway, were convinced there was much more than that."

"The whole staff? Talking about . . .?"

"You never realized, Denis, what a subject you were . . . still are, for those Agency women, and how they envied, even resented, Ms. Van Zan."

Guyane shook his head in bewilderment. "You talked to whom about this? To Mrs. Rodriguez?"

Fisherman laughed. "Certainly, but the language block interfered, and the key arrangement back then was to employ Van Zan. We had to rig a conference telephone hookup. I called Cynthia in California while you were admiring Picasso or Frida Kahlo somewhere and we grunted through preliminaries. Then when we needed an interpreter, Cynthia called your graciously bilingual mother. Madam Guyane rang my room to put me on the line, and translated Rodriguez's strong recommendation in Van Zan's favor. Although she wished both of you were still at the Agency, Madam Rodriguez was willing to see you out to AuxIndes to help our business. Then your mother called Cynthia and me, to interpret details between us. Madam Guyane asked me not to tell you right away: 'meddling momma,' or some such phrase. That's it."

"It, eh? How do I digest 'it,' I wonder. Anyway, some day you will be accountable for what you and those good women built."

His predilection for the great voices gave Masson an answer: "We have endured a postmodern enactment of your poet's *Waste Land*. AuxIndes has alternated between drought and storm, the thunder that threatens and the cloud that brings rain. Now more drought, soon thunder, eventually life-restoring rain. But what will you tell your compatriots in America that *you* are bringing back?"

"A lesson of sorts," Denis groped for answers. "Not heroic or notorious, but necessary. Our civilization has come to the verge of self-destruction. We have allowed it to condemn the most defenseless species—oceanic, vegetable, animal, vulnerable humans. Always with open eyes that see nothing, until the killers in their blindness immolate themselves."

"Like the greedy oil prospectors in Giraudoux's *Madwoman*, plunging down the tunnel to hell under Chaillot."

"Before they're finished unearthing fossil fuels, however, the process of uprooting may finish us all off."

"What will stop that?" asked Fisherman with an ironic chuckle. "You and I cried out against them weakly, and too late. Now, like Prospero in the *Tempest*, I've already drowned my book."

"Not yet," said Guyane, "you will have the Peasant and the Diva as stewards of your vision, to keep its balance before it collapses with all the rest." He hoped he hadn't just said too much, but Fisherman remained in his scholastic mode.

"In the end, Denis, humans will blame their self-destruction not on the secular culprits, but on some sort of divinity. Maybe artificial intelligence will masquerade for providential justice."

"Possibly," replied Guyane, following suit. "In place of what Scriptures called the wrath of God, science has already substituted the climate, a product of our headlong consumption of the earth and the eruption of CO_2 and methane."

"The white whale strikes," intoned Masson, from inside his literary universe, "after turning itself into carbon dioxide. And what of Ms. Van Zan?"

"Cynthia has her response—a child born in innocence, to be cultivated like a flower, a tree, communing with all that's going to be left in the natural sphere."

"It's to her that Lear asks at the end to undo his button."

"Perhaps, but not to me. I think I know who I am here, now, and in your country. It's time for me to resume the other struggle—against the exclusions of my own unbalanced society—perhaps to be of use to Haiti unless it's already gone under."

He paused, and watched Masson smile, then added, "Of course I'm forever at your service if I can help you pursue the claim to your rights."

Masson nodded slightly, betraying nothing. This time, his silence proved helpful, as Denis tried to fathom what he had himself just said, and what he would ultimately make of that decision. It had proved easier to take leave of Masson than he'd imagined, thanks to Roger's distraction by apocalyptic metaphor. Perhaps Fisherman's plunge into literature was providential, so that he no longer suffered delusions. Guyane preferred to believe that Fisherman was already considering the option to retire into a scholarly milieu, and to support someone else for the presidency, whenever the election occurred. If true, Denis finally understood what Vinaigrette had meant by imputing love between him and Masson.

Then Roger Masson grins, snatches a flyswatter, and slaps it decisively against the wall just above Denis Guyane's head.

CHAPTER 15

DOWNSTREAM PORTS OF CALL

Sophie Nuru, Fables à La Vinaigrette, current issue.

Readers of my *Chronicle* know how ferociously I avoid foolish consistency—wisely called a hobgoblin of little minds. I'm proud, though, of some regularity, for I have dissected this island's power games over the decades. *Steadily?* Yes, but does that somehow make me *consistent?* Is there a foolish goblin imbedded in *my* capricious mind?

No, I insist. Consider my *Mask,* that wizened elf with her big head and Puckish temper: what's revealed is a constant display of *in*consistency.

By the way, I constantly refuse to get any younger. Is that my fault, too?

Another challenge met: I've consistently shunned the tacky contaminations of family. I don't cook for people, never gush over babies, and refuse to spawn. My sole exception into parenting has nothing to do with childbirth, so it doesn't count, but I'll tell you anyway. Months ago, after her tour with Greenpeace, I tucked Anya, the renegade Wazimbwe, under my wing, nearly like a daughter.

Yes, unoffically, the golden Diva has become this bony goblin's ward.

Adopted, of course. Nobody would ever infer that I could naturally beget anything so lovely.

Why in any case? Because Anya needed shelter after she hastily surfaced. She was still breathing fire against the Karamau mafia during their vicious persecution of Fisherman's friends. Only Bamiara knew she was here. The ruffians in charge never noticed her swathed in a hijab—just another one of my protégées, they thought, from the miserable Arab North.

As for me, dismissed as a harmless old-regime radical, I'm not much of a target. My illusory motherhood kept Anya busy ghost-writing diatribes in this *Chronicle* against people who poison the planet. So I provided domestic cover for the Diva until international "patrons" awoke to the mess the Karamaus were making.

Then public opinion forced the usurpers out.

Although Anya's polemics sounded suspiciously like my own inimitable style, some readers were puzzled: Instead of revolution, was La Vinaigrette actually stooping to conserve something? WHAT? life on earth! Who, me?

That, in itself, should qualify as a triumph of inconsistency.

I welcomed Anya's denunciations of planet-level polluters, for I too oppose recourse to poisons—in some contexts at least. You can't use toxins to assassinate newborn puppies, for example, nor spiritual sorcery on putative witches. Why witches? Because this island is planted so perilously on the raucous ocean that our entire population shivers in fear of exposure to malign spirits—witchcraft that carries the plight of sterility.

People are not aware that sterility is all due to our climate. Anya gets it, so I'm not digressing here.

To defend against the plagues that threaten us, fertilization has become our national sport. They tell me boys are running after witches all over the landscape, so why is it that none of them seem eager to chase *me*? If sterility is the spell cast by witchcraft, it follows that suspicious minds should condemn me for the childlessness of males like Doménique Bienportant, and Masson, and Antoine Karamau (especially him).

I can't prevent the scurrilous tongues of AuxIndes from suspecting me of sterilizing mankind. Still, that's going too far: correlations I will own, but not causality. And it's just *some* mankind, the ones I select. Most of the time I only emasculate their institutions, not their persons.

On the contrary, my mission is to cross-fertilize everybody—to liberate them into their sexiest masks, whether they realize it or not. Am I a sorcerer? No. Consistent? sometimes, but a hobgoblin? Get over it.

Common confusion about my motives does afflict the island's "little minds." Your Vinaigrette remains a revolutionary (admittedly a bit out of practice), but she is mainly a writer of current history. The chronicler's role is to produce coherent readings of people's experience, even though human activity rarely follows patterns of logic or purpose. Yet, a chronicle's credibility demands organization, so that I need to reorder events whenever necessary—to link past with present, and if there is a future, to clarify its antecedents (When do we want it? NOW!).

Over the years Vinaigrette's *Chronicle* has followed our national parade from one regime to another—the pageantry of caricatures that we call history. My work expects readers to grasp imaginative metaphor, to hear the dark murmur of disturbed seas and irate air, to sense the turbulence in roots underground, even to respect the vigilance of our tombs—Cousins Spider and Raina, or the undead like Ishmael, hawking their mysterious omens.

Yes, I also had to impose such inconsistencies on that fact-ridden American visionary, Cynthia Van Zan. A warrior woman transplanted from ancient Dahomey, she could never really digest ambiguity. As jeune fille, however, Cynthia could innocently explore the ocean's baffling resilience, swim wide-eyed among sharks and sea urchins. After that exposure she inevitably shuddered over the shambles of human society and deplored our garrulous way of wriggling out. In spite of herself, while her patience lasted, Van Zan translated human chaos into visual metaphors; stunning illustrations born out of common logic.

Then, in five years, when she ran out of patience, she left us.

During that time here, Cynthia's graphic portrayal of those contradictions even converted a reluctant Anya Wazimbwe, the Diva who would translate them into words. That combination may yet save the planet.

Or maybe not, but we're waiting. And my bags are packed.

Taking no credit, accepting no blame, but with inconsistent hope, I've recently encouraged Anya out of *purdah* to minister over President Bamiara's new government. Yes, it should really be *her* presidency, not his. But Benjamin stayed the course "like a man" after Masson and Karamau agreed reciprocally to withdraw, and I was still keeping Anya in protective custody. Even after she discarded the hijab, Masson's BeauxIndes party decided to fix on Bamiara "the man," and we got through the election handily. I'll have to stick around for the next episode, when I plan to assure the woman's overdue turn.

Once the Peasant has been inaugurated, Anya seems to think that his benevolent administration can render human beings worthy of redemption. After peering deeper under the ocean surface, Van Zan probably knows better. If I weren't Vinaigrette, I would agree with Prime Minister Wazimbwe.

Yes, she's prime minister. It's not for nothing that I adopted her.

Now to reward me (hah!), Anya requires that I "enliven" my next *Chronicle* through a series of dialogues with "notable personages," bright or shabby—supposedly as a boost for my circulation. To appease the prime minister I will stoop to admit new characters into my narratives; but I decline to select my interlocutors consistently. I'll talk with whomever I choose.

And I'll leave my cozy lodgings (others might use a different adjective to describe them) to call on some who'd be uncomfortable or unwelcome here.

First (and certainly least), the erstwhile usurper Hannibal Karamau, that ludicrous ex-mayor who should be gone for good. After sulking over his election defeat by President Bamiara, he accepted an anonymous offer of "higher education" abroad. Higher than what? You could scarcely lurk lower than the Rapper while he was Antoine's political facsimile.

This week, Indesville must suffer Hannibal's unlucky presence. To be sure, he's no longer national dunce or clown mayor; he comes back merely to remind us of his insipid early career as a disc jockey. Still, Hannibal may not always be as dumb as we knew him during the 2008 mayoral campaign.

"Which I won!" the Rapper interjects, reading my thought when I confront him at his radio station. He is intruding behind a microphone there during his holiday from that unwitting university in France.

"Where I hope you study what you should have known before playing mayor."

"And becoming head of state only six years later! A rapid rise, no, Sophie?"

I think he is actually recording this, so I keep quiet and let him prate on. "Taking advantage of my prestige," he boasts, flipping through his screens, "station KBS wanted to get me back on the air during school break. By the way, what's your favorite song?"

"Don't bother," I say. "It's an opera."

He blinks at that, so I get to the point. I ask him how it felt last October to lose an election and to see Giselle Masson win the mayoralty on the same honest platform that he had once vilified in city elections. "Or that your uncle vilified *for* you. How does it feel now?"

"Oh, not so bad," Rapper says, pretending to be consoled. "Losing the presidency to Bamiara is different."

"Because he's a man, I suppose?"

Hannibal grins. "Roger Masson's supposed to be a man, too. But remember how he raged like a maiden scorned while he was president?—after I recorded my TV interview with your poor General Bienportant in exile."

"Domino a poor exile? Residency in a Mediterranean palace at taxpayers' expense?"

"Wherever. That interview made the little Fisherman so jealous! Our General, with my camera on him," Hannibal crows, "showed how healthy, manly, he could be. Especially when he mocked your fellow for rigging the recount and pretending to be *the* public servant."

"Masson didn't rig or pretend anything, and he wasn't my fellow; nor was Domino. I wasn't there for that ill-conceived interview of yours. Roger should have suspended this station's license when you faked those credentials—a political hack claiming to be a TV journalist."

"He should have tried; that would have helped me later against Bamiara. Instead Masson only howled about the interview until the Army made me head of state."

"Yes, a blessedly temporary travesty—and at gunpoint."

Hannibal laughs, then trying to catch me off guard, "I recall that you were supposed to nominate your charming daughter to run against me for president this time, but the Massons overruled you and went for Bamiara."

"They didn't. I won't accept overrule from anybody. Madam Wazimbwe has moved ahead anyhow, or don't you respect the status of a prime minister? You never treated your own with any consideration. But why do you call her *my* daughter?"

"Because she is, even if only adopted."

"More or less. It helps me keep her rich relatives from molesting her. What made you think I would have shoved her into the ring against you?"

"My uncle knew. He even designed a campaign to beat her—by outing you. He knew you'd been hiding her, while others believed she was off sailing with some do-goodniks."

"With Greenpeace, a commitment you couldn't possibly appreciate. She really was onboard their ship. I knew you would never think of looking for her there."

"No, and we missed her. I even wrote a rap song about her: 'Diva mia, pray for suffering polluters.' I'll bet she listened to it."

"She has better taste than that. And she's tougher, too. Your uncle Antoine realized that if Anya became president, she would take you all to the woodshed. She still might. We know where the money comes from," I lie, "to keep you in France, for instance."

"*Keep* me? As a student?" He laughs into the mic. "Students are penniless. They all are, aren't they?"

It's time for me to sneer, but I don't.

"Anyway," he says, "you asked if I'm learning the trade—to govern, right? My thesis next year will be a contract for the prosperity of AuxIndes, starting when I get reelected."

"Not reelected. Not re-anything for you, Hannibal. You weren't worthy of the presidency then, and you didn't give a damn about AuxIndes when you faked acting as head of state."

"You'll see, Sophie; everybody will see, when I'm back for good."

"For what good is that?"

Then I get on my feet and turn toward the door. He calls, offering his microphone. "Really, though, Sophie, what IS your favorite song?"

I shove the door open and leave, humming Verdi's *La donna è mobile.*

✽ ✽ ✽

Next, after taking restorative sniffs of vetiver, my goblin body softens, preparing for a call on Her Honor, Giselle Masson. Her vanquished opponent in the mayorals was a Rapper simulacrum, one

Genghis somebody who sought to retrace Hannibal's mindless path to victory. Unless Giselle's success is entirely attributable to Bamiara's coattails, the capital's voters have grown up in the last eight years.

No, that's saying too much.

At City Hall, Mayor Giselle ushers me into a sumptuous reception parlor designed by a predecessor for his own eternal glory (sorry, I don't recall his name). I'm a bit embarrassed that she's decided to receive me so grandly here, in her everyday work, the Honorable Masson uses a more modest office down the hall. Is Giselle mocking my revolutionary commitment? No, a Sirène never mocks; she entices.

(By the way, where IS that revolution now? Better ask Ishmael before my next issue of *Fables* is due.)

I'm rather disconcerted that, after her campaign loaded with projects for urban beauty and prosperity, the mayor reserves today's session with me to talk exclusively about her husband! As if she were still la *Fisherfemme*, not queen of a capital city.

Now, if I were to interview *him* instead of Giselle, would Masson focus as obsessively on his spouse? Somehow, I doubt it.

Were I to admit responsibility (I don't), perhaps I'm at fault for having started our conversation by praising him. Roger Masson got the mask dance mostly right, I say, even if few others appreciated his integrity. He was too straight to conceive how a shape-shifting Philosophe could keep everybody confused. By contrast, even dense old Domino suspected that Antoine was playing some sort of game all that time, but the ex-President did not take the threat seriously. Bienportant thought himself popular enough in his uniform to beat the Massons, even with Karamau playing both sides against each other. Wrong.

Losing that election to Masson in 2010 humiliated my Doménique permanently. The generous Fisherman let him retire honorably to Europe with his decorations. It was grueling for me to sit at Domino's deathbed for weeks listening to his endless simplifications, encouraging him to believe that I would publish them.

Then, after only five years in office, Masson himself had to pay the price. There was Karamau, secretly funded by the petroleum gluttons, flagrantly fabricating alliances with the implacable colonels. A few hired guns invaded the palace to purge what they'd been told was sexual promiscuity, while the whole army snored in their beds.

Now poor Fisherman, repatriated in theory but devoid of political ambition, must play second fiddle to Madame the Mayor.

And Giselle embellishes those insights. "Typically, Roger couldn't see the tricks coming until too late; he was looking at only one side of Karamau."

"The bright face of his mask," I add.

"That must be the way you see him, Sophie."

"Who? Me? Not my style, as you know."

She seems reluctant to mention the revolt of the uniforms, so I do it. "Your president husband was right to put a woman, albeit an enigmatic bisexual, in charge of defense. But he thought of feminism only formally, in terms of parity in status. The military perceived Zaphyra as a threat to universal norms—within their institution and the world at large."

She agrees. "Knowing no better, all those generals turned their backs while one battalion mutinied. That one was all Karamau needed. There Roger stood, my generous tycoon, offering banquets of seafood and bouquets of vegetables, even galettes from his new flour mill—all for fair prices, or even free, to masses of people who always only wanted more. And no one came to his rescue."

Time to be skeptical. "That philanthropic mask may have got him elected, Giselle. But once that was over your benevolent Fisherman had to dissolve into a different identity—as statesman, big boss. The Stranger."

"Oh, but as statesman Roger had impeccable intentions toward the public. He imposed taxes that redistributed wealth, endowed popular education, guaranteed a free press and dialogue with his rivals . . ."

"Yes, he even hired them."

" . . . especially over public health and housing, modern technology for farmers."

She pauses to catch her breath, and mine. "My noble husband, the merchant prince dreaming himself into solving every public problem."

"At best," I say, "the proverbial industrialist was changing his mask for the progressive politician's—as you are doing now. But nobody would believe him. So he alienated the rich families, and the shaky skeptics found plenty to doubt."

"Worse, Sophie. Everything Roger did was questioned. Was the Fisher King only fiddling with finances of the state—international loans, tax policy, customs regulations? Was he really there to serve the people who elected him, or to line his own pockets? Was he expecting the land owners to raid their Swiss bank accounts for taxes to grow a prosperous work force, or rather to expand his personal empire?"

"Adding to the doubts," I add, "those two Americans, who were they working for, your husband's business? the administration?—or the scary CIA? How could his staff shuttle between one headquarters building and the other without utterly mixing up the interests? How could *he*?"

"Although you warned him, Sophie, and some of his staff knew it, Roger never perceived that the levers of power were stacking these charges against him. And how rapidly they built up."

"I did try but he never believed it. Philosophe coming and going at the same time, always the same mask, but facing wherever he wished, the classic Trickster."

Giselle sighs. "When that battalion besieged our house, and his guards had flown for the hills, we talked with Karamau by telephone and heard all we needed. But not my outraged husband. Roger had no weapons, yet wanted to kill them all. He always had these inclinations toward meaningless violence—a sock thrower and a blasphemer when he thinks he's not being observed. Then we talked for hours, and you called, and he agreed to that exile wisely."

"It has turned out comfortably for you both. You're in charge of the city and he's been restoring some of the business. After all the exaggerations recited about him . . ."

"The lies, you mean."

". . . he lacked sufficient popularity to reclaim the presidency. But here *you* are, Madam Mayor, where you deserve to be."

"It would be more just if we had both recovered politically. The doubts about Roger persist, locally and internationally, long after the usurpers have proven themselves worse."

"That's worked in his favor, actually, and for you too, Giselle. Your romantic spouse could never succeed in all he expected to accomplish. Life in exile on the continent matured him while suspicions poured down onto the Karamaus and their clumsy conspiracy."

"Their failure did earn us some sympathy from the global banks and agencies, the big 'donor' powers." Here the Sirène laughs sarcastically. "And from all those vulnerable African chiefs who fear that what happened to us could repeat on their own turf."

"Although you always enjoyed some good will abroad, there was no action—until the uproar started at home. You should be glad not to have been here when Rapper closed your grain factory, the textile mills, and the fishing fleet, even the supermarkets, claiming that your husband had been selling the country to mythical Chinese moneylenders (or was it to the capitalist Americans?)." I scratch my head and continue.

"I'd been vainly agitating for a revolt in the streets," I add, "but luckily for you, all we got was nostalgia over those years of benign exploitation by the corporations, yours included. All the country—including rich squires, merchants, consumers, and the acquiescent press—moaned that nothing had come for them to replace Masson's productivity."

"Eventually," she tries to correct the account, "but it was the usurpers' blatant corruption and abuse that alienated everybody."

"Even before that, when the military repudiated your Fisherman's relations with 'Anglophonia,' the island became further isolated than it had ever been."

I see that Giselle is adroitly letting me "interview" myself. Now she adds with a frown that "the Karamaus consented to end Roger's exile just in time, you know, because Speranza was growing tired of us Frenchified fugitives."

"Lucky that. So today, alas, we have benevolent capitalism again, and with English creeping in *three* official languages."

"Sorry we can't simplify matters for you progressives, Sophie."

I reflect for a moment. "Meanwhile that wise child, Bamiara, stayed loyal to your husband without knowing how well it would serve himself. Your Peasant kept Hannibal and his uncle at odds with the exclusive clans that never trusted them or those palefaced Silhouettes. Anya was gleeful when her family and the rest of your beloved aristocracy refused to accept the foreign oil companies. What? they roared. More colonialism? Mining our sacred turf to grab something called fossil fuel—and not paying us off? And they're not even colored, those foreigners!"

"I'm glad you see the pattern, Sophie," concludes the Mayor, glancing at her wristwatch, a sign that I'm doing too much of the talking. Then, with a parting thought, she interviews herself: "Even you may not know how hard we had to work to keep Roger from climbing the hill on Day One after our return and tearing that statue down."

"I do know that he still envied the martyred Spider."

"And how often he swore to fire that empty pistol at Karamau's head," Giselle quips as she passes through the door.

My next stop, after several inhalations of the vetiver, requires reaching our new president—that faithful ersatz Peasant, Benjamin Bamiara. I have to wait a day and work through my precious prime minister, who hadn't included him in her roster of interviews for me. And whom I never ask for favors.

Except this once.

"Can you get me in, Anya, to talk very briefly with him?"

We're sipping coffee, which she makes sweeter than I. She is now more sparkling than ever. Her golden glow, aquiline features, smooth hair, cheekbones—how can those clods possibly stigmatize her as *my* daughter?

"Much as I owe you, *maman*, I'm not sure. Benjamin is up to his sideburns in interviews . . . but at least he won't suspect that you're looking for a sinecure. Not you. Can I tell him what you want to talk about?"

"I wish to know how Peasant—excuse me, President Bamiara, proposes to keep the lid on."

She grins. "Meaning on what?"

"You know well, Anya. We came as close under the Fisherman as this country will ever get to a progressive administration, bourgeois as it was. Every interested organization and government approved Roger's moves, but they ignored the pavanes, the fandangos of the old clans, the people you renounced and left behind. Those rich families tolerated Masson until they became threatened. How dare he question military tradition and its aristocratic barons? That was a change too far for them. Curses on your relatives, Anya, who disowned even you, their best, from the moment when you led the students against colonialist Babel."

"Yes, fortunately. Did they have a choice, those families, once we'd got rid of the Domino?"

"They didn't. Of course your uncles ostracized the Karamaus, for how could a low-born Philosophe and his ilk aspire to a place in their sphere? Masson was a better compromise, while he lasted.

Now, Bamiara has leapfrogged his old boss, and in shining bourgeois armor. But his options resemble the Fisherman's program. Can he hang on?"

"Maman, our Peasant worked those families cleverly during Roger's exile years. He only nodded at their dislike of the parvenu Masson, then turned them against Karamau, and won their admiration—without ever even mentioning my name."

"But you know those gold-hoarding clans," I say, "with their tombs chockful of dead generals. Fisherman was asking our Army to maneuver with allies from the Black continent, to abandon the comfortable neocolonial establishment. If the military brass don't support you actively, they undermine you, and if you offend their culture they do nothing to protect your legitimacy. Remember that, Madam Prime Minister."

"Yes, and thanks to you, I don't have to beg entrance to their tombs."

"You aren't atheist enough yet, Anya. You were always preferable to the mess made by that clown Hannibal, who wouldn't listen to his wily uncle. He chose to go a-borrowing on the open market for vanity projects. He dealt familiarly with weird people, and sang songs about everybody on his TV station. He just told me he'd broadcast a rap for you, while you were disguised as my domestic from Bangladesh. I know you never listened to it."

The prime minister scowls. "I did so! It was awful, vilifying our campaign against polluting monopolies. A Rapper who jingles about granting prospecting rights to toxic oil companies. While I was buried under veils in your basement and unable to answer—except indirectly, through your pen. Hannibal, a mere figurehead for Uncle

Antoine, did he imagine that his pop voice would assure people that he was in charge, that he could equate disarray with liberty? that he could simulate creativity without policy? Dammit it all, I will get you in to see Benjamin!"

Survivors from their student and fishery years are gradually returning to Bamiara's side, as they had done a decade ago for Masson. I'm proud of Anya for keeping her back turned away from the reactionary clans, refusing to urge her presumed birthright. And even proud of the others, discharged of their expatriation. Now they are taking key offices after having fled with glittering resumes into multilateral agencies: Bernard Chenille (the Papillon) in Public Works; Solange Sériel (whom the cynics call La Douce) who has left her European faculty to take over Finance; Olivier, who hated marketing, can now try to humanize the island in Cultural Affairs; Zaphyra is hammering stiff breezes into the Education Ministry while Bamiara manages the military on his own.

Masson himself is a phone call away, and Giselle the mayor, always stronger than people think. Together, they force me to reconcile with bourgeois democracy; it's a step above military fascism or corporate greed.

But not the final step, not yet.

Thanks to the election campaign, we know that Bamiara, who'd been popularly considered a closet gay, has had a wife and two children. There's one productive family my goblin mask doesn't condemn! It has lived quietly on the eastern shore, where wife Stéphanie trades in spices under her own name. Nobody, not even I, suspected why Benjamin spent his holidays on that coast. I'll bet Masson knew, but he doesn't tell us everything.

Sorry that I can't "interview" the whole establishment. Not Stéphanie on the coast or the number-crunching Solange Sériel; or that Haitian American whose smile sweetened Solange; perhaps Denis Guyane knew about Bamiara's family, and even stays in touch.

So there were things I didn't know. Not even me. I'm too agnostic to reach the ghost of Freddie the Spider, but he's somewhere, watching; so is Ishmael with his disembodied, alcoholic prophecies sent through the birds—what a mask he is—or was!

Unfortunately, my *Chronicle* can't embrace everything. Not my favorite exile, the American descendant of Behanzin. No longer jeune fille, Cynthia has become a barracuda with her film-projector talisman. I wish she were here to make our eyes dance. While Karamau is my boulder on the lawn, Cynthia's my pearl in the shell. She has power to frame the space around her, as Philosophe has to disrupt it. In spite of myself, I now think of her fondly as a mother, conceiving a new spirit to enrich her mask. That should edify Nigeria, with its polluted proximity to the water, its need of a Kondo in the sea. Oh, American amazon, I sense your absence palpably. Look how I've softened!

This afternoon, Anya tells me, President Bamiara has a date with Philosophe, supposedly to offer him "a new job." Flagrantly, Benjamin shifts that appointment off a day, deliberately making the erstwhile omnipotence guess for a while longer. I'm to see the Peasant in, of all places, the parking lot of that AuSecours market—evidently a symbolic space, where he faithfully organized remote broadcasts for his old boss in exile.

"Please ignore the police escort, *chère* Vinagrette," he says as I'm ushered into the limo next to him. "This crew never worked for

Karamau and won't. I insist they understand only Swahili or else get deported back to Zanzibar. Say anything you like."

I pop my main question, precisely formulated: "How will you satisfy popular expectations of progress without risking another upheaval from the power elites?"

"How?" he replies. "With sweet guile if need be. Learned from Philosophe himself, to keep the barons guessing. Tell me, who would be their champion this time? Not the military who've had enough politicking under Domino, and then lost face by failing the Fisherman; not Karamau, as you'll see, or the callow Hannibal who was ostentatiously never in charge of his own shoelaces. The rich have their resources without needing to accept blame for the economy. And the Internationals applaud our every move. Anya can take over if I stumble, and both Massons want us to succeed. Did you predict I'd lose the election? Nah, you're never wrong, I almost forgot that."

"Good for you to remember. Still, you haven't really answered the question—you do confront some obstacles."

"So be it. None of our handicaps matter so much when you take the trouble to embarrass the opposition. This innocent Peasant learned some positive things from Roger's election as President eight years ago, with its barrages of free publicity, its open indictment of corruption, and a tidy bankroll from the Fishery. I even profited from the earlier race we lost in the city where Karamau outfoxed Giselle's team. He showed us that it's how you present, not what you represent, that counts across the board."

"True, even for your bigshot capitalist friends?"

"Especially for them. And only if they think of me as *their* friend, not yours."

"That's for sure, Benjamin. You deserve this place after demonstrating that you understood the barons, while they believed Masson on the wrong track and Anya to be a traitor. By the way, I expect you to keep them from vilifying your Prime Minister."

"No easy chore for me, Sophie, but one I accept; she's still the best of us all."

"So be it. Tell me, did it help to mix with the ragtag BeauxIndes party every week in this parking lot, working for Masson without realizing that in the end you were serving yourself?"

"Verily, yea. Until Karamau perceived the threat from our rallies—too late, because he didn't see beyond that unwashed crowd into the patrician clans behind them; the few quiet ones who believed the island needed to be a 'community'—their term for whenever things quiet down. I had to persuade them that economics and environment were tightly integrated. I promised to defend the island against sun and cold, water and drought, as Roger defended its basic honesty against the corrupters. We can't hold back the sea surge that threatens to swamp us, but we will all prevail or all succumb—workforce, peasantry, and shareholders alike."

"So you advocated 'community' until the Trickster had to give his word that Masson would return? That took both of them out of the running."

"Yes, but while we waited for that mistake, Sophie, the party was raising protests by young AuxIndiens against the oil companies. They even got public opinion to urge the fish farm project that I had started for AuThon."

"I still prefer wild-caught seafood, Benjamin; the water has to be clean first. If I were you, I wouldn't trust those rich families or your precious internationals, not if Philosophe were after me."

He laughs. "But Karamau's fangs were pulled out one by one whenever the Rapper committed his oafish blunders."

"Antoine should have perceived that you would be the lucky surrogate, not my Anya whom he'd turned into a fetish. What kind of strong man is that? He was so frightened of her."

"He was mostly frightened of you. I took advantage of that."

"And I stayed away, best thing I've done in a while," I admit. "Karamau couldn't believe it. Ah, now your office said you were about to offer him a new job; is it one he can't reject?"

"It offers status and immunity from prosecution as long as it lasts, and it's located at a safe distance from the center. You'll see how that works out, in good time, Sophie."

With that, Benjamin presidentially presses something on his phone, and they drive me home.

So the new head of state elbows the national nemesis out of the way. He picks up where Masson had left off, reclaiming "darling" status with African leaders and the multinational crowd. He expresses little anxiety over the domestic power brokers who have never accepted leadership from anybody, and have not offered to take risks. The Wazimbwe even dream of reclaiming Anya to protect their privilege, while we know better. Or do we? Is it more than faith, after all? On her own, Anya will have to adopt Benjamin's technique, playing the elite factions off against one another. With the revolution still out of sight, I can only wish them well during an indefinite transition.

One other thought occurs to me as I comb through these palavers. I couldn't mention it to Giselle, but I have discovered new respect for her husband—for renouncing the amorous triangle, his early illusion. Instead, Fisherman "adopted" both Cynthia and Denis as his protégés, not his lovers. Then he let those children go off, as good parents must do, to find their own ways. So Roger Masson did have progeny after all, and he treated them as well as a father should. So far as I know, he never revealed his temptation to play jealous lover or his wish to be loved.

Next day, and final stop in the sequence of interviews has to be: who else? This time, however, I await him here, not any place *he* would find comfortable. Karamau rings my doorbell this morning, right on time. The Trickster is alone, swathed in his ebony redingote. He has no official trappings to entangle a visitor, no armed escort for intimidation. He does not remove his hat when I guide him into my now pristine studio (Anya made me clean it). He's never been here before.

"Is that lavender I inhale, Madam Nuru? Or frankincense? Very pleasant."

I shake my head. He's sniffing yesterday's coffee, and putting me on, pretending not to know those oils. In any case, they aren't the hot kind he once used against people's bodies.

Whether he likes it or not, I have to congratulate Karamau on his nomination, just announced. "Ambassador Plenipotentiary to the Somber Nation. Was that your first preference for an embassy?"

Philosophe doesn't bother to laugh. He raises both arms, as though on the cross. "Diplomacy itself would have been my last choice," he answers, "if I'd been given one. And that particular country would rank somewhere low on the list. I regret having learned so much English that I'll have to deal directly with its government. I should have preferred a more convenient spot dominated by Arabic or Portuguese, or Blah-Blah."

"So it's a new challenge for you, and should be welcome. You never ducked before, Antoine, even when you were being attacked as a (ho-ho) closet socialist. Bamiara might have treated you far more vindictively than this."

"He'd thought of it, I know that." Here Karamau does laugh, nearly. "Your charming Masson would have strung me up from a lamppost. I've actually come to ask you if I should thank Prime Minister Anya for keeping the noose off my neck."

"Ask her yourself, if she agrees to talk to you. I doubt it, though; she doesn't fake her feelings. And I believe ambassadors can report to presidents through the Foreign Ministry, so she just needs to know things, not entailing direct relations with you. After you get the other state's agreement, you're accountable to Benjamin."

Karamau nods gravely. "At least he's been clean, Mr. Bamiara, a peasant-patriot bathed in the aura of self-sacrifice. A friend to all, servant to the exiled victim, now redeemer of peace and harmony. He's had a female wife all this time. Even his skin darkened a shade once he announced his candidacy."

I had, in fact, noticed that alteration, not immaterial to Africa's descendants like Philosophe and myself. I pass up the chance to pun on the Somber Country where Karamau is headed.

"You forget policy, Antoine. As president, Bamiara gets credit for refusing the invasion of your hydrocarbon villains. He can invoke petroleum prices as a popular pretext to launch Anya's energy reforms. The multilaterals applaud him as he struggles out of the commitments and debts contracted by your nephew's pop-up regime. So now he can make space for new energies conveyed by wind, sunshine, and tides. Even for allowing the Army to stay asleep and play video games in its barracks—all it ever wanted to do in the first place."

"Of course," Karamau replies, "but as his diplomat, I'll have to appease the politicians sheltered in their stipends, immune to disapproval from rich and poor. They will persist in ignoring the goat farmers who remain in their arid southern homeland weaving those luscious rugs and starving. There will be no contesting the landed proprietors and tradesmen who want by any means to keep Masson's fingers away from their properties. I do follow the policies, you see."

"A complex web of them, Philosophe as thou art named. Your options seem to have liberalized, and your sentences have already got longer."

"Yes, Vinaigrette, but tell me, how will they end, those sentences?"

"A poor question, Ambassador Karamau: nothing really ends. For now, Bamiara is our head of state, the fourth you've had in the last ten years, counting your unworthy nephew. Benjamin has to clean up the mess bequeathed by his predecessors, starting with my old Domino, and by you. Too many children are out of school, inexplicably hungry in a country that can grow plenty of rice, corn, lima beans, and livestock. Your old police are keeping the Silhouettes in jail on some trumped-up charge; they're hoping just to be deported to France or Poland or wherever. Masson is in court to retrieve his confiscated assets. Anya has to dose the new President with feasible projects for a cleaner universe. Zaphyra, humiliated by your officers (yes, they were yours) is bullying their children with smiles; and Ishmael is quiet, I think."

"Bagatelles, all that. The issue at hand is: where am I?"

"You are still in government, Antoine, a recycling I cannot explain. You will soon be turning diplomatic tricks in some shadowy country where you can do little harm, but where they can't see you hide in the wide open."

The mask known as Philosophe laughs vigorously now, easing the weight he brought into my house. He has always known what spirit possesses him. So he rises, removes his hat, flourishes it in the air, and nods courteously. "Goodbye, Sophie," he says, taking a deep breath, before heading for the door. "I have inhaled your aroma: nothing beats vetiver oil as a camouflage for anxiety."

❈ ❈ ❈

New York, New Year's Day 2020

He'd enjoyed a few hours sleep when the phone howled at 6 a.m., Manhattan time. Caller-ID signified "NIGERIA," so Guyane merely groaned, turned over in bed, and let the call ring itself out. "More corny scams to the wrong target and at a very bad hour," he muttered to his welcoming pillow.

When he woke again, there was a message on the phone. A melodious voice that seemed, as always, to be echoing off his walls, his ceiling, his brain. It was indeed from Abuja.

"Sorry, Denny, it's afternoon here," sang the message, "and I forgot the time difference. You seem to be still with me. Happy New Year. And call me back, please, it's important."

Guyane shook off his torpor and swallowed a pint of water. New Year's Eve had allowed some superfluous carousing among professional colleagues who'd befriended him over the three years following his return from Lagos and Speranza. The group had a common interest in such matters as racial equity, First Amendment rights, reduction of violence in Haiti—and in abundant pinot noir. He brushed his teeth and called Cynthia back.

"Denis, we're fine. The digital book on student uprisings is out, selling well. I'm finishing my business with the press in Abuja. It's time to leave Africa and to come home. Can you put us up, me and Ocean, for a week or so starting next Wednesday? Until we get settled? If not, can you book us a flat nearby, with studio space? We really want to see you right away. Don't worry. We've got the money and winter clothes. Also, will your job let you meet our flight from London that afternoon? I'll email the details."

"Sure, Cynthia, I can and will, but why so sudden?"

"My shark skin urgently needs a place with water around me. You're still surrounded by water in Manhattan, aren't you?"

"For sure, Madam Kondo. While the bulkheads hold. But what's on your mind—scuba lessons or . . . ?"

"Don't ask how I know this," she interrupted, "but there's a compounded crisis on the way; the climate emergency will converge with a global public health menace, drug trafficking, and political chaos. Virtually no travel across borders; Black and brown people pushed to the brink of an existential volcano. Nowhere for islanders to go—except for the privileged few. Soon soaring heat and sea-level rise will intensify migration and reinforce a worldwide invasion by virus."

"Hmm. Sounds like something Masson has been reading."

"Or more likely, Baldwin's 'Aftertimes,' Denis. A new world is trying to materialize against all odds."

"That serious, huh?"

"Cataclysmic. You may have heard: Plage Mineure is already gone: swallowed into the sea. I've been in touch with the Chathams people at the dateline off New Zealand; also infamous Gorée the Senegalese slave port; and the stilt village, Ganvié in the lagoon between Dahomey and Nigeria (you never told me about that one!), and Sao Tomé nearby; the vanishing Maldives, and money-mad Mauritius. All endangered."

"Whoa, Cynthia. These islands are all friends of yours? Fisherman would retort that there's still Inishmaan, Ireland's magic satellite, where Synge sat in poetry on his rock. The rock remains. What about your Behanzin family, in Martinique?"

"Nothing from them, ever. Aftertimes will come to them soon."

"Not before I can get to meet them, I hope."

"Oh yes. You know, Denis, how islands are laboratories for the combustion of climate and plague. When some islands flood, others dry out, and all disgorge population, and conflict flares."

"Not news for us, Cynthia. What about AuxIndes?"

"I've heard from your adorable Prime Minister Wazimbwe, her eyes sparkling at you over the waves. She and Benjamin know that to neglect sea life is to condemn all earthlings."

"So the Diva speaks your language now?"

"Anya understands that we all live in repositories of poverty, whether we're surrounded by high seas or concrete—or by inaccessible wealth and power."

"Poverty may prevail yet, Cynthia. The rich are preparing life in their artificial islands of wealth, their real estate pods. But such fortresses won't subsist in isolation. Like your old Silhouettes on Plage Mineure, even those centers of refuge will need an envelope of the poor to do the work that maintains them."

"Right, Denis, but who or what will remain? All my friends have intelligence, but not all are human beings; some just swim or fly, and chatter; others push out their roots; some may be as artificial as those gated pods you mention. Which is why I'm coming back to Manhattan, the island of extreme poverty and extreme power."

"A nasty dichotomy; straddle it warily."

"Remember Marty Bondoo, the pianist? He's sent me some improvs from Corsica in the Mediterranean; I can use his tapes to animate anything I want. They sound like Ravel. Too bad you're so tone-deaf or the islands would be singing to you."

"Hah! I've been collecting some Bondoo discs. They make me think of you. But did you call today just to impugn my musicality?"

"Not really, but it's fun. 'Denis' won't metamorphose into *Dionysos* without my help. Now, the planet needs you, a linguist, a wordsmith, a right guy who happens to appreciate good wine. All the endangered creatures have to learn how to fill out the forms, for their survival."

"For life on the planet? That's never been easy, not even for people, Cynthia."

"True. We'll have to get our spirits going again, call our masks up from wherever they've been. I have an idea how to fight this perilous combination. To get the world to pay attention. Our way, professional, with film and story and music. A cultural change has to start from Manhattan, the power center that radiates poverty; then to other places, and . . . well, together, if you're available."

"Of course, Cynthia," he replied almost by instinct. "I'd be pleased to save the world with you—one island at a time, until we reach The Indies."

The END, for now